Praise for the Spellbinding Novels of Josie Litton

DREAM OF ME AND BELIEVE IN ME

"There's plenty of action, sizzling sensuality, strong clashes, and just the right touch of mystery here to tantalize any reader. . . . Strong characterizations, rapier-sharp dialogue, colorful historical details, and sizzling passion explode within the pages. . . . Ms. Litton is on her way to stardom."
—Kathe Robin, *Romantic Times*

"The characters themselves are magnetic and fully dimensional. Readers will be captivated as each relationship unfolds, and . . . anxious to devour Litton's next trilogy."
—*Booklist*

"[Litton's] is a fresh new voice with page-turning drama, sensuous love scenes, surprising humor, and a roller-coaster plot. . . . You will want to check out this new historical romance author."
—*Old Book Barn Gazette*

"Ms. Litton's talent shines like a beacon."
—*Rendezvous*

"If readers are as selfish and hedonistic as this reviewer, they would have wanted a triplet rather than wait a whole month for book three."
—*The Midwest Book Review*

COME BACK TO ME

"A heady mix of high adventure, breathtaking beauty, larger-than-life characters, and sizzling sensuality. The Middle Ages never looked so good."
—Amazon.com Delivers Romance

"A rare treat for romance readers."
—*The Oakland Press*

"A powerful plot starring two energetic and charming characters."—*The Midwest Book Review*

"Another fiery battle-of-wills romance to tantalize and intrigue readers . . . A powerful romance and a new author to cherish."—*Romantic Times*

"Litton excels at depicting realistically flawed, charismatic protagonists, and this tale . . . is a fitting finale."
—*Publishers Weekly*

DREAM ISLAND

"*Dream Island* brings to life a fascinating tale set on a mysterious island with an ancient history and a proud warrior culture. The author does such a masterful job with this work that the island of Akora becomes as memorable as her colorful main characters. And her engaging love story is magically woven into the fabric of this exotic tapestry."
—*Old Book Barn Gazette*

Castles in the
MIST

Josie Litton

Bantam 🦋 *Books*

New York Toronto London Sydney Auckland

CASTLES IN THE MIST

A Bantam Book

PUBLISHING HISTORY

Bantam paperback edition / November 2002

ISBN 0-553-58391-3

Published simultaneously in the United States and Canada

Bantam Books are published by Bantam Books, a division of Random House, Inc. Its trademark, consisting of the words "Bantam Books" and the portrayal of a rooster, is Registered in U.S. Patent and Trademark Office and in other countries. Marca Registrada. Bantam Books, 1540 Broadway, New York, New York 10036.

PRINTED IN THE UNITED STATES OF AMERICA

OPM   10 9 8 7 6 5 4 3 2 1

For readers,
with boundless thanks for all your support
and encouragement

PROLOGUE

THE WORLD SEEMED WREATHED IN SLUMBER when a solitary figure slipped into the library of the London house. Brianna shut the door quietly and checked to be sure it was closed before striking flint to tinder to light one of the oil lamps. By its glow, she scanned the library shelves. When she found what she sought, she took the book down carefully and set it on a nearby table.

The binding was tooled Moroccan leather embossed with the title: A History of Essex. She knew the book, having found it shortly after she first arrived in England months before. Then, she had accompanied her aunt to assist at the birth of Alex and Joanna's child. Now she had returned for her own sake . . . and because of the book.

Slowly, she opened it. It was a weighty tome thick with kings, queens, battles, and the like dating all the way back to the time of Alfred the Great. It had much to say about Hawkforte and the mighty family that ruled there. But it also spoke of other places, including one called Holyhood.

There was a picture of the manor of Holyhood, a simple line drawing depicting a graceful house. Brianna stared at it as fragments of memory stirred.

She had been there. She had been in that house, somewhere in the lost time before the terrible storm that took her parents' lives and left her a nameless orphan washed up on Akoran shores.

If she shut her eyes and thought of the house, she heard the distant sound of voices calling.

She was suddenly very cold, but the chill that rooted within her heart held a tiny spark of light. Her spirit yearned toward it, feeling the spark grow and warmth turn to heat. Her arms were wrapped around herself, but they felt strangely like another's arms, far stronger, drawing her powerfully.

In that embrace was protection and so much more, but in the house . . . The house held a secret, the key to a mystery that both terrified and tempted her. She stared again at the drawing and felt within herself the hardening of resolve.

H*E COULD SENSE HER AGAIN, ALMOST AS HE HAD on the road between this world and the next. She was the woman who had hovered near him, calling his name, slowing his journey into death and beyond.*

He had recognized her. She had been with him before, deep in the caves during the trial of selection when so much had been revealed to him. Then, he had had only the briefest glimpse of her, but he had never forgotten.

He knew her, knew her face and her voice, knew the scent and touch of her, knew how she felt even now, almost as though he already held her.

But he had not known her name. Until he awoke and saw the silver glisten of her tears and the fiery glory of her hair.

She was his. Of that, he was entirely certain. But she did not know it . . . not yet.

She would, he promised himself, and very soon. On the roof of the palace, beneath the stars, the Vanax of Akora turned his eyes to the north and saw with his warrior's heart the prize awaiting him there.

Chapter
ONE

S HE DID NOT COME TO HIM EASILY. HE LEARNED the curves of her body slowly in long nights and stolen days, the smallest, most exquisite details holding him enthralled even once he knew them with precision: the delicate hollow nestled at the base of her throat, the curve of breasts that were high and firm, the shadow of an indentation stretching between her ribs down to her navel . . . and so much more.

Her hands and feet fascinated him no less than did the more intimate parts of her. They were long and graceful, the hands well suited to difficult, precise tasks, the feet deceptively fragile. When he turned her over, it was to study the strong, slender line of her back swaying inward at her waist before flaring into the chalice of her hips. Her buttocks were round, firm, also muscled with a pair of twin dimples that made him smile, wondering as he did if she had ever noticed them.

He had not mastered her; never would he make the mistake of thinking that. Her face challenged him, and even now he did not know it absolutely. The mouth was too mobile to ever capture for long, the eyes too inclined to secrets.

Were that not enough, the woman Atreus held within his hands, which had carved her so carefully from pink-hued marble, had been without a name for far too long.

She had one now, he thought, as he returned the statue carefully to the velvet-lined box specially made to hold it. Very shortly, the box would be packed away in the last of the trunks being removed from his cabin. After a fortnight at sea, the journey made longer than usual by the clip of a gale brewing off the coast of Britain, the rhythm of the ship had changed as it entered the Thames. The tide was rising, lifting the great river and them with it. The damp chill of early winter, which had increased steadily with each day's sail farther north, eased a little as they were embraced by the heavily wooded banks of the river, but the air was still colder than any Atreus had ever known. Moreover, it carried an alien smell, not unpleasant, but a constant reminder that home was a thousand and more miles behind him.

It seemed a great distance, but he knew he had traveled farther, not in this world but in the passage to the next. Six months before, he had come very close to dying in an act of treachery and violence. The memory of that lingered—not in his body, which was entirely healed—but in his spirit. It steeled an already strong resolve and created within him a certain impatience. He wanted this journey over and done, its purposes achieved. Only then could he go on in the direction he knew he must take.

"That's the last of it, Castor," he said, and handed the small wooden box to his manservant, who waited by the trunks.

"Very good, Vanax. It appears we will dock shortly."

"Then I suppose it is just as well I am dressed." He glanced down and restrained a smile. "I am dressed, am I not?"

Castor surveyed him carefully. "I believe so, Vanax. That is to say, Prince Alexandros's instructions have been carried out and everything appears to be where it should be."

Atreus nodded. His half brother, who was himself half English, had provided both garments and guidance as to the wearing of them. Atreus did not doubt Alex's expertise in such matters; he merely wondered why anyone would go to such extraordinary lengths to garb himself.

He wore—from the skin out—linen drawers that covered him from his waist to slightly above his knees; linen stockings; gleaming black leather short boots; snugly fitted trousers of finely woven wool dyed a deep tan; a white linen shirt secured at the wrists by starched wristbands, and at the neck by a starched pointed collar encircled by the stock he had learned laboriously to tie; a tan waistcoat sporting its own high collar, and discreetly embroidered with dark gold thread; and, lastly, a dark brown cutaway coat.

The sheer quantity and variety of the garments amazed him. Surely protection from the damp chill could be achieved far more simply. As it was, not only was he wearing more clothing than he ever had in his life, he felt absurdly like one of the comically overwrapped packages given to gleeful children on their name days.

"It is not so bad, Vanax," Castor said in the tone of a man grateful not to be similarly afflicted. In a stab at consolation, he added, "In warrior training, we learn to adapt the cover of the surrounding countryside in order to conceal ourselves. Perhaps you would be more at ease if you thought of these garments in that manner."

"Perhaps I would be. Thank you, Castor. I'll come up directly."

When he was alone, Atreus stood in the center of the cabin. A big man, tall and broad-shouldered, with the lithe strength of a warrior, he found motion and action far more natural than stillness. Yet there were times . . .

He closed eyes of a dark brown bright with shards of gold and breathed slowly, deeply. The ability to separate himself from the distractions of the world was the fruit of long practice, first as a child following a path he could glimpse only dimly, later as a youth undergoing the rigors of the training Castor had mentioned, and finally in the fullness of his manhood, when he discovered that the stillness held within it great gifts of renewal and understanding.

"Come back. . . ." Her voice was soft, anguished, blurred by tears. He wanted to answer but could not. His body no longer responded to his will, which had become a thing apart, drifting on a current that seemed to bear him farther and farther away.

"Don't leave us." Formless, he frowned. Don't leave me. That was what he wanted her to say, for all that he had no idea why she should.

"Damn, Deilos!" It was later when he surfaced again into the pain that told him he yet lived. Pain and her anger, rage at the man who had done this to him. Deilos. No boyhood friend, but a companion turned traitor and would-be assassin.

Deilos, for whom there must be justice.

She smelled of honeysuckle. The scent and the thought of it on her skin pleased him. He breathed deeply, once more, and felt the . . .

. . . ship bump gently against the dock, recalling him to his present circumstances. The past slipped away, but the memory enshrouded him, inescapable.

He glanced around the cabin one last time and went out, up the narrow stairs to the deck where his men were gathered, also dressed in foreign garments, but of a simpler, more practical variety. Keen-eyed, hands resting on the hilts of swords that were in no way ceremonial, they parted for him. He heard the great rush of sound rising from just beyond the stone quay, the vast, tumultuous sound of a sea of humanity spilling from the docks, crowding the narrow streets, straining against the barrier of crimson-garbed soldiers. There was a band playing a raucous tune that involved a great deal of drumming and the clash of cymbals, but it was drowned out by the roar of cheers when he emerged.

He stood and took the full force of that wave of astonishing excitement and seeming pleasure for the arrival of a man the crowd did not know and could not possibly care about, save for the diversion he offered. He understood that well enough, yet it was still surprising. In the home of his heart, emotion was far more personal.

And yet, amid the mass of anonymous humanity, he caught sight of familiar faces set apart from the crowd. His spirit lightened. However strange the land to which he had come, it offered reunion with those he loved.

"Atreus! Atreus! Over here!" It was Kassandra, his half sister. Knowing as he did the need to present a properly dignified appearance, he could not help smiling at the sight of her. Wed but a few months, deeply in love with and loved by the tall, golden-haired man beside her, she glowed with happiness.

His men formed a guard of honor at the bottom of the gangplank. He walked among them and was caught in the fierce embrace of his half brother, Alex, who grinned and thumped his back hard enough to fell a lesser man. "Fine thing," Alex said, "you show up and immediately you're the most popular man in London. I should have expected it."

"You might also have warned me," Atreus said dryly. "I envisioned a quiet family welcome."

"For the Vanax of Akora on his first official visit to England? There was scant hope of that. Welcome, brother. It is good to see you."

"And you, Alex." He turned then and opened his arms to the young woman fairly bouncing up and down in her excitement. "Kassandra, sweet sister."

Hugging him, she said, "Joanna is devastated not to be here, but Amelia has had a little cough, so of course she could not leave her. Oh, not to worry, your niece is much better now."

"We have strict instructions to bring you home without delay," Alex said with the tolerant air of a well-married man. "Joanna is most impatient to welcome you herself."

"I look forward to seeing her," Atreus said, even as his gaze settled on the man standing a little to one side. Kassandra's obvious happiness disposed Atreus to think well of his English brother-in-law, but he had also taken the measure of the man on the training field and over a few carafes of wine. Royce had not disappointed him.

"It is good to see you," Atreus said.

"And you, Sire," Royce replied.

The Vanax of Akora, revered ruler of his people, winced. "Sire? Must formality descend upon us so soon? I had hoped to avoid it a little while yet."

Royce directed his attention toward the tall, burly man watching them both. Quietly, he said, "Unfortunately not. The Prince Regent is indisposed and sends his regrets. But Lord Liverpool, the prime minister, accompanied us."

Atreus looked at the man who had taken over the job vacated when his predecessor was assassinated earlier that year. Liverpool appeared to be what reputation claimed him to be: a solid, unimaginative, ploddingly dependable Britisher. Precisely one of those Atreus had come to . . . to what?

Impress, persuade, understand? Yes to all that, but far more, as well. Spurred by the new machines and factories spreading across the land, Britain was gaining wealth and power to a degree unprecedented in history. At war with both Napoleon and its own former American colonies, facing challenges at home that had brought bloody revolution to other nations, the sceptered isle sailed on, impervious to any interests but its own.

Such determination was to be admired, but it was also to be met with the greatest care. Atreus nodded. "Lord Liverpool, I have looked forward to meeting you."

The prime minister inclined his head gravely "Sire, you are most welcome. His Highness, the Prince Regent, and all of us in his government have anticipated your arrival most eagerly."

"As have I, Prime Minister. Apart from every other consideration, I have come to see what tempts so many of my family to make England their home, at least for a part of each year. You will forgive me, I hope, when I say the attraction apparently cannot be the climate."

The prime minister laughed uncertainly. Atreus was pleased. It was always best to keep one's adversaries, potential and otherwise, off balance. He might have pushed a little harder had not Kassandra diverted him.

"You remember Brianna, don't you, Atreus?" His sister drew forward a young woman in her early twenties, tall and slim, her hair the hue of red the painter Titian loved, the color hinting at deep passions even as the modest, confined style announced restraint. Her skin was the shade of cream, her eyes a light green shot through with gold.

And then there was that twin pair of dimples concealed beneath her demurely elegant garb. . . .

"Brianna, lovely as always." Because he saw no reason not to, the Vanax of Akora added, "You have been away from us far too long."

She colored and her eyes fell, but a moment later, her gaze met his. "I rejoice to see you so well, Sire."

Her voice was as he remembered, low and gentle but with the steadiness of true strength. They were speaking English, but he recalled that when she spoke Akoran, she had a slight, very charming accent. She also still smelled of honeysuckle.

"The carriages are over there," Alex said with a slight rise of a brow. Atreus caught it and smiled. Alex would find his behavior odd, but his brother would understand before long.

Atreus turned, and on impulse, waved to the crowd. The acknowledgment prompted a fresh outpouring of cheers only slightly muted when he stepped inside the carriage.

As protocol required, he rode with Lord Liverpool. Alex accompanied them as Royce escorted the ladies in a second carriage. Mercifully, the prime minister either felt no compulsion toward idle conversation or simply had nothing to say. Atreus was free to concentrate on the city, which at once shocked and astonished him.

It teemed with life, human and otherwise, crammed down narrow warrens and spread out over gracious avenues. In the space of what was really only a short ride, he saw poverty beyond anything he had ever imagined and grandeur that seemed intended to rival the gods. A city of contrasts, to be sure, and likely a reflection of the people who had built it. He would do well to remember that as he dealt with them.

He would, of course, for he always did as duty required. But that did not prevent him from turning his thoughts to pleasanter and far more personal matters. . . .

* * *

IF SHE COULD KEEP HER HANDS FROM SHAKING, everything would be all right. Only that, nothing more, just her hands. She ought to be able to manage that.

Seated in the carriage across from Royce and Kassandra, Brianna schooled herself to the appearance of calm. The reality of it was so far beyond her capabilities just then that she did not even consider it. Appearance would be victory enough.

He was here. Well, of course he was. She had known for several months that Atreus was coming. It was all arranged. The Vanax of Akora, chosen ruler of his people, would make a state visit to the royal court of the Prince Regent. The leaders would meet for purposes of mutual understanding and friendship. Difficulties between the kingdoms, arising from attempts by some in England to provoke an invasion of Akora during the past year, would be smoothed over. All would be as it should be.

But now Atreus was here and her hands were shaking. She gripped them tightly, even as her mind reeled from the impact of his presence. When last she saw him, he had still been recovering from the attack that almost claimed his life. Even then, far from the peak of his powers, he threatened to undo her. Of course, he could not know that. He couldn't . . . could he? The very possibility made her lightheaded, in itself disturbing, as she was not given to missishness.

"Brianna . . . are you all right?" Kassandra looked at her with concern. "You're rather pale."

"I'm fine, completely fine. There is no reason why I would be anything else."

The glance that passed between the married couple left no doubt that she had spoken too quickly and without thought. She wished her hasty words recalled even as she could not help but marvel at the ease of understanding shared by these two who had become her friends. Marvel and, truth be told, envy just a little.

"Atreus looks very well, don't you think?" Royce remarked with a slight smile.

"He does," Kassandra agreed, "to my great relief. When I think how close he came . . ."

"Do not think of it," Royce said and gently covered his wife's hand with his own. "All that is in the past. Dwelling on it cannot be good for you or our child."

Kassandra returned his smile. She was in the early months of pregnancy and entrancingly happy, all the more so since she had passed the point of starting each day with weak tea and dry rusks.

"I know this visit has a very serious purpose, but I do so hope Atreus will have a good time while he is here," she said. "He has so little opportunity for anything other than work." A loving sister, she added, "I sometimes think he would have preferred a very different sort of life."

"He did not have to become Vanax," Brianna said quietly. She wished her heart would be still so that her mind might rule. It, at least, could be trusted not to betray her. "He underwent the trial of selection voluntarily."

"I suppose that is true," Kassandra replied, "on the surface. But I don't think there really was any choice. He knew he was called to it."

Had he known? Brianna wondered. Perhaps, in some sense, but she was skeptical of the mysterious process by which the ruler of Akora was chosen. It remained hidden in legend and myth, wrapped in secrets and whispers. So much power flowed from it, almost total control over the lives and fates of every Akoran, yet almost no one knew anything about it.

"We must make sure he has time for himself while he is here," Kassandra was saying. "But it will be very difficult.

Joanna and I have given up counting the invitations, yet they continue to arrive in droves."

"The *ton* is beside itself," Royce said dryly. "I wonder if Atreus can have any conception of what awaits him."

"He will find out soon enough," Kassandra replied with a frown. "The reception at Carlton House is tomorrow evening and after that comes the deluge." A thought occurred to her and she brightened. "Brianna, your gown for tomorrow is magnificent. Madame Duprès has outdone herself."

Brianna shuddered just a little. She was deeply grateful to both couples for making it possible for her to be in England. Despite being born English, she had thought of herself as Akoran until earlier in the year when the chance had come to visit the land of her birth. The questions that arose then in her mind, and the unexpected yearnings she felt, had brought her back in search of what she hoped would be a resolution of some sort. For all that, fitting into British society was difficult. She had scant patience for its requirements, yet she was determined not to let down either herself or her hosts.

"Madame Duprès is a tyrant," she said. "But when it comes to the wielding of silk and satin, velvet and lace, she is also a genius. I suppose we must make allowances."

"Is it true you stuck her with one of her own pins?" Kassandra asked.

Brianna assumed a look of utter innocence. "You will have to ask the pin."

Royce chuckled, but she could not help noticing that he looked at her carefully. The Englishman missed very little, if anything. He and Alex were both big, supremely fit men who tended to move swiftly and silently, achieving their goals with very little discussion and nothing at all in the way of warning.

And then there was Atreus. . . .

The Vanax, ruler of her people and, though she was loathe to admit it, of herself. She must not think of him in any other way, no matter the treacherous stirrings of her heart. Put him beside the other two men and they would seem to be brothers, so closely did they resemble one another in size and strength. He and Alex actually were half brothers, sharing as mother an Akoran princess. But Atreus was all Akoran, heir to the family that traced its heritage back through more than three thousand years of proud Akoran history. And if she believed the legends—which she did not—he was even more than that, united with the land, the sea, the very air of Akora in some way that went beyond the understanding of mere mortals.

No wonder his word was regarded as law and his slightest whim accorded reverence. What she was beginning to think of as her plain British good sense scoffed at the very notion.

The carriages were passing beyond the gate guarding the graceful residence occupied by Alex, Kassandra, and herself. For the length of the Vanax's stay, it would also be his residence. In recognition of this, the royal banner of Akora fluttered in the breeze above the broad marble steps.

Descending from the carriage, Brianna lifted her eyes to the expanse of fierce crimson cloth emblazoned with the golden bull's horn symbol of the royal house. She had seen that flag every day for the better part of her life, since the storm that brought her, a shipwrecked and orphaned child, to the fabled shores of Akora. The hidden kingdom beyond the Pillars of Hercules was said to be where warriors ruled and women served. She had long since come to think of Akora as her home, but of late she was not so certain. Was she truly Akoran . . . or English? . . . Both? . . . Neither?

The realization stirred in her that the coming days and weeks might well bring the answer.

* * *

"A GOOD BEGINNING, DON'T YOU THINK?" ALEX SAID after the drawing room door closed behind Lord Liverpool. The prime minister had lingered the proper twenty minutes before taking his leave. Along with the usual pleasantries, he took with him a clear statement of the will of the Vanax of Akora. As a sovereign and independent nation, Akora would welcome full diplomatic relations with Great Britain. Also, as a sovereign and independent nation, Akora would defend its waters, its lands, its people, and its vessels wherever those might roam. No interference from Great Britain or anyone else would be tolerated. Doubt that, and meet the might of Akora's legendary warriors, rightly rumored to be among the most fierce in the world.

"Well enough," Atreus agreed. "Is Liverpool as lacking in imagination as he appears?"

"Entirely. He will convey your words to the Prince Regent accurately enough, but don't expect him to communicate the flavor of them. That you will have to do yourself."

"I intend to. Is this evening free?"

"Yes, but it could be your last taste of freedom for some time. After the reception at Carlton House, there is the ball here in your honor, but beyond all that, the *ton* clamors for your presence."

The Vanax of Akora said, "Accept those invitations you think absolutely necessary, but I do not intend to make myself overly available. Better, I think, to leave something of the mystery about Akora intact."

"I thought that might be your preference. Society has its uses, but it can be remarkably tedious."

Having shown Lord Liverpool out, Royce returned in time to hear this. "It will be Christmas in a week. We've been talking of spending it at Hawkforte." He turned to Atreus. "If that is agreeable to you."

"I don't suppose it's any warmer at Hawkforte, is it?" Atreus asked with a grin.

"I'm afraid not," Royce said with equal humor. "There's a good chance we'll see snow."

"Snow? I'd like to see that, and, of course, I've heard a great deal about Hawkforte. I'd be delighted to come, thank you."

Royce nodded. "Good—"

"I assume Brianna will be there?"

Alex and Royce exchanged a glance. "Brianna?" Alex repeated.

Atreus moved a little closer to the fire. He was well accustomed to physical discomfort, having experienced it often enough during the rigorous training that was a part of every Akoran male's upbringing, but the chill dampness was new to him.

"I expect a week will be sufficient to conclude my business here in London," he said. "It will have to be, for I am not inclined to linger very long after that. Too many matters on Akora remained unresolved."

Neither of the other men had to ask what he meant. They knew full well that Atreus's determination to modernize the Fortress Kingdom faced opposition from two sides—the members of Helios, "Sunshine," who wanted even greater change more quickly, and the followers of the traitor Deilos, who opposed all change and had been willing to go so far as to try to assassinate Atreus in order to prevent it. Most troubling of all were the indications that the two groups, or at least some members of them, had joined forces in the attempt to kill him half a year before. He had postponed Deilos's trial and the trials of the Helios members while he himself recovered, and to give public rage at them time to cool. But Akora's confrontation with the dissension within its own society could not be delayed much longer.

"After Christmas," Atreus said, "we will return to Akora directly from Hawkforte."

At the look of surprise evident in both men's faces, he added, "Hawkforte is on the sea, is it not?"

"Certainly," Royce said. "When you say 'we' . . ."

"Brianna and I. She will be returning to Akora with me."

There was a moment's silence before Alex said, "She hasn't mentioned that."

Atreus shrugged. "Hardly surprising, as she isn't aware of it."

"Is there some particular reason for her return?" Royce asked. "The letters she has shared from her family indicate they miss her but understand her wish to be here. However, if they've asked you to bring her back—"

"No, it isn't that. It's time for Brianna to return home." Well aware of the sensation he was about to provoke, the Vanax of Akora said, "And time for us to marry."

There was something undeniably satisfying about surprising two men so immune to surprise. Alex and Royce both stared at him in astonishment. The Englishman spoke first.

"I had no idea you were contemplating matrimony."

"Nor did I," Alex said. He looked at his brother intently. "You have said nothing of this."

"What needed to be said?" Atreus asked. "Surely it has always been understood that one day I would marry?"

"Yes, certainly," Alex agreed, "but considering the extraordinary lengths some of the most beguiling women on Akora have gone to in an effort to lure you into that happy state, and considering their universal failure to do so . . . let's just say this is startling news."

"Very startling," Royce agreed, "particularly since, to

the best of my knowledge, the young lady herself has not so much as hinted at this."

"Atreus," Alex began, his sharpening gaze evidence of the suspicion dawning in him. "Brianna does know what you intend, doesn't she?"

"I can't imagine how she would. We've never spoken of it."

The two husbands exchanged a glance. "You haven't spoken of marriage?" Royce asked. "But some understanding developed between the two of you when she was helping to take care of you after Deilos's attack?"

"Not at all," Atreus replied. "You may recall that Brianna left Akora to come here shortly after I regained consciousness."

Silence reigned through the space of several moments before Alex said, "She is a lovely young woman, but surely you should be better acquainted before contemplating marriage?"

Atreus shrugged. "There is nothing to contemplate. I have known for some time that Brianna is to be my wife."

"Known?" Alex repeated slowly. He looked at his brother more closely. "How could you have known?"

Atreus hesitated before replying. He rarely spoke of the central event of his life, which had transformed him from the man who would have been content to be an artist into the ruler of his people. But Alex and Royce were as close to him as anyone on earth. He owed them honesty.

In the quiet of the gracious London room, he summoned memories of an ancient ritual on a distant shore.

"When I underwent the trial of selection to become Vanax much was revealed to me. Among other things, I 'saw' the woman I now know to be Brianna and understood that she was to be my wife."

So seldom was the trial spoken of that the mere mention

of it clearly surprised Royce and Alex. They needed a moment to grasp what he had just said.

Gravely, Alex asked, "You have no doubt of the meaning of what you saw?"

"None whatsoever. If I do not marry Brianna, I will fail in my duty to Akora. Naturally, I cannot allow that to happen."

"You said the woman you *now* know to be Brianna," Royce said. "You didn't know who she was then?"

"I saw her face and form." He was not about to reveal how thoroughly he had seen her with all the intimacy of a lover. "But I didn't know her name. I had no idea who she was until a few months ago when I regained consciousness after the attack and found her caring for me."

Alex took a deep breath, let it out slowly. "That must have been a surprise."

"To say the least. There were times when I thought I would never find her."

With the candor of a brother who was also a friend, Alex added, "You must realize that Brianna may not share your conviction."

"It has been my observation," Royce said dryly, "that women prefer to be sought after for love rather than duty."

"That is only part of the problem," Alex said. "Brianna is not Akoran by birth. Her origins remain a mystery but I have the definite impression that she wants to discover more about them. That desire influenced her decision to return to England with Joanna and myself."

"I understood there was a certain risk involved in allowing her to come with you this time," Atreus said. "But while I recovered from the attack, I was in no position to resolve matters between us." He smiled faintly. "Fortunately, that is no longer the case."

"Then you intend to . . . persuade her?" Royce inquired.

"That is my preference," said the man who was absolute ruler of his people. "But I have waited long enough and there are matters at home that demand my attention. One way or another, Brianna will return with me and we will be married." Graciously, he added, "You are, of course, all invited to the wedding."

"And if Brianna does not agree?" Royce asked quietly.

"That would be regrettable," the Vanax said. Steel in his voice, he added, "But we all must do our duty."

He accepted the brandy his brother offered and joined in the toast that followed. The winter wind blew down the chimney just then and raised a spray of sparks. Atreus glanced at them, noting in passing that the flashes of fire shone with bright delicacy and were not easily extinguished. Indeed, the harder the wind blew, the more the sparks rose to meet it and the more determinedly they burned.

Y OU WERE VERY QUIET AT DINNER LAST
night," Joanna said. She looked across the
breakfast table at Brianna, who was buttering a
croissant. The three women were seated in the
morning room of Alex and Joanna's residence. Beyond the
high windows, the December day bloomed.

"I'm just a bit tired," Brianna said. Much as she appreciated the concern of her friends, she kept her attention on
her plate.

"The ship brought letters for you from home," Joanna
said. "Good news, I hope?"

Brianna did look up then, smiling at her friend. Joanna
was ever the mother, attentive to everyone's well-being.
While yet she wondered what might trouble Brianna, she
would seek to draw it from her. "Very good. My father
writes that we have five new colts."

"Marcus must be pleased," Kassandra said. "Your family raises the best horses in all of Akora."

"I will tell him you said so when I reply. My mother, in her letter, says Father is working too hard, but she doesn't sound terribly concerned. They are all well, including Polonus, who also wrote."

"He is your younger brother?" Joanna asked.

Brianna nodded. "Two years younger. He is unsettled yet and restless." She had not meant to say that, but reading Polonus's letter the previous night, she had gleaned the impression that her brother, for all that he said little of substance, had much on his mind. She sympathized, knowing that they shared many of the same perceptions and hopes. But she worried, too, that Polonus's dreams of the future left little room for necessary patience. His was a young man's nature, vigorous but rough-edged, prone to thoughtless error.

"Perhaps you are also a bit apprehensive about this evening?" Kassandra ventured. "If so, you have no reason. You are more than prepared to enter society. Indeed, you might have done so months ago."

"I know," Brianna said, glad to think of other things. "And I deeply appreciate all you have done to help me find my place in the land of my birth. But I wonder if tonight is not the right time. After all, I would not wish to detract in any way from Atreus's presence."

"Oh, you won't," Joanna said frankly. "It's unlikely that many members of the *ton* will notice anyone else. Indeed, I expect them to overlook Prinny himself."

"That will be a new experience for him," Kassandra murmured. "Where are the men, by the way?"

"They rose early," Joanna said with a smile. "At least, Alex did." Her smile deepened. "He didn't depart quite as soon as he expected, but I believe they had plans."

Kassandra rolled her eyes. "If they return bloodied and bedraggled, I think we have every right to protest."

"Why would they do that?" Brianna asked. Atreus had come so close to losing his life. Surely he would not place himself at any unnecessary risk.

Yes, he would. She had lived long enough among Akoran warriors to know that full well. The plain truth was that he would regard as amusement what she would see, at best, as needless danger.

"They are men," Joanna said, and shrugged. She brightened as a serving maid arrived, holding Amelia.

"My apologies, my lady, but the little one won't stop fussing."

"Never apologize for bringing her to me," Joanna said, holding out her arms. "There, sweetheart, what troubles you?"

Nothing, so far as Brianna could see, for the baby quieted as soon as she felt her mother's touch. Instead of crying, Amelia busied herself looking around at everything.

"She is such a fascinating child," Kassandra murmured.

"Your goddaughter?" Joanna said. She laughed. "Of course you feel that way."

"For more than just that reason. I have the uncanny impression that she *sees*. . . ."

"Naturally she sees."

"Not just sees, *sees* . . . more deeply, more completely . . . something."

Joanna's arms tightened around her daughter. "What are you saying?"

"Nothing terrible," Kassandra said gently. "You know that full well. It's hardly as though there haven't been women with unusual abilities in this family before."

"She is only a baby," Joanna protested even as she glanced worriedly at her daughter. "Surely it is far too soon to know anything of that sort."

Amelia made a little sound very much like a chuckle.

"Gas," Joanna said firmly. "She does not understand a word we say and she has gas."

"She looks very cheerful for a baby with gas," Kassandra observed. To Brianna, she said, "Am I being completely inscrutable, or do you understand what I'm saying?"

Slowly, Brianna said, "I know you both can do unusual things. Joanna can find that which is missing and you . . ." She hesitated before saying gently, "I have thought that your gift, as it might be called, truly must seem like a curse sometimes. To see the future—"

"Possible futures," Kassandra corrected gently. "Such vision served us well when Akora was threatened, but now, thankfully, the future is as mysterious to me as to anyone else. Yet we know such abilities are inherited. They date from the misty beginnings of Joanna's own family and spread to Akora when a member of that family arrived on our shores centuries ago."

"But these abilities are unpredictable, are they not?" Brianna asked. She looked at Amelia, who stared back solemnly. "And in many generations, they haven't been present at all."

"That's true," Joanna agreed. "They seem to appear when they are needed. At any rate, Amelia will be whatever she will be."

Brianna smiled at the baby. "Right now, she looks sleepy."

As though in response, Amelia yawned. A few moments later, her head slumped against her mother's shoulder. Joanna rose to return her to the nursery. When they were left alone, Kassandra said, "You're not really nervous about this evening, are you?"

"A little," Brianna admitted, although not for the reason her friend might assume. Going out into British society held no particular qualms. An evening in the library would be far more congenial, but at worst, she expected to be bored.

An evening in Atreus's presence . . . that was another matter altogether. She had gotten through dinner the previous evening, but only with difficulty. What was it about the man that made her stomach flutter so?

He was undeniably handsome, but she had lived most of her life among Akoran men, who tended to be extremely fit and virile. He was commanding, but that was hardly surprising. He was the absolute ruler of Akora. It would be odd indeed if he did not wear the aura of command. Besides, she didn't especially like commanding men . . . did she?

He had almost died a few months before. Her Aunt Elena, the most gifted of Akora's healers, had fought the greatest battle of her life to save him. Brianna had helped, although she considered her own contribution to be very small. But she would have fought just as hard and cared just as much for anyone else. Wouldn't she?

The way he looked at her . . . A shiver whipped down her spine, bringing with it truth. There was something in the way the Vanax of Akora looked at her that ignited her unease, as though he knew her in some way that was not possible.

Clearly, she needed diversion, and quickly.

"Would you care for a ride?" she asked Kassandra. Thinking of her friend's condition, she added, "We can keep it nice and gentle."

"Not too gentle," Kassandra said. "I'm fit as the proverbial fiddle. Now if only Royce would understand that."

"It's only natural for him to be concerned," Joanna said as she returned from settling Amelia down. "Did I hear something about a ride?"

Brianna nodded. "It's a perfect day. Not too cold, and

there is no wind. If we're going to be cooped up all evening, we might as well get out and enjoy ourselves now."

"I agree entirely," Kassandra said with a grin. "Give me half an hour to go home and change."

Joanna tugged the bell pull. A young maid appeared almost at once. "Sarah, be a dear and tell Bolkum we need three horses saddled."

The young woman dropped a quick curtsey. "As you say, my lady."

Within the hour, the three friends rode out. They were accompanied by an escort of half a dozen guards who remained a polite distance behind them, far enough to allow the illusion of privacy, but close enough to respond in an instant to any hint of danger.

"I've tried to convince Alex that this isn't necessary," Joanna said with a sigh. "But he won't be swayed."

"Neither will Royce," Kassandra said. "If one of them didn't insist, the other would, and the end result would be the same."

"They do have some reason for concern," Brianna pointed out. "There is great unrest in England."

"That might not be so," Joanna said, "if the Prince Regent showed more interest in the welfare of his subjects."

Her bluntness did not surprise Brianna, who was well accustomed to Joanna's speaking her mind. Nor was she alone in this.

"I wasn't aware he showed any interest at all," Kassandra said dryly.

Joanna nodded. "Too true. The self-indulgence of society from top to bottom is remarkable. Yet there are people who really are trying to make things better."

"May Fortune favor them," Kassandra said. "How glad I am that on Akora we have the blessing of wise government."

Brianna hesitated. She truly valued the friendship of

both women and would never wish to cause them distress. Moreover, discretion was her natural preference. Yet the urge to respond proved irresistible.

"There are similarities between Akora and England," she said.

A slight wind blew where a moment before there had been only calm. Brianna tightened her hands on the reins. She did not like wind.

They were turning into Hyde Park, within sight of the long curved lake called the Serpentine that gleamed in the winter sun. Nearby were the ancient, gnarled trees that framed Rotten Row—really the *route de roi* or "way of the king," the name long since corrupted. The broad dirt road where the fashionables came to see and be seen was unexpectedly crowded, given that it was barely mid-morning.

Brianna was wondering about that when Joanna said, "What similarities?"

"What? Oh, similarities . . . well, Akora and England both have hereditary monarchies."

Kassandra drew her horse around a cluster of riders in the center of the road and said, "Not really. No one can become Vanax who has not undergone the trial of selection, no matter who his family may be."

"So it seems," Brianna acknowledged, "but no one has ever become Vanax who is not directly linked to the Atreides family."

"I thought," Joanna said, "the explanation for that is that only members of the Atreides family can survive the trial of selection. Haven't there been others who have attempted it and perished?"

"Ten, at least, that I know of from our history," Kassandra said. "But, of course, that is over thousands of years. There may have been more."

This time, Brianna did keep silent, but the thought was in her mind that no one really knew how those ten men—or any others—had died. All that was certain was that power remained with the Atreides family, absolute power resting now in the hands of Atreus.

"Does there seem an unusually large turnout for the hour?" Kassandra asked.

Relieved to be on more neutral ground, Brianna nodded. "I was thinking the same myself. I wonder what accounts for it?"

"Good Lord," Joanna murmured, "there's Lady Melbourne." She nodded in the direction of a stout but still elegant figure aboard a handsome gray. The lady inclined her head in acknowledgment and turned her mount toward them.

Kassandra permitted herself a small groan. "Now you've done it. She'll want something, you can be sure."

"I know, it's just I was so startled to see her. She never rises before midday, yet here she is, and not alone. For that matter, most of the *ton* seem to have decided to go riding."

"*Dear* Lady Joanna," London's most renowned, not to say feared, hostess called out as she approached. "And *dear* Princess Kassandra. It is such a delight to see you both." Her glance strayed to Brianna, but only briefly. Untitled, unfortuned, and unknown, Brianna knew herself to be of absolutely no interest. For that she was immensely grateful.

"We are all *so* looking forward to the grand event tomorrow," Lady Melbourne declared. "I understand *absolutely* everyone is invited, which is terribly splendid of you. But tell me, have you come to join the gentlemen?"

Joanna, perhaps feeling herself responsible for the encounter, replied. "The gentlemen?"

"Your husbands, of course, and your guest, His Highness, the Vanax of Akora. Such an impressive title, I'm sure, and such an impressive gentleman by all that is being said. I gather those who were at the dock yesterday to welcome him were most astoundingly impressed."

"How nice," Kassandra murmured. "But we are here simply to ride. As for my husband and brothers—"

"Oh, come, do not tell me you are ignorant of their whereabouts! Word spread several hours ago that they were here." Deflating only slightly, Lady Melbourne added, "Of course, no one has actually seen them, although everyone has certainly been looking."

Brianna struggled to hide a grin, failed, and discreetly turned her head away. Even so, she was hard-pressed not to burst out laughing when Joanna said, "Has anyone checked the groundskeeper's lodge?"

"Why ever would they be there?" Lady Melbourne demanded.

"It is an Akoran tradition," Joanna explained solemnly. "Isn't it, Kassandra?"

"What? Oh . . . yes . . . of course. A tradition . . . to . . . to . . ."

"To pay a call," Brianna suggested.

Kassandra looked at her gratefully. "Yes, that's it, to pay a call on . . . whatever person happens to be responsible for wherever one happens to be. That's it. It's a courtesy, really."

"Do you mean to say that the Vanax of Akora would call on a groundskeeper before he has even met the Prince Regent himself?" Lady Melbourne appeared utterly dumbfounded by the possibility, but ready to seize on it all the same.

"Oh, yes," Kassandra said solemnly. "Most definitely he would. Atreus always upholds tradition." She looked to her companions. "Isn't that true?"

They both nodded vigorously.

"Completely," Joanna murmured.

"Without fail," Brianna offered.

"Dear ladies, thank you so much!"

With no further pretense of desiring their company, Lady Melbourne dug her heels into the gray and sped off at a trot well beyond the capabilities of most women her age. But then she never had allowed anything to stand between herself and a social triumph.

Seeing her speedy redirection, other riders quickly drew the desired conclusion and followed. Soon enough, the surrounding stretch of Rotten Row was deserted save for Brianna and her friends.

"That was too bad of us," Kassandra said with a laugh.

"Matter of self-preservation," Joanna insisted.

"You don't think there's any possibility they actually could be somewhere about here?" Brianna asked.

"Good Lord, no," Kassandra assured her. "Atreus is the very soul of courtesy, and I'm sure he would be happy to meet the groundskeeper. In fact, I'm sure he'd prefer him to a great many of the people he is going to meet. But there's no chance of the three of them being here. Royce would have realized the fuss any appearance here would cause, and Alex as well. No, they've gone off somewhere else altogether."

"And laid a false trail while they were about it," Joanna said. At Brianna's puzzled looked, she added, "I'd wager this was one rumor that didn't get started on its own. Those three wanted to get up to something and they didn't want anyone noticing, so they sent everyone off in the wrong direction."

"But why?" Brianna murmured.

"Exactly what we intend to find out," Kassandra said, with Joanna's full agreement.

Male laughter and the scent of excellent tobacco greeted their return to the house. As they removed their outer garments in the entry hall, Joanna asked, "Have the gentlemen been back long, Mulridge?"

The stern, black-garbed housekeeper who had come to greet them shook her head. "About half an hour, my lady." She looked to Kassandra. "Lord Royce wasn't too keen to hear you'd gone riding, ma'am."

"Contrary to my dear husband's opinion, I am not made of spun glass."

Another round of male good humor reached them from the inner sanctum of Alex's office. Kassandra grinned. "Besides, he doesn't sound unhappy."

"Up to something," Joanna murmured. For good measure, she added, "and thinking they got away with it."

"We can't have that," Kassandra said, and swept past the curved marble staircase toward the ornately carved door leading to her brother's office. She had just reached it when the door was opened by her own dear husband.

"Thought I heard your voice," Royce said. He looked her up and down, appeared satisfied by what he saw, and took her hand, raising it to his lips. "Have a nice ride?"

"Quite nice, if rather crowded. The oddest thing happened. It seems all of society decided to go riding this morning in Hyde Park. Can you imagine what prompted that?"

Royce chuckled and stood aside so that the ladies might enter. As he did so, Alex and Atreus got to their feet, extinguishing the cigars they had been enjoying. Though she made a sincere effort not to do so, Brianna found herself unable to look anywhere other than at the Vanax of Akora. He stood, tall, broad-shouldered, clad in a loose white silk shirt open at the collar and tucked into buff riding breeches. His thick hair, black as a moonless sky, looked riffled by the wind. Burnished skin stretched tautly over high cheekbones, a blade of a nose, and a decidedly firm jaw.

He was unrelenting in his masculinity, a challenge to any woman who crossed his path, yet also far more. She knew there were people—including those she truly loved and respected—who revered him as uniquely wise and just. She could not share their views, but she could grant that he had extraordinary courage. Never had he been known to flinch from any enemy or challenge. Looking at him, she could not imagine that he ever would.

"Brianna," he said softly, yet his voice seemed to possess an odd resonance that echoed deep within her. He came toward her, across the Persian carpet, his eyes never leaving hers. "Did you enjoy your ride?"

Breathe . . . she had to breathe . . . but when she did, the air was filled with tantalizing traces of leather, tobacco, and pure man.

Really, that was no help at all.

"Very much," she said, and prayed she did not sound as befuddled as she felt.

"Good." His mouth curved slightly, as though something amused him. He had the most fascinating mouth . . . hard yet generous. . . . She wondered how it would feel—

"Hyde Park was crowded?"

"What? Oh . . . yes . . . everyone was there, or so it seemed."

"And I have to wonder why," Kassandra said. "What gets society out of bed before noon?"

"A rumor that the Vanax of Akora would be riding in a certain place?" Royce suggested lightly. "A word spread here and there by ever-eager delivery boys who don't mind making an extra shilling or two?"

"We thought as much," Joanna exclaimed. "While everyone was looking there, where did the three of you actually go?"

"Moors Field," Atreus replied. "And my apologies, ladies. If we'd any notion you would choose to go riding in Hyde Park this morning, we would have sent society in another direction."

"Never mind that," Kassandra directed. "Just tell us why you went to Moors Field. Isn't it that rather desolate place over toward Bishopsgate?"

"Any place is bound to be desolate when it's used for artillery practice," Alex remarked. He gestured to the silver tea service set out on a nearby table. "Shall I ring for more?"

"Oh, do," Joanna said. "We'll sip tea, toast our feet, and hear all about what the three of you saw."

"Nothing we don't already have," Atreus said. "And that, of course, was the point."

Brianna sank down on the nearest settee. Tea was definitely in order. With any luck, it would rally her wayward thoughts. "I understood the threat of a British invasion was past?"

It was the turn of the Vanax of Akora to be surprised. As he took the seat beside her, Atreus asked, "How did you know of that?"

Before Brianna could reply, Kassandra said, "You forget, brother, she was with us through all those terrible weeks when we did not know if you would live or die. Indeed, it is fair to say that we would not have managed half so well without her. Naturally, Brianna became almost a member of the family."

Atreus nodded slowly. "Almost. . . ." His smile was most unfairly devastating and his eyes . . . If she were not very careful, she could get lost in them. "Then I presume I can count on your discretion," he said.

Brianna cleared her throat. "You do not wish to alarm the people."

"I do not wish to trouble them with a threat that is over and done with," he corrected gently. "We went to Moors Field because the British are the masters of artillery. They're kind enough to test it in front of anyone who is interested enough to look."

"That seems rather foolish of them."

"Perhaps, but considering the number of French spies in England, there is a certain sense to it. The information those gentlemen send back to Napoleon must be demoralizing, at the very least."

"You said Akora has everything the British have. Are we then also the masters of artillery?"

He smiled at the question but did not dismiss it. Instead, he said, "We are the masters of our fate, as we have always been. What is useful to us, we build for ourselves or acquire. Always we understand that power, especially power that deters, is the surest guarantee of peace."

"Akora has always known peace."

"And you think that means it always will?"

"I don't know," Brianna admitted. "I haven't really thought about it." The truth of that startled her. She had thought long and hard about the need for change, but the virtues of stability . . . that was another matter altogether.

"Akora is so separate from the world," she said.

"The world is changing. Surely you've been here long enough to see that?"

"Akora is not England."

"Akora is part of the same world," the Vanax countered. "It would be the worst sort of mistake to imagine ourselves immune from the turmoil evident elsewhere."

"Then why don't you—" She broke off, suddenly horrifyingly aware of how very close she had come to blurting out far too much truth.

"Why don't I what?"

"Nothing, I just was . . . surprised by what you said."

"But not alarmed, I hope? You understand Akora will be fine?"

As she understood nothing of the sort and could not find it in herself to lie, Brianna said, "I certainly hope so."

The others were listening far too intently. She was glad of the diversion when Joanna poured the tea.

Brianna was quite proud that the hand with which she accepted the delicate cup and saucer did not shake at all.

Proud, and more than a little surprised.

A short time later, although not quite short enough to suit her, the ladies excused themselves to begin their preparations for the evening.

"It's quite unfair," Kassandra said as they departed. "We will primp and crimp for hours, while you men will toss yourselves together at the last possible moment."

Royce lifted his cup in salute. "But we will spend the entire evening in awe of your beauty."

"Oh, well, then, I suppose it's worth it," Joanna murmured. "Come along, ladies." They had scarcely reached the stairs before she added, "Bravo, Brianna."

"Definitely bravo," Kassandra agreed. "Well done."

"What is well done?" Brianna asked, genuinely confused. She had no notion of what they meant.

"Standing up to Atreus as you did," Kassandra explained. "Not just instantly agreeing with him. He gets far too much of that, you know. There are very few he can count on to actually challenge him or even . . . *gasp* . . . to disagree."

"I meant no discourtesy. . . ."

"Of course you didn't," Joanna said, "and no one would ever take it that way. Atreus likes people who have minds of their own."

Softly, Brianna said, "But in the end, it is only his that counts."

"It is true," Kassandra said, "that once he makes a decision, debate stops. But Atreus comes to his decisions carefully and thoughtfully. He has always been open to an intelligent argument supported by facts. On more than one occasion, he has changed his initial opinion when such an argument persuades him to see a matter differently."

At the top of the stairs, Brianna paused. She could walk away now, say nothing more. But these women were her true friends. She felt as close to them as to any member of her family.

"It is good to know his mind is open," she said, "but there are some who believe all of Akoran society should be more open."

"You mean those people in Helios?" Joanna asked. "The sunshine people?"

"The name means 'sunshine,' " Brianna agreed. "The point seems to be that light should be shone on deliberations that are now shrouded in secrecy."

"It's all a great deal of fuss about nothing, if you ask me," Kassandra said. "You can't drag everything out into the open and debate it. There will always be delicate matters best settled privately among people of discretion."

"Helios seems harmless enough," Joanna said.

Kassandra shrugged. "Perhaps, but let us not forget that there are still several members of Helios in jail because of their possible involvement in the attempt on Atreus's life earlier this year."

"There is no evidence against them," Brianna said.

Joanna shook her head. "Actually, there is. It just hasn't come out yet."

"There is evidence," Kassandra agreed, "and that will become obvious to everyone when the trials are held."

"I see. . . . Do you have any idea when that might be?" Brianna's hands were tightly clenched in the folds of her riding habit, where her friends could not see them.

"Soon, I believe," Kassandra said. "Atreus wanted time for public sentiment against Helios to calm, at least somewhat, and he also had to make this trip. I imagine he will act when he returns to Akora."

They parted a short time later, each to the ministrations of her lady's maid. But as Brianna suffered herself to be brushed, perfumed, gowned, and generally fussed over, her mind remained elsewhere, dwelling on the implications of all that had been said.

And on the encounter with a man she had presumed she knew, but now suspected she might not know at all.

Chapter
THREE

THOUSANDS OF GOLD-ENCRUSTED CRYSTALS reflected the light of almost as many candles, arranged in vast chandeliers hanging from the ceiling and in wall sconces between the high windows of the ballroom. So brilliant was their combined radiance that night truly seemed transformed into day. As though to further deny nature, the room was filled along the edges with orange trees set in immense silver tubs. A week before Christmas, some of the trees boasted fragrant orange blossoms, but many had been forced so effectively that they already bore fruit.

"Astounding," Brianna murmured, though truth be told she could have chosen any number of other words to describe such unbridled extravagance. The Prince Regent's willingness to spend almost incomprehensible wealth on his personal whims while many of his people struggled to put food in their mouths was beyond her ability to grasp.

"Isn't it?" Joanna said softly. "Alex and I met here last year during the unveiling of this latest incarnation of Carlton House. Prinny is inordinately proud of it, as you no doubt can tell."

Brianna glanced down the reception line in which she stood, observing the rotund man who looked like a weary and dissipated cherub, but who was, in fact, England's ruler, in place of his mad father. The contrast between the prince and the man standing directly beside him could not possibly have been greater. Not only was Atreus almost a foot taller than the Prince Regent, as well as in superb physical condition, his very presence radiated intelligence, gracious charm, and genuine interest.

How he managed to maintain such cordialness bewildered Brianna. They had been standing in the receiving line for close to an hour, and still the cream of British society kept coming, gloriously garbed, giddily excited, and eager for a few precious seconds with the man who had them all agog. The gentlemen were open enough in their admiration, but the ladies . . . the manners of many of them were positively shocking. They could not have been more obvious about their willingness to offer the Vanax of Akora far more private entertainment.

Not that she cared, not a whit. It had absolutely nothing to do with her. On the contrary, the better occupied he was, the less likely he would be to disturb her with those too-knowing looks.

"And you are? . . ." Yet another inquisitive lady eyed her dubiously. Brianna sighed. She had tried to sit out the receiving line, but the others wouldn't hear of it. Much as she appreciated their efforts, she was well aware that no one had the slightest interest in meeting her.

"Our dear friend Brianna," Joanna said with a frosty

smile. There was some consolation in knowing that Joanna loathed such events every bit as much as Brianna was coming to do. Kassandra, born a princess, seemed more inured to them, but not even her patience was inexhaustible.

"How nice," the lady murmured with perfect insincerity and hurried on, eyeing Atreus with eagerness that could only be called alarming.

Mercifully, a short time later, the Prince Regent declared, "Enough! By Gawd, I swear some of 'em are coming through twice. Damn cheek!" He waved off the remainder of the line, still stretching out of sight, and eyed the anxious majordomo who hovered nearby.

"Music, and make it lively. No room to dance, as usual, but can't be helped." To Atreus, he said, "Have to give it to you, milord, you've drawn out some of my peers I haven't seen in a dog's age. Thought one or two of 'em was dead, actually. Rather a shame."

"I'm sure it is your own company they seek, Your Highness," Atreus replied diplomatically.

"Not likely. You go in for much of this sort of thing on Akora?"

"In a way. We have a saying that if you want to see someone, look for him at the palace because everyone turns up there."

Prinny shot him a glance that suggested that the Prince Regent's mind, agile in his youth, still had some life in it. "Palace, is it? Thought you more of a rough bunch, bit primitive, actually, if you don't mind my saying. See now that was wrong."

Atreus smiled faintly. "It is in part to correct such misconceptions that I have come, Your Highness."

"Very wise . . . ought to have things clear. Avoids trouble in the end." A gong sounded. "Dinner," the Prince Regent announced with his first real show of enthusiasm.

"And about time. We'll feed you well, sir, I can promise you that, at least."

"I've heard a great deal about the splendor of your table, my lord," Atreus replied. He joined the prince in leading the company down the curving staircase toward the rooms on the garden level where dinner would be served.

A short distance behind them, close enough to be aware of what was being said, Brianna bit her lip. She knew full well that Atreus had heard what she had heard—that the meals at Carlton House were extravagant to the point of being grotesque. They were also exercises in endurance, comprising dozens upon dozens of courses, each richer and more elaborate than the last. Some were "corner dishes," laid out on the table so that the guests might help each other and share particular favorites. Others were "removes," offered but once. She tasted only a few of each, contenting herself with a little sole in pastry, a bit of lamb in jelly, a few bites of buttered lobster, and rather more of the potatoes with parsley, which were quite good. She let pass the raised giblet pie, ham pudding, curry of rabbit, haunch of venison, and considerably more.

Even so, she expected to find the experience interesting, and was not disappointed. Surprised, to be sure, but not disappointed. The table was being relaid for dessert when she became aware of a gentleman seated on the opposite side who appeared to be staring at her. As she could imagine no reason why he should do so, she assumed herself mistaken, but a short while later, when she happened to glance in his direction again, she received the same impression.

He was, she judged, a man of between forty and fifty years, pleasant enough, with thinning red hair brushed back from a high forehead. His expression was intent, but not offensive. He appeared startled, enough so that he ignored the dishes set before him and even neglected to respond to a remark made by the person to his left.

Uncertain as to what, if anything, she should do, Brianna was diverted by the conversation at the head of the table. Once or twice, she glanced at the man again and found him still watching her, but quickly enough another matter commanded all her attention.

She had not imagined Atreus would take any particular note of her presence. In that she had been quite wrong. The Prince Regent was occupied forking jellied oranges into his mouth when Atreus said, "I am not alone in being new to Carlton House, sir. I believe it is also the first time Brianna has been here."

When he was able, Prinny responded. They had been introduced earlier in the evening, so he knew who she was, but understandably enough, he had accorded her no notice. Until now. "Is that a fact? And what do you make of it, young lady?"

Surprised that Atreus had brought her deliberately to the Prince Regent's attention, Brianna said, "It is extraordinary, Your Highness. Truly, I have never imagined such a place."

The Prince Regent beamed at what he assumed to be a compliment. "Worked damn hard for the results I got, tell you that. Architects are a rum bunch, slack off if you let them, but I wouldn't hear of it. 'No stinting,' I said, 'do it bigger and do it better.' They listened finally, but I have to tell you, another man might have given up."

"But not you, Sire," Brianna murmured.

"No, not me. Didn't want to hear any of that carping about money, either. Very distasteful, that." He made a face rather like a child denied a sweet. To Atreus, he said, "Don't suppose you have that sort of problem, do you? You've got no Parliament to contend with, so Hawkforte tells me. Used to be like that here, in the old days. Wouldn't have minded being around then."

"It's not quite that simple on Akora," Atreus said lightly. He caught Royce's eye and raised a brow.

"I was responding to His Highness's inquiry about the nature of Akoran government," Royce explained. To Prinny, he said, "As you may recall, Sire, while I did say there is no formal parliament, the Akorans have an age-old process of consultation and compromise that goes on more or less continually."

"Must get rather tiresome," the prince remarked when he'd thought about it for a moment or two.

"It becomes second nature after a while," his royal guest assured him. The conversation moved on, but Brianna remained vividly aware that from time to time, Atreus's attention returned to her. She felt his gaze even as she refused to meet it.

So absorbed was she in that effort that it came as rather a shock to realize that the red-haired gentleman seated halfway down the table was still watching her. Indeed, he continued doing so until the vast, overblown meal finally sputtered to an end. As they were rising from the table, he melted off into the crowd. She did not see him again during the remainder of her visit to Carlton House.

It was after they had returned to Alex and Joanna's residence that the evening proved to have yet one more surprise. Atreus had just stepped down from the carriage when he turned and offered his hand to Brianna. She responded instinctively, and felt the warm strength of his fingers curl around hers. Pleasure spiraled through her, and hard on it, alarm.

"Did you enjoy the evening?" he asked.

She heard the question but had some difficulty concentrating on it, because rather than simply let go of her,

Atreus had tucked her hand into the crook of his arm and proceeded up the stone steps to the wide double doors.

"It was very interesting," she managed.

He laughed, a rich, deep sound that did absolutely nothing for her presence of mind. "You are a diplomat."

"Not at all. I just try to have some care for the other person's feelings."

"That is the essence of diplomacy: know the other person, know what he will respond to positively or negatively, and act accordingly."

"I'm sure there must be a great deal more to it than that."

"Everything else is elaboration. That gown is quite attractive. I suppose the English style is a welcome change after all that white."

White being the color for virgins on Akora, Brianna had assumed she would wear no other until her marriage. But coming to England had meant adapting to a different way of life. The truth was that she loved the gown of deep blue that, in all modesty, she knew went very well with her hair and eyes.

Or she had loved it until Atreus's remark made her actuely aware of herself in a manner all too intimate.

"Thank you. . . ." The doors were opened by Akoran guards on duty in the entry hall. At sight of the Vanax, they bowed.

Atreus nodded to them, and looked at Brianna expectantly. "Your cloak," he said.

Embarrassed at being caught so befuddled, she struggled with the frog closing at her throat. Finally, she got it undone and removed the cloak. He took it from her with a slight smile, handing it to a footman.

"A nightcap?" Alex suggested.

"Not for me," Joanna said with a smile. "Morning

comes much too soon and with it darling Amelia, but you three go ahead."

"I must beg off," Brianna murmured. "I'm all but asleep on my feet."

"You did extremely well this evening," Atreus said. "It is understandable that you would be fatigued."

She looked up . . . and up yet farther. The man really was almost too tall. He also looked amused in a way she was beginning to find irksome. "I did nothing."

Atreus appeared about to reply but before he could do so, Joanna intervened. "That's enough," she said briskly. "Come along, Brianna, time for bed. Alex, dearest, I'll wait up."

"You don't have to do that, sweetheart," her loving husband said.

"Yes, I do," Joanna said as she mounted the steps with Brianna in tow. Over her shoulder, she added, "We need to have a little chat, husband. Good night, Atreus. It's so very good to have you here."

Wondering what Joanna wanted to talk with Alex about, Brianna could find no acceptable way to ask her. Perhaps she truly was weary, but her mind also felt over-stimulated. Long after she parted from her friend, dismissed her maid, and slipped alone into the wide, high bed, her thoughts kept returning to Atreus.

He attracted her, confused her, filled her with longings, and made her just a little afraid.

It was really too bad of him to do that. She had quite enough to cope with as it was.

And yet, try though she did, she could not find it in herself to blame him.

He liked people who had minds of their own? She was just beginning to believe that perhaps he did.

He did like her gown . . . and her in it. She was quite sure of that.

He was remarkably patient and disciplined. His handling of the Prince Regent had been masterful.

And his handling of her? She had been handled in some way she could not define, but knew was there all the same.

Atreus, Vanax of Akora, scion of the Atreides, wanted something from her. She could not imagine what that could possibly be, but as sleep gently claimed her, she was quite certain she would find out before too much longer.

B EFORE THE FIRST FAINT GRAY LIGHT OF A WIN-ter dawn challenged the stars, Atreus arose. Having long ago learned the value of taking some time for himself before being overtaken by the day, he always awoke early. As was also his custom, he spent the first few minutes of the day in prayer and meditation.

As was increasingly the case these days, he thought of Brianna. Some of those thoughts were pleasant, to be sure. Others were not. She was who she was, the orphaned child. He had to accept that, come to terms with it. Above all, he had to decide what to do—or not do—about it.

But on that morning, he came no closer to any such decision. Bathed, dressed, yet still frustrated, he turned his thoughts to what might actually be accomplished in the hours ahead.

The brothers met for breakfast in the morning room. They were discussing the previous evening, and, in particular, the Prince Regent, when a guard interrupted them.

"Your pardon, Vanax. Prince Alexandros, there is an English gentleman outside who asks to see you."

"At this hour?" Alex said. He took the proffered card and studied it. "William, Earl of Hollister. The name is familiar but I can't say I know him."

"Is it not the custom to pay calls at this time?" Atreus asked.

"Definitely not. Hollister either has scant regard for the proprieties or he believes the matter of great urgency."

"Shall we find out which?" Atreus suggested.

Moments later, the Earl of Hollister was escorted into the morning room. He appeared composed, but under some significant strain. At sight of Atreus, who rose along with Alex to acknowledge him, the slender, red-haired man also looked surprised.

"Your Highness . . . I didn't realize I would be disturbing you. My apologies."

"Not at all," Atreus said.

"Have a seat," Alex said. Rather pointedly, he added, "At this hour, we do not stand on formality."

"It is early," Hollister acknowledged as he took a place at the table. The other two men resumed their seats. "I am most sorry. Frankly, I've been up all night mulling over what to do. Obviously, I could have waited to come to you, but as busy as I am certain you must be, I was concerned I might miss you."

"The matter you bring is of such urgency?"

Hollister smiled wearily. "Yes and no. It has waited sixteen years, yet I do not believe it should wait a day longer."

The brothers exchanged a glance. Quietly, Atreus said, "Sixteen years?"

Hollister nodded. "Sixteen years ago, my cousin, Lady Delphine Wilcox, née Hollister, disappeared along with her husband, a Mister Edward Wilcox, and their daughter, who would have been eight years old at the time. The assumption has been that they were all lost at sea."

"An assumption you are no longer making?" Alex asked.

"I cannot make it any longer. You see, I received a tremendous shock yesterday. I found myself seated across the table from a young lady who bears a striking resemblance to my late cousin. Indeed, so great is that resemblance that I felt I might be looking at a ghost."

"Brianna," Atreus said quietly. His wife-to-be, ghost of his own memory. And his own guilt.

Hollister nodded. "I have been told that is her name, and as far as I am concerned, that seals the matter. It is the same name given to my cousin's child. The young woman is described to me only as a lady of Akora and a friend of your family, but in fact she is Lady Brianna Wilcox, the title hers through her mother's line. She has a family right here in England. A family, I might add, most eager to receive her."

No longer able to conceal his agitation, Hollister looked from one to the other of his hosts as he said, "I am at a loss to understand how this could have occurred. While I am sure we are all grateful that Brianna is alive and well, particularly given Akora's reputation for being hostile to outsiders, how could you fail to make any effort to return her to her rightful family?"

Alex remained silent, but Atreus said, "We did make an effort. Sixteen years ago, when Brianna arrived on Akora, she was severely injured. She did recover, but with gaps in her memory that have never healed. She knew her name was Brianna Wilcox and it was obvious when she spoke that she was English. But she knew very little else. Inquiries were made here in England, but nothing ever came of them. It did not appear that anyone was looking for a lost couple named Wilcox, or their lost child."

He sat back, his gaze steady on Hollister. "And now perhaps you would like to explain how that could have been? How could a family lose a daughter and granddaughter, and conceal that fact so effectively that our agents did not uncover it?"

"Your Highness—"

"Explain that," Atreus cut in. "Or this matter ends

right now. As Vanax, I am ultimately responsible for the well-being of every Akoran, including Brianna. There is no possibility that I will allow her to have any knowledge of a family that is being less than completely truthful about what happened to her."

Hollister paled but remained resolute. Slowly, he said, "It was all very regrettable. My uncle, from whom I inherited the title, disapproved of my cousin's choice of husband. An estrangement followed. My uncle was a very strong-willed man, accustomed to having his own way. He made the couple's situation in England untenable, with the result that they fled to the Continent. Delphine was never spoken of again. Years later, after his death, I found evidence in my uncle's papers that he was aware of her disappearance and had made inquiries in an effort to find out what had happened. But he told no one of that and tolerated no mention of her. I imagine that was why your agents learned nothing."

"What a terrible waste," Alex murmured.

"Indeed it was," Hollister agreed, "but one I have every intention of rectifying." He looked to Atreus. "I give you every assurance, Your Highness, that Brianna will be received into our family with true joy and ever tender consideration for her welfare. She will have a home, a family, and, I might say, excellent prospects."

"She has a home and a family now," Atreus said quietly. "As for her prospects . . ." He broke off. The Englishman presented a problem. If Brianna were left in ignorance of her origins, she might never know true peace. That would be harmful to her. In the kingdom where it was said warriors ruled and women served, every Akoran male was raised with the strict admonition that it was forbidden to ever harm a woman. Atreus accepted that fully even as he accepted that he had other, potentially conflicting responsibilities.

If Brianna was informed of the possibilities open to her in England, she might wish a life for herself that Atreus could not allow her, lest he fail in his preeminent duty to Akora.

"I will consider this," he said as he rose. "Until I have come to a decision, you will not approach Brianna in any way. Is that understood?"

Hollister also got to his feet. He nodded stiffly. "It is, Your Highness, but may I say, I hope most fervently that you make the right decision. To leave an old wrong uncorrected cannot possibly benefit anyone."

When Hollister had left, Alex turned to his brother. "Hell of a situation."

"It is that. I would like you to gather all possible information on the Hollister family. I want to know everything about them—history, reputation, wealth, everything."

"Then you are considering telling Brianna?"

Atreus hesitated. "I am considering it," he said finally. "What are the odds that Hollister will not respect my instructions but will attempt to approach Brianna on his own?"

"Small to nonexistent, at least for the next few days," Alex said after a moment. "Rising after that. He strikes me as a man on a mission, truly determined to right that old wrong."

"And perhaps commit another against a land about which he knows nothing, and for which he has no reason to have any care."

"It is a delicate matter," Alex said. "I have two recommendations: that we inform Royce at once and enlist his help. It is possible that he already knows a great deal about the Hollisters. Also, that you make Brianna aware of your intentions. As I suspected might happen, Joanna and Kassandra sense that something is in the air. Joanna asked me directly last night if you have a personal interest in Brianna."

"Have I been that obvious?" Atreus asked with a grimace.

"I wouldn't have said so, but the ladies . . . let's just say they have instincts that surpass our own in certain situations."

"I agree to your first recommendation," Atreus said promptly. After a moment, he added, "But not to the second. When I inform Brianna that we are to be married, I do not wish to be overly distracted by other matters. Once my business is concluded here—"

"You will be free to turn your considerable persuasive abilities in her direction," Alex said with a grin.

"Something of that nature. We are going to Hawkforte next week. That should be an opportune time to settle this matter."

"And an opportune place. There's something about Hawkforte. . . ."

"I recall you telling me that you proposed to Joanna there."

"Yes, I did, and it's where Royce and Kassandra resolved their differences and decided to wed."

"Well, then, I couldn't ask for better."

Having determined how events should proceed, Atreus turned his attention elsewhere. He had a meeting later in the morning with Lord Liverpool and several other government ministers. In the afternoon, he would receive half a dozen of the wealthiest and most powerful business leaders in England, all eager for trade opportunities with Akora. That evening, he would attend the ball Alex and Joanna were giving in his honor. It promised to be a busy day.

All this he accepted. Duty was life, life duty. From tenderest childhood, he had never questioned that. The trial of selection that had made him Vanax had only confirmed what had been within him from the beginning.

And yet, despite all that, his thoughts kept returning to Brianna, remembering the caution he saw in her eyes, the natural grace of her movements, her body tensing slightly when he was near, the deep reserve he sensed within her.

Standing at the window, looking out at the winter garden, he found himself thinking not of Liverpool or the Prince Regent, indeed, not even of Akora. He thought instead of the flash of forest-green eyes, the fire buried within hair like dark red silk, the quizzical tilt of her head . . . the sudden lilt of her voice. . . .

Startled by the direction of his mind, usually so disciplined, now suddenly wayward, Atreus turned away from the window. He did not see the small brown sparrow that darted out to peck at the crumbs that had suddenly appeared.

A T THE WINDOW OF HER BEDROOM, OVERLOOKING the garden, Brianna broke up a little more of the scone from her breakfast tray and tossed it to the bird. The air coming through the open window was chill and she shivered a little, but her thoughts kept her too preoccupied to allow much notice of her discomfort.

Standing at the window, she had watched the red-haired man depart. The glimpse she had of his face showed features set in great seriousness, and, she thought, resolve.

Who was he? Why had he called at such an early hour? She had not been at the window when he arrived, so she could not know if he had been received or turned away. But in either case, he had come. There must be a purpose behind such action, just as there must be a reason for his scrutiny of her the previous evening.

Hope, tentative and fragile, stirred within her. She had

lost so very much—home, family, and, to a great extent, identity. Yet so much had been given to her—home, family, and an entirely new life. She longed at once to know the truth of herself and be true to the person she had become.

She tossed a final handful of crumbs and shut the window. The bird continued to bob and dart for some time, but Brianna did not watch him. Other matters required her attention.

Chapter
FOUR

I DON'T KNOW," JOANNA SAID AND FROWNED AT
the admission. "I confess I took no notice of a red-
haired man at Carlton House yesterday. Kassandra,
does he sound at all familiar to you?"

Pointing her stockinged toes a little closer to the fire,
Kassandra replied, "There is something very vague in the
back of my mind, but I just can't grasp it. What time did
you say he called?"

"It was shortly after seven A.M. when I saw him leave,"
Brianna said.

"Who calls at that hour?" Joanna asked, looking at her
sister-in-law.

Kassandra shrugged. "No one I've ever heard of. Was
Alex awake?"

"He was, and already up and about."

Remembering the habits of her brothers when they
were on Akora, Kassandra said, "I wonder if he and Atreus

were breakfasting together. They often meet early to go over business."

"They may well have," Joanna agreed. To Brianna, she said, "I shall make inquiries."

"Discreetly, if you would not mind," Brianna requested.

Both wives laughed. "Assuredly," Kassandra said.

A tug on the bell and a brief wait brought Mulridge to them. The black-garbed housekeeper did not look surprised to be summoned. On the contrary, she appeared to have been expecting it.

"The red-haired gentleman arrived shortly before seven A.M.," she reported upon being asked. "He presented his card to one of the Akoran guards, who took it to the morning room where the gentlemen were breakfasting. A few moments later, he was admitted to them. He remained for about ten minutes."

"I am always in awe of your knowledge, Mulridge," Kassandra said sincerely. "Not only of this household, but also of my own."

"Thank you, ma'am."

"Can you put a name to him?" Joanna asked.

Mulridge hesitated. "You could ask the gentlemen."

"We could," Joanna agreed. "But it's so much more interesting to know something they don't know we know."

Mulridge, who to the best of any of their knowledge had never been married, looked thoughtful at this. At length, she said, "I can see how that would be. All right, then. I can't be sure but I think he might be one of the Hollisters."

"The Hollisters?" Joanna asked. "Their seat is at Holyhood, isn't it? That isn't so very far from Hawkforte. How remarkable— Brianna, are you all right?"

At the mention of the red-haired gentleman's possible identity, Brianna had felt no reaction at all. But hearing the name of Holyhood . . . that was another matter altogether.

Months before, she had stood in the library staring at a drawing of the house called Holyhood, and felt deep the stirrings of precious memory within her mind. She had so very few memories, at least of the first eight years of her life. Every tiny fragment was to be cherished.

She knew that house. She had been inside it.

And now someone from Holyhood seemed to be reaching out to her.

She had lived for sixteen years on Akora. She had grown to womanhood there. She understood the delicate balance between the way of the warriors and the way of the women. She was well schooled in the art of drawing from men the best of themselves.

Training and instinct, both, called her to be gentle, patient, forbearing.

Training and instinct be damned.

"Where is the Vanax?" she asked.

Joanna answered her. "He has meetings this morning with government ministers, and meetings this afternoon with business leaders. Then, of course, there is the ball this evening."

The ball. The event for which the entire household had been readying itself for the past fortnight.

"Much as I would like to just sit here," Kassandra said, "I think we'd best get to it."

Joanna sighed and stood. "Coming, Brianna?"

"What? Oh, yes, of course." She was happy to help, but in the back of her mind was the thought that the ball would not last forever. Eventually, she would confront Atreus.

HOWEVER, BY MID-AFTERNOON IT SEEMED AS though the preparations for the ball would never be completed. Floors were receiving their final coat of wax, windows their final polishings. Every piece of furniture was being dusted and buffed, every carpet beaten. What seemed like every flower from every hothouse within a fifty-mile radius of London was being set out in a bowl or vase, wound round a trellis, or arranged into a bouquet favor for the ladies. Mouthwatering aromas floated up from the kitchens, but there was no time to eat a morsel. Footmen and maidservants hurried back and forth, their steps growing ever more rapid as the day wore on. Fires were lit in every room to stave off the winter chill, protect the flowers, and prevent any creep of dampness.

In the midst of all this, Madame Duprès swept in to oversee the final touches to the ladies' gowns. Even she appreciated the enormity of what was underway, and was mercifully brief.

In the wake of her departure, a flurry of emergencies occurred.

"It never fails," Joanna muttered as she rushed to calm an all-but-hysterical housemaid who had scorched one of the linen tablecloths. "Milk," Joanna called out. "Just put milk on it. It's fine, there are others."

"Drain's backed up in the kitchens," Kassandra remarked as she hurried to see what could be done about it.

"The musicians are here," Mulridge informed Brianna, who was the only one of the three left in the entry hall, "but unless I am very much mistaken, one of the violinists is drunk."

"Pour tea down him," Brianna instructed, "and if that fails, instruct the footmen to take him to the stables and dunk him in one of the horse troughs."

Mulridge nodded approvingly. "Very good, miss."

"Cook says the lemons are poor," Kassandra reported when she emerged from the kitchens looking just a bit worse for the wear. "And there isn't enough parsley."

"For heaven's sake, don't tell Joanna," Brianna said as she came from soothing a frantic florist who had only just realized that the roses—the several hundred roses—had not been dethorned. "She's had quite enough to deal with and now she's gone off to tend to Amelia."

"She wanted to review the table settings one last time, to take account of any quarrels, feuds, or rivalries that have erupted in the last twenty-four hours. I'll just bring the chart up to her."

"Do you think this was really a good idea?" Brianna asked as she climbed the stairs with Kassandra. The flurry of activity below was beginning ever so slowly to subside. The silver had its final polish, as did the crystal, and the tables were finally being set. The musicians—including the violinist—were tuning up, and the smoking fireplace had been seen to. Everything she could possibly help with was done or in competent hands. The time had come to catch her breath and ready herself as best she could.

"Inviting both Whigs and Tories? Whether it's a good idea or not, it's past time someone did it. Alex and Joanna are probably the only ones who could have."

"Even so, it promises to make for an interesting evening."

Kassandra's laugh was a reminder, should any be needed, that she was a princess well schooled in courtly intrigue. "I wouldn't miss it for the world."

Joanna stuck her head out the door of her bedroom, caught sight of the seating charts in Kassandra's hand and sighed with relief. "Oh, good, you've brought them. I've just had a note that Lord Bromley and Lord Duchamps found out this morning that they've been sharing the same mistress for the past year, and neither is pleased about it."

"However," Kassandra said, "it will give Lady Bromley and Lady Duchamps something to chortle over."

"Lady Melbourne sent the note," Joanna said as she balanced Amelia on her shoulder. "I can scarcely believe she has done me a kindness."

"She has accepted you," Kassandra said. "You have her admiration."

"As you certainly should," Brianna agreed. "Everything downstairs looks wonderful."

Joanna shot her a grateful smile. "Thank heavens. I was never any good at this sort of thing—despised it, actually. But marrying Alex, I had to learn something about entertaining. Still, hosting Prinny, the Whigs, *and* the Tories is a bit daunting. I wouldn't dream of doing it for anyone other than Atreus."

Ah, yes, Atreus, who had drifted at the edges of Brianna's mind all day and was now back front and center. Atreus and Hollister. Hollister and Atreus. And Holyhood, mysterious Holyhood, wrapped in a fragmentary dream.

There was time—just—for a hot soak before her maid arrived to ready her. Brianna sat in front of the dressing table as her hair was brushed to silken smoothness, then fashioned into a crown of curls falling from her head to just brush her shoulders. Shoulders, she thought, left rather bare by the gown of Madame Duprès' creation.

"Since the ball is in honor of the Vanax," the dressmaker had decreed, "your gown should be in the Greek style, *n'est-ce pas?*"

"Wouldn't it be better if it were in the Akoran style?" Brianna ventured.

"There is a difference?"

The Greek style—or what passed for it—was all the rage, courtesy of the French. Enemies of the British though they were, they remained the undisputed masters of all things fashionable.

"In Akora," Brianna said, "we dress more simply."

"Oh, *non*, then that will not do. Simplicity is for dairymaids."

Which was how Brianna came to behold herself in the

mirror wearing a gown that she supposed could be called Greek, if only just. Whatever its inspiration, it was quite undeniably beautiful, although rather more daring than she had realized during the earlier fittings. Perhaps she should have paid better attention.

Had the fluted shoulder caps always bared so much of her shoulders, or the deeply squared neckline exposed rather more of her breasts than seemed proper? Was the silk, a shade almost precisely that of sea foam, really as gauzy as it looked? No, fortunately that at least did not seem to be the case when she hurriedly stepped in front of a lamp to check. But even so . . .

"Oh, miss," the maid, Sarah, said, "you look absolutely lovely."

"I feel rather drafty." Brianna took one last look in the mirror and decided there was nothing to be done for it. The hour was striking nine o'clock, and the guests would be arriving at any moment.

Thanking Sarah, she hurried from the room and was halfway down the corridor when a door opened. Atreus stepped out and, seeing her, stopped.

"Brianna—" His eyes lingered on her. "I would have thought last night that you could never look lovelier, but I would have been mistaken."

She heard his words, but as though from a distance. All her attention was focused on the man himself. The corridor was wide and long, its ceiling high, yet he dominated it. He was dressed in the British fashion, as he had been at Carlton House, but with a blood-red waistcoat that added just a hint of barbaric splendor to what would otherwise have been simple elegance.

It was deliberate, she supposed, as was everything he did. A subtle reminder to all and sundry of the exotic world from which he came. And to which she knew he wished speedily to return.

She had waited all day and was not inclined to wait any longer, but before she could say anything of what was uppermost in her mind, Atreus took her hand and raised it lightly to his lips.

"You do Akora proud," he said.

"As do you." Her voice was remarkably steady. In that, she took true pride.

He grinned, and for just a moment looked a shade abashed. "I thought the waistcoat overdone."

"Oh, no, it suits you well."

He kept her hand as they continued toward the stairs. She pretended to scarcely notice, but was aware of little else. "The British make such a fuss over fashion," Atreus said. "I believe the greatest offense I could give to the Prince Regent is to appear in plain and simple garb."

"He does set great store by appearances," Brianna managed. She was startled by the readiness with which he touched her, and even more so by her own inability to object.

"Which, I suppose, is why the appearance of both Whigs and Tories here tonight will be of such import?"

"Such is my understanding, although to be truthful, their feud seems rather childish."

"The Whigs were the Prince Regent's great friends these many years," Atreus said. "They encouraged his excesses, praised his pretensions, and generally did their utmost to ingratiate themselves, all with the assumption that if and when the mad king was put away, Prinny would throw out his father's Tories and hand power to them instead. However, as seems so often the case, assumptions made when power was only a dream changed when it became reality."

"He decided the Whigs' desire for a negotiated peace with Napoleon would weaken the British throne, *his* throne?"

"So it seems. Royce and Alex both tell me that Prinny agonizes endlessly over the possibility of revolution coming to Britain, and is said to have dreams in which the mob is screaming for his head."

"Less brandy and more exercise might go a long way toward easing his rest," Brianna said tartly.

"No doubt it would, but self-restraint is not in his nature. Earlier this year, so I understand, he asked Royce to undertake a rapprochement between the Whigs and Tories. It really can't be done, not in any meaningful sense, because they are so far apart politically and so keenly driven by ambition. However, bringing them together tonight under the same roof will give the appearance of unity, and really that is all Prinny wants."

She looked at him as they descended the stairs. "It never could have happened without your coming here. Nothing less would compel both sides to tolerate each other, if only for a few hours."

"Then I suppose I should be honored."

"No," she said. They had come to the bottom of the steps. The others—Joanna and Alex, Kassandra and Royce—were already there and looking at them with unfeigned interest.

"It is the British who should be honored," Brianna said, and gently but firmly removed her hand from his.

WHETHER OR NOT THE BRITISH WERE COGnizant of the honor done them, they were immensely titillated, as was more than evident within a very short time of the first guests arriving. Although Atreus and Alex both wore British garb, they had taken care to station Akoran warriors wearing tunics and carrying swords throughout the vast entry hall and into the ballroom. The warriors were, as always, imperturbable, although one or two had to restrain a smile at the delighted astonishment with which they were greeted.

Amid murmurings of "Achilles come to life" and the like, the guests milled about, awaiting the arrival of the Prince Regent. Prinny had a habit of arriving at such gatherings at an hour he regarded as fashionably late and his hosts tended to view as frazzling. But on this evening, a bare quarter hour after the appointed time, the carriage emblazoned with the royal crest appeared. Immediately, all others made way for it, though this required the strenuous efforts of drivers and outriders alike, pulling and tugging at the horses to force them out of line.

Prinny strode in with the expectant air of a child anticipating delights. He went directly to Atreus and greeted him warmly. "Damn fine night for this, wouldn't you say?"

"I would," Atreus agreed. "On Akora, we only have nights like this in the mountains. I find it invigorating."

"I have to say I feel a fair dose of vigor myself. Lady Joanna, what's this I hear about there being dancing tonight?"

"If it please Your Highness," Joanna replied in a friendly manner. Brianna had never heard her treat the Prince Regent in any other way, and he seemed to appreciate it.

"It would please me," Prinny declared. "Never any room to dance at the usual crushes."

"Ah, but that's why we invited only a select few," Alex said. He was standing beside Joanna and looked very well, Brianna thought, as did Royce, although neither of them had anywhere near the appeal of Atreus.

"I could hear the teeth-gnashing all the way here," the prince declared and appeared well satisfied by it.

There was a clamor just then by the entrance, as some of those who had assumed they would be arriving before the prince rushed to get in without further delay. Prinny was well known for looking unkindly on anyone who came late, which he defined as after himself.

Lord Liverpool was part of the crush, as was a smaller, slender man easily recognizable as Charles, Second Earl of Grey. So it was that the leader of the Tories and the leader of the Whigs found themselves pressed up against each other like sardines in the same barrel, for what must surely have been a few uncomfortable moments.

They sprang apart as soon as they were able, and each gentleman straightened his attire while studiously avoiding looking at the other. But Prinny had seen and he chortled.

"Worth coming just for that. Royce, I've a suspicion this was your idea."

"You did ask that I do whatever was possible to bring both sides together, Sire," Royce said with a grin.

The prince chuckled again, requiring the somewhat dazed guests clustering around him to do the same. This brought on hearty royal laughter, which continued even as they went into supper.

Joanna had deliberately kept the menu far simpler than what would have been found at Carlton House or, indeed, under any roof of the *ton*. However, she had also seen to it that every ingredient was of the finest and freshest quality, requiring none of the sauces commonly used to conceal staleness. The prince was surprised at first, then intrigued.

"By Gawd," he announced after a savory, oak-smoked salmon was served on a bed of hothouse greens, "can't remember when I've tasted better. Is this the Akoran way with dishes?"

In actuality, the menu, for all its relative simplicity, was far more complex than would have been served at almost any Akoran meal, but Atreus refrained from saying so. Instead, he merely inclined his head. "We are a simple people, Majesty."

"Oh, no," Prinny said, eyeing the next course of beef in a light red wine sauce. "I'm not about to make the mistake of thinking that again. No, you're refined, that's what you are. You've had enough time to refine down what it is you are, what's important to you and the like."

Seated only a little way down the table from the royal pair, Brianna just managed not to raise an eyebrow. Generally, the Prince Regent was so absorbed in his own complaints and fears that he was capable of seeing very little else. But on occasion, the mind that was still surprisingly sharp seemed to come back to life, however briefly.

He had the Akorans dead right, she thought, if he meant refinement in the sense of a steel blade refined to its maximum sharpness. It was just as well that Akora and Great Britain seemed destined to be friends.

Certainly, as the evening wore on, the atmosphere was conviviality itself. Lord Liverpool went so far as to nod cordially in the general direction of the Earl of Grey, who was seen to respond in kind. The two gentlemen did not actually speak to each other but neither did they come to blows. That had to be considered a victory of sorts.

Lady Melbourne, that helpful lady known more commonly as "the Spider" because of her instinct for spinning webs of intrigue, certainly thought so. She went so far as to overlook her normal disregard of anyone as inconsequential as Brianna, to address her in passing. "Lovely evening, absolutely lovely. Just what we all needed."

Supper ended, and the cautiously amicable crowd adjourned to the long gallery where dancing would be accommodated. The musicians—apparently all sober—were installed on a balcony overlooking the chamber. They struck up a quadrille, followed quickly by a cotillion. The prince led Joanna out first, as befitted her status as hostess, and partnered Kassandra next. Atreus, who had learned the dances at Alex's insistence, made his bow to Lady Liverpool, who was quite overcome by the honor but acquitted herself well all the same. Lady Grey not being present, she was said to be occupied at home with her many children, the honor of the next dance with the Vanax of Akora fell to Lady Melbourne. Brianna thought she caught a glimpse of the beguiling beauty that lady had been as she chatted happily with Atreus whenever their paths crossed in the dance.

There was a moment's stillness, followed by a murmured rush of excitement, for the next tune the musicians offered was nothing less than a waltz. Alex and Royce did not hesitate but moved directly to discourage any gentleman who might have thought to engage either of their wives. Brianna was just wishing that she had a partner herself, for she knew the waltz and loved it, when Atreus appeared before her.

"I'm not overly familiar with this one," he said. "Do you think you might assist me?"

She could hardly refuse, could she? Not when his gaze was so entrancing and her hand, somehow, was already in his. He led her out to the murmured notice of the crowd. Her last thought before he gathered her closer was that Lady Melbourne and the rest of the guests would be reassessing her, moving her about in the constantly churning rankings of their minds. She did not think she liked that at all.

But dancing with Atreus—*waltzing* with Atreus—that was another matter altogether. His hand was warm and steady at her waist, he held her precisely the proper distance away, and he moved . . . sweet heaven, he moved with a grace no man should possess.

The gallery and all it contained flowed around her, unseen, unimportant, the mere frame for the moment and the man. It would not last, of course; nothing ever did. But just then she could wish the hour would stop, dawn never come, and herself never be anywhere save in the arms that held the world at bay.

Chapter

FIVE

IT WAS NEARLY DAWN BEFORE THE LAST OF THE
guests departed. Fog had crept up from the river, not
in modest wisps, but in thick, swelling clumps,
steadily thickening until only the light of the torches
held by outriders permitted the carriages to depart. It was,
Atreus thought, a fitting end to a day he felt he had crawled
through, for all that it had held some delightful surprises.

One surprise, really: Brianna, whose loveliness he was
convinced could not be surpassed. He had known she was
beautiful, but finding in her a strength and sweetness of
spirit was a happy discovery.

As for the rest . . . Liverpool and the government ministers were men with slow, plodding minds, but once they
grasped an idea, they held on to it limpetlike. Wearing
English garb, speaking fluent English, reminding them
seemingly in passing that his family was united through no
less than two marriages to one of the most ancient and hon-

ored families in the British Isles, he had led them to think of him not as an exotic barbarian but as almost one of their own. At the same time, he made clear that Akora was a proud and fierce nation, unflinchingly united in the determination to defend its sovereignty. By the time the meeting was over, the mood had changed from stolid suspicion to convivial acceptance.

So much for that encounter. The wealthy businessmen were another matter. If the ministers were rocklike in the inflexibility of their minds, the *cits*—as he understood they were called—were like fire, darting here and there in insatiable search of fuel. He could well believe them capable of marching over whole continents, remodeling them to suit their needs as they went.

But they would not come to Akora, of that he left no doubt. The Fortress Kingdom would not welcome them. However, Akora would come to them as it already did, paying well for what suited it, and with the prospect of greater business to come. They could be content with that or . . .

For such clever gentlemen, nothing more needed to be said. If they didn't know the exact count of foreign vessels that had disappeared in Akoran waters in recent years, they could likely come close to it, and reach their own conclusions about the folly of challenging warriors rightly reputed to be among the fiercest in the world.

That left the Prince Regent.

Atreus sighed deeply. How any man born to such privilege and opportunity could waste himself in the pointless pursuit of pleasure was beyond his ability to understand. He acknowledged that and did not try.

Passing through the entry hall, he nodded to the guards on duty there. "Prince Alexandros has just retired, Vanax," one of the men said, "but he left instructions to awaken him if you wished to talk."

"There's no need. I'll be going to bed shortly myself."

"Do you require anything, lord?"

"Thank you, no." He bid the men good night and went down the hall to the library. A fire had been left burning, for which he was grateful. Warming his hands before it, he considered pouring himself a brandy.

All thought of that evaporated when a faint sound, all but imperceptible, alerted his warrior instincts, which were never very far below the surface. Turning in an instant, Atreus took three quick strides across the library and reached out, seizing hard hold of the figure lurking in the shadows near the windows.

His first reaction was shock at realizing he was holding a woman. His second, purely male response, was to take note that she was beautiful. Hard on that came recognition.

"Brianna? . . ."

Surprise riveted him. He was at once concerned that he might have hurt or frightened her, and puzzled as to why she would be in the library at such an hour. Was she unable to sleep and in search of distraction? Yet she appeared fully dressed, still in the pale sea-foam gown he couldn't help but notice emphasized the high curve of her breasts and slim waist. Her hair remained caught up by a matching ribbon and left to tumble over her shoulders, although a few stray wisps of curls had come loose around her face. The scent of her delicate perfume—honeysuckle, again—was highly distracting.

"I assumed you had gone to bed," he said, but gently, releasing her as he spoke.

She looked at him steadily, even as she rubbed the wrist he had held. "I would speak with you, Vanax. There was no time earlier, but now I think I must."

The seriousness of her manner and the use of his title put him on guard. Cautiously, he said, "Of course, but this cannot wait until morning?"

"I would rather it did not."

"I see. . . ." He gestured to the cabinet near the windows. "Would you care for a brandy?"

"No, thank you." She took a breath; he saw her do that and suspected she was gathering her courage. A moment later, he was sure.

"I would like to know what William, Earl of Hollister said to you."

He was both surprised and not. The moment he recognized her, he realized the matter must be grave indeed for her to seek him under such circumstances. Even so, he was not fully prepared for what he could only think of as her audacity.

In a bid for time as much as for information, he asked, "May I ask how you come to know of this?"

"I saw him leave this morning." She glanced at the clock on the mantel and corrected herself. "Yesterday morning. I recognized him as the man who stared at me across the table at Carlton House. I made inquiries and learned his name."

"And you concluded that his visit to me had something to do with you?"

She did not answer directly but said, "The Hollisters' county seat is at Holyhood."

"I believe it is."

"I have been to Holyhood."

This truly was unexpected, and for a moment, Atreus was at a loss for how to deal with it. Finally, he said, "How could you know that?"

Briefly, she told him. Her voice was low and tight as she described finding the drawing of Holyhood and realizing that she recognized it.

"I have been there," she said again. "I don't know exactly when or why, but I am certain of it. William

Hollister acted oddly when he saw me, and then he came here. I want to know why."

Atreus reminded himself that there were times when leadership consisted of being able to change strategies swiftly.

"Hollister believes you bare a close resemblance to his late cousin."

"His cousin? Who was she?"

"Her name was Lady Delphine Hollister. She married a man named Edward Wilcox. They had a child called Brianna."

"Oh, my God . . ." Her hand flew to her mouth as she staggered back, just one step, before catching herself. Even so, Atreus was at her side instantly. "I'm sorry," he said and meant it. "I should have told you more gently. Here, sit down."

She allowed herself to be lowered onto the settee. Atreus sat beside her. He could feel her shaking and was swept by the need to soothe her. She seemed unexpectedly fragile in his arms. Such was her spirit that it created a misleading sense of her strength.

Or so he thought until she straightened suddenly, pushing him away. On a breath of sound, she asked, "When were you going to tell me?"

"Tell you . . ."

She turned to face him, her gaze bright and hot. "Hollister came to you because he recognized me. He knew what I have not known for sixteen years, my identity, and he told you. When were you going to tell me?" Ominously, she added, "Or were you?"

Wind rattled the windows.

Atreus stood. Looking down at her, he said, "Brianna, do not challenge me."

In a heartbeat, she, too, was on her feet. "Why not? Because you are Vanax? All wise and all powerful? You have no right to decide such things!"

"I have every right and every responsibility. Now calm yourself and sit down."

She faced him angrily a moment longer, but to her credit, she did regain control quickly. Even so, she did not sit. "I prefer to stand," she said.

He allowed her that small victory, but he was alert now, aware that she was not in the least compliant. Had he wanted a compliant wife? He couldn't recall ever thinking about it and realized with a start that he had simply presumed his wife would accept his authority in all matters.

Brianna, it seemed, did not.

Cautiously, he said, "After hearing what the earl had to say, I determined to learn about the Hollister family. I wished to know what you would encounter, should you come into contact with them."

"You sought to protect me?" Her tone made it clear what she thought of that.

"Is that so difficult to accept?"

"I do not wish to be protected. I wish to *know*." She sighed deeply, some of the anger going out of her. Softly, she said, "I don't think you can imagine how important this is to me. All your life, you have belonged. There has never been any question of who you are, where you come from, nothing of that sort. But for me . . . there have always been questions, or at least for as long as I can really remember." Looking at him, she added, "I love my family, I truly do. My parents are wonderful people, as are my brothers, my aunt, all of them. And I love Akora. I am deeply grateful that I came to such a wonderful place. Yet it is not enough. I need to *know*."

He had to tell her. Scarcely had she done speaking than Atreus knew that. All thought of withholding knowledge from her was gone. As a purely practical matter, she seemed fully capable of rooting it out for herself anyway. But beyond that, he could not ignore the pain and longing in her. Never could he do that.

"Sit down," he said again and this time, perhaps sensing that she had won, Brianna obeyed.

BECAUSE HE DISAPPROVED OF THE MARRIAGE," Atreus said a short time later, "your grandfather repudiated your mother. So far as the present earl knows, there was no further contact between them."

Brianna took a sip of the brandy Atreus had insisted on giving her. The fiery liquid challenged the chill that had crept over her as she listened to the story. "Hollister is wrong. There must have been at least one meeting between them and it must have been at Holyhood, otherwise I could not have the memory I do."

"It would seem so," Atreus agreed. He appeared grave, his eyes shadowed by concern.

He also looked devastatingly handsome and utterly male, the broad sweep of his shoulders and the proud tilt of his head drawing her gaze again and again. A lock of ebony hair fell over his brow. She curled her fingers to deny the all but irresistible urge to brush it gently aside.

She knew his body, had helped care for it when he himself was helpless. But that seemed in a different life, far removed from the man who sat beside her now. She knew the shadow of his lashes against his lean cheeks, the curve of his jaw, the various scars that accentuated rather than marred his beauty. And he was beautiful, though likely he would scoff at the notion. He might even blush, as she had seen him do once when she complimented him on the waistcoat. A man to turn the heads of women, yet unimpressed, perhaps even unaware of his own power of attraction.

How wayward her mind had suddenly become, yet she could not seem to help it. Nor could she quite believe that she had dared to challenge him as she had done.

All day she had held hard to her resolve. She would confront him. She would demand to know what he knew. She would not be cowed by his power, his presence . . . the sheer, devastating impact of him.

So much for that notion.

All the same, she had faced him, and miracle of miracles, he had told her what she wanted to know. And now he sat very close, his hand over hers, offering her comfort.

"My parents died . . ." she said softly and shied away from that terrible, twisted pain, ever so fresh and real, the hidden shadow over her life.

Outside, beyond the high windows, the fog was thinning, blown on the wind that would not be denied. She tried to ignore it, and was surprised to find that in Atreus's presence, she could do so.

"But you lived," he said gently. "Surely you know that is what they would have wanted."

"I have almost no memory of them. They were my parents, they gave me life, and I have every reason to believe they cared for me for eight years. But I have almost nothing of them."

His hand tightened. "What do you remember?"

Too much, too little. "A few snatches of a voice singing . . . my mother's, I believe. A wonderful moment, whirling through space, when I think my father lifted me on his shoulders. A little more like that . . . so little."

"Not so. You have yourself."

She looked at him, into his eyes, feeling his strength. "What do you mean?"

"I realize that your family on Akora has helped you to grow and become the person you are, but much of that person must come from your original parents. If you look inside yourself, surely you will find something of them."

She did not look into herself, at least not very often. What she might find there was too frightening. "I had not thought of that. . . ."

"Then do so now. Think what makes you different from your Akoran family. Not necessarily anything very large or obvious, but small things."

Small things were safe. Those she could contemplate. "I have a greater fondness for my own company than do any of them. They are gregarious, while I am not."

"There you are, likely you were born that way. What else?"

"I cannot eat strawberries, they give me hives. No one else reacts that way."

"Strawberries? I will have to remember that."

She might have asked why, but the possible answer alarmed her.

No, not true, she was well and thoroughly tantalized. "Atreus . . ." He was very close, his strength and warmth beckoning her.

"Brianna?"

"Did you intend to tell me?"

"It is . . . not so simple."

So very close, there on the settee close to the fire with the fog swirling outside and the night wearing on. So very . . .

"I had thought to wait," he said, and she did not know what he meant.

But it did not matter then, because his mouth was on hers, hot and hard, not gentle as she had imagined, but hungry and demanding. And wonderful, utterly and completely wonderful, answering some need within herself she had not even known was there.

Sweet Lord, the man could kiss! Never mind that she had not been kissed before, at least not remotely like this.

She was a properly brought up young woman of Akora, which was to say properly educated, which meant she had a rather vast storehouse of theoretical information about the doings of men and women.

Never did anyone on Akora make the mistake of believing that ignorance and innocence should march side by side. Quite the contrary.

Yet all the same, none of that had prepared her for the sheer, overwhelming reality of Atreus. Not even to the smallest degree.

She was swept by delight even as a hot, terrible hunger leaped within her. She could not think, could scarcely breathe, and none of it mattered. Nothing mattered except his mouth, the strength of his arms around her, and the sudden, shattering sense of *rightness* that claimed her.

In that moment out of time, nothing else existed. She had become someone she did not know, could scarcely even recognize.

Until he drew back abruptly, his eyes very dark, staring at her. Roughly, he said, "Go to bed."

"W-what? . . ." Breathe, she had to breathe.

He stood up, walking quickly to the windows, putting distance between them. His hands were clenched at his sides, his back to her.

"Go to bed, Brianna."

She was dismissed. Ordered to bed like an errant child. Fury and more than a little embarrassment surged within her . . . but only briefly.

A properly brought up young woman of Akora . . . properly educated . . .

"Atreus—"

"My . . . self-control is not what it should be," he admitted, his reluctance to do so palpable. "I am sorry for that. Really, you must go."

Fury fled. So, for that matter, did embarrassment, at

least mostly. She was stunned, more than a little confused, and deeply apprehensive. What a strange turn of events! What an unexpected complication thrown into her life, just as she prepared to grapple with the sufficiently complicated question of her identity.

Realistically, there could not possibly be anything between her and the Vanax of Akora. All the same . . .

Sweet Lord, the man could kiss.

"Good night . . . Atreus."

He did not look at her but she saw him nod. His voice was deep and oddly gentle when he said, "Sweet dreams, Brianna."

QUITE TO BRIANNA'S SURPRISE, HER DREAMS *were* sweet, remarkably so. She woke from them to the thought that it had all been a dream. It could not possibly have happened—not her daring or its result, and most especially not that kiss.

And yet, there was a languor deep within her, heavy and torpid, contrasting sharply with the excitement that drove her from the bed to stand at the high windows looking out at the new day.

The fog was gone. Frost rimed the windowpanes and a brisk, entirely natural winter wind swayed the bare branches of the trees in the garden. The sky hung heavy and leaden, hinting that there might be snow.

One of the ever-efficient maids must have been in already, for the fire was lit and the water in the china pitcher steamed. Grateful for both, Brianna dressed. She chose a high-waisted day dress in pale yellow wool, embroidered around the hem with tiny flowers. The dress was her challenge to the gray day. Letting down the hair she had forced herself to stay awake long enough to braid, she brushed it hastily and secured it at the nape of her neck with a green silk ribbon that matched her shoes. Tossing a lacy shawl of the same verdant color over her shoulders, Brianna stepped out into the hall.

Silence reigned. Somewhere deep in the house, the staff was going about its duties. She saw no one until she went down the stairs to the entry hall. As always, Akoran guards were on duty there. They nodded to her cordially as she passed.

Not until she reached the morning room did Brianna realize that it was much later than she had assumed. An early riser all her life, she thought at first that the clock on the mantel must be wrong. It could not possibly be almost two P.M., could it? Hesitantly, she tugged the bell pull near the door.

The maid, Sarah, appeared almost at once. "Good afternoon, miss."

With an eye on the clock, Brianna asked. "Have I truly slept so late?"

"It seems so, miss," Sarah said kindly. "Lady Joanna was rather concerned, but she thought you needed the rest. Her ladyship said to tell you that she and Princess Kassandra have gone off to Bond Street to do a bit of Christmas shopping. You're welcome to take one of the carriages and join them, if you like."

Much as she enjoyed the company of her friends, shopping held little appeal for Brianna. Instead, she thought of the library, a cheerful fire, and a good book. The moment she did so, she also thought of Atreus. Indeed, he instantly overshadowed every other consideration, including whatever it was Sarah was saying.

"Tea?" the maid repeated. Eyeing Brianna, she added, "And something to go with it? Help you to wake up a bit. Cook's trying out a new pan for making those French things, crepes, I think they're called? French or not, they're tasty. Perhaps you'd like one or two? Oh, and the head gardener's sent strawberries from the hothouses at Hawkforte. Still can't get over that, strawberries in December."

"No strawberries," said a deep voice from the direction of the door.

Brianna whirled, finding herself looking at Atreus . . . yet not Atreus. Or at least not as she thought she knew him. A night's growth of beard shadowed his jaw, his thick black hair was unbrushed, and his shirt, open at the collar, was no longer entirely tucked into his breeches. He was leaning against the doorframe, his arms crossed over his chest. There was a light in his eyes. . . .

"Sarah," he said with a smile, "would it be possible to get coffee?"

The maid blushed, caught herself, and nodded. "Certainly, Your Highness, coffee . . . right away. Oh, and miss, did you want something?"

With her stomach doing slow flips? "I don't think so, Sarah, but thank you."

Stepping into the room, Atreus said, "On the chance the lady will change her mind, kindly bring the crepes, but no strawberries. Brianna is allergic to them."

"Oh, fancy that," Sarah breathed, reddening yet further. She hurried off, but not without a backwards glance at the pair left facing each other in the sudden silence of the morning room.

The clock was ticking very loudly. Perhaps there really was something wrong with it. Clocks shouldn't be that loud, should they?

"You look like spring," Atreus said.

The clock forgotten, Brianna went searching for her composure, which she appeared to have mislaid.

"Thank you," she murmured. He looked amazing and wonderful, but she wasn't about to say so. That much sense she still had. "Have you been to bed at all?" Oh, brilliant! Show a very personal concern for him and better yet, speak of bed. So much for sense.

"No," he said with a rueful grin. "I decided last night was a good time to read through the rest of the reports Alex and Royce have prepared on what must be every possible detail of the current situation in England. Sometime after dawn, I dozed off in the library."

"Every possible detail?" she asked, simply because she had no idea what else to say. This new, seemingly relaxed Atreus was every bit as appealing as the sensual man she had encountered the night before. Indeed, far too appealing.

"Care to know something, anything, for that matter, about the Luddites, that army of peasants and workers protesting industrialization? Their grievances seem more than justified, but their objectives are unrealistic in the extreme."

He moved around the table, pausing to toy with a knife set at one of the places. Spinning it idly, he looked at her. "Or what about the outlook for the war against Napoleon? There have been so many setbacks the British might be forgiven for thinking they cannot win. Yet the military situation is swinging in their favor."

"What about America? They're at war there, too."

"That's a different matter. Alex and Royce both think England will lose—again—and I agree. At any rate . . ." He let the knife drop and looked at her. "Forgive me, I should not presume you are interested in such matters. What do you make of that Byron fellow, the poet?"

"Poetry bores me, for the most part. But I find the doings of nations interesting."

"Am I destined to underestimate you?"

She was saved from replying by Sarah's return. The maid was a little out of breath, understandable enough, considering that she had made record time.

"Your coffee, Your Highness," she said as she set the tray down. "And your tea, miss. The crepes will be along shortly. In the meanwhile, Cook sent these scones, muffins, a basket of fruit, tea, jam, and . . . oh, yes, a bit of lemon cake, just to tide you over."

"Very good of Cook," Atreus said solemnly.

"I'm to say there are eggs, if you like—any kind—and a quite good bacon, but Cook doesn't recommend the ham, she's sending it back on account of being too salty."

"Crepes and all this will do nicely."

"Yes, sir . . . Sire, I'll tell her."

"Amazing," Brianna murmured when Sarah had hurried off.

"What is?"

"Cook is actually a Missus Dursten from Hawkforte. She thinks the world of Lady Joanna, adores Prince Alexandros, and would turn cartwheels for Amelia, which now that I think of it, would be a rather alarming sight. As for the rest of us . . . let's just say Missus Dursten has rules particularly as regards the timing of meals."

"Really?" Atreus looked at her with patently false innocence. "She seems most accommodating to me."

"As I said, amazing."

They both laughed. She really was enchanting, Atreus thought. Although it was still startling to see her in anything other than white, the colors she wore were most becoming. Her hair kept putting him in mind of fiery silk, and her skin . . . Too easily he remembered how meltingly soft she felt.

He held out a chair. As she sat down, Atreus asked, "Do you really prefer tea?"

"I have developed a taste for it, or perhaps it is only that the taste has returned."

Taking a seat across from her, Atreus nodded. "Have you remembered anything more?"

"Not that I am aware. Is there any particular reason why you thought I might?"

"Your Aunt Elena told me that sometimes a sudden shock will restore memory. Finding out about your parents certainly was that."

Rather than dwell on the fact that she had received a second shock the previous night when he kissed her, Brianna asked, "How did you come to discuss such a matter with my aunt?"

Atreus hesitated. She was to be his wife. He could expect to speak to her of matters he did not readily discuss with very many others. "When I regained consciousness after the attempt on my life, there were some gaps in my memory. Elena believed they would heal with time, and she was right. But she also said that sometimes a shock restores memory."

"She tried for years to help me regain mine," Brianna said softly.

Atreus waited until she had sipped a little of the tea. "Elena also told me that in certain cases there can be a reason why memory does not return."

She set the cup down with a clatter. "Did she? How interesting."

He had wondered at the time if Elena might have been speaking of her niece, but that made little sense. What could Brianna possibly not want to remember?

"Crepes, Your Highness, miss," Sarah announced as she bustled in. "Good and hot, filled with crab Cook says is very nice, and with a little drizzle of her creamy mustard sauce on top." With a grin for Brianna, she added, "Not a strawberry in sight."

"Excellent," Atreus said. "Thank you, Sarah."

The maid finished serving and hurried off again, no doubt to spread the word belowstairs that the Vanax of

Akora was as courteous as he was handsome, Brianna thought. He was all that and more. So much more.

"There is a theater party this evening, isn't there?" Atreus remarked.

"I believe so."

He yawned suddenly, prompting her to ask, "Will you be awake for it?"

"Oh, yes," he replied with a laugh. "In warrior training, we go for days without sleep." His smile deepened. It was really a quite devastating smile, very unfair under the circumstances. He was unshaven, wearing clothes he had literally slept in, and his eyes were reddened with fatigue. He was also far and away the most devastatingly attractive man she had ever met. Completely unfair.

"At the time," Atreus said, "I wondered if I would ever have any particular use for that experience."

"You questioned the usefulness of some aspect of your training?"

"I question a great many things. Why does that surprise you?"

She answered honestly. "I think of you as upholding tradition, not questioning it."

"Yet having lived in the palace, you must be aware that I am intent on bringing change to Akora."

Careful, her mind whispered. Be very careful. "I know you will accept improved weapons and the like from outside Akora because to do otherwise would leave us vulnerable. But every Vanax throughout history has made sure that our warriors could defend us properly against any enemy. There is nothing new in that."

"There is much more involved than mere weapons," Atreus said. "There is a new way of thinking taking hold in a few places—Britain and America primarily. People have perceived that they can do more, aspire to more, that they don't have to simply accept that which has always been.

They are finding new solutions to age-old problems and with every step they take, they are gaining greater confidence in their own abilities. It is nothing short of a revolution."

"You sound as though you approve of it." She could not conceal her surprise.

"I neither approve nor disapprove. I accept the reality of what is happening and its implications for Akora. Some of what comes from all this will be good and some will be bad, that is inevitable whenever human beings do anything. But above all, it *is* and we must deal with it."

Careful . . . But she was hard-pressed to restrain herself, so startled was she. "You must realize that Britain and America have something in common besides their willingness to embrace new ways."

He was looking at her, too closely, she thought. "And what would that be?" Atreus asked.

Care be damned. She spoke from the heart. "They provide more freedom for their people and greater openness in their government than is common elsewhere."

"They do," he agreed, but then added, "in their own limited way. Akora is far more open."

"How can you say that? Akorans can't even vote."

"Neither can most Englishmen or Americans. Only a small percentage have any say in what governs them. But on Akora, it is entirely different. Everyone can come to the palace, and some days, I think everyone has. Men and women alike can speak in assembly and speak to me directly, if they so desire. Do you have any idea how much of each day I spend reading suggestions, comments, or simply remarks sent to me by ordinary Akorans, or meeting with those people themselves? Last year, before I was injured, I traveled one day out of every three to visit different parts of Akora and hear whatever people wanted to tell me."

She had not realized all that, and it gave her pause. Even so, she said, "But you don't have to act on what they say. You can simply do whatever you like."

"Whatever I like?" He looked at her in astonishment. "You can't possibly believe that. I have to do what is right for Akora. My own preferences count for nothing."

"What stops you from deciding that what you want *is* what is right for Akora?"

"I survived the trial of selection because I will do what is right for Akora above all other considerations."

"The ancient, mysterious trial of selection about which almost no one knows anything. Why can't there be more openness about that?"

"It is not so simple. . . ."

"You went through some sort of ritual, something happened. And when it was over, you were acknowledged as Vanax. That doesn't seem so complicated that it cannot be discussed."

"Does it truly not? Yet it speaks to the very heart of Akoran faith, to the beliefs that have sustained us for thousands of years. I wonder if it is because you are not Akoran-born that you seem not to understand this. I wouldn't have thought that could be, but—"

The possibility seemed to trouble him, or perhaps he was merely perplexed. Brianna could not be sure and had no time to consider it, for just then, there was a clatter in the entry hall and the sound of familiar voices. Very quickly, they were joined in the morning room.

"It is *so* cold," Kassandra exclaimed. Her cheeks were red and she hurried to warm her hands by the fire. "But Bond Street was wonderful. The shops are marvelously festive. Brianna, you should have come with us. But you were up very late, weren't you?"

She and Joanna exchanged a glance. As one, they looked

to Atreus, who had stood at their arrival and regarded them with affectionate caution.

"Ladies," he said, "if you will excuse me, I'm expecting several more government ministers shortly and I could do with a shave before receiving them."

Barely had he departed than Joanna took the seat on one side of Brianna and Kassandra claimed the other.

"Did you have a chance to ask Atreus about Hollister?" Joanna inquired with seeming casualness.

"It came up—"

"What did he tell you?" Kassandra asked.

Brianna took a breath. As much as she appreciated her friends' interest, she was at a loss for words. Had she truly spoken so frankly to Atreus . . . to the Vanax? Her own daring astounded her, but so did his seeming honesty. He did not strike her as a man determined to wield power at all costs. On the contrary, he was far more thoughtful and sincere than she could have imagined.

"Brianna," Joanna said gently. "What happened? Tell us. . . ."

"You did talk, didn't you?" Kassandra asked. "What did he say?"

"It is not so simple," Brianna murmured, and she was startled to realize that she had echoed Atreus's own words.

Chapter

SIX

I CAN SCARCELY TELL YOU THE JOY IT GIVES ME
to know that Delphine's child lives," the Earl of
Hollister said. "Your mother and I were as close as
brother and sister. I have never become reconciled to
her loss or given up hope that she might be returned to us
one day."

*A voice singing brightly . . . calling to her . . . shouting
above the roar, "Hold on, Bri! Hold on!" A voice long si-
lenced.*

"How I wish she could be here with us," Brianna said
softly. They were seated in the drawing room, facing each
other across an elaborate tea neither had touched. The
sight of little salmon sandwiches, almond cookies, scones,
jam, and pats of butter shaped like roses made Brianna's
stomach heave. She was that nervous, though she kept
telling herself there was no reason to be. Hollister was a

kind and caring man. Moreover, he appeared every bit as anxious as she.

Though he made an obvious effort to prevent it, his gaze slipped to the man standing a little distance away near the windows overlooking the garden. Atreus had said very little after the initial introductions, but his silent presence dominated the room. He stood, austerely garbed in black, observing them both.

"Did you also know my father?" Brianna asked.

The rush of air around her as she was lifted high, her own startled laugh. Arms strong and protective . . . gone.

"I regret that I did not. However, I have every confidence that since Delphine chose him, he must have been a very good man."

She would not cry, absolutely not. However much she had longed to find someone with knowledge of her parents, she would get through this meeting with dignity. Even so, it was very hard. . . .

"I wonder if I might develop a taste for tea," Atreus said. He was there suddenly, taking the seat beside her. His gaze met hers. "Would you mind pouring, Brianna?"

"No, of course not," she said, finding a fragment of pride in the steadiness of her voice. Not quite so her hands, but she managed well enough. Only a few drops marred the pristine whiteness of the lace doily beneath the teapot. "Sandwich?" she asked, holding out the plate.

Atreus eyed them dubiously. "With all respect to Cook, I prefer salmon grilled over an open fire and accompanied by a decent wine."

"Wouldn't say no to that myself," Hollister allowed. "Do much fishing?" he asked Atreus.

"We have problems occasionally with sharks. I've gone after them."

"Sharks?" The earl laughed a bit nervously. "I'm more of a trout man, myself. We've some very nice trout streams at Holyhood." To Brianna, he said, "Your dear mother had a fine hand with a line. Perhaps you'll prove as skilled."

"Perhaps . . ." Her gaze returned to Atreus. She was not looking for his permission, definitely not. But she wanted some sign from him, some indication that he understood her longing.

And she did not want to think about why that mattered to her.

"Holyhood is near Hawkforte, is it not?" Atreus asked.

Hollister nodded. "It is that. Indeed, legend has it that Holyhood belonged to the lords of Hawkforte for many generations."

Brianna had not heard this. "Did it really?"

"Oh, yes." Hollister had the look of a man turning to a favored topic. "There is a fascinating story regarding Holyhood at its very beginnings. It may even be true."

"What is that?" Atreus asked.

"Well, there is a beautiful lady involved, of course. There always is in this sort of story. She is said to have been the sister of the first lord of Hawkforte and to possess a rare gift that made it possible for her to feel the pain of others and heal them. According to the tale, she came to the notice of a fierce Viking lord who had wearied of a lifetime of battles and wished to make peace. A misunderstanding of some sort occurred between them, the details are unknown, and he took her from Holyhood by force. But very soon, he came under the spell of her beauty and gentleness, while she came to respect his courage and honor. It is said they fell deeply in love. Together, and with the help of others, they made the peace that had been only a dream into reality."

"The original lord of Hawkforte is said to have wed a Norse woman as part of a search for peace," Atreus remarked. "There is also said to have been a third marriage of another Viking lord and an Englishwoman who possessed a rare gift."

"You are familiar with those tales, Sire?" Hollister asked.

"As Hawkforte is twice united with my own family through marriage, I have made it a point to know its history."

"The family of Hawkforte is the noblest in the realm," Hollister said matter-of-factly. "My own family's greatest honor is our claim to descent from them."

"I had not really thought about that," Brianna said. "But that would mean I am related to Joanna and Royce." She looked to Atreus. "A descendent of their family came to Akora and married into your own, so actually we are all related."

The implications of that settled over her slowly. Kassandra and Joanna had spoken of their gifts as part of a shared family legacy. Now, it seemed, that legacy included her as well. Was it possible she might find, among people who had experienced such things, some understanding of the terrible shadow that haunted her?

"So it seems," Atreus said. He set down the tea, still untouched. "Although the connection is very distant." To Hollister, he said, "Have you informed your family?"

The earl nodded. "My wife, Lady Constance, is quite beside herself. She also knew Delphine, you see. We were all friends in the old days, and she is thrilled beyond measure at the thought of welcoming Brianna to Holyhood." With a hint of apology, he said, "Perhaps I should say just a little more about that. We have three fine sons, the eldest of whom is married and recently made a father himself. Constance was delighted to acquire a daughter-in-law and now, I believe, she hopes for another daughter of a sort. She is already making . . . plans."

"What sort of plans?" Atreus inquired before Brianna could pose the selfsame question.

"Oh, just the usual. . . . An appropriate introduction to society, that sort of thing."

"Brianna is already in society. She has been to Carlton House and has been received by the Prince Regent."

"Well, yes, I suppose, of course she has. I believe Constance has in mind something more personal, a proper introduction for Brianna herself."

"What purpose would that serve?" Atreus again, the shark hunter, deadly.

Hollister coughed. It appeared the tea did not agree with him. "The usual . . . young lady . . . life ahead of her . . . only appropriate she meet the right sort of people."

"Actually," Brianna said quickly, "I think I'd be better at fishing."

Atreus chuckled even as Hollister fought a smile. After a moment, the Vanax of Akora said, "We will keep Christmas at Hawkforte. As Holyhood is nearby, Brianna may visit you then." He paused. "If she so wishes."

"I do so wish," she said firmly, although she was feeling anything but. Lady Constance and her plans were more than a little daunting. Acquiring an English family appeared to entail rather more than she had anticipated.

"Well, then," the earl said. "We will look forward to that." He stood, offering his hand to Brianna. "My dear, may I say again how very happy I am . . . well, just that you are here and that after far too long a time, you are returned to us. It truly is the fulfillment of a dream."

The man's sincerity could not be faulted. "Thank you, my lord," Brianna said as she, too, stood. "I am so very happy to know you."

A warm handshake later, Hollister departed. Brianna was left alone in the drawing room with Atreus. She took a breath, willing herself to calm, but thoughts of Holyhood chased through her mind along with memories of that astounding kiss.

"Are you all right?" Atreus asked. He was close, too close, and looking at her far too perceptively.

"Yes, of course. The earl seems very kind."

"If a bit anxious."

She glanced toward the windows and the gray winter garden beyond. "You have that effect on people."

"I do?" He sounded genuinely surprised. "Hollister has no reason to be made anxious by me. Royce was very forthcoming about the earl and his family. Their finances are sound, their behavior sensible, no slander taints their name. The previous earl was considered a difficult man. This one is viewed far more kindly."

The bird was back, accompanied by several others. On impulse, she chose a scone from the tea tray and walked over to the French doors leading to the garden. Opening them, she stepped out onto the stone terrace. It was very cold, but the chill was a welcome antidote to the heat of her emotions. Better yet, there was no wind.

"You should have a cloak," Atreus said as he joined her.

She shrugged and tossed crumbs to the birds. Pale light filtered through the bare branches of the trees. "Are your meetings going well?"

"Tolerably so. I'm looking forward to moving on to Hawkforte."

"And to an English Christmas? I've heard they are wonderful."

"That, too. Brianna . . ."

She bought time dusting her fingers clean.

"Come inside," he said and stepped back through the open doors. She hesitated, but the scone was gone, the birds were darting off elsewhere, and the cold was making itself felt. All the same, she went reluctantly, with caution.

"Your Highness . . ."

He raised a brow. "Atreus."

"I am accustomed to thinking of you formally. You are the Vanax."

Something moved behind his eyes, a flash of . . . anger . . . rebellion? She could hardly credit that and, at any rate, it was gone in an instant. Besides, she had other matters to distract her. Atreus's fingers were strong and warm on her wrist as he drew her to him.

"I am also a man," he said. His lips brushed lightly . . . so lightly, over the high curve of her cheek, drifting downward in a slow, tantalizing, yet inevitable caress that had her heart pounding long before his mouth claimed hers.

H E SHOULD NOT BE DOING THIS. HE SHOULD have the sense and the discipline to refrain from touching her, particularly after discovering how incandescent she was in his arms. There would be time for that later, but this was now, and the taste of her threatened to undo him. All the more so when he felt her surprise give way swiftly to passion that matched his own. He was far too experienced a man not to perceive that, and far too sensual not to be enticed by it.

She was a virgin, he was reasonably certain of that. It was rare for an unmarried woman of Akora to engage in any intimate relationship. Not unheard of, but rare. She was cautious, he knew that already, and she had pride. Both would prevent her from straying.

But she had also come of age in a world that never mistook ignorance for innocence. She had received the same training all Akoran girls received, which was to say she had all too good a grasp of the nature of men, their needs, their yearnings, and their vulnerabilities.

So it had always been, back to the distant beginning. So he supposed it always would be.

Fire scoured through him. Temptation he already knew far too well threatened to drive out all restraint.

Voices sounded in the nearby hall. There was laughter.

"Alex and Joanna are back," Atreus said. He spoke with difficulty, his breath not entirely his own.

She did not reply, only stared at him as though stunned.

That was something at least. Heaven forbid he be alone in the mindlessness of passion.

Gently, very gently, he set her from him. Barely had he done so than the drawing room door opened.

"Atreus?" Alex asked. He stopped abruptly, his gaze sweeping over them both. Understanding and perhaps even amusement shone in his eyes. "I see Hollister has left."

"Yes, he has." Atreus took a breath. By chance, his gaze fell on the mantel clock. With an effort, he wrenched his mind back to the well-trod path of duty. "I am engaged to do . . . what with the Prince Regent?"

"Accept the salute of his favorite regiment, then attend a small supper to which he has invited a good portion of the diplomatic community—or at least that much of it with which England is still on speaking terms."

"Another delightful evening," Atreus murmured, but he was resigned to it. Four more days in London before they went to Hawkforte. Another week and they would depart for Akora. Ten days to reach there if the sea was kind. A few more days for Brianna to be reunited with her family and final plans to be made. Less than four weeks in all before he could properly wed her. He could last four weeks . . . just.

"What did you think of the earl?" Alex asked Brianna.

"He seems very kind . . . and rather fascinating."

"Fascinating?" Atreus had thought Hollister a rather

mild, not to say bland fellow. What could possibly be fascinating about him?

"He is the only person I have ever seen with red hair," Brianna said with a small shrug. "Besides myself, of course."

So simple a remark, so striking. In her life, at least so much of it as she could really remember, she had never seen anyone who looked like her. What must that mean? Even as he turned the thought over in his mind, he said, "There are other people on Akora with red hair. Not many, to be sure, but they are there."

"I don't doubt it, I just never met any of them. To encounter someone with whom I share such a trait is . . . comforting, although I couldn't begin to explain why."

Perhaps she couldn't, but Atreus had a clear sense of what it meant to be set apart from everyone else, different in a fundamental way. He knew all too well the loneliness that could breed.

Loneliness Brianna had lived with for far too much of her life. And which Hollister stood ready and eager to end.

Hollister, and Lady Constance with her damnable prospects.

"The Prince Regent," Alex reminded.

"He's not actually king, is he?" And therefore not necessarily due the full extent of Atreus's own impeccably royal patience.

Alex shrugged. "The king is mad and locked up somewhere. The son occupies the throne in his stead. Prinny's as close to a king as England comes these days and he expects to be treated as such."

"He's too drunk most of the time to have much idea how he's being treated."

"If he's still conscious, he knows," Alex warned. "But don't despair, it's only a few more days. Royce reports that the Prince Regent and the entire *ton* are besotted with you. Byron is threatening to write a poem."

"Perhaps there will be war between England and Akora after all."

Brianna laughed. She didn't mean to, but she couldn't help it. She was shocked by such sudden intimacy. It was too much to contain.

He was, as he had said, a man. Not the Vanax, at least not only, and not like anyone she had ever known.

And then there was the way she felt when he kissed her . . . or touched her . . . or happened to glance in her direction.

"You find this amusing?" Atreus asked, very low, his voice rumbling through her.

Breathe.

"I think," she said, "you are doing your duty marvelously." All those hours spent listening to the older women, catching what they said and what they did not say, hearing the memories and the warm affection in their voices. "And I think that"—she moved toward the door and somehow, she really had no idea how, she was turning, just glancing over her shoulder and remembering to smile—"you should have an especially good time once you get to Hawkforte."

She was in the hall, shaking, and feeling as though she had swallowed butterflies at the sight of his surprise turning quickly to fierce will.

What had the women said, something about the passions of men being their greatest vulnerability . . . and their greatest strength?

Atreus was a man, and a man who knew passion. She had not realized that, had not even suspected it. He had been only the Vanax to her, a figure of incalculable power and an obstacle to how she believed Akora should be. None of that had changed, yet everything was different.

There didn't seem to be enough air in the hall.

They would go to Hawkforte and then he would return to Akora. She would, too, someday. After all, she had family there and she loved them dearly. But she had her own past to find here in England with the help of William Hollister and his countess. Perhaps also her future, although she shied from peering too far into that.

She had waited a long time for this. She would make the best possible use of every moment. Only a few days, less than a fortnight, and Atreus would be gone. That was good, it was. She could not allow herself to think otherwise.

But the thoughts came all the same as she climbed the stairs. Instinct drew her to the nursery. Joanna was there with Amelia, who was chortling in her bath. Her friend took one look at Brianna and held out her hand, drawing her into the circle of feminine warmth and comfort.

L ATER, IN THE HOURS WHEN EVEN LONDON SLEPT, it began to snow. Slowly at first, only a few flakes drifting past the chimneys and over the tile roofs, settling quietly on the cobblestone streets. But soon the snow became thicker, softening the hard contours of brick and mortar, stone and iron, whirling in little eddies at the bidding of the wind.

By morning, the world was transformed. In the breakfast room, Brianna stood so close to the window that the tip of her nose felt cold. Had she ever seen snow before? She had no memory of it, but surely such a marvel could not be forgotten entirely. On impulse, she opened one of the French doors and reached out, scooping up a handful of feathery soft coldness. It glimmered in the sunlight and melted on the tip of her tongue.

Breakfast ignored, she hurried upstairs, found a cloak and gloves, and darted back down. She was just about to step outside when Joanna joined her. "Come on," Joanna said with a grin, "I'll race you."

Decorum forgotten, they rounded the corner into the garden, laughing, only to slide to an abrupt stop. They were not alone. Alex was there already and so was Atreus. They were . . .

"Hah! Think you're fast?" Alex demanded. "Beat this!"

A large ball of snow struck the chest of the Vanax of Akora. Atreus drew back his arm and returned the favor with equally good aim. Alex scooped up another handful and dispatched it almost in the same motion. Atreus dodged, sent another missile flying, and got another in return.

The contest was fast, furious, and thoroughly good-natured. It was also, apparently, irresistible. Joanna dove for a ball of snow, and lopped it straight at her husband.

Her aim was either very true or very lucky, for she struck Alex full in the face. He stopped for just an instant, eyed her with unholy glee, and launched himself straight at her. Joanna needed scarcely a second to choose discretion over valor. She picked up her skirts and ran, dodging in and out among the topiary bushes, laughing all the while.

"Good morning," Atreus said. He was slightly reddened by the cold, his chest plastered with snow. He looked very young and . . . carefree? Yes, that was the word. He looked vastly more relaxed and content than she had ever seen him.

"Good morning," Brianna replied. Somewhere nearby, Alex and Joanna were still chasing each other, but she was scarcely aware. The garden and indeed the world narrowed down to Atreus, the light in his eyes and the sudden, stunning jolt of pleasure she received from simply being near him.

"So this is snow," he said.

"Hmmm." Panic fluttered at the edges of her mind. She

wasn't about to make an utter fool of herself, was she? "Snow seems to agree with you."

"It does," he acknowledged, "as does the fact, not at all to my credit, that the Prince Regent thinks he has the ague."

"Ague? He is ill?"

"He thinks he is, which I have been given to understand happens on a regular basis. He's taken to his bed, dosed himself with laudanum, and sends his heartfelt apologies. Brother monarchs . . . warm fraternal feeling . . . utmost respect for Akora and so on. The long and short of it is that our meetings are at an end."

"You can leave London?"

He nodded with the enthusiasm of a schoolboy unexpectedly released. "I can—and just in time, for between us I will say this was harder than I anticipated. How any man born to such privilege can show such neglect of his people is beyond my comprehension."

"I think," she said, "he knows in his heart that they just want him to be a symbol of sorts and he resents it. He yearns to be necessary, not merely tolerated."

"God help this country if it ever actually needs his sort."

"I agree, but how would you feel if you were in the same position? Suppose being Vanax meant nothing really and was only for appearance?" *Careful . . . oh, so careful.*

"Then I would not be Vanax," he said without hesitation.

"What would you be?"

A moment passed, no more. It was quieter in the garden. Joanna and Alex had found some other occupation.

"A sculptor," Atreus said. "I would spend my days carving stone."

"Would you be happier?"

"I *am* Vanax. I can't escape it. Happiness must lie in being true to ourselves, don't you think?"

Did she? "I don't know that I've ever really thought about what makes people happy beyond being safe and with those we love."

He closed the small distance still beween them, snow on his chest and in his hair, heat in his eyes. "If that were enough for you, you would never have left Akora."

She did not step back, she would not, but the urge was there. "My situation is unusual."

"True enough, but you'd still seek more, wouldn't you?"

He was too close, too perceptive, too . . . everything. She bent down, reaching, not knowing what she did. At such close range, it wasn't as though she could miss.

Joanna had run, sensible woman that she was, but Brianna stood her ground, mainly because she was so stunned by her own action that she couldn't move. Atreus spit snow, swallowed astonishment, and did what a lifetime of warrior training had prepared him to do.

"Ummmphh!" Her feet sailed out from under her and she was on her back, in the snow, her fall softened by the strong arms that promptly braced on either side of her, trapping her.

"You are shockingly lacking in decorum," he said and smiled.

"I don't like being intimidated."

"Intimidated? You're joking. When have you ever been intimidated by anything or anyone?"

"I haven't, generally, but you—"

She broke off, warned by the very male light in his eyes that she was treading in a direction she most definitely did not want to go. "Never mind. Let me up."

"Are you cold?"

"Yes."

"Well, then." He turned suddenly and without warning, reversing their positions so that he was on the ground and she was on him, clasped in a gentle but quite remorseless embrace.

His eyes were even more golden than she had thought, and, despite the time away from Akora, his skin still looked kissed by the sun. The air was cold, but Atreus was warm, and she, snug against him, was on fire.

"Let me up," she said again, sounding unconvincing even to herself.

"I claim a forfeit."

"A what?" She had brothers in her Akoran family. She knew the rules by which they lived. "You cannot. I hit you fair and square."

"You did not. I had no warning."

"Since when is that required?"

"It is the time-honored custom of warriors to declare their intentions. You struck from ambush."

"I was standing right in front of you!"

"All the same . . ." His arms tightened, drawing her closer. "Is a forfeit so very much to ask?"

"You do not ask, you claim, and it depends on the forfeit."

He was going to kiss her, she knew it, and the knowledge brought a deep, churning excitement. She wanted this, wanted him, and for once she did not want to think at all.

"Kiss me," he said, and at her startled look smiled with an odd gentleness. "Kiss me, Brianna, instead of my kissing you. Is that so much to ask?"

"There is no difference."

"Oh, yes, there is and we both know it, a very great difference."

She could not, she had never, it wasn't right, she . . . had faced the storm, had arrived all but dead on a golden shore, had fought back to life, had made a place for herself, had dared to dream of the past revealed and the future unfolding. Through all that, she had come to this place, to this moment. To this man?

She was bound to do it wrong, for truly, she had no experience except what he himself had shown her. Was that enough?

"If I kiss you, will you let me go?"

"I will," he said and added, because he was a truthful man, "for now."

Brianna heard that but did not heed it. Nothing mattered except that he was there, so very close, and she wanted so very much to find out what it would feel like to . . .

. . . kiss him. Tentatively at first, her lips just barely brushing his before returning, lingering, savoring the taste and touch of him. His mouth was warm and firm, enticing. The freedom she felt suddenly, freedom *he* had given her, and the man himself combined in sweet intoxication. Reason dissolved, doubt vanished, caution lasted just a little longer, but proved no match for the hot wind of desire whirling through her.

She kissed him thoroughly, deeply, and with skill that surprised them both. So exhilarating was the experience that she would have gone right on kissing him had not Atreus's arms tightened around her so fiercely that she could scarcely breathe. He stood suddenly, lifting her as though she were of the same approximate weight as thistledown, and set her apart from him.

"That," he said firmly, "was not a good idea." His gaze held a degree of wariness Brianna found quite satisfying.

"You named the forfeit," she reminded him sweetly.

"There are times when I think the education of Akoran women would benefit from some reexamination."

"Do you? I suspect many an Akoran man has entertained that notion, but oddly enough, you can't seem to hold on to the thought long enough to do anything about it."

She had gone, perhaps, just a tiny bit too far and was rapidly considering a strategic withdrawal when happy chance intervened. Royce and Kassandra strolled round a corner of the house, took one look at what they had come upon and grinned.

"Brother dear," Kassandra said, "you have snow all over your back. Anyone might think you'd been lying in it."

"*Anyone* might tend to her own affairs," Atreus muttered.

Royce laughed in male sympathy. "I hear Prinny's abed and you're a free man."

"So it seems. How soon can we leave here?"

"I've already sent word to Hawkforte to expect us this evening, if that suits you?"

"Perfectly," Atreus said, and once again counted the days to Akora.

Chapter
SEVEN

THEY WENT TO HAWKFORTE BY SEA. THE roads were much better than they had been only a year or two ago, Royce said, though not so good as they were likely to be a few years hence, given the frenzy of work being done on them. But the weather was mild, no sign of the previous night's storm remained, and they all agreed it would be far more pleasant to sail. That is, all of them except Brianna, who voiced no opinion. She stood on the deck of the twin-masted sloop, wrapped in a cloak of emerald-green with a fur-trimmed hood framing her face. While the others chatted, she kept herself apart, seemingly content with her own thoughts.

But her shoulders beneath the cloak were stiff. The brief glimpse Atreus had of her before she turned away suggested that whatever those thoughts might be, they were not born of contentment or anything approaching it.

He gave her a few more minutes, then went to stand

beside her. Leaving the Thames estuary, they had turned south. The wind favored them and they were speeding over the water. Gulls whirled overhead, their raucous cries piercing the silence, while here and there, on small bumps of land rising out of the water, seals raised their heads to watch the sloop go by.

"A fair day," Atreus said.

"It is that." Her voice was as tight as the grasp of her gloved hands on the deck railing.

"You are a brave woman."

His blunt assertion had the desired effect. She gave off staring at the water and turned to him instead. "Why would you say that?"

"You are here, on a boat at sea. Given what happened to you as a child, you could be pardoned for never wanting to step off land again."

He had not meant to speak of it at all, not now and perhaps not ever. But the words were said all the same and he was glad of it. They must, in some way at least, speak of what had happened to her, however difficult that proved to be.

Her laughter was uneasy. "Is such perception a part of being Vanax?"

"I think it comes more from looking at the world a particular way."

"As an artist?"

That was very quick, he thought. Most people never realized that so much of what he was, stemmed from the life he would have made for himself had he not been Chosen. "It has to do with seeing details both small and large." He touched her shoulder lightly. "You are tense and I ask why. It occurs to me that you did not come to the palace until very recently for a reason. You had to cross the Inland Sea to get there. What finally prompted you to do so?"

She shrugged, and as she did, moved beyond his touch.

"I tired of being imprisoned by my own fears and memories."

"A good reason," he acknowledged, letting her go for the moment. "How much do you remember?"

Carefully, she replied, "Of the storm that brought me to Akora? Almost nothing. It's just fragments, pieces I can't fit together."

He tried not to sound relieved. "Perhaps it would be better not to try."

"I've lost so much that I'm reluctant to let anything else go."

"Understandable enough, but the past can never be changed. Even the present is so fast fleeting that we can only glimpse it as it speeds by. That leaves the future for us to make our own."

"To me it's all intertwined. I don't seem able to think about a future for myself without first knowing my own past."

It was not the response he wanted, but he accepted it all the same. Her future was already decided, though she did not know it. She would soon enough and she would accept. He would make certain of that.

But for the moment, it was enough to ease her fear. Pointing out over the water, he asked, "How many colors do you see there?"

"Colors? The water is gray."

"Is it? What of the foam in our wake?"

She craned her neck slightly, looking back. "That's white . . . except where it's pale green . . . and some of the water is dark blue, almost black but the black has green in it."

"Where the sun hits, it's bright gold."

"You want me to see that it's beautiful, don't you?"

"I want you to see it for what it is, not what you may remember or fear."

She looked at him long enough for Atreus to wonder if she would reply. She did, but not directly. "Do you also paint?" she asked.

"I tried my hand at it in my youth."

"Your youth?" Her smile was teasing. "Are you so very old, then?"

He was six, almost seven years older than Brianna. Not so very great a difference, especially not given her intelligence and courage. Because of who she was—and who she would be—he answered more openly than he might otherwise have done. "The years before I became Vanax seem a very long time ago, almost as though they were part of a different life. I left behind a great deal, but I held on to what mattered most."

"What was that?" she asked softly.

"My family and the love I have for them, the values I want to protect, and—" He reached out, catching a stray wisp of fiery hair that had slipped from beneath her hood, twining it between fingers scarred by chisel and drill. By sword, as well, for he was, first among all else, a warrior.

"—and the stone," he said. "I couldn't leave that behind."

Her hand covered his, gently disengaging his fingers. He allowed her do so, but instead of letting go, she turned his hand over in hers, studying the fine lines pale against his burnished skin, running her thumb lightly over the calluses on his palm. He breathed deeply, reminding himself they were not alone, but feeling her touch to the very center of his being.

The wind blew, and overhead, the gulls whirled. The fast-fleeting present of which he had spoken so surely seemed to slow and almost to stop. But finally, in the fullness of fickle time, the proud towers of Hawkforte rose above them.

* * *

IT LOOKED, ATREUS THOUGHT, OLDER THAN ANY-
thing he had seen yet in England. The road from the
small harbor where they had docked led directly through
the open gates set in high walls draped in moss, lichen, and
the deep red of winter ivy. In front of the walls were the
contours of what must have been earthen berns that were
likely older still. Within the walls was a vast courtyard
paved with precisely cut blocks of stone that avoided mud
and kept down dust. There were buildings on all sides,
many very large. At a glance, he saw stables that could easily accommodate a hundred horses along with all they
would require—fodder, tack, smithies, and the like—as
well as armories sufficient to deter the boldest enemy.

"Impressive," he said with a smile. "Are you expecting
the French?"

"Only if Napoleon truly is mad," Royce replied, "and I
doubt that. Let's just say we respect the old ways here at
Hawkforte."

"How very Akoran of you." Ahead of them was a graceful stone hall connected to a high tower. "The original
buildings?" Atreus asked.

Royce nodded. "Carefully maintained and frequently
updated, but still very much as they were nine centuries
ago. The wings on either side were added later, of course,
but they are also very old."

They entered the great hall, where Atreus stopped in
frank admiration. The walls, soaring fully thirty feet,
sported an array of banners, weapons, and shields that was
impressive even by Akoran standards. At the same time,
the pleasant arrangement of seating areas near the immense hearth and the huge but graceful table awaiting
guests bespoke a woman's influence.

The hall smelled of pine and other woodsy scents, no
doubt because of the garlands being hung everywhere in

celebration of the coming holiday. A dozen or so servants were at work. They nodded cordially to the new arrivals and several looked at Atreus with frank curiosity. He could not help but notice that they showed none of the bowing and scraping he had seen among the retainers at Carlton House. Instead, these were men and women of obvious pride. Again, he thought of the similarities to Akora, where no man or woman was considered superior by virtue of birth or possessions.

"You are at home here, my sister," he said to Kassandra.

She nodded and shared a smile with the husband who stood close beside her. Alex and Joanna were nearby, Amelia nestled in her father's arms. The baby had slept almost all the way to Hawkforte but just then she woke, looked around, and after what appeared to be a moment's thought, let out a piercing howl.

"She's hungry," Joanna said.

"And she will shake the rafters until something is done about it," Alex added with a grin. "We'll join you for supper."

They all dispersed, Kassandra to supervise the unloading of the many trunks, crates, and bundles brought from London, and Brianna to help her. Royce showed Atreus to his quarters in the west wing, comprised of a spacious apartment with pleasant views of the sea. Castor was already there, unpacking Atreus's belongings. He set the small wooden case that held the statue on a marble-topped table near the vast bed before nodding cordially to both men and departing.

"I trust you'll be comfortable," Royce said.

"I'm sure I will be. Thank you for inviting me."

"It's my pleasure. I hope you'll come back many times. After all, this is Kassandra's home now, and she naturally misses you. But also, if you are serious about Brianna—"

Atreus raised a brow. "If?"

The tall, golden-haired man smiled sardonically. "You are, aren't you? You're going to marry a woman you hardly know simply because you believe you're supposed to do so."

Atreus leaned against the window frame, crossed his arms over his chest, and regarded the brother-in-law he considered a friend. "What would be better, do you think? *Not* to marry her even though I believe I am supposed to do so?"

Royce was not a man to refrain from speaking his mind when he thought it necessary. "What about taking some time to get to know each other better, even to fall in love?"

Respecting as he did that his brother-in-law knew vastly more about such love than he did himself, Atreus nonetheless said, "And if we do not fall in love, what then? Not marry? But Brianna is to be my wife. If I had known sooner who she was, we would already be married. There is no point in waiting any longer."

"Not for you perhaps," Royce said quietly, "but what about Brianna? She is only now discovering her true identity. What if she wants the life that can be hers here in England?"

Atreus did not answer at once. The very question Royce posed had plagued him ever since Hollister's appearance. No matter how he turned it over in his mind, there was only one answer.

"Knowing Brianna as I am coming to, seeing her for the woman of honor and courage she obviously is, I don't believe she would make that choice."

Royce nodded, but the sympathy in his gaze mingled with concern. "You'll find out quickly enough if you're right. Hollister will know by now that we've left London, and I don't think he'll waste any time."

Indeed, he did not, for scarcely had dawn broken the following day than the invitation from Holyhood arrived.

* * *

"IT IS VERY ODD," BRIANNA SAID. "I HAVE WANTED this for so long, dreamed of it, really, but now that I am on the verge of fulfilling my greatest hopes, I . . . am not so certain anymore."

"You're taking a big step," Joanna said soothingly. "It's only natural to be anxious about where it will lead you."

"It's not just that. I thought I knew what I wanted: to come here to England, to find out more about myself, if possible to find some trace of family here. Now all that is actually happening. I should be delighted."

Kassandra said, "I remember a time when I felt . . . oh, bewildered, I suppose you could say, or confused."

"So do I," Joanna said. "Not all that long ago, as it happens."

The ladies were breakfasting in the high tower, that part of Hawkforte given over to the private quarters of the lord and his lady. The views were breathtaking, but they afforded them little notice, absorbed as they were in tea, toast, marmalade, and confidences.

"Men," Kassandra observed, "provoke confusion. They cause it much the way a high wind results in scattered leaves needing to be swept up."

Brianna nibbled at her toast, looked from one to the other, and said, "What has this to do with men?"

The wives looked at each other. "Why do you imagine you're confused?" Joanna asked.

"Because I love my family in Akora and I am having serious doubts about trying to make any connection to my English relatives?" Brianna suggested.

It was Kassandra's turn to say, "Brianna . . . dear . . . there is the matter of Atreus. We all know he is—"

She looked to Joanna who said, "A man. Very much a man. And you and he . . . well, it's fairly obvious—"

Kassandra again, "—that the two of you are drawn to

each other. There's nothing wrong with that. Nothing at all. But believe me, Joanna and I have both discovered how very . . . confusing such men can be. They aren't the ordinary sort of male, not remotely. All three of them can be quite overwhelming. They have that in common, and we"—she looked to Joanna, who nodded—"we understand it. You will, too, if you just let yourself."

She had brothers in her Akoran family, one especially to whom she was particularly close. But she had no sisters with whom to talk of such matters. Her Akoran mother, however, was a warm and loving woman, much given to laughter and frank talk.

"He kissed me," she blurted out, and instantly corrected herself. "No, that is not true. He kissed me twice and the next time, I kissed him."

"You kissed him?" Kassandra said, seizing on what was of greatest interest. "Good for you. How did he react?"

"He put me from him."

Joanna chuckled. "Excellent. I adore Atreus, of course, but he has always struck me as much too controlled. It's past time someone shook him up."

"I'm hardly doing that," Brianna said, bewildered as to how her friend could come to so wrong a conclusion. "At most, he's amusing himself."

"Not Atreus," his sister said emphatically. "He knows how to relax when work is done and duty discharged, yet here he is, in the midst of delicate negotiations with the British, engaging in a little dalliance? I think not."

"Neither do I," Joanna declared. She took the ribbon held forgotten in Brianna's hand and twined it expertly into her friend's hair. "There, you look lovely."

"Quite ready for Holyhood," Kassandra agreed.

Joanna nodded. "And for anything else."

Much as she appreciated their reassurance, Brianna remained silent, trying to come to terms with the notion

exploding in her mind. She and Atreus . . . Atreus and she—
The very thought stunned her. It was absurd . . . impossible . . . simply wrong. She should dismiss it out of hand.

And she would, any moment now, when some small
semblance of reason reasserted itself.

While she waited for that to occur, as it surely must, she
went from the high tower, down the curving stone steps,
through the great hall and out into the crisp winter day
where her past awaited her.

M Y DEAR!" LADY CONSTANCE HELD HER ARMS
wide as she hurried to greet her guests. She spared a
smile for the others descending from the carriage, but it
was upon Brianna that her attention focused. "William
told me how greatly you resemble your mother, but even
so, he understated the matter. You are the very picture of
Delphine."

"Am I?" Brianna managed with difficulty, for Lady
Constance was hugging her quite fiercely.

Stepping back just a little, that good woman studied her
even more closely before nodding emphatically. "You have
your father's brow, perhaps, but otherwise you are entirely
Delphine. She was the loveliest creature, always smiling,
and with a voice so sweet she put the birds to shame. You
sing, I presume?"

"Not unless I wish to inflict punishment on those
around me," Brianna said ruefully. Having survived her
first few moments with Lady Constance, she was now able
to observe her, and could not help but like what she saw.
Whereas the Earl of Hollister seemed mild and restrained,
his countess was anything but. Her manner was open and
sincere, she displayed none of the pretension found among
so many of the *ton*, and the fine wrinkles etched about her

eyes and mouth appeared to owe their origins to frequent smiles rather than the sour resentment of age.

"I am sure you are being far too modest," Lady Constance said. She looped an arm through Brianna's and only then, having sufficiently secured her, gave her attention more fully to the other arrivals.

"Dear Lady Joanna and Lady Kassandra, how very nice to see you both, and my lords, you are also most welcome." Her gaze turned to Atreus, whom she did not hesitate to assess frankly. "Your Highness, if you will forgive that I do not stand on ceremony, it is a great honor to have you here."

To her credit, Lady Constance appeared to mean exactly what she said. The presence of the Vanax of Akora was an honor. That it was also the social coup of a season that had left the *ton* gnashing its collective teeth over so illustrious yet elusive a royal visitor did not seem to matter to the countess.

"Let's not have everyone standing on the doorstep, dear," the earl said good-naturedly. With a tolerant eye on his wife, he ushered the guests into Holyhood.

Brianna took a quick breath, willing herself to calm. She had gazed so many times at the drawing of Holyhood in the book she had found in Joanna and Alex's London library that the exterior of the residence was entirely familiar. But once she walked through those doors, when she actually stood inside the house, what would she find then?

Atreus was at her side. Precisely how he had supplanted Lady Constance was not clear, but his nearness was undeniably comforting. Unlike Hawkforte, so meticulously preserved down through the centuries, Holyhood must have been rebuilt many times. The present house appeared to be no more than a few decades old. The entrance hall was a spacious rotunda rising to a dome several stories above. The marble floor was laid out in the design of a star, the walls were dimpled with alcoves holding statues in the

Greek and Roman styles, and the ceiling high above was lavishly painted to resemble the night sky. Graceful marble columns framed the double staircase that curved up almost out of sight.

"My late uncle had this house built," Hollister explained. "It replaced a structure dating from the Tudor era."

"Very impressive," Atreus said, but he was looking at Brianna. She appeared pale and strained, not at all as he had expected. Instinctively, he took her hand. Even through the leather glove she wore, her skin felt cold.

"Is something wrong?" he asked quietly.

"No, not at all." She met Lady Constance's curious look with a smile. "I would love to hear more about my mother."

"Oh, you will, my dear! But better than that, we have a wonderful surprise for you, don't we, William?"

"Yes," the earl said, but he, too, was watching Brianna.

"Come along," the countess said briskly and led the way into the drawing room, where a cheerful fire dispelled the winter chill. Servants were setting out tea, but Brianna scarcely noticed. Her attention was riveted on the portrait of the woman above the mantel.

All the breath went from her. She was staring at . . . herself? No, not precisely, there were differences that taken all together added up to a distinct person, yet one she so closely resembled as to leave no doubt of the identity of the woman she gazed upon.

"My mother," Brianna said softly.

"It was painted the year she and your father met," the earl said. "After their elopement, the portrait vanished. The assumption was that your grandfather had it destroyed. However, when Constance and I arrived here, we discovered it in one of the attics and returned it to its rightful place."

"That was very good of you," Brianna murmured. She was dreadfully afraid she might cry, but she was also filled with a sudden lightness of spirit. Her mother, the woman who had brought her into the world and cared for her the first eight years of her life, was suddenly far more than shattered memory and the whisper of a lost voice. She had been real, she had lived right here in this house. And just then, smiling down at them, she seemed present once again.

"It is only proper," Lady Constance said. "Your grandfather behaved very badly, if I may say. This was Delphine's home and she should always have been welcome here."

But she had not been, although she had returned once with her husband and child.

A long hallway swept by shadows . . . a light at the end of it . . . the smell of cinnamon . . .

"What a dear child . . . the image of her mother . . . that horrid old man . . ."

". . . hush, Bridie, hold your tongue . . ."

"Sit down, dear," Lady Constance said gently, but Atreus was already guiding Brianna to a nearby settee.

She sat and only then realized that she was holding tight to his hand. Flushing, she let go. Her gaze fell on the array of tempting dishes set out on the low table before them, and she seized the distraction they offered. "You must have a wonderful cook."

About to pour, Lady Constance paused. "Why, yes, we do. Perhaps this is a good time to mention that the older members of the staff would appreciate an opportunity to meet you. They knew your mother, you see, and they're thrilled that you're here."

"I would be delighted to meet them," Brianna said softly.

"Splendid," Lady Constance said. "After tea, then?"

Brianna nodded and let the conversation flow on around her. The Earl of Hollister was interested in Atreus's impressions of London and drew him out on the subject. Brianna listened absently, but other voices drew her more strongly.

"*Edward, we must try . . .*"

"*I agree, but I do not want you hurt . . .*"

"*For Brianna, her heritage . . .*"

"*Son of a French whore . . . dare to . . . my daughter . . .*"

"*Father!*"

"Wilcox is not a French name." Brianna had spoken aloud without realizing it, the sound of her voice startling even to her own ears.

"What did you say?" Kassandra asked.

"Wilcox is not a French name," Brianna repeated reluctantly. To her hosts, she said, "I'm sorry, this must seem very strange to you. I should explain that I have actually been to this house once before as a child. Being here again stirs memories I did not know I had."

"Good heavens!" Lady Constance exclaimed. "William, did you have any idea of this?"

"None," her husband replied. "Are you saying that Delphine and Edward returned to this house at some time, bringing you with them?"

Brianna nodded. "They did. They met with my grandfather but that meeting . . . did not go well." She paused, fighting the sadness welling up inside her. "There was shouting . . . I think I heard my grandfather's voice. He said something about the son of a French whore."

The Hollisters exchanged a somber look. William shifted in his chair. "I had hoped this would not come up, but perhaps it is better to keep nothing concealed. Edward Wilcox was the son of an Irish soldier and a French woman. Your grandfather was often intemperate in his speech. His choice of words should not be taken to mean there was anything improper about that lady's behavior. However, Wilcox did grow up in France and at one time was employed by the French government. The late earl utterly loathed the French. He found it inconceivable that his daughter would marry a man whose loyalties he regarded as suspect."

"Were they?" Brianna asked, though she feared the answer. "Suspect, that is?"

"I have no reason to think so," William assured her. "As I have said, I never met your father, but I am confident that Delphine would not have chosen him if she had any doubts as to his character."

"Do you have any idea how old you were when your parents came here?" Atreus asked.

"I must have been younger than eight, for I was that age when I came to Akora. Yet I was old enough to hear and remember some of what was said that day even though the memory of it eluded me until now."

She looked at the portrait of her mother, as longing overwhelmed her. What she would give to know what Delphine had felt and thought, what she had hoped for and dreamed of, what she would have taught her daughter had her life not been cut tragically short.

"Where were we before we came here?" she wondered aloud, as though the child she had been could answer. "Where did we go when we left?"

"France?" Joanna suggested. "If your father was half French and had lived there, perhaps he found it more congenial than England."

"Had they remained in this country," William said, "Delphine's father might well have made even greater difficulties for them. He certainly had the power to do so and he was, by all evidence, extremely angry about their union."

"France?" Brianna turned the idea over in her mind,

seeking any sense of familiarity. Had she and her parents lived there?

"*Parles-tu français*, Brianna?" Royce asked.

"I don't know," she answered at once. "There are people on Akora of French heritage, but none of them lives near my home. And as I did not travel until recently, I had no chance to hear their language, so I have no idea if I can speak it or not."

Silence drew out long enough to become noticeable. Finally, Atreus said, "Brianna, Royce spoke to you just now in French and you understood him well enough to answer, albeit in English."

"*Peut-être tu as parlé anglais avec tes parents,*" Royce continued. "*Mais tu as parlé français avec d'autres.*"

"I understand you," Brianna said slowly even as the realization stunned her. "*Je comprends . . .*" She had come to Holyhood hoping to learn something of her past, but to discover so much, so suddenly, was dizzying. "Perhaps we did live in France and, as you say, I spoke French with other people, at least enough to learn a little of that language. How remarkable. Until now, I had no notion of it."

"There, you see," Lady Constance declared. "Being here is the best possible restorative for your memory."

"I am inclined to agree," Lord William said. "After you greet the servants, perhaps I may interest you in a tour of the estate?" He nodded to the others. "Of course, you are all welcome to join us."

"How very kind of you," Kassandra said. "But I have so many preparations for the holiday yet to see to at Hawkforte—"

"And Amelia is still getting over that pesky cough," Joanna added. At Alex's startled look, she relented slightly. "Or at least, she might be."

"However," Kassandra continued, "there is certainly no reason for Brianna not to remain. It will be daylight for hours yet. Lord William, would you mind escorting her home?"

"Not at all, I would be delighted." He looked at them both gratefully. "Very kind of you, ladies, very kind, indeed."

Neatly done, Atreus thought. A bit obvious, but all the same, effective enough. He could, of course, simply declare that he wished to tour Holyhood himself. The whim of a royal visitor would take precedence over any other consideration. Tempting though the idea was, he would not indulge it. His sister and sister-in-law had arranged this between them, on that score he had no doubt. Much as he might wish their instincts not quite so sharp, he could not fault their care of Brianna. She was their friend, and they wanted what was best for her.

So, too, did he. Indeed, that was more of a consideration with each passing day.

How much did she remember? How much could she? How much did he?

"Atreus . . . it's the French! Damn them!"

"Hold the line, men! The wind is with us!"

"Closer . . . closer. Warriors of Akora, do not flinch!"

"Fire!"

Boys, they had only been boys, but not after that day. Never again after that.

"Atreus?"

He met Brianna's gaze, smiled readily. He accepted the tea Lady Constance offered and even tasted it. He conversed, although he little attended what was said.

And at length, he left. But memory, that relentless fellow, lumbered after him, an ill-omened shadow darkening the day.

Chapter

EIGHT

THE CHURCH BELLS RINGING IN THE CRYSTAL-
line air of a winter morning announced the joy
of the day. Hearing them, Brianna stirred deep
in her bed. She was warm, comfortable, and
disinclined to move, yet excitement prickled at the edges of
her mind.

Christmas.

It was here, it had come, and she felt suddenly a child
again. With a laugh, she threw back the covers, gasped at
the chill, and seized her robe. Bundling into it, scrabbling
for slippers, she paused just long enough to poke up the fire
before hurrying over to the windows.

It had snowed. A fresh dusting of white brightened the
ancient stone walls and blew in little eddies around the
high towers. Smoke curled from the chimney pots above
the tiled roofs. As Brianna watched, a cat strolling across

the courtyard stopped to bat at drifting flakes before recalling its dignity and moving on.

And still the church bells rang.

She dressed quickly and secured her hair with ivory combs that were the gift of her Akoran parents. Thinking of them, she hurried from the room. She missed her parents and her family, her home, her friends. She missed Akora. But she was also enthralled by Holyhood and the life that could be hers if she remained in England.

In the three days since Brianna's first visit to Holyhood, she had spent many hours with the earl and his countess. Lord William was very proud of the estate and greatly enjoyed showing her around it. For her part, Lady Constance delighted in talking of Delphine, who had been her dearest friend.

"I was five years old when we met," Lady Constance said. "Delphine was seven, so naturally, I looked up to her. She loved to read and was rarely without a book, even then."

"I, too, love to read," Brianna said. "It was my exploration of Joanna and Alex's library in the London house that led me to the drawing of Holyhood."

"What a shock that must have been for you. Yet how fortunate that you have been able to recover at least some of your memories."

It *was* fortunate. Yet just then, what had been was of less importance than what would be, beginning with the warm, enfolding pleasure of Christmas that grew and deepened throughout the day.

Atreus went out with Alex and Royce to cut fresh boughs of pine for the great hall. The men returned hours later, laughing and smelling of the woods through which they had tromped. Brianna was just coming into the hall from the kitchens. She stopped, caught suddenly by the sight of the man she could no longer think of safely and impersonally as the Vanax.

Atreus turned just then and saw her. His shoulders and chest were dusted with snow. The cold had ruddied his skin and riffled the thick black hair swept back from his brow. He looked younger than usual, as though he truly had left the cares of state behind in London.

Yet his expression, when he caught sight of her, was serious. He set down the bundle of boughs he was carrying and nodded.

"Happy Christmas, Brianna."

"And to you, Atreus, Happy Christmas."

He continued staring at her as her self-consciousness mounted, all the more so when the corners of his mouth twitched. "You have flour on your nose." Before she could react, he ran a finger down the bridge of her nose and over the tip, gently, carefully brushing the flour away.

"We've been baking cookies," she said, all too aware of the pleasure his touch evoked.

"I thought I smelled cinnamon." He took a breath. "Almonds, too, and . . . chocolate."

"We could use a hand here," Alex called. He was up on one ladder, Royce was on another. Between them, one of the larger boughs sagged. "That is," Alex added good-naturedly, "unless you'd rather discuss recipes."

Very softly, so that only she could hear, he said, "If your cookies taste as sweet as you smell, you can be certain I will savor them."

That made it more than a little difficult for her to keep her mind on very much of anything throughout the remainder of the day. Still, she tried, helping Joanna and Kassandra with all the preparations for the evening before slipping off to bathe and dress.

She came down again to find the great hall empty, except for Atreus. He stood near the fire, one arm braced against the mantel. He appeared lost in thought, but some sound must have alerted him, for he turned suddenly.

"Where are the others?" she asked, even as she absorbed the sheer impact of him. He was dressed formally as befitted the occasion, and in the English style as befitted the season. The intricate designs stitched in gold on his waistcoat were all that relieved the otherwise austere elegance of his garb. Even in a room as large as the great hall of Hawkforte, he looked very big and very much in command.

As she studied him, Atreus studied her. He could have told her that Royce and Alex had agreed, in the spirit of male solidarity, to keep their wives well occupied so that Atreus could have time alone with Brianna, who had proven disturbingly elusive of late. He might have added that such connivance was hardly unfair, given the ladies' own great skill at it.

Instead, he said, "You look beautiful."

Her skin, normally a shade of cream, turned rosy. She wore a gown of rich blue silk, and fastened around her slim waist was a sash of white satin embroidered with holly leaves and berries. Her hair, unrestrained, tumbled over her shoulders. She was, he noted, without jewelry.

"Thank you," she said and looked toward the steps. When still no one appeared there, she smiled a little anxiously. "The decorations are lovely, don't you think?"

"Very festive. Come here."

"What?"

"Come here." When she hesitated, he smiled gently. "I have something for you."

"Oh . . . I thought we were all going to exchange gifts after supper."

"We are, but I wanted to give this to you privately." He reached a hand into the pocket of his frock coat and withdrew a flat box made of wood inlaid with mother-of-pearl.

Handing it to her, he said, "It would please me greatly if you would wear this tonight."

She came closer and, still with hesitation, accepted the box. Her eyes met his before falling to the contents that were revealed as she lifted the lid.

"*Oh . . .*"

The box contained the sky, or at least a piece of it taken at the height of day and at the deepest point of color. It glowed as though the radiance trapped within it was alive. All about it, gold, brilliant as the sun, curled in soft, perfect tendrils, grasping . . .

"The Tear of Heaven," Brianna whispered. She could not conceal her astonishment. She had heard of it, of course. The sapphire set in gold and worn as a pendant was famous on Akora. Legend said it had been found in the caves beneath the palace centuries before, polished into a magnificent gem by a master's hand, and kept always within the Atreides family, passed down from generation to generation.

"I could not possibly," she said, thrusting it back into Atreus's hands. What was he thinking? How could he possibly do such a thing?

And yet she knew. Somewhere in her heart, the knowledge was already there.

"Why not?" he asked, not at all deterred. "I regret it doesn't match your eyes, but it does compliment your gown."

He was teasing her, as a man will when he wants to calm a woman. Or distract her from serious matters.

"We both know," she said firmly, "that no one would give such a gift for so frivolous a reason."

"Frivolous? That's a word I don't hear often enough, at least not about me."

"I did not say you were frivolous—"

"Would it be so terrible if I was? The idea has a certain appeal."

She wasn't going to smile, absolutely not, but he was looking at her with such frank male enjoyment that she couldn't get her bearings. "Atreus, be serious. The sapphire belongs to your family. I cannot possibly accept it."

"Now there you have it wrong. My mother and sister have their own jewels. The Tear of Heaven is mine, but it doesn't suit me. It will look much better on you."

He was being impossible. Utterly, completely, impossible . . . to resist.

"You may wish to make light of this—" She broke off when he took both her hands and drew her to him.

"Brianna, if I wish to make light, it's because this is unexpectedly difficult. I thought I had it worked out, but I find looking at you—"

Looking at a woman of true loveliness, not only in her face and form, but in the strength and courage of her nature. She was more, much more, than he had imagined. He was pleased by that, of course; any man would be. But she also presented certain complications he could have done without.

"Perhaps you should not be looking at me," she said softly. Inherently honest, she added, "And I should not be looking at you."

"Or perhaps we should simply accept that we are drawn to each other." He brushed a light kiss over the fingers curled around his own and noted the sharp intake of her breath. Before she could release it, he pressed his advantage.

"Brianna, I am convinced you are the woman who is meant to be my wife." She paled, but he went on. "I understand this must all seem very sudden to you, but I cannot linger here. I must return to Akora, and once there, I must turn my attention to the problems that need to be resolved. I would like to do that with you at my side."

There, he had said what he intended, and it was true, so far as it went. They were drawn to each other. The few heated kisses they had shared left no doubt of that. Moreover, he did believe she was meant to be his wife. If he saw no reason just then to tell her the source of that belief, it was merely to spare her confusion. She had enough to cope with as it was.

"This is too much," she said, as though affirming the direction of his own thoughts. "I cannot turn my mind to it. I came to England to find out who I am, and now you propose to make me someone entirely different."

"I do not," he said, no, truly swore, for he did not want her any different from the way she already was. Brianna, just that and nothing else. The depth of that realization was startling but he went on, determined to make her understand. "I do not," he repeated emphatically. "Your past does not determine who you are any more than being my wife would do. Your life is your own, and you decide the direction of it. But tell me this: What can you find here in England or anywhere else that will have more meaning than what awaits you on Akora?"

"To be your wife?" Her gaze sharpened. "You may regard that as the highest aspiration, but—"

"I meant what it will mean to be my consort. There has been no such person on Akora in the years you have been there, so you may not realize the power of that position."

"But I do not seek power," she said.

He believed her, but he also understood what she did not. "Neither did I. Those of us who do not seek power may be best suited to wield it."

As she considered that, he took the pendant, and before she could object further, fastened it around her neck. The finely wrought chain was short, the jewel hanging from it nestled in the hollow at the base of her throat. She raised a hand, touching it, and stared at him.

"I have not agreed to this."

He fought the urge to simply enforce his will. That would not do with this woman. She deserved—and de-manded—better.

"Then agree to consider it." And to help her do so, he lowered his head and kissed her, just there on the nape of her neck where he knew she would be especially sensitive. It was not fair, he knew that, but just then, fairness did not matter quite so much as it should. He wanted her. Not the nameless woman of his vision. Not the exquisite statue in the velvet-lined box in his quarters. Brianna herself, the woman who trembled beneath his touch even as challenge lingered in her gaze.

"Your family," she said when she could breathe again, "will misunderstand if they see me wearing this."

"No, they will not. They will understand that I have asked you to become my wife, and that you are consid-ering it."

"Atreus, I don't know if I even *can* consider it. There is something I must tell—"

She was meant to be his wife. Moreover, were that not so, he would still want her so powerfully as to tolerate no denial. Whatever concern she had, whatever she thought she needed to say, would likely only complicate matters further.

"Hush," he said and enforced the command in the most time-honored Akoran way. There, where warriors ruled and women served, but where the prohibition against ever harming a woman ruled every moment of every man's life, men had, of necessity, learned to be extremely persuasive.

He kissed her with blatant possession, his hands sliding down to clasp her hips as his tongue plunged deeply into her mouth. Instinct drove him to set gentleness aside and let passion rule, if only for the moment. He would pay the toll in frustration and think it well spent if he left her with no doubt of the pleasure that awaited her once she was his.

Drawing back just a little, still pressing her hard against him, he murmured, "Feel, Brianna. Stop thinking or reasoning, and just *feel*."

Sweet heaven, she could do nothing else. The sheer power of him, his strength and will, his taste and touch, engulfed her. She could not get close enough to him. Any distance, any barrier was intolerable. Nothing existed except the hot, hungry need to take him deep within her, to make him a part of herself, to receive from him the essence of life itself.

"Atreus—" His name on her lips was half prayer, half plea. She dug her fingers into his shoulders as passion leaped yet higher. Her back was against the wall, she was dimly aware of cool air on her legs, and his mouth . . . his hot, skillful mouth was . . . withdrawing? No, she could not bear that. He must not stop. She—

"This is madness," he groaned, and she found a tiny glimmer of relief in the knowledge that she was not alone in the maelstrom of need.

Quickly, he stepped away and stared at her. He was breathing hard as he ran a hand through his thick hair. "God, let it be a swift wind that blows us to Akora."

By which she divined that he was impatient for them to wed . . . and bed. While she was far too honest not to acknowledge that she wanted the same—what a pale word was *want*—the former still stunned her.

"Atreus, I must—"

Was it merely the chance coincidence of the moment or did fickle fate take a hand? In either case, they were no longer alone. Kassandra and Joanna came into the hall first, chatting loudly enough to herald their arrival. Royce and Alex were directly behind them. Both couples looked relaxed, in good humor, and ready to begin the evening's festivities.

Brianna turned away for a moment, fighting for calm. There was no hope of completely concealing what had happened between her and Atreus, but pride demanded that she regain control of herself. She took as long as she dared without drawing even more attention to herself, and mustered a smile before turning to greet the others.

Barely had she done so than Joanna and Kassandra both gasped. Their husbands did not, but they were no less intent.

"Oh, Brianna!" Kassandra exclaimed, beaming a smile. "The Tear of Heaven—"

"It looks very good on her, does it not?" Atreus interjected before his sister could follow her happy expectations any further. "It is my hope she will agree to keep it."

"Agree—?" Joanna looked from one to the other of them, her surprise evident but quickly bridled. "Oh, well, that's fine, then . . . isn't it?"

"There is a great deal to be said for considering an important decision before actually making it," Alex said, even as he struggled not to grin at his brother. Atreus had assumed that the heart of a woman could be commanded by the will of a man.

"I believe it's called looking before leaping," Royce said, also smiling. "I understand it's highly recommended."

"I've always thought so," Atreus said, in the tone of a man reassessing his assumptions. Matters had not developed as he had hoped, or even expected, yet he had no doubt of the ultimate outcome. Brianna would be his. Was she not the woman he had seen? Did she not turn to fire in his arms? Between one and the other, there could be no doubt.

That being the case, he was inclined to indulge her. If

she needed a little time to come to terms with her future, so be it.

A *little* time.

A fresh fall of snow drifted by the mullioned window-panes. Flames leaped in the immense stone fireplace that dominated the north end of the great hall. Tall silver candelabras illuminated the high table covered with white linen and set with gold plate.

The scents of pine and woodsmoke mingled with the aromas of the holiday feast. They dined on goose accompanied by a dozen perfect dishes, a small meal by the profligate standards of the Prince Regent, but a feast to those ordinarily given to simpler fare. All the same, Brianna ate very little. Not that she was without appetite. On the contrary, she simply forgot. Thoughts of Atreus . . . of herself and Atreus . . . of Atreus and herself . . . of Atreus . . . were all far too distracting. She had only to look at him to feel the sweet, hot surge of desire unlike any she had ever known. Truth be told, looking wasn't actually necessary. The mere thought of him was quite enough.

She raised her glass, absently noting the candlelight reflected in the straw-hued liquid, and sipped. Across the table from her, Atreus was laughing at something Royce had just said. The man she had thought of as unrelentingly stern and serious looked relaxed, approachable, and overwhelmingly seductive.

He was strong, determined, a hunter and a warrior, accustomed to having his way. Yet he could also be gentle, lighthearted, and patient. He offered her an honorable marriage, the promise of passion, and more.

What would it mean to be not only Atreus's wife but the consort of the Vanax of Akora? What might she be able to do?

The wine was cool on her throat and far easier to swallow than the notion that she might wed for power. The very thought repelled her. But if she followed her heart and power came unbidden . . .

What might she be able to do?

She sighed, turning the stem of her glass between her fingers, and contemplated the many faces of temptation.

The meal ended with Christmas cookies, poached pears, fruitcake covered in white marzipan icing, and a sweet wine—the fourth, or perhaps it was the fifth wine, to accompany the meal. Brianna had declined almost all, but it didn't seem to matter. Her mood had improved greatly over the course of dinner. Indeed, she looked back with some wonder at how very tense she had been.

When the table was cleared, they all settled near the fire, where the gifts were piled, some wrapped in lovely fabrics, others enclosed in beautiful boxes.

"The biggest first," Royce decreed, and indicated the mysterious object so large that it had been placed on the floor. The Lord of Hawkforte lifted it easily, depositing it at his wife's feet. "For you, Kassandra," he said gently.

She removed the wrapping carefully, exclaiming with delight when she revealed the glowing leather of a magnificent saddle.

"For the day when you can ride again as you like," her husband said. Ruefully, he added, "Which is to say, like the wind. Only promise me, you will never go too far from me."

"Oh, Royce," his princess murmured as her eyes filled. She managed a watery smile as she hugged him.

A short time later, it was Royce's turn to be surprised when his wife presented him with a . . . What was that? Brianna wondered. It was about the size of one of the portable writing desks that went everywhere, about a foot wide and twice as long. But it was also about two feet high and seemingly comprised of numerous moving parts, most crafted from metal.

"Can you guess what it is?" Kassandra asked her husband.

Royce held it in his hands, turning it this way and that. Realization dawned, and with it delight. "It's a steam engine? That's what it is, isn't it? It's a model steam engine?"

Kassandra beamed. "It is, indeed, and I have the maker's oath it will truly work. You may study it to your heart's content while you conspire to build one for yourself."

"Do you really intend that?" Alex asked.

"I'm thinking of it. Steam power will prove revolutionary, I'm convinced of it."

"Forgive me, love," Joanna said with a grin. She handed her husband a much smaller box of ivory tied with a scarlet ribbon. "This is nothing so modern."

That did not trouble Alex, for he was well pleased by the set of chess pieces carved from deep green jade and black onyx, and intrigued by the cleverly hinged board that accompanied them.

His own gift to Joanna took everyone by surprise, most of all Joanna herself. She received it with a mix of astonishment and delight. "I had no idea you knew," she said.

Alex laughed and dropped a light kiss on her brow. "Knew what my lovely wife has been sneaking off to do these past many months? Knew why you have come to bed occasionally with a smatter of charcoal on your cheek?"

"Have I? Oh, Lord!" Joanna blushed but admitted to the others, "I have been drawing, and Atreus, I hold you responsible."

Her brother-in-law, who clearly held her in great affection, laughed. "Do you? And how did I manage that?"

"You made me realize that art is not an indulgence, that it can be as necessary to life as the very air we breathe." She looked to the wooden box her husband had given her, filled with charcoals in an array of colors, as well as paints, brushes, and papers. "Thank you, my love," she said to Alex. "I shall endeavor to produce something utterly impractical."

When the laughter had died away, Brianna found herself gifted in turn. From Royce and Kassandra, she received a copy of the book that contained the drawing of Holyhood, as well as several other volumes that also spoke of the history of her English family. Her pleasure in the gift was equaled only by the books she received from Joanna and Alex who, knowing her love of history, had chosen very well indeed.

"The venerable Beale," Alex said, "and the equally venerable Sir Thomas More, but no Byron."

Brianna hugged the books, delighted by them, and by the thoughtfulness of her friends. When she had given them their own gifts, she looked to Atreus. He was watching her, his gaze intent and more. He was looking at her as a man looks at a woman he has claimed.

Through the haze of relaxation and enjoyment, resentment stirred, but weakly. He could look however he would. Her fate was her own to choose.

Even so, she could not help but enjoy his pleasure in the gifts his family had chosen for him, including a superb collection of maps, some hundreds of years old, that traced the mistaken, confused, and often outright ridiculous notions about Akora held by those who could not simply admit they knew nothing of the Fortress Kingdom.

"Look at this," Atreus said, indicating one of the older maps. "We appear to be the abode of dragons."

"My favorite is the one that shows Akora surrounded by rings of fire," Alex said.

This raised chuckles all around, which gave way to exclamations of pleasure as Atreus revealed the gifts he had brought from Akora. For Joanna and Kassandra there were exquisite glass vials bound in silver and gold filigree,

holding the rarest, most precious scents created by the
kingdom's famed perfumers. Alex and Royce were equally
well pleased with the superb Akoran swords they received,
weapons of perfect balance and lethality, the hilts carved
with ancient symbols that bound the warrior to fight always with honor.

When all the rest of the gifts were given, and each well
admired, Brianna stood. A little shyly, she said, "I must ask
your indulgence. My gift for Atreus is outside."

This drew expressions of surprise and curious looks.
Wrapped against the cold, they left the great hall and
walked through whirling snow toward the stables.

"I really didn't know where else to put it," Brianna said,
"so it wouldn't be seen."

Taking the lamp Alex had brought along, she held it
high to reveal the contents of a stall. An ordinary stall,
swept clean and empty save for a block of stone the height
of a man.

Atreus stepped forward. As he did, his expression was
transformed. Slowly, he reached out a hand. "What is
this?" he asked softly.

"Quartz," Brianna replied. "Rose quartz, Lord William
tells me. He has been showing me all around Holyhood.
Near the manor, there is a cliff that rises above a rocky
strand. At the base of the cliff is very soft clay in a remarkable shade of purple. The people thereabouts make pots
from it. Above that clay, rising out of it, is a wall of quartz."

"How did you get this out of there?" Atreus asked as he
ran his hand caressingly over the translucent surface.

"Over the years, chunks of the quartz have broken
away. When I asked Lord William if I might have a piece to
give to you, he insisted I take this one, even though it was
the largest."

"It is magnificent," he said. "I've worked with marble,
gneiss, granite, alabaster, all sorts of stone, but never

quartz of this size and purity." Even as he spoke, his hands caressed the stone as though seeking the shape he would coax from it. "Thank you, Brianna. This is wonderful."

Relieved that so unusual a gift was so great a success, Brianna could not help but notice how right Atreus's powerful hands looked moving over the stone with skill and certainty. He touched her in something of the same way. Was that also right?

Her own hand strayed to the sapphire at the base of her throat. The gem felt heavy and cold, yet it warmed beneath her touch. The Tear of Heaven, a name redolent of sorrow. Were she to keep it, with all that implied, would sorrow be her fate?

Or would her tears more likely be those of happiness?

"The ship comes tomorrow," Royce said. He looked at the quartz. "This will need to be moved very carefully."

Atreus nodded and the men went on to talk of how that would be done. Brianna scarcely heard them. She was thinking of the ship that would take Atreus back to Akora.

And of whether or not it would also take her.

Chapter
NINE

CHRISTMAS HAD COME AND GONE. IT WAS the day after, though daylight remained hours off. Brianna desperately needed sleep. Her eyes were dry enough to burn, and a tremulous chill had seized her very bones, this despite the remnants of the fire glowing redly and the mound of covers cocooning her.

The Tear of Heaven was no longer around her throat. It was back in the inlaid box where she had first seen it, and that box was on her dressing table.

Would she ever wear the gem again? Should she?

A sigh born of deep frustration rivaled the muted sounds of night. In a sudden burst of impatience, Brianna hurled herself from the bed and into her robe. She could not bear to be still. The hour notwithstanding, she had to find some occupation.

Candle in hand, she left her room, making her way along corridors and down stairs to the great hall. She continued on to the east wing, where the wide double doors of Hawkforte's library stood open. She could see all the way through to the high windows framing a full moon hanging low in the sky. The light of that moon revealed the man seated at a table near the windows.

Atreus, as sleepless as she.

She took a quick step back and was about to withdraw, when Atreus stood and looked in her direction. Tender amusement laced his voice. "You forgot your slippers."

She glanced down at her bare toes, up again at him. He had crossed the distance between them with silent swiftness and was directly in front of her.

"I couldn't sleep," she said.

"Neither could I. Come over by the hearth."

"But there is no fire."

"Easily remedied. This is an excellent library. Have you had much chance to explore it?"

"Some," Brianna said. She watched him as he turned his attention to the hearth. He moved with the easy, economical grace of a man used to doing such tasks. She wondered where he had learned to build a fire. In the mountains above the royal city of Ilius, perhaps, where the boys went to begin their manhood training and where the nights could be cold indeed?

The muscles of his broad back flexed as he fed wood in slowly. When the fire caught, he stood, dusting off his hands, and nodded toward the table where he had been sitting. "Would you like to see something?"

She nodded, not quite trusting herself to speak. Alone in so intimate a setting, it was all too easy to indulge thoughts of what life would be like as his wife. Instead, she turned her attention to the objects he had been studying.

"What are these?" she asked.

"Take a closer look." He held out an ivory cylinder tipped in gold at both ends.

Brianna turned the slender wand over slowly. Symbols were carved into the gold. She recognized them as Akoran, but written in a style not used for centuries.

"Did you bring this with you?" she asked.

Atreus shook his head. "It's been here at Hawkforte for about seven hundred years, along with the letter it contained, and these other items." He gestured to the collection spread out on the table. Brianna saw a small statue of a horse cast in bronze, a short blade of lethal steel, a bottle of carved alabaster that might have held scented oil, and a box bound in gold and inlaid with pearls that was large enough to have held all the rest.

"Was all this sent by the Hawkforte who reached Akora so long ago?"

Atreus nodded. "The letter that was inside the cylinder still exists, but it is too fragile now to be handled. The man who sent it was named Falconer. He wrote to tell his family here that he would not be returning."

"That must have been very difficult for them."

"Even so, they also must have been glad to know he was alive. Royce tells me that when he and Joanna were children, they studied these things endlessly. They became fascinated with Akora, with the result that Royce went there and Joanna followed in search of him. What one man did seven hundred years ago directly shaped the lives of people he could never even have imagined."

The carved horse was cool and smooth in her hands. Whoever had made it had caught the motion of the animal in midgallop. It reminded her of the horses her Akoran parents raised on Leois, the island of plains where horses flourished.

A sudden, piercing stab of longing darted through her. She set the carving down and looked at Atreus.

"Do you think of the consequences of your actions for generations yet to come?"

"Occasionally, but mostly I just try to do right for the people I am entrusted to lead."

"And for yourself?"

"Yes, that as well."

She was warmer now that the fire had caught. Its flames cast a circle of light into the room. She should find a book and go, but the solitude of her room had little appeal. Even so, to stay where she was would be foolish in the extreme.

Which left her to wonder why she found herself sitting on the rug in front of the fire, staring into the flames. "There is something I have to tell you," she said.

Atreus lowered himself beside her. He tossed another log on the fire and contemplated the requirements of honor. She was a young, inexperienced woman. She was also highly sensual, though he doubted she fully understood that yet. With very little effort, he could make her his. His body reacted enthusiastically to the idea. No surprise there. But his conscience required some convincing.

She would not be harmed, he'd make damn sure of that. When all was said and done, she would be vastly more content and certain of her path in life. That being the case . . . He rose before he could ponder the matter further and went to close the library doors. When he returned, Brianna was looking at him.

"Did you hear what I said?" she asked.

Said? Something about wanting to tell him . . . what? The instinct of a warrior, ever alert to danger, prickled along the back of his neck. He concealed his sudden unease and sat beside her again. Smiling, he brushed away a non-existent strand of hair from her cheek. "Don't you find it tempting sometimes to just relax and enjoy yourself?"

His touch was light, even teasing, as was his manner, but it didn't seem to matter. Her own response was entirely serious. She could not look away from him, could scarcely breathe, and her body—her body seemed to have developed a mind of its own.

She'd been warned of this. Her mother and the other women had made it clear: Men could banish sense, shatter control, and make rational thought impossible. There was a reason why she was supposed to be cautious of all that. Now if only she could remember what it was—

Instead, she was leaning into his hand, accepting his caress. What had seemed so important a few moments before was now in real danger of slipping beyond her grasp. Before that could happen, she forced herself to pull away. The loss of his touch was almost painful, a further shock to her already overburdened emotions, but she steeled herself to bear it.

"I have to tell you something."

His beautiful mouth curved at the corners. The light in his golden-brown eyes was hot and tantalizing. "Does this have to do with strawberries?"

"What?" She remembered how his mouth felt, the sheer, stunning pleasure it brought. "Strawberries?"

"You're allergic to them," he reminded her. "But not to this—" He took her hand, his thumb moving back and forth over the inner curve of her palm. She felt his lips very close . . . and gasped when he nipped lightly at the soft pad of flesh between her thumb and fingers. "Or to this." His tongue stroked back and forth, again and again.

She was trembling and hot, much too hot. "Atreus—"

"There was a time when I thought you would never call me anything but Vanax or, worse yet, Highness."

"You are that. You are—"

His arm was around her waist, powerful and compelling yet still oddly gentle. His other hand was slipping beneath the collar of her robe, easing it off her shoulder. And his mouth, his far too skillful mouth, was drifting down her throat to the place where the Tear of Heaven had rested.

And would again, if he had his way.

"You are the Vanax," she managed though her voice sounded very faint and breathless. "The Chosen, Akora's absolute ruler, you decide everyth—*oh! . . . that feels so good . . .*"

"It will get better," he swore and immediately proved it. His hand, which had slipped beneath her robe and gown, cupped her breast, lightly squeezing, stroking, even as his mouth claimed hers in a deep, drugging kiss.

She was on her back suddenly, with no memory of how she had gotten there, and her robe was gone. Worse yet, the thin fabric of her gown, all the concealment she had left, suddenly felt intolerable. She wanted to strip it off, throw it into the fire and make equally short work of his shirt and breeches. She had a sudden image of their clothes going up in flames, and burst out laughing.

Atreus raised his head, smiling as he gazed down at her. "I amuse you?"

"No, yes . . . oh, heavens, I can't think—"

"Good." He lowered his head again.

She had a tiny moment to consider that it was not only the women of Akora who were very well educated in certain regards, before coils of need tightened within her, becoming all but unbearable. She twisted beneath him, distantly aware that her gown had crept up to bare her legs, and moaned when she felt the thick, hard bulge between his thighs.

But there was still something she needed to say. Something that mattered.

And she had to tell him, had to without further delay, without regard for the pleasure he offered, the passion and the promise of a future she wanted, heaven help her, wanted so fiercely she longed to forget all else.

Tell him—

"Atreus!"

"Easy, sweetheart, you'll have everything you need, I promise."

His shirt was gone, his chest bare, and her breasts felt the tantalizing touch of the crisp mat of hair that arched between his flat nipples and down over the rippling muscles of his abdomen to vanish into the waistband of his breeches.

What she needed . . . what she wanted . . . what she was—

Tell him!

"Helios—"

The single word, faint and breathless, scarcely penetrated his raging hunger. But he was a man, protective and caring, and instinctively he moved to soothe her.

"Don't worry about that, sweetheart. It's of no concern. You have nothing to fear from them—"

"No, you don't understand—"

"They are misguided, foolish, but few are truly dangerous. Don't worry—"

"They are not! They are right to want more openness, more freedom—"

Her skin was soft, smooth, enticing. She was bowed beneath his hands, very close to the full grip of passion. And he, he was rock hard, wanting only to bury himself deep within her. In another moment—

"They are right?" He raised his head, staring down at her. "You can't believe that."

She stiffened. He saw the dark flush of her cheeks, the unsteadiness of her breath, evidence of the struggle raging within her.

And he knew. Somewhere in his heart, the knowledge was already there.

"I do believe it," she said and broke away from him.

He saw her lips move, heard the words, and even understood them, on the surface at least. But what lay behind the words, the truth they revealed, that made no sense at all. She could not be a member of the rebel group that wanted to transform Akora beyond all recognition *and* the woman who was meant to be his consort. That simply wasn't possible. Was it?

"Brianna—?"

She had her back to him as she pulled her robe on. Holding on to a nearby chair, she stood unsteadily and turned to face him. She sighed deeply. "I am a member of Helios."

He, too, got to his feet, never taking his eyes from her. He saw when she took a breath, when her eyes closed for an instant, when resolve hardened within her. And he knew then what he should have known all along. She was not merely the vision he had seen in the cave. She was not simply the exquisite statue carved by his hands. She was Brianna, a woman of courage and complexity.

"Some of your friends may have conspired to kill me."

"No one from Helios would ever have done such a thing!"

"You think not? There is all too much evidence that says otherwise."

In the firelight, her eyes were bleak. He had to fight the urge to reach out to her. Instead, he demanded, "Brianna, how could you? *Why* would you? Helios has no thought for the traditions of Akora, for the values that have served us so well through all the centuries. They would discard everything, and for what? Some childish notion of freedom without responsibility?"

"For a chance to help shape our country's future," she countered. "That is all any of us has ever wanted. Too much of what happens on Akora is done in secrecy, beginning with the selection of the Vanax himself."

"The selection of the Vanax is a deeply spiritual process directly linked to the very essence of Akora." Atreus was shocked, disbelieving, and more than a little frustrated.

His body ached and his heart— He preferred not to think of that. "You have no idea what you are talking about. If you did—"

"Why have I no idea?" she demanded, clutching her robe closed. "Why do so very few know what lies behind a choice that affects us all? You complain that the goals of Helios are childish, but when are we allowed to be truly adult? You control our lives—"

"I do not! I *serve* Akora and all Akorans. If you do not understand that, you understand nothing at all."

"Then perhaps I don't, for I see one man given virtually absolute power in a ritual that has been clothed in secrecy for far too long!"

Atreus snatched up his shirt and pulled it on but did not bother fastening it. He was too busy staring at her in true bewilderment.

"I remind you," he said stiffly, "that our ways have preserved Akora for thousands of years, while all about us other nations rose and fell, entire peoples disappeared, and far too often, chaos reigned. Is that the future you want for Akora? That we should be as fragile, as *temporary* as everyone else?"

"Of course not! I love Akora and want only what is best for it!"

"Really? And who determines what is best? You? Your Helios friends? The same people who thought what was best for Akora was to conspire with a madman to kill me and take over the government?"

"That hasn't been proven! You yourself said they are still to be tried. *You* will preside over that trial. *You* will decide their fate. But you've already made up your mind, haven't you? Where is the justice in that?"

"I *will* put aside my personal concerns, for that is the essence of what it means to be Vanax. They *will* receive a fair trial. If they are innocent, they will go free. If they are guilty, they will pay. Where is your difficulty with that?"

"If what you say is true, I have none."

"If? Do you think I lie?"

"No! I simply doubt any man can truly put aside a matter so personal as his own life and near-death."

"I am not any man. *I am Vanax*."

Silence, except for the crackling of the fire. Flames leaped suddenly, pulled up the chimney by a gust of wind that battered against the windows and howled round the high towers.

Wind where there had been none before, wind born out of stillness, wind that sounded like a howl of grief.

"No!" Brianna paled. She put her hands to her ears as though to shut out the sound.

"What the hell?" Atreus strode over to the window, which had broken open, pulled it shut, and secured it. By the time he had done so, the wind seemed to be dying. Slowly, Brianna lowered her hands, but she remained pale and obviously distressed.

Under any other circumstances, he would have gone to her at once, reassured and comforted her. But given what had just passed between them, he remained where he was. Even so, he watched her with great care and even more bewilderment. She was—what? Terrified? Stunned? Both, perhaps, but why? It was, after all, only the wind.

"What troubles you?" he asked.

"Nothing! No, not nothing . . . you . . . me . . . Helios." She shook her head as though trying to clear it. "It doesn't matter. I'm going to bed." She went toward the library doors. Her hand was on the knob when she looked at him. "Do you want the Tear of Heaven now or in the morning?"

"I want you."

He saw the shock ripple through her, saw the dark,

swirling shadows behind her eyes. "You cannot," she said, "not now."

"I should not," he corrected. Then, incredibly, he laughed. The sound startled them both. "But it seems I'm not the sensible fellow I've presumed myself to be."

Brianna had opened the door, but she did not go through it, not yet. "Did you really think that?" she asked shakily. "You are an artist."

"Therefore ruled by passion? I am a man. It has been my observation that passion must yield to reason, at least most of the time." He came toward her, through the shadows, giving her no time to think. "Let us reason together."

"Don't . . ." She held out a hand, fending him off. "Don't touch me again."

"Why not, Brianna? Have I hurt you in some way?"

"No, we both know you have not. But when you touch me, I cannot think."

"Is that supposed to be discouragement? Come back with me to Akora."

"For what purpose?"

"You said you love Akora, and your friends there are about to go on trial. Come and see that they receive justice."

He came closer, closer still, so close she was reminded of the warmth of him, the heat and of what that made her feel.

"Come with me, Brianna. Be my conscience, if you must."

"You don't need that."

"Don't I? Have you any idea what I remember? The endless pain that devoured me? The desire for death, simply to end that pain? The temptation of the world beyond this one, and of how difficult it was to return here? And the fear, let us not forget the fear, for I surely have not. Fear that I would not be healed, not be a man, not be able to move at all, not be whole in mind or memory. There are still nights when I wake with that fear."

"Atreus—" Her voice choked. Her hand, reaching out blindly, caught his. "I was there," she said. "I have some sense of what you suffered."

"Yet I must judge the very people who may have helped bring that about. I must put aside all personal considerations and be Vanax. Come with me."

"I belong to Helios."

"You belong to yourself, and to Akora, and—just possibly—to me." He drew her closer, slowly, steadily. "What do you fear, Brianna? Why did the wind distress you so much?"

The question was out before he could stop it. She looked not pale but ashen, not startled but sickened. A woman in the grip of nothing short of horror.

"Brianna—"

She dropped his hand, turned to the door, threw it all the way open. As though in slow motion, he saw the silken curtain of her hair rise behind her as she fled.

"Brianna!"

He was a warrior, a hunter when need be. He was bred for both, trained and honed. And he was a man, hard with the hunger for her, driven by ancient instinct.

He caught her at the foot of the stairs. Her eyes were wide, shocked. If she thought of resistance, he gave her no chance to act on that thought, but lifted her high against his chest and took the steps two at a time.

No man may ever harm a woman.

He would not harm her, he damn well would not.

He would have her, and in the process, she would have him. Together, they would defy the demons taunting them both.

He knew where her room was. He had passed it one day

while Royce was showing him around the manor. One of those seemingly endless days she had spent at Holyhood.

He kicked the door open and saw the bed bathed in moonlight, the covers thrown aside as she had left them. Swiftly, he shoved the door closed, crossed the room, laid her on the bed and came right down over her. A steely thigh thrust between her own. "Tell me no, Brianna. If that is in your heart, say it now."

She stared up at him, color in her cheeks and her eyes burned free of shadows. "Say what? That I want you as you want me? That right now I don't care anything about tomorrow or an hour from now or anything but this moment?"

Her hands were beneath his shirt, stroking the hard contours of his chest. Her hips rose, caressing the bulge of his erection. He groaned and closed his eyes for a moment, summoning control.

He would need it, for Brianna twisted beneath him, her every movement, every breath, and the soft, urgent little sounds she made, driving him right over the edge. He was a man of discipline. He had gone days without sleep, endured bitter cold, scorching heat, hunger, and thirst and come out of all that to fight and win in the hand-to-hand combat that was a part of every Akoran warrior's training. He had confronted intricate problems and reasoned them through to solution. He had schooled himself to patience in seemingly infinite hours with his counselors and all those who sought to advise him. He could damn well do this!

"Brianna, sweetheart, easy . . ."

"No! I can't stand this. Atreus, please!"

Her gown was gone, stripped away by one of them, he had no clear notion who, but it didn't matter, she was naked against him, her skin smoother than the alabaster he had carved, every curve and plane alive, real and more arousing than he could bear. And yet he had to bear it, for his pride as a man and his genuine care for her demanded that he do nothing less.

Sheer survival drove him to take her mouth hard and fast, thrusting his tongue into her as he reached down between her silken thighs and found unerringly what he sought. There he stroked, again and again as his tongue moved to the same rhythm, as her skin heated against his, as she bucked and moaned, and finally as the coils of every tightening pressure released suddenly, hurling her into ecstasy.

It was not enough, not for him, certainly and, he decided, not remotely for her. His big hands clasped her wrists, holding her in place as he moved down her body, savoring every exquisite inch of her. His mouth was skilled, relentless, and utterly effective. She cried out helplessly and reached for him, but he would not risk her touch. Instead, he turned her, pausing long enough to enjoy the dimples. They were even more enticing in person than they had been in his imagination. Lightly, tantalizingly, he blew on the base of her spine and was rewarded when she cried out. Again, her hips rose, straining toward him. He reached down, making quick work of the buttons of his breeches, and freed his organ. He was hard to the point of bursting, but still he held on. Only a few droplets of pearly fluid glistening over the hard, round tip of him revealed how very close he was. With relentless care, he rubbed between the silken folds of her cleft, entering her just the smallest way, enough to feel the intense contractions of her muscles straining to draw him in fully.

Again pleasure took her, and still he waited, turning her to face him, whispering to her how beautiful she was, how enticing her passion, how utterly he wanted her. She was sobbing his name, crying out to him when he finally slid between her thighs, still slowly, still exercising restraint despite the savage pounding of his heart and the desperate, driving need of his body.

All that shattered when, at last, he thrust fully into her, past the barrier of her virginity, driving hard and deep. She was tight, hot, and slick with desire. Her arms embraced him, her lips shaped his name and she . . . she claimed him fully and utterly, taking from him the very essence of life, in a completion so intense that blackness swirled at the edges of his mind.

When Atreus came to himself, he was lying beside Brianna, holding her in the shelter of his arms even as his hands moved, learning and soothing her all at once.

"My God," he said softly.

Her lips smiled against his heated skin. "Mmmmm."

"I've never experienced anything remotely like that." He spoke with simple truth.

She turned slightly, looking up at him. "As I believe you know, I haven't either. I must say, what I had assumed was a quite comprehensive education has fallen short of the mark."

"We could devote ourselves to rewriting the texts."

"That has merit. We should consider it."

He laughed, hugging her close and feeling in her embrace a sense of rightness also unlike anything he had ever experienced.

Except in the caves, where he had gone to discover his destiny and awoke facedown in the dirt to realize that he had found it.

He looked again at Brianna. She was asleep, just that suddenly, between one breath and another. On the cusp of utterly male satisfaction, he should have followed her.

And would have, but for the belated stirring of his conscience.

He had done what was right and necessary. He had not harmed her. Yet he could not deny the greater truth.

He had taken her innocence, and in doing so, had bound to him the one woman on earth who should have wished him as far from her as it was humanly possible to be.

How could she not, when her parents' deaths haunted her still? The deaths he had caused so long ago on that day when a boy became a man.

"Atreus . . . it's the French! Damn them!"

"Hold the line, men! The wind is with us!"

"Closer . . . closer. Warriors of Akora, do not flinch!"

"Polynx is dead! Menelos as well! Atreus, what do we do?"

There was blood splattered on the cannons, a great gaping hole in the side of the ship. Men he had known, respected, looked to, were dead at his feet.

He stepped over them, saw the confusion in faces as young as his own, heard his voice hard and steady over the roar of battle.

"Reload! Do not hesitate! We are the line! We will not break!"

It was his eye that gauged the distance, his hands that moved the cannon barrel, just slightly. Just enough.

His order. His will.

"Fire!"

He lay in darkness, holding her in his arms, and thought of his own lost innocence, gone not in sweet, heady passion but in the blood, sweat, and terror of battle. Gone beyond all recapturing, no matter that being with her made him feel washed clean and whole again in a way he had not hoped to experience.

He turned his head and touched his lips softly to her brow, tasting on his kiss the salt of tears too long unshed.

THEIR FACES WERE SOFT WITH SURPRISE, their eyes wide and shadowed. Brianna looked from one to the other with mounting guilt. "Please try to understand," she said. "I know this must seem very sudden, but I truly must return to Akora."

Uncharacteristically at a loss for words, Lady Constance looked to her husband. "Of course we wish only the best for you, my dear," the earl said, "but is there some urgent need that prompts this decision?"

She had taken an irrevocable step that might determine her entire future? She was torn between desperate desire for the man she thought of with every breath and fear that she was betraying her highest ideals? She was haunted by old memories that were creeping ever closer?

"I miss my family."

"Oh, my dear." Lady Constance reached over and took

her hand. They were sitting in the family drawing room at Holyhood. Outside, the crisp winter day was fast fading. Earlier, Brianna had met the younger generations of Hollisters, including the very youngest, a devilishly darling tot named William in honor of his grandfather. Warmly welcomed by them, she liked each and every one. With very little effort, she could come to think of them as friends and perhaps even as family.

A cheerful fire burned and tea was at hand. Holyhood had all the little touches of a home . . . her mother's home. Hers, if fate had called her in that direction.

"We understand completely," Lady Constance said. "It is only natural. You have discovered so much about yourself. Perhaps you need time to consider all that has happened."

"I do, but please do not think I am less than appreciative of all you have done and all you offer me. Finding you, discovering Holyhood, means the world to me."

"The doors of Holyhood will always be open to you," Lord William said. "As they should have been to your mother and father." He stood and held out his arms to her. She went into them gladly, both touched and relieved by his response.

"Indeed, they are," Lady Constance said as she came to join them. With a gentle hand pressed to Brianna's cheek, she said, "You know, my dear, I was a young woman once. I know how longings can pull us in different directions. But believe me, there is no trustier guide than your own heart." She looked to the portrait over the mantel. "I am convinced your own dear mother would tell you just this."

Brianna blinked back sudden tears. All day she had teetered between determined calm and exuberent emotion. Had she truly done what memory and the satiation of her own body announced? Had she woken in a bed that still held Atreus's warmth and scent? Had she turned to him instinctively in the moments before she realized he had withdrawn, leaving on the pillow beside her the Tear of Heaven, mute reminder of all that lay before them?

So it seemed, and she had no regrets to show. Quite the contrary. Concerns abounded—he was the Vanax, she was Helios. He was Akoran, she was—or might be—English. He was a man, she a woman, and for all the incandescent pleasure they had found together, wariness of losing herself to him ran deep. But she had no regrets, not a single one. Indeed, she was hard-pressed to conceal her smiles.

The plain truth of it was that the Vanax of Akora was an extraordinary lover. She had heard whispers to that effect during her time in the palace, but the women who had known him were models of discretion. Were it not for their tendency during the darkest days following the attack on him to gather in corridors and sob copiously, she might never have overheard their observations.

Now he lived, gloriously and entirely, and he wanted her. That reality was still very difficult to comprehend, yet she must come to terms with it for both their sakes.

"My dear," Lord William said gently, "we must spend a little time talking of practical matters."

She was still thinking of Atreus and scarcely heard him.

"Before your grandfather died," the earl said, "he had something of a change of heart."

Lady Constance nodded. "To be fair, it may have happened years earlier, but still too late to bring back his lost daughter. At any rate, he made provision for you."

"Provision?" Brianna repeated, looking from one to the other.

"The late earl left a settlement for you," Lord William explained gently. "A sum of money to become yours when you married—in which case, of course, it would be under the control of your husband. But he added another, somewhat unusual provision. His will allows that if you are still unmarried at the age of twenty-five, the settlement becomes yours without restriction."

"But he could not have known that I was alive."

"He hoped," Lord William said gently. "At least, I imagine he did. He did not confide in me. I will tell you that had your grandfather not made the provision he did, I would take it upon myself to do so. It is only right."

"That is very good of you, and I suppose it was of him, but I really have no idea what this means."

"It means," Lady Constance said, "that should you choose to return to England, you may marry very well, or, if you prefer, you may live a very comfortable life of independence."

"And," Lord William added firmly, "you may do either with our complete support, the support of your English family."

Brianna did understand then, and with that understanding came piercing sorrow for what might have been. "If anything like this had been offered to my mother——"

"Delphine and Edward might still be alive," Lady Constance said. "Dear child, it does not do to dwell on such things, but we can, indeed we must, learn from the mistakes of the past."

Brianna blinked back tears and summoned strength. "I have lingered longer than I should have, but I am so very grateful for your understanding."

"It will be dark soon," Lady Constance agreed. "Why don't you spend the night? We could have at least a little more time together. We will send word to Hawkforte, of course. No one there need be worried for you."

The invitation was tempting, but she was torn. The plain fact was that she was anxious to see Atreus and equally anxious about how she would react when she did. Pride urged her to face him, but the kindness of the earl and countess, and her genuine desire to spend more time with them before departing England, tipped the balance.

"I would like to stay," Brianna said with a smile. "Thank you for asking me."

A messenger was dispatched forthwith to Hawkforte. A short time later, the younger Hollisters joined them again and the evening proceeded in a spirit of warm conviviality.

ATREUS CRUMBLED THE NOTE. HE LOOKED OUT over the towers of Hawkforte to the blaze of glory that was the setting sun. Behind him, Royce said, "There is no reason for concern. The Hollisters will make her perfectly comfortable and this is certainly preferable to her being on the road after dark."

"But not as preferable," Atreus replied, "as her having returned long before now, or better yet, not having gone at all, particularly not with only a coachman to accompany her."

"You're welcome to a horse," Royce said.

It was tempting, far too much so, but he was not about to go pounding up to the doors of Holyhood to—what? Prevent her from being lured away with the promise of the life that could be hers if she remained in England? He did not doubt for a moment that the earl and his countess would do just that if they could.

"When will the ships be here?" Atreus asked.

"Around midday tomorrow, given the tide."

"I have enjoyed your hospitality but I hope you understand, I am not inclined to linger."

Royce smiled sympathetically. "Of course not. By the way, Kassandra and I have been talking. She would like to return to Akora for the birth of our child."

Atreus did not conceal his surprise. "I thought you both wanted the baby to be born here at Hawkforte. Brianna's aunt, Elena, is planning to come to help as she did when Amelia was born."

"That was the intent," Royce acknowledged. "But recently, Kassandra began thinking of the baby being born on Akora. If that is to happen, I would prefer she go there now rather than closer to her time."

Atreus nodded. He understood that Royce was setting aside his own preferences to honor his wife's, a choice of which Atreus entirely approved. "Are you able to go with her?"

"I will be," Royce said in the tone of a man prepared to overcome any obstacle. "But I need a few days in London to arrange matters. I realize you do not want to extend your stay but—"

"I am also not in such a hurry to leave that I would inconvenience my host or neglect my duty to my sister. Take whatever time you need."

Royce nodded. "I leave for London in the morning. Prinny will simply have to understand that—"

"That the Vanax of Akora requires your presence for further discussion of trade and related issues. I will give you a letter for him to that effect."

Royce laughed. "Nicely done, and thank you, that will make my task considerably easier."

Atreus wrote the letter after supper. Shortly thereafter, he retired. Sleep promised to be elusive and he wasted no effort seeking it. Beyond the high windows of his quarters, moonlight gleamed on white-flecked water. He tossed on a black woolen cloak and went out into the night. The air was blowing from the sea. It was cold and brisk, invigorating rather than unpleasant.

He walked out across the lawn that fronted that side of the manor, past the gardens sleeping until spring, to the tumbled stone walls. From there, he could see the old town and the harbor beyond. But it was not in that direction that he looked. Instead, he turned toward Hawkforte. The manor seemed to float above the dark mound that was the land, as though a part of it, yet also something more.

By Akoran standards, Hawkforte was young. It had stood for a mere nine centuries or so, whereas Atreus worked and lived in rooms his ancestors had occupied for millenia. Yet Hawkforte radiated a sense of unbroken continuity, of a place and a people that had never wavered, never weakened, and most certainly never yielded. All about it, the world had shaken and convulsed over and over while Hawkforte held strong. In that, it was very much like Akora.

Such places seemed to hold echoes of the past. He was not a superstitious man, far from it, and despite his experience with the trial of selection, he was not a mystic. Yet on more than one occasion, he had gone around a corner of the palace, entered a room, done something entirely commonplace, and had a sudden sense that he was not alone, that there were others all around him, unseen yet still entirely real, doing the same things, for the same reasons. He had experienced nothing of that sort at Hawkforte, nor would he expect to. And yet there was a sense of . . . something. Perhaps that was not so surprising. He was, after all, a member of the family not only by marriage but through the distant Hawkforte ancestor who had found his destiny on Akora.

A gust of wind blew suddenly off the sea, returning him to the present moment and reminding him . . .

Brianna feared the wind.

The thought leaped fully formed into his mind. He saw her suddenly, in a flash of memory, in the library at Hawkforte, her hands over her ears, crying out as the wind that seemed to come from nowhere howled all around them.

She believed her parents had perished in a terrible storm at sea. Perhaps that was why the wind frightened her. Certainly, he had no reason to think otherwise. But the memory lingered, joining all the other thoughts of her.

Having claimed her, he deeply disliked being without her. She should be there with him, close to his hand. He wanted to protect and care for her, to coax her smiles and hear her laughter.

He also wanted to bed her, quite urgently.

The wind blew and Atreus sighed. He was tired enough to feel not entirely connected to the world around him, as though some portion of his mind floated elsewhere. Beyond the old stone walls, down toward the shore, he heard what sounded like voices, but when he looked in that direction there was no one. Or was there? For just a moment in the moonlight he thought he caught a glimpse of a woman, and beside her, the tall, broad-shouldered shape of a man bending close as though to hear what she said.

The illusion, for surely that was all it was, vanished in an instant. The moon moved behind a cloud. Atreus waited a little longer, contemplating the night, before walking back across the broad lawns to ancient Hawkforte.

FROM THE WINDOW OF ONE OF THE MANY GUEST rooms at Holyhood, Brianna watched the cloak of clouds rising out of the west. It was very late. All around her, the great house dozed. Nothing moved except for the cat sitting on the wall of the stone terrace just beyond the window. In the act of cleaning its whiskers, it stopped suddenly and looked out toward the sea, appearing for all the world to watch something passing by. But there was nothing to be seen, apart from the ripple of water that must have been caused by the eddy of the tide.

Brianna let the curtain drop and turned back to the room. The fire still glowed cheerfully. On a nearby table, a tray held a pot of hot chocolate, a silver bowl of whipped cream, and a crystal shaker of ground cinnamon. In front of the fire, a large chair beckoned. A little distance away was the bed, curtained in silk, heaped with pillows, and provided with a mattress so thick she thought she could become lost in it. There was a dressing table with a mirror in a silver frame, an exquisite Aubusson rug in hues of ivory, rose, and spring green, and a pretty cabinet painted with twining vines and filled with books.

It was a lovely room, warm, feminine, and entirely comfortable. No shadows lingered in it.

It had been Delphine's room. So Lady Constance had told her, gently, when that good lady bid her good night.

"If you would prefer another . . ." Lady Constance offered.

But she had not. She wanted to be in her mother's room, surrounded by the things that had been part of Delphine's life, looking through the windows at the same view Delphine had seen. It was, in all likelihood, the closest she would ever be to her mother.

Unless she remained in England, among those who had known and loved the woman who was only stray wisps of memory to her.

The smooth linen sheets of the bed were cool, but her feet found the porcelain bottle filled with hot water nestled at the bottom. On the few cold nights that ever came to her family's home on Leois, her mother filled similar bottles and saw that they found their place in every bed.

Her Akoran mother, Leoni, the woman whose face was the first she saw when she regained consciousness. Who had not left her side for weeks as she struggled against the lure of death. Who had held her when she wept, soothed her in a thousand ways, steadied her when she took her first steps into a new life. And her father, Marcus, the strong, calm, good man who had not hesitated to welcome an orphan child into his home and his heart.

How she missed them! Through all the months in England, the desperate need to find herself, to know who she truly was, had held every other emotion at bay. No longer. Now she knew. She was Lady Brianna Wilcox. She had a name, a heritage, and a past she could no longer deny.

"—*Delphine . . . the wind*—"

"—*only a baby, Edward*—"

"—*when she cries . . . is upset*—"

"—*don't say that*—"

"*Papa, look, Papa! I made the boat go!*"

"*Momma, don't be mad*—"

"—*The tree in front, ma'am, knocked down*—"

"—*that child*—"

"—*all the wash on the line*—"

"—*the shutters ripped right off*—"

"*Edward, we must leave here . . .*"

"—*again*—"

"—*again*—"

"—*that child*—"

They had moved from place to place, never staying anywhere for more than a few months. Flashes of memory came . . . a room, a house, a street, fading before she could more than glimpse them.

"*My family . . . stories . . . strange occurrences*—"

"*Not your fault, Delphine. Never think that, sweetheart*—"

Voices overheard in the dark, when they thought her asleep, voices of love and concern.

Voices gone from her for so long now.

She was crying and had been for a while. Her tears fell against the smooth pillow in her mother's bed, in her mother's room, in her mother's home. In Delphine's memory—and Edward's—Brianna wept, for all that they and she had lost.

She had needed to do that for a long time and when she

was done, she slept. Deeply at first, then lightly, skimming through dreams, then not at all, for it was morning and someone was knocking on her door.

M ORE COFFEE, YOUR HIGHNESS?" LADY CONSTANCE smiled as she offered the pot. That good lady looked entirely at ease, as though it were an everyday occurrence for royalty to appear on her doorstep before the sun was above the treetops. Fortunately, she was an early riser, as was the earl, looking only mildly nonplussed by their un-expected guest.

"Thank you," Atreus said. "And may I also thank you again for your hospitality. It was my intent to arrive at a more civilized hour."

But a hard gallop, flat out from Hawkforte on a spirited mount, had a way of eating up miles.

"Not at all, my lord," the earl said genially. "As you know, I myself have a predilection for early morning calls."

Atreus's laugh ended suddenly when Brianna walked into the morning room. She had dressed, not hastily but with a certain degree of distraction, after being informed by the flustered maid that "His Highness, the Borax of Akora" had arrived. Atreus's importance was appreciated belowstairs, even if the precise details of his title were a bit fuzzy.

He looked very much at ease chatting with Lord William and Lady Constance. He also looked . . . utterly male, powerful, compelling, and far too tempting. Those broad shoulders beneath his riding jacket . . . all too easily she remembered how they felt beneath her seeking hands. He was freshly shaven, but she recalled the roughness of his cheeks in the secret hours of the night. And his mouth . . . better she not think of that at all, and what chance had she of not?

He was standing, coming toward her, and she could do nothing but stay rooted where she was, staring at him.

"Brianna—" His voice was deep, caressing, tinged by concern. "We missed you."

Was that the royal "we," she wondered, in the tiny part of her brain where thought was still possible.

"Lady Constance and Lord William were kind enough to offer me breakfast. I thought you might like company returning to Hawkforte this morning."

She supposed that meant she was not to stay any longer. That was also her choice or she would have stood her ground. All the same, and as a matter of principle, she did not think it wise for him to have matters all his own way.

"I promised William I would stay awhile."

"William?" Atreus looked to the earl, surprised by so great a degree of familiarity.

That worthy pressed his lips together in a futile effort to hide a smile. "I believe Lady Brianna refers to my grandson. They met yesterday, and he is much taken with her."

"As I am with him. We are engaged to go frog hunting."

"All the frogs are hibernating at this time of year," Lady Constance said.

Brianna shrugged. "I did not assume we would be successful."

"I, too, would like to go frog hunting," Atreus said.

Both Hollisters looked in his direction. It fell to the earl to say, "Are you quite certain of that, Your Highness?"

"Absolutely. In fact, I can't think of anything I would rather do."

"I see. . . . In that case, I'm sure William will be delighted to have you come along. In fact, now that I think of it, why don't we all go frog hunting?"

"An excellent idea, my dear," Lady Constance said, proving yet again that she was an admirable wife. "I will inform the staff. The day is bright, a winter picnic would be just the thing."

"You don't look quite fit for frog hunting," Atreus said a short while later as they were preparing to go out. "Your eyes are red-rimmed."

Brianna secured the frog closing of her cloak—rather apt, she thought—and said, "You are supposed to say my eyes look like limpid pools or something of that sort."

"Limpid pools? Really? Sounds rather dim, and your eyes definitely aren't. Have you been crying?"

"I have been remembering."

"What?"

A single word, uttered in the tone of command. He wanted an answer, but did he fear it? Not Atreus. Surely, fear was foreign to him.

"About my parents, just snatches of conversation." She was not about to tell him about the wind. Indeed, she could scarcely bear to think of it.

"You should not have stayed here."

"On the contrary, being here, knowing who my mother was, knowing that part of me, all that is exactly what I most desired."

"And is it still?" he asked suddenly. "Having attained all that, is it still your greatest desire?"

Brianna turned, looking at him over her shoulder. "No," she said and went out into the bright day.

Chapter
ELEVEN

THREE DAYS LATER, BRIANNA WATCHED THE
towers of Hawkforte slip away into the early-
morning mist. The day was warm for winter.
The seals basking on the rocks drowsed so
deeply they scarcely could be bothered to lift their heads at
the fleet's passing.

The Vanax of Akora did not sail alone. Two warships led
the way and another two followed. Even in such troubled
times, no one would be mad enough to challenge the warriors renowned as the fiercest in the world, but the display
of power was a useful reminder all the same. It would be reported by every captain who passed within sight, spoken of
in crew messes and in capitals alike by men who would tell
and retell tales of the tragic end met by anyone foolish
enough to challenge the Akorans.

The fifth vessel that completed the fleet was larger, built
for comfort as well as combat. But it also carried a full

complement of warriors and armaments. On its deck,
Brianna looked up, her eye caught by the royal standard
flying from the top of the center mast. It signified the presence on board of the Vanax of Akora. The same Vanax who
was up in the rigging, thirty feet above the deck, helping to
unfurl the sails.

She wasn't going to look, not again. The shock of her
first sight of him in so perilous a position had yet to pass.
But she could hear his voice drifting down to her as he
laughed—*laughed*—with the men up there with him.

She was looking despite her best resolve. Sunlight
glinted off his thick black hair rumpled by the breeze. The
weather being typical of an English December, he and the
other men still wore woolen trousers and shirts. They were
all tall, powerful, supremely fit, but her eyes saw only him.
He had about him the aura of command even as he joked
with the men and shared their tasks.

The ship dropped into the trough of a wave and Brianna
grabbed for the deck railing. The mast seemed to slant
alarmingly above her. A cry rose in her throat, choked off
only because she knew it would be both foolish and embar-
rassing. Atreus and the other men seemed scarcely to notice the ship's movement. They continued as they were,
releasing the rest of the sails and, it seemed to her, lingering a little longer as though enjoying the view.

Finally, well after she thought he should have, Atreus
dropped back onto the deck almost in front of her. He appeared unaffected by his exertions, his strength and stam-
ina that of a man at the peak of his powers. Obeying an
instinct she scarcely understood, Brianna drew her cloak
more closely around herself. A hood covered her head,
framing her face in soft white fur. The cloak itself was a
shade of green Madame Duprès claimed matched her eyes.

She looked, Atreus thought, quintessentially feminine—lovely, strong, and proud. And wary, most definitely

wary. Here was a good example of why a man should not lie with a virgin unless it was accepted by both that she was his to cherish and protect for all time. Brianna had not accepted that, not yet at any rate. The lack of such acceptance was causing her unhappiness, if she but knew it.

All the same, she had come on board under her own power. He had not, as he thought he might have, had to compell her presence. Would he have done so? Going to England, there was no thought in his mind but that she would return to Akora with him. Learning to know her better, to see her as the woman she truly was, made him marvel at such a blithe assumption. Was it Alex who had tried to warn him? He should have listened to his brother, who had good reason to know the difference between the woman a man imagined he wanted and the one he found himself loving.

A sudden burst of laughter drew his attention. Alex and Joanna were also on deck, a little distance away. Alex held Amelia, who was working her way out of her blankets with admirable determination. She had one arm free already and waved it in her father's face. Nearby, Royce and Kassandra enjoyed her antics.

The presence of his family was always welcome, Atreus reminded himself. He genuinely loved them all. It was just that he would have liked some time alone with Brianna. Actually, quite a lot of time.

She turned her head just then and he saw how the winter sunlight danced along the smooth curve of her cheek. The statue in his cabin notwithstanding, stone wasn't the right medium for her, but neither was clay. Nothing could truly capture the woman herself.

"Is that *marinos* I smell?" Brianna asked.

Atreus took a quick sniff and grinned. "It is and not a moment too soon. When was the last time you had *marinos*?"

"Too long," she said over her shoulder, already heading in the direction of the tantalizing aroma. An iron hearth enclosed with flagstones was the center of attention for a circle of warriors. Several large, battle-scarred veterans were supervising the preparations while fending off the suggestions of their fellows.

They made way courteously for Brianna, who smiled her thanks and took an appreciative sniff. With the tantalizing aroma came a cascade of memories, tripping one over the other. Her mother at the outside hearth behind their house, where the cooking was done except on rainy days, trading sallies with her father as they argued over the proper proportion of seasonings. Her brothers seated at the big table of rough-hewn teak set under a striped awning, their hands flashing as they shelled the small shrimp and crayfish netted only an hour or so before in the Inland Sea and brought home in sacks kept moist with seaweed. Herself fending off the eager cats who vied for tidbits of the plump whitefish that was skinned, filleted, and added in bite-size chunks to the simmering pot.

Longing to be among them again welled up in her. She turned away quickly but not in time to elude Atreus's keen gaze. He followed as she stepped over toward the railing, and laid a hand gently on her arm.

"Brianna, are you all right?"

She managed a faint laugh. "Now that I'm actually on the way home, I'm more homesick than ever."

"We will be there soon," he said gently. He kept his touch light and resisted the urge to draw her to him. The lack of privacy rankled. "Although I would wish it sooner yet."

She knew precisely what he meant because she felt it herself. "Atreus . . . what happened between us—"

"Was meant to happen. If you regret it, that is unfortunate, but in time you will—"

"I didn't say I regret it. I just don't think it settles anything."

He was a calm man, a man of care and deliberation. In conflict as well as in council, he kept emotion reined and relied on reason.

But four days before, his self-control had gotten lost in Brianna's bed. It seemed he had yet to find it again.

"The hell it doesn't." Before she could draw breath, he moved to block her from the sight of anyone else on deck, at the same time pulling her against him. His voice was low and hard. "No woman ever gave herself more completely or generously to any man. No ceremony of joining could make us more truly one than we became then. Do not deny this, for you know it is true."

More softly but no less firmly, she said, "It is also true that much lies between us. Do not deny that."

More than she knew. He would not think of that, not now. "Nothing will lie between us. I will not allow it."

"You do not control everything, Vanax of Akora. Most certainly, you do not control me."

She flattened her palms against his chest as though to push him away. Before intent could become deed her touch softened. With a warrior's instinct, Atreus seized the advantage, but his response was no crude battering of the citadel. He acted with the skill of a master strategist, brushing her mouth lightly with his, making her inhale sharply with surprise. He withdrew and returned, deepening the kiss even as his arms closed implacably around her.

"Yield, Brianna," he murmured. His tongue found hers, stroked, teased, withdrew again. "Surrender and accept your victory."

"I can understand why you are so formidable in council," she said unsteadily. "You are a master confuser."

"I have never felt an impulse to kiss one of my councillors, and you have no reason to be confused."

She sighed and in a poignant gesture leaned her forehead against his chest. "Yet I am, deeply confused."

His big hands stroked down her back soothingly. "It will sort out, truly. You will see when we reach Akora."

Brianna looked up, meeting his gaze. "My beliefs are very different from yours. I accept that we both want only good for Akora, but we see very different paths to that good."

"You must trust me to do what is right."

"A child trusts a parent to make the right choices, the right decisions. Eventually we must put childhood behind us."

"I do not treat my people as children, but neither do I expect them to be burdened by responsibilities that are rightly mine."

"But don't you see, that's exactly the—"

She broke off suddenly. As one they turned toward the hearth. The warriors who had been gathered around it were gone, no doubt in a well-intentioned effort to give them some obviously needed privacy. No one was tending the *marinos*, which had begun to scorch.

Passion and politics were all well and good, but the stomach counted, too. "For heaven's sake," Brianna muttered and hurried to stir the pot.

T HE WIND HELD STRONG. SOON THE COAST OF England was but a memory. Shortly after turning south out of the Channel, they spotted a convoy of French warships. The vessels came close enough for them to see sunlight glinting off the metal casings of the spyglasses being used to survey the Akoran ships, but no closer. The French knew better than to stray too near, nor did they tarry.

Breton fishermen proved more daring. They steered

their skiffs within shouting range and exchanged greetings with the Akorans before continuing on toward the vast cod fisheries to the north.

As the bull's head ships kept course south along the coast of France, they shared the lanes with more crafts of every description, including, as Royce noted ruefully, several vessels flying the American flag. Their intrepid captains and crews had run the blockade the British were attempting to maintain on their embattled nation.

"It's not going well for the Americans," Alex remarked after they watched one such ship vanish into the distance. "They lack men, matériel, and money to prosecute a war."

"But not determination," Atreus replied. "That they seem to have in plenty, and they fight on their own lands. I would not rule out their victory."

The fate of the Americans, whatever it might be, did not occupy them long, Over dinner that evening, the talk turned to what awaited them on Akora.

"Deilos remains defiant," Atreus said. "He refuses to cooperate with investigators or acknowledge any of his crimes."

"That is ridiculous," Kassandra said. She looked to her husband, who sat beside her at the large table where they were all dining. "We all know he tried to provoke a British invasion of Akora to turn people against you and bring himself to power. Royce was there when Deilos not merely admitted that but boasted of it to me."

Atreus grinned as he looked at his brother-in-law. "Deilos does have a few things to say about you, Royce. He remembers your last encounter quite well."

"What happened then?" Brianna asked. She knew something of the story but suspected there was much more to be told.

"I didn't kill him," Royce replied.

"You were right not to," Atreus said. "His trial will re-mind all Akorans that what we have is not imperishable."

"What about those people from Helios?" Joanna asked him. "I know quite a few of them were arrested right after the attack on you, but haven't most been released?"

Atreus nodded. "All but four who are suspected of con-spiring with Deilos."

About to deny that any such conspiracy could exist, Brianna caught herself. In the days since her declaration to Atreus, she had wondered if he would tell his family of her involvement with Helios. Firm though she was in her prin-ciples, she dreaded what would surely be the shock and disapproval of those she regarded as good friends. The re-lief she felt at their continued ignorance was fragile, for she knew the secret could not be kept indefinitely.

Looking at her, he said, "Of course, it is possible they are innocent."

"I thought there was significant evidence against them," Kassandra said.

"That was the conclusion of the investigators," Atreus acknowledged. "However, there is no presumption of guilt."

Carefully, Brianna asked, "If that is the case, why have they been held? They could have been living in their own homes with their families these past months rather than waiting in jail."

"The evidence," Atreus replied, "suggested that if they were free, they might continue to act on Deilos's behalf. Therefore, I agreed with the magistrates that they should not be released."

"Someone conspired with Deilos," Royce said. "I am convinced of that, and I don't mean the men who were foolish enough to fight for him."

"What do you mean?" Alex asked quietly.

"To make use of Helios as he did, he must have had someone on the inside."

"Not necessarily," Brianna countered. "Deilos used the symbols of Helios to his own purpose, but those were no secret. Anyone could have appropriated them to any end."

Joanna took a sip of her wine and smiled. "Your fairness does you credit, but I think it is also your gentle heart speaking. You want to believe the best of people."

"I cannot take any such credit, truly. The fact is—"

"Brianna is right," Atreus said. "There may be some other explanation for what occurred. If that is so, the trial will reveal it. As I must sit as judge, I hope you will understand that I do not wish to discuss this further."

They all nodded and the conversation moved on, but Brianna remained largely silent. Atreus's support touched her even as she realized he had spoken to prevent her from doing so. Just then she was more concerned with what he had said about the presumption of innocence. Could the members of Helios truly receive fair judgment from him? She hoped so, for their sakes . . . and for her own.

T HE FOLLOWING DAY, THEY WERE FAR ENOUGH south to have left the northern winter well behind. Kassandra and Joanna were delighted to put away English garb and change to the much more comfortable Akoran styles. So was Brianna until she drew her favorite tunic from her trunk and realized it was . . . white.

The color of virgins.

After a brief tussle with her conscience, she resigned herself to the necessity of deception. To appear in any color other than white would be a public declaration of what had passed between her and Atreus. She was in no way prepared to do any such thing. But let him so much as raise an eyebrow when he saw her . . .

To his credit, he did not, but he did smile as his gaze lingered over her. "You are lovely in anything you choose to wear, but Akoran garb suits you best."

"It is more comfortable," she said shortly even as she made a valiant but futile effort not to stare at him. Atreus, too, had changed. He wore a pleated linen kilt and sandals. A plain leather headband that looked as though he'd had it for years kept his hair out of his eyes. The sole hint of his rank was in the gold band secured around the powerful muscle of his upper left arm. He looked supremely male, drawing her in a way she could scarcely resist—and indeed had difficulty remembering why she should.

If he were not Vanax . . .

She dismissed the thought for the foolishness it was and turned to other matters.

"You did not tell your family about me."

He shrugged, drawing her wayward gaze to the broad sweep of his shoulders. "It is between us."

"Thank you for that. I realize they will know eventually, but their good opinion matters a great deal to me."

Atreus leaned back against the deck railing, his arms folded over his broad chest, and regarded her steadily. "And mine, Brianna? Does my good opinion also matter to you?"

"Of course it does." More than she was willing to admit just then, far more.

"Yet you and the others in Helios would do . . . what? Remove me from office? Substitute some man of the people who made easy promises or offered quick solutions? Is that what you want?"

Stiffly, she said, "No one I know in Helios or anywhere else has ever suggested that you should not be the leader of Akora."

"Deilos believed otherwise. He thought to kill me and take power for himself."

"Deilos was never part of Helios."

"But he may have sought to use Helios. Tell me, how did you become involved with it in the first place?"

She hesitated, torn between determination to do nothing that might threaten her friends and desire to make him understand what drove them.

"I knew people who were involved, we talked about things. I suppose they were trying to find out if I was sympathetic. Eventually I was invited to a meeting."

"A meeting? Do those happen often?"

"It depends; everything is rather informal. That's part of why I simply can't see Deilos having any involvement with Helios."

"Because he doesn't seem inclined to sit around a campfire late into the night, drinking wine and sharing grand visions?"

She looked at him in surprise. "How did you—? Never mind; let's just say he would clash with everyone else."

"Perhaps not everyone. Among the mostly young people who belong to Helios—they are mostly young, aren't they?—there may be a few who yearn for greater discipline and direction, exactly what Deilos would provide."

"Just because people are young and idealistic doesn't mean they can be duped. Helios is completely dedicated to peace. Some of the men don't even want to take part in the usual warrior training because they believe it makes our culture too focused on violence."

It was his turn to be surprised. "Warrior training is directed entirely to defending ourselves. What can be wrong with that?"

"I don't think it is wrong but others see it differently, and that's the point: people should be able to have different views and express them freely."

"People can do that now. Any man who doesn't want to

take part in warrior training only has to say so and no squadron would take him."

"But that's the problem. A man should be able to say that without being looked down on."

"What should he be, admired for refusing to do his part to protect his home and family?"

"Why should there have to be admiration or condemnation, one or the other?" Brianna countered. "Why can't there just be respect for different viewpoints?"

"Because such respect won't repell an enemy, not from outside nor within. Deilos must have believed the gods were gifting him when he discovered Helios."

"You don't know that he discovered us or what he thought if he did."

"Quite right," he acknowledged ruefully, "and I need you to remind me of that from time to time."

The admission took her aback. She was just thinking how very reasonable he was being when he inquired, "Are there men in Helios who are actual men?"

"Atreus!" Her exasperation could not have been more evident.

"Oh, all right," he relented slightly. "I suppose I can see, if only barely, that it may take courage to refuse to do what most consider normal and necessary. Perhaps if a man is sincere in his conviction, not acting merely out of cowardice, he can contribute to Akora in other ways."

"You believe that?"

"No . . . but I am open to the possibility that it might be true. Certainly it would be worth investigating."

"Why don't you say these things publicly? Why are you seen as such a . . . a monolith determined to uphold Akoran traditions and only allow as much change as you think best?"

"A monolith? Really?" He looked amused.

"Atreus, I am not joking. That is how you are seen."

"By Helios?"

She nodded. "You are a figure of such extraordinary power, so distant from all the rest of us."

"Did it ever occur to any of you that I don't particularly want to be that way?"

"No," she said honestly, "it never did. You seemed completely removed from ordinary human concerns, invulnerable—at least until you were injured."

"Then what did you think?"

"That it would be terrible if you died," she said softly, the memory of her own fear for him still far too fresh even months after the attempt on his life. "Your family would suffer such pain, but beyond that we would all be the poorer for losing you."

"Thank you, I appreciate that." He spoke dryly.

"Atreus . . . Helios is not your enemy."

"I don't think it is necessarily, but ideals are a two-edged sword. They can lead people to do great things but they can also make them susceptible to great lies."

"Are you saying that you yourself are not governed by ideals?"

That stopped him, if only briefly. "You argue like a councillor."

"Thank you, I think. You know, the Council is part of the problem. Everyone on it is a great lord of a land-holding family and almost all are of a venerable age. Deilos was the youngest when he was on the Council."

"And we saw how well that worked out."

Encouraged because he seemed so unexpectedly willing to talk with her, she said, "Seriously, why couldn't the Council be bigger and there be more variety of people on it? Men who aren't of the great families, younger people, even women."

"Women? I've been meaning to ask you about that. You

recall your Akoran history? Thousands of years ago, an ac-
cord was reached between the priestesses of the old way
and the warriors of the new. The warriors would rule and
the women serve, but in return no woman would ever be
harmed. Does that all sound familiar?"

When she nodded with tolerant patience, he continued.
"The second part of that, about women never being
harmed, is at the center of Akoran life. There is no shame
greater for a man than to harm a woman. However, the first
part—the warriors rule, the women serve part—when will
that actually go into effect?"

A smile twitched at the corners of her mouth. She let it
come as she gave the answer that was a standing joke
among all Akorans. "Any day now. We just need a little
more time to adjust to the idea."

"More than three thousand years?"

Her shrug was somewhere between an apology and a
philosophical acceptance of the nature of all things. "It's a
big adjustment."

"To suggest that you've already had vastly more than
enough time would be to do you harm?"

"I'm afraid so."

"I thought that might be the case. Still, no harm trying?"

"Not at all. Now about enlarging the Council—"

Anyone coming onto the deck just then would have
been startled by the sight of the Vanax of Akora laughing
unrestrainedly as he hugged the woman who was, beyond
doubt, his *amora*.

SEVERAL MORE DAYS PASSED, THE AIR GREW
balmier, and sleep became ever more elusive. At night,
lying in her cabin, Brianna counted the stars painted on the
ceiling above her bed and thought of Atreus.

Man and Vanax. Lover and ruler. She had fought for his

life, wept at the thought of his death, and rebelled at what she considered his tyranny. But he was not what she had believed, not at all. He laughed, he teased, sometimes she felt from him a certain wistfulness for the life he would have preferred and a reluctance for power that surprised her. Most surprising of all, he listened. He didn't promise great changes and she didn't expect him to, but he *listened*. Moreover, he dangled the notion that as his consort, she would have power. It was an enticing promise from a man already far too seductive.

Sex and power.

Her cheeks warmed. Never, not once, had she thought of marriage in such terms, and to do so now shocked her deeply. Yet there it was, stark and inescapable. Marry Atreus. Share his bed. Share his power. What more truly could any woman want?

Love.

She had seen the love her Akoran parents shared, and there were times, late at night when her mind wandered in the realm between wakefulness and dreams, when memory came more readily and gently. Then she remembered that Delphine had loved her Edward and he her. She had seen that, too.

She could love Atreus. At the thought, her eyes opened. She had not realized they were closed and that she was drifting. Love Atreus. Oh, yes, so easily. She was halfway there already, wasn't she? And about that she absolutely would not think at all.

Morning came, finding her stiff, weary, and in no fit mood for company. She went up on deck in time to see the last faint stars flickering out. The sea that still surged dark and threatening through the distant reaches of her memory showed only the ripple of a steady wind. A few men were still asleep on deck, others had gathered around the day's first pot of coffee. She sniffed appreciatively but did not approach them. Instead, her gaze was drawn to the solitary figure seated in the stern, one arm resting on the ship's rudder. Atreus.

Slowly, she walked to him. His black hair hung loose, just brushing his bare shoulders. He had not yet shaved and the night's growth of beard reminded her all too vividly of the stolen hours they had shared. Indeed, the closer she came to him, the more it seemed she could feel the smooth, hard curves of his shoulders, the teasing roughness of his beard, the warmth of his lips. . . .

Beneath the graceful drape of her tunic, her nipples hardened. She took a breath against the flood tide of feeling that threatened to engulf her.

"Did you sleep well?" Atreus asked, not taking his gaze from hers.

"Not particularly. You?"

He smiled faintly. "Scarcely at all." The light in his eyes left little doubt as to the cause of his restlessness.

"Sit down," he said gently, and moved over on the bench to make room for her.

She did but only because she wanted to, not because her knees felt weak. Her thigh brushed against his. She jerked away as though from fire.

He sighed but made no move to compel her. Instead, he said, "Look there, starboard off the prow."

She looked, saw nothing, looked harder and sensed as much as saw the faint rise, little more than a soft curve against the horizon. What the eye might miss so easily the heart knew at once.

"Akora," she murmured, and felt confusion dissolve into joy.

Chapter

TWELVE

T HE CLIFFS THAT ROSE A HUNDRED AND
more feet against the sky offered no hand- or
footholds by which they might be scaled. The
rock supported only a thin scattering of
shallow-rooted scrub brushes that could withstand the
wind, but they would rip away under the weight of a
would-be climber. At the foot of the cliffs, breakers
crashed directly against immense boulders. There were no
beaches to offer a safe landing, no bays that could serve as
harbors.

No wonder outsiders called Akora the Fortress Kingdom. Even approaching it as she was, on an Akoran vessel
flying the royal banner, Brianna could understand the awe
and amazement felt by *xenos* foolish enough to venture too
close. The volcanic explosion that had ripped the island
apart more than three thousand years before had sent a
wall of lava smashing into the sea, where it rapidly cooled,

forming the wall behind which Akora remained hidden from the world. A wall threatened by a world that was changing rapidly, filling with new weapons and new ideas, yet still held strong by the courage and determination of its people.

Would that be enough? The question was uppermost in her mind as the royal vessel tacked in closer to the coast. She saw the narrow break in the cliff wall just ahead, that led to the southern inlet. The entrance looked small and unpromising, but appearance was deceptive. There was ample room for a ship even vastly larger than theirs to enter and follow the inlet around, out of sight of any off-shore observer, to where it joined the Inland Sea.

There, the drowned heart of Akora shone darkly in the light of fast-fading day. Sea birds sought their nests, adding their plaintive calls to the whisper of the wind and the clank of the rigging. Far in the distance, she could just make out three low humps, all that could be seen of the trio of small islands that, with the royal island of Kallimos and her own island home of Leios, made up Akora. Instinctively, her gaze turned westward, in search of Leios, but it was too far off to be seen. All the same, it tugged at her heart. Her parents would be there, her mother perhaps preparing the evening meal, unless they had gone to eat with friends, in which case Leoni would have brought something delicious. Would they be thinking of her? She had been gone months, almost half a year. Many letters had flowed back and forth, but that was scant substitute for sharing the ordinary routine of days.

And her brothers, what were they doing? Especially Polonus, closest to her in age and the one she worried about. She had advised caution before she left, but she doubted it was in his nature.

Off to the east, she saw Kallimos, only the southern tip of it, to be sure, but the light was already on in the guard tower there. As she watched, the light flashed—on, off, on, off—the rhythm varying according to the signal code used by Akorans for centuries. Near her on deck, a crewman opened a metal fire box, the flame within amplified by polished mirrors, and responded. On, off, off, on, off. The signals continued back and forth for several minutes until the guard tower faded into the distance.

Aware suddenly of a presence beside her, she said aloud, "What did they say?"

"The usual," Atreus replied. He had joined her near the railing. "We have identified ourselves and given our port as Ilius. The tower we just passed is now flashing that news to the next tower in the chain, which will pass it onward to the next, and so on. Word should reach Ilius within a half hour or so."

"That quickly?" It would be hours yet before the wind and tide brought them to the royal city.

"The system was designed to give ample warning of any enemy entering this strait or that to the north."

She looked up at him and felt yet again the little shock that always seemed to course through her at the sight of him. That he was there, so close to her, was startling enough. But every little detail of him—the arch of his brows she had traced with her finger in the night, the slight indentation of his chin, the white scar on his forehead that was a reminder of how close he had come to death—all the tiny testaments of their intimacy still held the power to stun her.

"Has that happened often?" she asked.

"Has what happened?" He appeared as distracted as she knew herself to be. There was some satisfaction in that. Not much, but some.

"Enemies entering the Inland Sea."

He thought for a moment. "It has happened four times,

I believe. The most recent incident was five hundred and ten . . . no, five hundred and twelve years ago."

"Really?" She was not surprised that he knew so precisely, this man who seemed to embody the heart and soul of Akora. He, above all others, would know their history. "What happened then?"

"It's a long story," he said and drew her attention to the flickering lights appearing suddenly on shore as they passed. All along the coast of Kallimos, the island whose name meant "beautiful," Akorans were responding to the spreading news of their Vanax's return. The torches were their greetings, set against the gathering darkness.

"You've only been away for a few weeks," Brianna said as she watched the fiery welcomes blaze their message out across the water.

"I've never been away before," he reminded her. "And who knows, I may never be again."

She, who had traveled far more than he, looked at him in surprise. "That's right, isn't it? You only went this time because of the diplomatic situation."

"Not exactly . . . there were other considerations."

"Because so many members of your family were in England?"

"No, actually it had more to do with you." He leaned against the railing, looking at her. "I went to England to put a final end to any foolish thoughts of a British invasion of Akora, but I also went to bring you back."

She had heard him correctly—she was quite sure of that—but his words made no sense. "I don't understand . . . until you came to England, we did not know each other. It's true that I helped to care for you after you were injured, but we had very little contact once you regained consciousness." A possibility occurred to her. "Did my parents ask you to bring me back? In their letters to me, they were very understanding of my wish to be in England, but perhaps they have become impatient?"

"Perhaps they have, but if so, they did not confide that to me. You say we did not know each other. But I did know you. I have known you for a long time."

More torches were burning along the shores. Brianna stared at them, imagining the jubilation of the people welcoming Atreus home—the man they believed possessed unique powers bestowed upon him during the mysterious trial of selection. That was superstition, of course, yet she could not repress a shiver of apprehension.

"That is not possible," she said with certainty she was far from feeling.

"What are you afraid of, Brianna? That there is more to the world, to Akora—and to us—than you want to acknowledge?"

"I am not afraid. Why would you even say that?"

"Because it is fear I felt in you in the library."

She turned away quickly, but not before he saw the sudden, roiling shadows that moved behind her eyes. His instinct was to seize hold of her and demand she tell him the source of her fear, so that he could banish it. But caution, and an ever-growing understanding of her, held him back. She was not a woman to be readily brought to hand. Her pride and courage would not allow it.

Instead, soothingly, he touched her arm. "Brianna, come with me. There is something I want to show you."

He was not pressing her, though she was quite certain he wished to do so. Surprise and what felt dangerously like gratitude undermined her caution. Just as long as they spoke of something other than fear.

"What is it?"

"It's hard to describe. I'd rather you just saw it." His hand slipped down her arm, his fingers catching hers. With a smile that stole her breath, he led her across the deck, down the narrow steps, and along the corridor to his quarters. She hesitated just a moment before entering and felt foolish for doing so, but the intimacy of their surroundings evoked heated memories.

Atreus's belongings were, like hers, packed in expectation of their arrival, but one of the trunks stood open. There was a small box on top. He brought it to her. "Take a look inside."

She was shaking her head before he even finished speaking. "I cannot accept any more gifts."

"It isn't a gift. I would never give this away, but I do wish you to see it."

Relieved and more than a little intrigued, she lifted the lid of the box carefully. The interior was lined with velvet and fitted to hold a small statue carved in pink marble.

A statue of a woman.

Curious, Brianna lifted it. At once she saw that it was exquisitely made by a master hand. Her gaze rose to Atreus. "Your work?"

He nodded. "I made it about eight years ago. Take a closer look."

She did because she could not resist. The statue really was astonishing. It was so lifelike that the coldness of the stone startled her. He must have known the model extremely well to capture so vividly every detail of her form.

Every tiny, meticulous detail.

This could not be. It truly was impossible. Yet by the evidence of her own eyes, she was holding a statue of herself—a shockingly exact depiction in stone of her face and body. As she was now, not eight years ago when he said the statue had been made.

"A coincidence—" She could barely utter the word, so stunned was she, but she clung to the notion as to a lifeline. One Atreus tore from her in an instant. "You don't believe that, but if you really do have any doubt, turn her over."

She did, only to regret doing so the moment she saw the pair of twin dimples placed on the statue precisely where they were on her own self.

The stone that had felt cold suddenly seemed to burn her hands. She thrust it back into the box and thrust the box at Atreus even as she glared at him. "This isn't at all funny. You made the statue in the past few weeks. You must have!"

He set the box down carefully before replying. "I made it eight years ago. You don't seriously think I'm lying, do you?"

"No," she admitted on a breath of sound. For all that there were differences between them, she believed him to be a truthful man. His keen sense of honor would allow nothing less.

"I saw you," he said, answering the question in her eyes. "Eight years ago, when I underwent the trial of selection."

"You saw me? . . ."

"Sit down," he said gently, and drew out a chair near the table, which was now cleared of the books and scrolls that had been packed away in anticipation of their arrival.

He pulled up another chair and sat opposite her. Taking her hands in his, he said, "Every man who undergoes the trial of selection experiences it somewhat differently. We know this because there are records kept, passed only from one Vanax to the next. Even so, there are common elements for all. We . . . see, for want of a better word, through a perspective beyond ourselves. What we see varies, but in my case, I saw the woman who was to be my wife. I saw you."

"You thought you saw someone who looked like me."

"Down to the precise angle of your brows, the very slight asymmetry between the left and right sides of your face, the exact curve of your chin? And then there are those exquisite dimples."

When she flushed, he said gently, "I saw *you*, Brianna. There was no doubt that you were real and that you were meant to be my wife. When I emerged from the trial, I assumed I would find you quickly and we would wed. I was looking forward to it. The only problem was that I didn't know your name."

"My name—"

"Remained a mystery, but not one that concerned me overly much. I remembered the old saying that if you want to meet someone, look for him at the palace, because sooner or later everyone comes there."

Understanding dawned, and with it the first faint stirrings of belief, however fragile and reluctant. "Except that I didn't—"

"You remained on Leios." He smiled wryly. "Years went by. Every once in a while I'd see a red-haired woman and think for a moment that she was you, but she never was."

"Until you were injured."

"I regained consciousness to find myself looking at the woman I had been searching for all that time. The moment I saw you, I understood I hadn't been meant to find you until then."

"How could you have known that?"

"Because you looked exactly the same as when I saw you during the trial. Eight years before, you were only a girl of sixteen. I'm sure you were lovely, but you were not yet the woman I saw, the woman you have become."

It made sense, everything he said, there was a strange logic to it. If he was in the grip of some personal delusion, it was amazingly coherent. "Why didn't you say anything?"

"I discovered that you wanted to return to England. While I was reluctant to let you go, I also knew I needed time to recover fully. I have to admit, I didn't anticipate that you would stay as long as you did."

"Nor could you have suspected that I would find my English family."

"True, Lord William and his countess caused me a few uneasy moments."

Her mind still reeled. All that had happened, everything that had passed between them, was shaped by a ritual she knew almost nothing about and held in profound doubt. *Everything.* "What about my involvement with Helios? How can you possibly reconcile that with what you believe about me?"

"I can't," he admitted. "I simply have to trust that what I saw is what is meant to be."

"But you don't have to simply trust. You don't have to live your life on blind faith."

"Blind?" She had feared he might be offended, but instead he looked amused. "Brianna, believe me, there's nothing blind about my faith. Consider this: Perhaps it is your involvement in Helios that is part of why you are so suited to be my wife."

The thought, and that it should be his, were so startling that for a moment she could only stare at him. "But . . . you are opposed to Helios."

"I am opposed to heedless change that threatens Akora's security. But I have been thinking, you *are* meant to be my wife, therefore there must be some purpose to your feeling as you do. Perhaps I am called to broaden my own thinking, to consider possibilities beyond those I already entertain."

"You mean, you would see things Helios's way?" The very idea filled her with amazement. Could it be?

"No," Atreus said, disabusing her at once. "Helios has articulated nothing except the desire for some general degree of greater openness. That is hardly sufficient policy to run a government or a nation. However, there may be some elements to the general idea of openness that could be worth exploring."

Disappointment filled her, but only of a faint sort. She had not truly thought he would capitulate so easily. Nor, truth be told, would she wish him to. He was, after all, a man convinced of the essential rightness of who and what he was.

But not, apparently, of everything he thought. " 'Some elements,' " she repeated. "Does that mean you could envision some sort of compromise?"

He smiled again and stood, drawing her up with him. "Are we negotiating?"

"Isn't that what men and women do?"

"Sometimes. . . . Brianna, I have been very patient." His arms were around her. She could feel the warmth—no, really the heat—of his big, hard body, which was no longer strange to her. He was close, so close. She could have tried to move away, and might even have succeeded, but she wanted him to kiss her, wanted to feel his passion and her own rising together, wanted—

His mouth brushed the hollow at the base of her throat. Startled and instantly infused with pleasure, she gasped. He raised his head, looking at her. "The Tear of Heaven belongs there. Let me see it soon."

She could breathe, of course, how absurd to think she could not. She just needed a moment.

And, thankfully, she got it, for just then a shout went up, followed swiftly by another. She needed that moment to realize the source of the excitement and when she did, it became her own.

The moon, rising above the hills, revealed the royal city of Ilius.

* * *

JOURNEY'S END CAME WITH CRAWLING SLOWNESS. The tide took them swiftly, pulling them into port. They sped through the water, but too slowly, every moment grudged. Brianna stood on deck with the others, watching as the city grew closer. Ilius, city of dreams. So it was said, for it was a dream that built it, a dream that imagined a seared and terrible landscape turned into a place of beauty and hope. So it had, century after century, emerging from ashes and despair to symbolize all the best of Akora.

The city rose from the deep harbor, climbing through white-cobbled roads framed by flower-draped houses and shops, higher and higher until it reached at last the flattened top of the hill where the palace stood. In the moonlight, the immense red and blue columns supporting the massive roofs looked washed with silver.

Generation after generation had added to the palace while carefully maintaining all that was built before. It grew, Atreus had always thought, like a living creature carved from time itself.

And it called to him irresistibly. It was the home of his heart, the place where he had taken his first breath and would, in the fullness of the years, take his last. It was the only place he truly wanted to be.

Beside him, Brianna said softly, "It is so beautiful."

She reached out across the small space separating them and took his hand. Together, they watched the city come to them.

Although they arrived at the hour when most people were usually in their beds, it seemed as though every man and woman in Ilius, and more than a few of the children, had stayed up late to welcome their Vanax home. Torches burned so brightly as to banish night. The beat of drums and the lilt of lutes joined the cheerful din of voices that reached out over the fast-narrowing water to embrace them.

Just before they settled beside the stone quay, Brianna gave a happy cry. There among the crowd she saw her own beloved parents, Leoni and Marcus, accompanied by her mother's sister, the renowned healer Elena. Her first thought was delight that they should be there, but hard on it came concern. Quickly, she turned to Atreus. "Do they know—?"

He understood immediately. "About us? No, they don't. But everyone knew I intended to return soon. Perhaps they hoped you would be on the same ship."

Moments later, his guess proved correct. Scarcely had Brianna set foot on the quay than she was in Leoni's arms, with Marcus beaming beside them.

"Oh, my dearest!" her mother exclaimed, hugging her fiercely. "Elena persuaded us to come to Ilius on the chance you would be arriving. I scarcely dared to believe her. Polonus is with us, but he's gone off somewhere; the others are at home. We have missed you so much! You look so wonderful! Doesn't she look wonderful, Marcus?"

"Wonderful," her father agreed. His voice was oddly husky and, for just an instant, Brianna thought she saw the sheen of tears in his eyes.

"Papa," she said and embraced him, laughing and crying at the same time. In all the months away, she had not allowed herself to really think how much she missed them, these warm, loving people who had welcomed her into their hearts. Now, safely back with them, her emotions could not be contained. How easily they could have been angered by her determination to seek out her past rather than simply accept the life they had given her. How secretly she had feared they would. But there was nothing in their warm embrace save unconditional love and acceptance, exactly what she felt for them.

"Oh, my," she said shakily, when she finally managed to

stand a little way apart. "I don't usually sob all over every-one."

"No harm done," Elena said as she smiled at her niece. "It is so very good to see you, Brianna. Welcome home."

"And welcome to the Vanax," Marcus said, drawing her attention to the happy crowd surrounding Atreus. Truly, he seemed engulfed by the throng. Were he not of such considerable height, she would not have been able to see him at all. Nearby, she caught sight of Alex and Royce, and assumed they had Kassandra, Joanna, and Amelia safe beside them. Several counselors she recognized were there as well, along with palace guards attempting, in their good-natured way, to keep some degree of order.

That seemed a losing proposition, but Atreus did not appear to mind. He willingly gave himself up to the tide of joyful enthusiasm that bore them along the high, winding road and all the way to the palace gates.

There, torchlight gleamed on the immense twin statues of lionesses framing the entrance to the vast courtyard before the palace. Brianna was just close enough to see Atreus raise his hand as he passed them and touch the foot of the nearest lioness. It was a gesture familiar to many Akorans who had themselves done the same whenever they returned from a journey, be it to the other side of Ilius or of the world.

As they entered the courtyard, the crowd fanned out, filling every corner. Servants hurried from the palace, bearing more torches and the first of what quickly became many tables. Laughter bubbled in her. How very like Ako-rans to seize the excuse for an impromptu party. More musicians were joining those from the quay. Already, several groups were dancing. Barrels of wine were rolled out and quickly tapped. Food appeared as though magically—from the palace, to be sure, but also from kitchens and pantries throughout Ilius. Everyone, it seemed, had brought something to share. Soon the tables groaned under an array of breads, cheeses, meats, chickens, fresh fish, soups, salads, and, of course, a multitude of different versions of *marinos*, each of which had to have its due. Lastly, and especially appreciated by Brianna, were the bite-sized almond candies lightly dusted in cinnamon or powdered sugar and a favorite for finishing off meals.

When had there last been such a celebration? she wondered as she licked her fingers. The straw-colored wine that flowed so abundantly had proven tart and sweet on her tongue. It left her just slightly mizzled, or perhaps that was from the sheer, giddy excitement of being home. Blessed, beautiful home.

Her parents were off dancing, looking for all the world like young lovers. Atreus was nearby, talking with several men she recognized as counselors. Over their heads, his gaze found hers. The intimacy of his smile made her forget the press of the giddy crowd.

He looked . . . wonderful. Vividly alive, delighted to be home, and very much in command.

Half a year before, he had almost died. When it became clear at last that he would not, there were prayers of thanksgiving throughout Akora, but shock and horror had lingered, enough to restrain the expressions of relief. Not so now. The impromptu explosion of unfettered joy going on all around her was the true celebration of Atreus's life, his survival, and, in every sense, his return to his people.

A sudden *whoosh* drew her attention just in time for her to see a stream of light rise against the night sky, hover for a breathless instant, and explode suddenly in a shower of glowing embers.

Fireworks. Another rocket burst against the heavens, followed quickly by a steady stream. Fountains of multicolored stars rained down, while great spinning wheels of fire whirled across the sky. Giant, incandescent flowers exploded in shards of light that dissolved slowly into darkness.

Brianna was enthralled, so much so that she was hardly aware of the young man who came up beside her until he touched her arm and said with some amusement, "Bri, come back to earth."

"What? Polonus? Oh, Polonus!" She laughed and embraced her youngest brother, a slender young man with gentle brown eyes and a soulful air. He was two years older than herself, yet she had always felt the elder, or at least the more responsible, when it came to this brother who seemed forever to be led astray by his good intentions. She had missed all her family, to be sure, but Polonus had always held a special place in her heart.

"Mother said you were here, but had gone off somewhere. How are you?"

"Well enough, and you?" Before she could reply, he said, "We've missed you, Bri, really, a lot. It hasn't been the same without you."

"I've missed you, too, more than I ever suspected was possible."

"Yet you went. Was the journey worthwhile?"

"Yes," she said softly, "it was. I found what I was searching for."

At once, his expression lightened. "Did you really? Good for you. I had a feeling you'd do a better job of it than the authorities managed, assuming they even tried."

A little of her exasperation with this old subject flavored her response. "Polonus, there is no reason to believe that anything other than a true and honest effort was made to find my English family. There were extenuating circumstances, as I have discovered, that doomed any such effort to failure."

"If that is the case, well and good, but I fear you are

inclined to be too trusting. Matters have not improved here. Our friends remain imprisoned."

With a quick glance around to be sure everyone near them was too preoccupied to hear, she said, "I know, but the trial will start soon, and I am persuaded it will be fair."

Her brother took a step back, staring at her. "I can guess who's *persuaded* you. You've drawn even closer to the Atreides family, haven't you? Bri, I warned you about that."

It was a warning that had both surprised and irked her. It reminded her that in the past year or so, Polonus seemed ever more inclined to think he knew best. Whereas once he had valued her opinions, more recently he was likely to dismiss them. It was a tendency she had hoped he would overcome, but now that seemed not to be the case.

"They are not our enemies, Polonus, far from it. They are all good and honorable people who want only what is best for Akora, just as we do."

"If that is so, why has Helios been banned?"

"Banned? What are you talking about? Helios hadn't been banned when I left here. In fact, almost all of those who were arrested after the attack on Atreus had been released already."

He brushed off her objection. "Perhaps we weren't banned officially, but how many people do you think are willing to be part of an organization whose members are suspected of conspiring to kill the Vanax? I just came from a meeting where there were fewer than a dozen of us. A year ago, there would have been a hundred, or even more, but now—"

He stopped suddenly, staring at her. "Atreus?" His expression hardened. "I've never heard you call him anything but the Vanax."

She loved Polonus, she truly did, but there were times when she no longer seemed to know him. Where was the boy who had poured out his heart to her, revealing how he feared and loathed the very thought of warrior training and yearned for a gentler life? For that matter, where was the man who had returned from the training he dreaded, still convinced that it was wrong, and anxious to chart his own course? When had he become so rigid in this thinking and so ready to judge others?

"Atreus," she repeated. "He is a man, a human being, like any of us. If you and the others in Helios could know him better—"

"As you have come to?"

She frowned, yet her voice remained gentle. "Yes, as I have. He is neither close-minded nor arbitrary. He is willing to listen and to consider alternatives, even though they may not appeal to him initially."

"And then he goes right on and does anything he damn well pleases."

"He says otherwise. He says the good of our people must always come before his own wishes."

"For pity's sake, Bri, of course he says that! We agreed, you and I and the others, that it's all pretense and posturing to keep people complacent so they don't demand more control of their own lives."

"I know we thought so, but what if it isn't true? What if he really means what he says? Really lives by it every day, in everything he does?"

"Next you'll be saying there's something to that absurd fiction of the trial of selection."

"I didn't used to think so," she admitted, thinking of the statue and of Atreus himself, of his fundamental decency and honesty. "Now I'm not certain."

"I never believed you could be led astray like this, but you have a woman's mind; you are weak."

Her shock could not be contained. "Do you hear yourself? How can you say such a thing?"

"I do not speak to hurt," he said quickly, honoring the age-old prohibition against a man doing harm to any woman. "But to instruct. It is well known that women are less logical in their thinking, more given to emotion, therefore more easily led to false conclusions."

"Well-known? That is nonsense! Who has told you such things?"

"I don't need to be told by anyone. A man with eyes to see and a mind to think comes to such conclusions for himself."

"Then the man needs to rub his eyes and clear his mind, for truly he is allowing himself to become deluded!"

"It is not for you to say such things."

"Not for me—"

"Or for any woman. You would do well to remember your place."

And with that, the brother she loved and thought she knew turned on his heel and vanished back into the crowd.

Brianna stared after him in utter bewilderment until someone, rushing passed with a laden tray, pressed another glass of the tart, sweet wine into her hand. She drank it absently and was glad when a fresh burst of fireworks distracted her.

SOMETIME TOWARD DAWN—SHE THOUGHT IT must be then because there were only a few stars left in the sky—she found herself sitting with Leoni on the steps of the palace. Quite a few people were with them, some even stretched out and asleep. Marcus was off helping some of the men put away tables. A few bunches of diehard revelers were singing, but generally it had gotten quiet.

Leoni, her ever practical and thoughtful mother, had secured a pitcher of the wine that had proven so popular.

She refilled her glass and her daughter's as she said, "Wonderful celebration, just what we all needed."

Brianna nodded. "The people are so happy."

"None can possibly be happier than I." Leoni leaned over and patted her daughter's hand gently. "There were days I feared you might never return."

"Oh, Mother—" Tears clogged her throat.

"Now, now, none of that. I didn't mean it in a bad way. If you had stayed in England, I would have known in my heart it was what you needed and been glad for you. All the same, I can't remember a more joyful moment in my life than when I saw you get off the ship."

"I should have returned sooner."

"You returned when it was right for you to do so, and if you feel you have to go again—"

"I found what I was looking for."

"You found—?" Leoni's hand tightened on hers. "Your parents—?"

"You and Marcus are my parents," Brianna said softly. "Only true parents who genuinely love me would have understood my need to go."

Leoni made a soft sound, somewhere between a sigh and a sob. She was silent for a moment, regaining control of herself, before she said, "We understood that you needed to know yourself, just as we all do."

"I am Lady Brianna Wilcox, or at least that is who I am in England."

"So much you learned? Tell me, how did all this come about?"

"Thanks to a man with red hair," Brianna said and laughed at her mother's surprise. As the level of wine in the pitcher diminished yet farther, she relayed all that had happened in England. Well, almost all. Of Atreus she said nothing.

But he was in her mind, moment to moment, breath to

breath. After a while, Marcus came back, and, laughing, took happy Leoni away. Brianna assured them she would seek her bed soon. She stayed on the steps a little longer. The stars were gone and clouds were moving up out of the east. They came heralded by a fresh wind. Such was her contentment that she took only distant notice of it.

The thought came to her that she should find Atreus and tell him what a wonderful party it had been. She stood, just a shade unsteadily, and ran up the steps to the palace.

TREUS WAS NOT IN HIS QUARTERS. BRIANNA stopped just inside the double doors that led from the center corridor of the palace's family wing. The area was familiar to her because she had spent so much time there while helping in the struggle to bring Atreus back from the brink of death. His rooms were spacious, decorated with murals, as was the Akoran custom, and comfortably if rather simply furnished in keeping with the preferences of the man himself—of whom there was no sign. She saw only the servant, Castor, whom she had come to know and who appeared to be unpacking the last of Atreus's trunks.

"You wish something, Lady?" he asked, glancing up from his task.

Suddenly self-conscious, she said, "I . . . shouldn't have come. I don't really know what I was thinking."

Castor's gentle smile suggested that her thoughts were

not really so great a mystery. "Sometimes the Vanax has difficulty sleeping. On such occasions, he is often to be found in his studio."

"His studio—?"

"Do you know where that is?"

"I don't . . . wait, yes, I do. I can find it. But perhaps I should not disturb him."

"Perhaps you already do, Lady."

That struck her as insightful and oddly reassuring. She nodded in thanks and withdrew. Back in the corridor, she stood for a moment trying to recall which way to go. There were those who said the palace was a labyrinth, and she thought them not far wrong. Any structure that had grown over thousands of years was bound to have more than a few twists and turns. She seemed to take most of them before finally finding her way to the secluded hideaway Atreus used as a studio.

It was in a part of the palace that was very old, the stone floor sloping down in the center, where centuries of feet had trod. The room itself was large, with a high ceiling and tall arched windows carved into the outside walls. Through them, she could see the storm clouds building ever more steadily toward the west.

But it was on the man standing in the center of the room that her attention focused.

Atreus's back was to her. He wore only the white pleated kilt of an Akoran warrior, leaving the upper part of his body bare. Morning light, filtering through the oncoming storm clouds, fell over the powerful muscles of his back and shoulders that flexed as he moved. He stood, feet planted firmly apart, in front of a low table. So intent was his concentration that he gave no sign of noticing Brianna's presence.

She shut the doors quietly behind her and walked a little farther into the room. The air smelled of stone dust, earthy clay, the oncoming rain, and the flowering grape vines twining around trellises just beyond the windows. At the far end of the studio stood a massive block of stone from which the head and arm of a man appeared to be emerging. Nearby was the smaller but far more complete statue of a horse, standing perhaps five feet tall, and so exquisitely detailed that she half-expected the animal would break into a gallop at any moment.

Everywhere she looked, she saw works of such beauty and passion as to steal her breath. Here was a side of Atreus she had known existed, but had not remotely understood. A side so private that she felt a trespasser in a place she had no right to be.

Her instinct was to withdraw as quickly and quietly as possible, and so she might have done had not Atreus turned suddenly and looked at her. For a moment, he was silent, only watching her. Finally, he asked, "Is the party over?" There was a smear of clay on his chest.

"It's been over for a while." She nodded toward the statue of a dancer about to soar into the air. "That's lovely."

"Do you think so? I'm trying to capture a sense of great strength and focus wrapped in deceptive delicacy."

"I'd say you're doing a good job of it."

He laughed and took up a cloth to wipe his chest and hands. "Thank you. Later today, the stone from Holyhood will be moved in here. I'll need to study it for a while before I can begin to feel what is in it, but I will strive to make something worthwhile come from it."

"I'm sure you will." She walked closer, drawn to him, and looked again at the clay dancer. "You didn't see this in stone?"

Atreus shook his head. He came to stand beside her. "She is for bronze. Clay is just the first step. After that comes wax, then clay again, pressed into the wax to form a hollow mold, and finally the bronze itself poured into the mold. There are other ways to create such a statue, but I happen to like this one because it means there will ever only be one of her. No copies will be possible."

"Which demands more patience, bronze or stone?"

"Both require patience, but so does everything of any worth." He dropped the cloth over the statue and looked at Brianna pointedly.

"Are you being patient with me?" She could only assume it was the wine that made her so bold.

"I'm trying. Did you have a good time at the party?"

"Very nice, thank you." She was a properly brought up young woman, damned if she wasn't. There was something else she was supposed to ask. . . . Oh, yes— "Did you enjoy yourself?" It had, after all, been a party for him.

"I did," he said solemnly, although, oddly, he seemed to be struggling not to smile.

"You should smile more. You have a wonderful smile . . . but you don't let it out anywhere nearly enough."

"That's very remiss of me."

"There, that's better. Just what I said . . . wonderful."

"Would you like to sit down?" He cupped her elbow gently.

"Actually, that might be a good idea. I'm a little more tired than I realized."

"Must be all the excitement of the day, coming home and all that. How is your family?"

"Mother and Father are just the same, nothing's changed, and that's marvelous. Polonus . . . is Polonus." There was something about her brother, some reason why she shouldn't say very much about him to Atreus, but she couldn't seem to worry about it just then.

There was a narrow bed under her, not more than a cot, really. "You sleep here sometimes?"

He was very close to her, warm and hard. She was acutely aware of his strength, so contained, so entrancing.

"If we were married, I wouldn't much like your sleeping here."

"Fine with me. That's settled, then."

"Atreus, be serious."

"I could be," he acknowledged. His arm came around her, turning her to face him as he drew her closer. "I could be very noble and upstanding. I could take into account that you've probably had just a bit more wine than you're used to and escort you to your quarters."

She was staring at his mouth as he spoke, remembering how it felt when he kissed her. "This isn't because of the wine."

"Are you quite sure of that?"

"It may have given me a bit of courage, that's all."

His fingers brushed over her cheek, down along the fullness of her lips, teasing, tempting. "I don't imagine you ever lack for courage."

"You'd be surprised—"

"I already am, by all this, by how much I want you, by how you fill my thoughts and my dreams, by how I cannot envision a future without you."

She caught the tip of his finger between her teeth, bit down lightly. "You will admit there are complications?"

A shadow moved across his face—a face that was, she decided, the epitome of masculine beauty. "Forget them."

"I can't—" But it seemed she could, or at least she could scarcely recall whatever it was that seemed so important. Nothing seemed to matter except Atreus and the surging hunger rising in her like the wind itself blowing through the arched windows.

He stood, drawing her with him, and ran his hands over her shoulders. Strong, skillful hands scarred by sword and chisel, capable of drawing beauty from stone and earth.

Capable, too, of swiftly undoing the ties that held her gown in place. She gasped as it fell suddenly, baring her to the waist. The small sound of surprise was lost in Atreus's devouring kiss, no teasing temptation, but the urgent possession of a man rapidly approaching the limits of his control.

His arm was steel around her waist, holding her in place. His mouth was fire, slipping down her throat, over the swell of her breasts to catch first one nipple than the other, suckling her. She cried out, gripping his shoulders.

"Atreus, please—!"

He crouched slightly, his tongue tracing the shadows of her rib cage, his hand pushing the fabric of her gown down farther, over the swell of her hips until it fell in a pool at her feet. Beneath it she wore only a tiny triangle of cloth over her sex, scarcely enough to preserve modesty.

Not remotely enough to deter Atreus. His reached beneath the thin band to push it down her legs, but it snapped under the force of his grip. He made a sound deep in his throat and wrapped his arms around her, holding her tightly against him.

The world dissolved. Unable to stand upright, held there only by Atreus's strength, Brianna endured the quicksilver torment of his tongue delving between the soft, swollen folds of her womanhood, finding the point of exquisite sensibility, pleasuring her unbearably.

He brought her to the brink and directly over it, hurtling her without warning into a dark ecstasy from which she emerged only faintly to discover that he had only just begun.

"I have waited too long," he said thickly as he stood and gathered her into his arms, laying her on the cot as he dropped his kilt. Swiftly, he covered her, grasping her legs and wrapping them around his lean hips. Between one heartbeat and the next, he plunged into her.

Her first response was shock—he was very large—but she was ready, and her body took him eagerly. She watched through the haze of her own pleasure as passion took him. At the end, he threw back his head, the veins in his powerful throat straining, and shouted her name.

Time passed; she had no idea how long. They lay entangled on the cot, their bodies cooled by the wind that blew stronger yet. Deep, abiding contentment filled her. She ran her fingers through his thick hair, cradling him against her.

As he lay against her breasts, she felt him smile. He raised his head and gazed down at her. "Now I truly feel that I am home."

He rose, dropped a quick kiss on her belly, just above the damp tangle of red curls between her legs, and walked over to a table against the wall. When he returned, he held two goblets.

"I think I've had enough wine," she said faintly, far too occupied admiring him to be much aware of what she was saying.

"This is orange juice with a touch of honey."

She drank thirstily, staring at him as he did the same. Was there an inch of his magnificent body that was not astoundingly beautiful? Did he have any idea at all of how he appeared in her eyes?

She set the goblet on the floor beside the cot and propped herself up on her elbows. "Are there any statues of you?"

He looked surprised. "Of me? I'm not dead yet."

"What on earth does that mean?"

He drained his goblet and sat down beside her. "Have you been to the caves beneath the palace?"

"I've heard of them, but I haven't been there."

"We must go together, and soon. There is much I wish to share with you." He trailed his fingers over her shoulder and down along the curve of her breast to her rigid nipple. She shivered helplessly.

"But not quite yet," he said and lifted her, resting her on his lap facing him with her legs spread to either side. The position was shockingly intimate, all the more so as his hardness probed the swollen, sensitive folds of her womanhood.

"Too much?" he asked gently.

She shook her head. There would never be too much with him. Her hunger for him was too great, threatening to devour her. Slowly, he lowered her, holding her so that she could not move except by his will. Sweet, enticing frustration rose in her. She had to have more . . . *had to*.

The powerful inner muscles of her body clenched around him, drawing him deeper. He gasped and for just an instant, she thought he was about to yield. But this was Atreus, and he was not a man to give in easily.

She cried out softly in surprise when he stood suddenly and, still deep within her, took a handful of strides across the room. Something smooth, hard, and cold was against her back. She glanced up, seeing high above her the statue of the man barely emerging from the stone. Atreus moved, and the wind blew harder, filling the room, filling her.

The wind, deep inside her, irresistible, undeniable, stronger and stronger, until she could hear nothing but the frantic gasp of her breath, the pounding of her own heart and the remorseless, savage wind.

"*No!*" She screamed even as her body convulsed. Atreus heard her and froze, but only for an instant. Her completion drew from him his own, on and on, seemingly without end.

When next he knew, they were on the floor in front of the statue. Brianna lay curled in a heap, her knees drawn up almost to her chin. Her eyes were closed and she was shaking.

A low curse broke from him. Instantly, she was in his arms, held tight against him.

"Brianna, sweetheart, tell me what's wrong. God, if I hurt you—"

She opened her eyes and looked at him, but sightlessly, with no sign of understanding. Swiftly, he rose, carrying her, and stripped the blanket off the cot, wrapping her in it. Sitting on the cot, holding her, he stroked her face gently and he called to her.

"Brianna, hear me, tell me what's wrong."

The storm, which had threatened all morning, was breaking over them. Atreus was distantly aware of rain slashing in through the studio windows, carried by wind that seemed to grow stronger with every passing moment.

Leaving her very briefly, he went over to the windows and pulled the wooden shutters closed against the fierce, tearing grasp of the wind. As he did, he saw the white froth on the waves kicked up in the harbor and the flash of windborne debris rolling down the road from the palace.

Akora was no stranger to rain-laden squalls that came out of the west, hurtling across the Atlantic. But this tempest was from the east, suggesting it was more dangerous, a great spinning wheel of raw power that could hammer down everything in its path. The saving grace of such storms was that they usually arrived with at least some warning. Not this one. Much of the Akoran fleet was at sea. The crews would have to make a run for safe harbor or risk riding out nature's fury in the open.

Brianna moaned softly. Atreus returned to her hastily and took her in his arms. Wrapped in the blanket, held close against him, with the wind a little muted by the shutters, she seemed to recover somewhat. This time, when he looked at her, she saw him.

"Atreus? . . ." Her voice was very faint. "I'm so sorry. Oh, God, I'm sorry!"

Sorry? What in all Creation could she possibly have to be sorry about? Carefully, determined not to frighten her further, he cupped her face in his hands. "Brianna, look at me. Listen. You have done nothing wrong. It was I. I should have had more restraint."

She looked at him blankly for a moment before shaking her head. "You don't understand." Her gaze moved toward the shuttered windows. "Out there . . . it's my fault."

He had to turn her words over in his mind before he could understand them at all, and then they made no sense. "The storm . . . is your fault?"

The wind. She feared the wind. He had seen that at Hawkforte, had tried to talk with her about it, but she had eluded him. Not now. Now she would reveal all to him, the better that he could soothe and care for her.

"You won't believe me." She spoke sorrowfully, as though remembering an old hurt.

"Give me a chance." Adjusting her on his lap, he tucked her head against his shoulder and spoke calmly. "It isn't really the storm, is it? It's the wind."

She nodded mutely.

"You're afraid of the wind."

"Not always. Wind is just a part of nature, usually. But sometimes the bad wind can come."

"Bad wind? Wind that does harm?"

"It can. Sometimes it just blows the laundry off the line or upsets the cows. But other times—"

A long, deep tremor moved through her. "It started when I was a child. We moved so often because of it."

"Because you were afraid of the wind?"

She shook her head. "Because I caused it."

He must not have heard her correctly. "You caused it? That's not possible."

"It shouldn't be, but it is."

"Brianna, you were only a child. There must have been

other reasons for your family moving, you just didn't know it."

"I heard my parents speak of it. They didn't want to believe, either, but it happened too many times for there to be any doubt."

She must have misunderstood, he thought. She had been so young, and her memory remained fragmentary.

"But later," he said, "when you came to Akora, surely Leoni and Marcus do not believe this?"

Another long tremor shook her. "Akora . . . when we came—" She breathed in sharply and suddenly, without warning, twisting free of him. Wrapped in the blanket, she stood alone, an oddly forlorn figure, staring up at the figure emerging from the stone.

"My father was holding his arm up like that just before the waves closed over him. I think he was trying to say something to me."

The horror of that vision implanted in her mind struck Atreus to the core. Of all the vast multitude of subjects about which they might speak, her parents' deaths were the last he would choose.

"Brianna, I am sorry if the statue makes you think of that, but—"

She did not seem to hear him. "I was so upset that day. I hated being on the ship. I wanted to go home, to the last place where we had lived. I had a friend there, despite everything. I think her name was Emmeline."

"You remember that day?" She could not possibly. He would know already if she did.

"Only pieces. I remember being so upset, and then I remember the wind."

The wind. Understanding dawned, but with it came sheer incredulity. He stepped in front of her and took hold of her shoulders, compelling her to look at him. "You cannot possibly believe that you had anything to do with what happened to your parents."

Her numb misery had passed, replaced by a bruised resignation. "There were other storms, other times. Some village children surrounded me one day, shouting that I was a witch. The wind that came then knocked trees down. Another time a roof was blown off."

"Coincidence, nothing more."

She smiled wistfully. "Leoni and Marcus know. Not all, for I would never burden them with that. But they have seen it happen often enough."

"You actually believe this." He had to say that out loud and hear himself say it before the words had any reality. She lived with this, had for years. It haunted her.

It was said in warrior training that a man could feel such horror and shock as to make him unable to feel anything at all. Atreus had experienced that once before, a long time before, in a moment of his life he would vastly prefer to forget. He, too, knew what it was to be haunted by memory and by guilt. But in his case, the cause was real. He had killed her parents. That he had done so in all honor to save Akora changed nothing so far as he was concerned.

But her guilt . . . surely a burden so misplaced could be taken from her.

W HERE ARE WE GOING?" BRIANNA ASKED AS HE carried her out of the studio and into the maze of corridors. He had paused just long enough to don his kilt, but was barefoot. She remained wrapped in the blanket, nestled against his chest.

"You need to sleep."

Perhaps she already did sleep, for when she was next aware, he was pushing open the doors to his apartment in the private family wing of the palace. It was very quiet.

Castor had gone and no other servants were in evidence. After the long, roisterous party, the whole palace and indeed the city beyond seemed wrapped in slumber.

"I shouldn't be here," she murmured, but Atreus did not heed her. He drew back the covers of the bed, unwrapped the blanket, and laid her down gently. The linen felt cool against her heated skin. She shivered, but stopped when strong arms enfolded her. With a soft sigh, she gave herself up to them.

Brianna slept, Atreus did not. He lay awake as the world drowsed and morning turned to afternoon. The rain ended, though the scent of it lingered on the air. A few sounds filtered up to him, chiefly the voices of palace guards, who, however fatigued they might be, would never allow that to interfere with their duty. Except for the usual exuberant dogs and the occasional rooster with a poor sense of timing, quiet wreathed the city.

He was glad of it, for in the silence he heard his own thoughts more clearly.

He had to tell her. Just as he could not withhold from her the information William Hollister had given him, he could not leave her believing what she did about herself.

She thought she was responsible for her parents' deaths.

The sick and twisted irony of that wrung a bitter laugh from him.

When she knew the truth . . . as she must . . . what then? She was meant to be his wife. He had known that eight years before and he was more convinced of it than ever. But whereas he had once considered their union inevitable, now he could not be so certain.

His sister Kassandra bore her name in memory of the prophetess of Troy, whose warnings of doom went unheeded. Like her, Kassandra had been able to see the future. That "gift," which had so often been a curse, was gone from her now, its purpose fulfilled. But while she possessed it—or more correctly, while it possessed her—she had realized that the future was made of infinite pathways that became reality or did not, according to the choices people made.

Perhaps his life with Brianna was one such path that would not be taken.

Scarcely did the thought surface than his arms tightened around her. He had sought her because of his duty as Vanax, but it was as a man that he had found her. A man who loved her.

Did he love her enough to let her go? If it came to that, if there was no other way?

She stirred slightly, as though some measure of his thoughts disturbed her dreams. He whispered to her gently and she stilled, but not before her hand crept over his wrist, her fingers finding their way to rest just where his life's blood pulsed.

Chapter

FOURTEEN

AT DUSK, THE SERVING WOMAN SIDA BROUGHT
them food. She came no closer than the an-
techamber, calling out softly to let them know
she was there, and left the tray on a table before
withdrawing discreetly.

Atreus fetched it, returning to the bedchamber wearing
only a bemused smile. "Sida seems to have great faith in
our appetites."

Observing the plentifully laden tray, Brianna said, "I'm
starving." She sat up just a little self-consciously, drawing
the sheet around herself. The admission surprised her, but
then so did everything else.

She had told him. He knew the truth about her, even her
most desperate, hidden secret. And he was still there with
her, looking at her for all the world like a man who approved of what he saw.

"Atreus—"

He set the tray down on the bed and joined her there. "Later. What would you like?"

It was cowardly, she supposed, but she was glad enough to put such dark concerns aside for just a little time. Besides, the aromas wafting from the tray made her stomach rumble. She spied medallions of chicken in a creamy mustard sauce, fresh greens lightly sauteed with a hint of vinegar and caraway, crusty rolls filled with walnuts and raisins, spears of lightly fried sweet potatoes, and lastly, cups of cool, sweet custard dusted with nutmeg.

"That . . . and that . . . some of that . . . oh, just some of everything."

He laughed and did as she bid, filling plates for both of them. Filling, too, goblets with the light wine that accompanied the food, which Brianna eyed warily. There was also a carafe of chilled water beaded with droplets of moisture, and she helped herself from that.

Pouring the water, she was distracted by Atreus—his nearness, his nakedness, his smile, the heated memories he provoked. . . .

"*Oh.*" A little of the water sloshed over her hand and fell on the coverlet of the bed. She grabbed a napkin and tried to blot it up just as Atreus did the same. Their hands brushed as their eyes met.

"It's all right," he said gently.

"No, it isn't. I should have told you the truth about myself the moment you said anything about my becoming your wife."

"Brianna . . . nothing can ever change that. I will always believe you are meant to be my wife."

"Oh, Atreus—" She couldn't help it, his acceptance of her brought tears to her eyes.

He brushed them away slowly, the glistening drops clinging to his fingertips. "Finish eating," he said gruffly. "There is something I want to show you." Without further explanation, he rose, walked over to a chest near the wall, and removed a tunic.

A short time later, clad in one of the shirts Atreus had worn in England, Brianna found herself being led toward a narrow door about halfway down the corridor of the family wing. The hastily improvised garb fell below her knees. When they entered a winding stone staircase, Atreus let go of her hand long enough to strike flint to tinder and light a small lantern he took from a peg just inside the door. Holding the lantern in one hand and hers in the other, he moved toward the steps.

"Where are we going?" Brianna asked.

"To the caves beneath the palace. You said you've heard of them?"

She had heard, whispers of mysteries and rituals, even including the trial of selection itself. It was not forbidden for anyone to visit the caves and so far as she knew, many people had done so. She had thought of going herself, but had never made the time. Now she had to wonder why. What did she imagine might be there that she did not wish to confront? Something that might challenge her beliefs about what was real and what was not?

Although she had no fear of the dark and had never experienced discomfort in close quarters, she was glad of the lantern Atreus carried and gladder still of the warm strength of his hand around hers. They continued downward, past what she knew must be the ground floor of the palace. The air grew cooler and slightly damp.

Finally, the stairs ended and they emerged into what she could just see beyond the circle of light must be a large chamber. A moment later, she gasped, and stumbled back a step when she found herself staring into the nearby face of a statue so finely carved that it appeared for a moment to be a living man.

"Meet Thaddeus," Atreus said. "He was Vanax about seven hundred years ago."

He had, she thought, a very strong but kind face. "How did he do?"

"Quite well, for all that he didn't want the job and apparently never fully accepted it."

"How is that possible? Isn't the Vanax the Chosen?"

"Yes, but we aren't all interchangeable. Some have fit much more comfortably into the position than have others." He turned slightly, illuminating another statue with his lantern. "For instance, that's Praxis. He was Vanax two thousand years ago, give or take a century, and he enjoyed it thoroughly. No hesitations, no doubts, no regrets, that was Praxis."

Gazing at a face of undeniable serenity, Brianna said, "Do you know them all?"

"Each and every one. We leave private records for our successors. The first two years after I became Vanax, I read them compulsively."

"You were seeking guidance," she said with sudden insight.

He nodded. "That, and I felt alone in a way that surprised me." Slowly, he turned, illuminating more of the statues. "To be an artist is to be alone a great deal of the time. That's necessary in order to create, and it never bothered me. But being Vanax . . . that's a different kind of aloneness. I had difficulty adjusting to it."

The thought of him alone and ill at ease in his new position tugged at her heart. Scant weeks before, she could have reminded herself that he had undergone the trial of selection voluntarily, but now that made no difference. Whatever choice he might have had did not erase the challenges he had faced.

And would still face.

She was considering that when another statue caught her attention. "Is that a woman?"

"It is, her name was Demetre."

"Was she the wife of a Vanax?" That might explain the woman's presence in a chamber that clearly was intended to honor those who had ruled Akora.

"She was a priestess and a renowned teacher. Did you know that your aunt Elena will be honored with a statue here as well?"

"That's wonderful. She is an extraordinary healer."

"She is also somewhat resistant to the idea. Perhaps you can help convince her."

As they spoke, they continued walking through the chamber. At its edge, Brianna felt the floor beneath her sandals change from worn stone to dirt. She breathed in sharply as the lantern illuminated an immense cave. Crystalline cones rising from the ground and descending from the ceiling shone in gleaming shades of white, pink, green, and blue. They seemed to divide the vast space into aisles, all leading to an enormous slab of rock near the center of the cave. On it, she thought she glimpsed a large red crystal that looked remarkably like a ruby, except it could not be by virtue of its size . . . could it?

There was no opportunity to ask, for they passed quickly through the cave and entered a passage that seemed carved out of stone. At the far end of it, Brianna saw a strange glow. As they grew closer, it proved so bright as to make the lantern unnecessary.

"Small creatures live here," Atreus explained as he set the lantern aside. "They cling to the rocks. It is their bodies that produce this light."

"Where are we?" Ahead of her was water, and, oddly, what appeared to be a . . . beach? As they drew closer, the air warmed noticeably. Tendrils of steam wafted past. Her nose twitched. The steam smelled slightly salty.

"The water is heated and laden with minerals," Atreus said. "It is possible to drink it, and we think it helped to sustain those who took shelter here after the volcano exploded. But there is also another source of water." He gestured to a small building, little more than a row of columns holding up the pointed roof. In the strange light, it seemed to glow eerily.

"A temple?" she asked.

Atreus nodded. "As incredible as it may seem, all of this appears to have been on the surface close to the sea. It was a sacred place, and people naturally gathered here, seeking protection. They may also have been thinking of trying to put out to sea to escape the volcano, but they never got the chance. According to the records we have, as the volcano continued to erupt, the ground underwent an immense upheaval that may have signalled the island being ripped apart. This area was literally folded into the earth—surely a terrifying experience for everyone who happened to be here, but also the means by which their lives were saved."

"How astonishing that anyone survived." Truly, she could not imagine how anyone did, or how they managed afterward.

"I used to think that, until I came here eight years ago."

"Eight years?" She looked at him sharply. "That was when you underwent the trial of selection."

"Yes, right here."

"Here? But—" That he would bring her to such a place, and, moreover, that it was a place anyone could choose to go, surprised her.

"I want you to understand," Atreus said softly. He raised her hand, still clasped in his. The brush of his lips across her fingers was featherlight. "As much as anyone can who does not actually undergo the trial, I want you to know what it means."

She had revealed to him the most hidden and secret part

of herself. That he was willing to do the same, to share what most set him apart from all others, touched her deeply. Stepping closer to him, she said, "Atreus, I will try to understand, I truly will. I will do my utmost to set aside what I think may be my natural skepticism and accept that your beliefs are genuinely a matter of faith."

Perhaps it was the odd light, but he looked amused. "I appreciate that. Of course, this does have to do with faith, with the spiritual life of Akora. I knew that when I agreed to undergo the trial, but in reality I had no idea at all of what would be involved."

"Your grandfather didn't tell you anything before he died?" Brianna asked.

"Not a word." He sat down on the beach, drawing her with him. The sand felt warm. She slipped her sandals off and wiggled her toes.

"On the evening of the appointed day, I said good-bye to my parents, to my brother and sister, and to several close friends. As you may imagine, none of us knew for certain if I would return alive. I did know I was supposed to spend the night in the caves, so I came down here."

"What happened?"

"Nothing."

"You mean the trial—?" He couldn't possibly be telling her what she had always suspected. With a start, she realized that if he did, she would feel not vindicated but disappointed, even diminished. When had her views changed so greatly? In his arms? In the warmth of his strength and smile?

"Nothing happened at first, not for what seemed like a long time. I wandered around, and finally found myself here. After all the anticipation, to experience absolutely nothing was a great disappointment. I was bewildered, and concerned that perhaps I had done something wrong." His laughter held the memory of the man he had been, young, idealistic, and uncertain. "Perhaps I was of such inconsequence that I wouldn't even be killed. I'd have to go back up to the palace and somehow explain why I was still alive, yet not the Chosen."

"How awkward for you," she murmured.

"So it seemed. At any rate, when still more time passed and nothing happened, I grew annoyed. I decided that as long as I was here, I would make use of the opportunity." He nodded toward the mineral stream. "I'd bathed there a time or two and found it pleasant. Care to give it a try?"

"You mean right now?"

"When better? It is what I did next and I would like you to share the experience, as much as possible."

Leaving her to decide, he rose, dropped his kilt, and waded into the water. She was treated to a tempting view of his broad, sculpted back tapering down to buttocks that were frankly enticing. She stood, drew the shirt off over her head, and followed him. He turned, his gaze blatant and all-encompassing. She held her head high and tried not to stare at the water lapping just below his naval.

"Oh . . . that's hot."

"Too much so?" His arm drifted around her, his hand stroking her hip.

"No . . . it's fine, just a bit of a shock." As was so much else in her life these days.

"Relax, it's supposed to be soothing." When she looked at him doubtfully, he removed the leather thong that secured his hair. Carefully, he lifted hers, coiling it with studied attention, and securing the silken mass at the crown of her head.

The sudden coolness at the nape of her neck was strangely arousing. She even shivered slightly as the tiny hairs there rose suddenly. In an instant, without warning or reason, she felt as though someone was watching them.

"Is there someone here?" she asked.

"What makes you think that?"

"I don't know." Certainly there was no evidence of anyone, no sound or movement. Feeling rather foolish, she said, "I just thought for a moment . . . it doesn't matter."

At any rate, the fleeting impression was gone. She felt entirely alone with him, as though nothing existed in the world except the two of them. It was a delicious sensation, truly there was no other word. But it also made her acutely self-conscious.

"How long did the people stay here?" she asked.

"About two weeks. When they finally dared to venture above, they found their world utterly devastated."

"Nothing was left."

Atreus nodded. "No feature, no contour of the land, no building, no field, nothing that looked in any way familiar to them. No vegetation remained, nor was there a single tree or bush. They had managed to save a few of their animals, but otherwise everything was gone."

"What must they have thought?" she murmured. In the lessons she'd learned as a child, the original survivors were legendary figures of courage and fortitude so vast as to be scarcely comprehensible, but before all that, they had been men and women, surely not so very different from everyone else. She could scarcely imagine the depths of despair they must have encountered.

"They thought they had been abandoned," Atreus said. "They were wrong, but it would be a while before they discovered that."

This she had not heard before. "What do you mean?"

"Later. Might I ask a favor?"

In the eerie light of the cave, he looked like a young god rising magnificently from the waters. The dark hair that brushed his broad, bare shoulders framed features of utterly male beauty. His sensual mouth, evoker of pleasure that even now resonated within her, curved upward slightly as his eyes moved over her lazily.

He could ask. The real question was whether she had any possible hope of refusing.

"A favor?"

"Help me fulfill a fantasy."

YOU HAVE QUITE AN IMAGINATION," BRIANNA gasped.

Her arms were braced against the rim of the pool. The water lapped around her, stirred by the steady, rhythmic movement of their bodies. Her buttocks were nestled against his groin. He was deep within her, masterful and enticing, bringing her to the brink over and over only to pause, to wait, to begin again.

She tried to undo him, clasping him with her inner muscles, but he only growled a laugh and sank his teeth lightly into the nape of her neck. The sensation was exquisite and sent a fresh rush of heat through her. She cried out, her voice echoing against the walls of the chamber.

"Enough, Atreus, enough!"

"Never, not with you." He took firm hold of her hips and bent her farther, allowing even greater penetration.

Lights flickered before her eyes—from the creatures of light or the fevered bursts within her own brain? It scarcely mattered. She was consumed by pleasure, at once shattered and set free by it, soaring beyond all constraint.

Stunned, and returning only slowly, she was glad of Atreus's strength still holding her upright. With a groan, he dragged them both out of the water and slumped beside the pool. He was breathing hard, but a low chuckle broke from him.

"I would not have thought reality could surpass fantasy."

She smiled, too spent to speak, and curled against him.

Some time later—how much she could not have said—Brianna woke to the murmur of voices. She sat up quickly and looked around for Atreus's and her own clothes, but before she could find them, the voices vanished as though they had never been.

Slowly, she settled back down again, but sleep had fled. Beside her, Atreus lay on his back, one hand resting lightly on his chest. His breathing was slow and deep. He was unlikely to wake soon. To gaze at him at her leisure was a temptation she could not resist. His body fascinated her. He was so obviously different and yet they seemed designed to complete one another.

Very lightly, scarcely breathing, she traced the curve of his shoulder. Directly beneath taut skin was the power of bone and sinew. Long cords of muscle contoured his arms and legs. Here and there, she saw scars she had not noticed in the tumult of their lovemaking. Some looked old—the legacy, she supposed, of warrior training.

Dark hair arched between his flat nipples and down over his abdomen, to thicken at his groin. At the moment, he was not aroused, hardly surprising given their recent activities, but that part of him still fascinated her. It represented the power of the male, yet it rendered him so vulnerable.

In England, touring the Tower of London, she had seen displays of the armor worn by medieval warriors complete with elaborately decorated codpieces protecting that which men were said to value above all else. Some of the codpieces were so enormous that they must have advanced before the men, like boastful heralds of their potency. She, Joanna, and Kassandra had giggled over the display, outraging the loitering guard, who clearly had not believed they should be there to begin with.

At the memory, a soft laugh bubbled up in her. She

stifled it at once and held her breath, hoping Atreus would not awake. He did not, and she breathed more easily. But her fascination did not ease. To the contrary, moment to moment, she was ever more entranced by him.

And, inevitably, the mere brush of her finger was not enough. He was so deeply asleep, surely he would not notice if she . . .

Carefully, she leaned closer. His skin held the aroma of the mineral spring, a salty, pleasant scent, mingling with the musky scent of their lovemaking. She placed a hand on his chest, close to his own, and felt beneath her palm the beat of his heart.

Not so very long ago she had thought how easy it would be to love him. The reality turned out to be easier still. She loved this man—man, not Vanax—flesh and blood, muscle and sinew, pride and courage, passion and tenderness. Loved him with a heady exaltation that bubbled up past all control.

One kiss . . . just that, nothing more . . . surely he would not know. Watching him carefully, alert for any tiny flicker that would herald his awakening, she touched her lips just there to the high-boned curve of his cheek. His skin was warm and smooth . . . enticing. . . .

She jerked away, suddenly aware of how very close she was to losing all restraint. That wouldn't do at all . . . would it? If he were awake, he would be in control, as he invariably was when they made love. But what if he were not in control? What if she was?

The thought was tempting and more. She simply could not resist it. Slowly, still watching him, she moved closer. He would wake soon. He was a man honed to battle and would not still be asleep had he not exhausted himself so devotedly. She would have very little time.

How best to use it? How daring, exactly, did she feel?

Very, so it seemed. She wanted to touch him as he

touched her, to know him in every way. Before her nerve could fail her, she leaned forward and blew very carefully on that part of him that fascinated her the most. Just a tiny puff of air riffling the dark whorls of hair nested there.

He stirred and she moved back a little, but a moment later he was still again and her courage returned. Where her breath had gone, the very tip of her tongue followed. It wasn't enough. She wanted more of him. Slowly, she traced her tongue down the length of his shaft before returning to swirl over the smooth, round tip. Very lightly, carefully, she raked her teeth over the ridge of highly sensitive skin.

He groaned and she opened her eyes to find him looking at her down the length of his body, caught in what could only be described as an indelicate position. Also a delightful one. Mistress of the situation, she offered no quarter, but boldly continued as she had begun. Not until she tasted the first salty droplets of tribute did she relent just enough to raise herself and straddle him.

"You certainly are full of surprises," Atreus rasped as he gripped her hips.

"You might want to keep that in mind." Pulling the leather tie from her hair, she tossed the fiery strands over her shoulders and rode him.

A RE YOU AWAKE?"
It was much later, although how much he could not know. Time had a way of getting lost in the caves.

He sighed deeply as his arms tightened around her. "I shouldn't be, yet here I am."

"Will you tell me more about the trial?" She was impatient to know, indeed could not sleep for it.

"Oh, that." The most important event in his life, and it had gone clean out of his head. Truly, the influence of a good woman could not be overestimated. "I was still reluctant to return to the palace, so I went in there instead." He turned his head toward the little temple.

"What's in there?"

He stood, grace to his honor without falling over, and held out a hand. "Come and see."

They entered the temple together. It was very small and filled with the infinitesimal creatures of light. In the stillness, the loudest sound was that of water trickling.

"Look there," Atreus said and drew her closer to one wall.

As she had in the chamber of statues, Brianna found herself looking into a face, but this one was wreathed in moss, incalculably ancient, with an expression that was barely discernible yet suggested gentle strength. From the wall around the face, water fell in a steady stream.

"You've heard of this," he said.

She looked from the stone face to him. "Have I? What—?" About to ask, she caught the water in her hand and tasted it even as memory stirred. So did a smile. "The joining water?"

Atreus nodded. "Enjoyed by uncounted couples on their wedding night and said to possess remarkable powers of . . . encouragement."

She dropped her hand. "In that case, we really shouldn't drink any."

He arched a brow. "Why not?"

"If we get any more *encouraged*, it's likely to kill us."

He laughed, the sound filling the small temple. "I think it's more legend than reality. I've drunk the water and noted no upsurge of passion."

"So you came in here?"

"Yes, I'd been here before, quite a few times. It was— and remains—a favorite place of mine. I sat down just over there."

"And then?"

He hesitated, but the die was cast and on it rode the only chance he was likely to get. "I leaned back against the wall. It was warm."

She tried it for herself. "It is cool now."

"As you would expect it to be, but that day it was warm. After a while, I wondered why. The whole temple was warm, hot even. I thought something must be wrong and that I should leave. But when I tried to rise, I could not. And then the volcano exploded."

"The volcano? What——?"

"I felt it happen, all of it. I felt the fissure open in the earth, the immense rush of lava filling it, shooting upward, exploding into the air, ripping the earth farther apart as it went. I heard rock scream and water shriek. I saw temples fall and people die. I experienced shock and sorrow beyond any I had ever known."

He spoke simply, even matter-of-factly, because that was how it had become for him in the years since, in his complete and absolute acceptance of what had happened to him. But for Brianna it was, naturally enough, different.

"You had a hallucination of some sort," she ventured.

"No. I wasn't actually experiencing it. There was something else, vastly beyond me. I was just a tiny speck standing off to one side."

Hesitantly, she asked, "Are you saying this place holds some sort of memory of what happened?"

"It does, but not in the way places can seem haunted by echoes of the past. This is a living memory."

She did not understand, he could see that. But she was trying to, struggling toward it. She had a good mind and she had been raised Akoran. He waited, watching, and when he judged the time right, he took her hand in his. He placed his other hand palm flat, fingers splayed on the wall of the temple, near the stone face.

"Don't be afraid," he said.

He drew a breath and followed it inward, seeking the stillness he knew would be there, just as he knew what he would find beyond it, here in this place. The vastness against which he just barely brushed, the touch of power beyond comprehending, the boundless sense of joy and pride, of loneliness ended and purpose affirmed, and within all that gentleness, warm and welcoming as a mother's embrace.

Brianna inhaled sharply. Her hand tightened on his but she made no effort to pull away. Shielding her, he went just a little further, let her feel just a little more before slowly withdrawing.

A long sigh escaped her. She looked at him with eyes darkened by awe. "What was . . . is that?"

"Some people call it the spirit of Akora."

"Some people—?"

"I think it is more. There are places all over the world that people regard as holy, where we feel closer to something far beyond ourselves. Akora is one of these, but not the only one, although it may be that here we can come closer than anywhere else."

"It's astonishing. And you felt it, you experienced it directly."

"For me, it was a glorious and life-affirming experience, but I can understand why someone not suited to it would not survive contact with such power." He looked down at his hands. "When I returned to the palace, there were burns on my palms where they were in contact with the wall. Oddly, they didn't hurt and they faded in a few days, but I learned then that the same marks have appeared on every man who became Vanax."

He waited through her silence, summoning patience, surrounding it by hope. She raised her head, met his eyes.

"You really are the Chosen. It's really true." Her

amazement was clear, but so was her heartfelt acceptance, even her joy.

He moved quickly. "Yes, it is, just as it is true that from that time I have known, you and I are meant to be husband and wife."

"You still believe that, even knowing what you do now about me?"

"Brianna—" He reached out, needing to touch her when he said what he must. "You are mistaken in what you believe about yourself."

"Mistaken? Atreus, if you still cannot accept the truth about me—"

"It is not truth. In my family, there have been women with strange gifts, including sometimes the ability to summon primal forces of the earth. I don't dismiss the possibility that you are like them, especially given your own connection to the family of Hawkforte. But you did not cause your parents' deaths."

"You cannot know what happened, you were not there."

"Yes, I was." His hand tightened on her arm. He had planned what he would say, thought it out. Even so, the words threatened to choke him just as the memories did. "I was fifteen years old and in warrior training. The company I was with was on naval maneuvers in the waters near the southern strait when we spied French ships approaching. It wasn't the first time that happened, or the last. We ordered them to turn about, but the admiral who led them refused. We learned later that they were badly off course, the admiral feared Napoleon's wrath and decided an incursion against fabled Akora would restore him to favor. He was tragically mistaken."

"The storm—"

"There was a strong wind, but no storm. The French ships were sunk in battle."

Her skin was very cold. Before his eyes, the color fled

from her face, leaving her eyes wide and dark. "My parents—"

"We had no idea civilians were on board until you were found."

"Oh, God." She was shaking so hard he feared she would fall. To prevent that, he moved to draw her closer, but before he could do so, she wrenched away. Staring at him, she demanded, "You are telling me that my parents were killed by Akorans?"

The people who had taken her in, made her their own? The people she . . . loved?

"We were defending ourselves."

She scarcely heard him, spoke as though to herself. "But such a battle would have been known. Leoni and Marcus must have known. Everyone must have, but no one—*no one*—ever told me."

"You said Leoni and Marcus did not know you thought yourself responsible."

"Even so, they did not tell me the truth of how my parents died. Of how I came to be with them instead."

"What point was there in telling you when your life was to be here, especially after it became clear there was no one in England. Or so we thought."

"But there was, there was! And I wouldn't have known that either, but for my own insistence." She backed away from him, her arm held out to hold him off. "So many lies."

"Not lies."

"Yes, lies! Lies of omission, things not said that should have been. All these years I've loved Akora, but to find that my parents died because of it . . . My father went into the water, desperate to find my mother, but he could not, and he looked . . . oh, God, the way he looked as the waves closed over him."

The nightmare of that horrible day rose up within her and with it came stark, inescapable truth. "You could have been honest with me from the beginning but instead, you . . ." She looked down at herself, standing naked as he was, their bodies so familiar to each other now after the long, impassioned hours of lovemaking. "You sought to bind me to your side. To fulfill what you think is meant to be, because nothing else matters, does it? Nothing except what Akora demands."

Her mouth twisted in pain. "I doubt no longer that you are Chosen, but you might well wonder if that has made you less than human."

She was gone, fled from him. He stood alone in the temple as he had eight years before, but this time he knew he had failed.

Chapter

FIFTEEN

S HE HAD AWAKENED FROM A DREAM INTO A
nightmare. Atreus was the Chosen, the legends and
beliefs of Akorans were true, some power that
touched them all made itself known in these islands. She had felt it in the temple, experienced it through
him. The revelation was astonishing, and it would have
filled her with joy had it not been overshadowed by the discovery that her parents had died because of it.

Though she shied instinctively from so harsh a conclusion, it remained inescapable. It was the vital spirit of
Akora, whatever it might truly be, that inspired and em-
boldened Akora's people to preserve the Fortress Kingdom
against all intruders.

Her eyes burned. She turned her face into the wind.
Perhaps it would dry the tears she seemed helpless to stem.
For the first time since awakening sixteen years before to

the sight of Leoni hovering over her bed, she felt utterly and completely alone.

Akora, the home she loved, was the reason her parents had died. Those she had trusted and loved the most had let her believe a lie about those deaths. The twin blows were almost more than she could bear, yet bear them she must, for there truly was no escape from them.

She could leave Akora, not immediately or easily, but she could go. A life awaited her in England. She knew that, but it brought no solace. Wherever she went, whatever she did, the hurt and grief would follow her.

She could not leave herself behind, and an integral part of that self now was the inescapable truth that she loved Atreus. Yet it was that very love that made it impossible for her to dwell any longer in the realm of lies. He had set out to wed her not because of the woman she truly was but because of what he believed she was supposed to be—his wife. He had done it masterfully, luring her with passion and power. And she had been all too receptive, all too willing. Were it not for her commitment to Helios and the questions that raised within her, she might well be his wife already.

Her head throbbed. She put it in her hands and closed her eyes, but found no relief. Stumbling out of the caves, she had gone directly to her quarters to bathe and change, but had scant memory of doing either. Now she sat, perched on the highest tier of the stone seats surrounding the empty stadium. Half a year before, she had been sitting very near to where she was right now, caught up in the thrilling excitement of the Games and of the chariot race then underway. Atreus had been in the lead, very close to winning. She remembered jumping to her feet, her heart pounding, thrilled by and for him.

Just afterward, the stadium—and, it seemed, the world

itself—was torn apart by a massive explosion that brought down the wall directly beside Atreus.

They said the traitor Deilos was responsible. They said he opposed the reforms the Vanax wanted to bring to Akora. That he thought himself worthy of being Vanax in his place.

They said some of those of Helios had helped him.

More lies? She didn't know and couldn't think. The sun was too bright and the wind was growing stronger.

Damn stupid wind. From her tenderest years, when first she suspected the truth about herself, she had dreaded it. Now it seemed only a pointless nuisance. Other gifts, Atreus had said, present in the women of his family and of Hawkforte. Gifts of calling the primal energies of the earth, but presumably *to some purpose*. Something beyond mere annoyance.

But now with her . . . oh, no. If she had to receive a "gift," did it have to be for no good use? And if she had to fall in love with a man, did he have to be—

Her mind recoiled from the path of self-pity. She jumped up, left the stadium, and set off in no particular direction through the city. Soon, she found herself joining the stream of people heading toward the palace. There was a purposeful solemnity about them. She had little time to wonder why before the answer presented itself.

"Bri, I didn't think to find you here."

Polonus pushed his way through the crowd to reach her side. She smothered a sigh and strove to conceal all signs of her unhappiness. Even without their conversation at the party, she could not imagine confiding in him. Despite their earlier closeness, he was one of those who had let her believe a lie.

Yet he knew her well enough to realize something was amiss, without a word from her. "What's wrong?" Polonus asked. For a moment, his young man's self-centeredness seemed set aside as he looked at her with genuine concern.

It was not enough. She wished only to remain hidden within herself. "Nothing."

"You're very pale."

She continued walking, not looking at him. "I have only just returned from England. There is little sun to be had there at this time of year."

"Even so, you looked better the other day. Look, I'm sorry if what I said upset you."

"You did not sound yourself. That was upsetting. The rest, frankly, was nonsense."

He flushed but did not protest. Instead, he said, "This has been a very hard time for me, but now at least with the trial starting—"

"The trial? Does that begin today?"

He looked at her with puzzlement. "Of course, that's where everyone is going. Where I thought you were going. Aren't you?"

"Yes, of course I am." They were her friends in Helios as well as his. Atreus had used the trial as one more way of drawing her back to Akora. Perhaps now he expected her to stay away, in which case he was in for a surprise.

She would go, she would hold her head high, and she would see if there truly was such a thing as justice to be found on Akora.

On the flow of the crowd, she entered the vast courtyard in front of the palace, the site of the party less than two days before. All sign of that revelry was gone. Perhaps in anticipation that the crowd would be as large as it was, a decision had been made to hold the trial in the courtyard. No other place on Akora could begin to accommodate so many people.

The quickest among them realized at once that they would have the best possible view from the stairs leading up to the palace, and moved to occupy them. Polonus drew Brianna along, finding places for them near the dais set up at one end of the courtyard. A table had been placed there, along with a simple, high-backed chair.

"No throne?" Polonus murmured.

"He doesn't need one," Brianna said. "Atreus's power doesn't come from symbols." She understood that all too well now.

Polonus glanced around quickly, as though mindful of who might be nearby. "It comes from the ignorance of the people."

She knew better, but she had no wish to argue with him. Below them, near the dais, she saw Kassandra and Joanna sitting with their husbands. They did not see her and for that she was grateful.

There was very little time to wait. Without announcement or fanfare of any sort, Atreus came from the palace and took his place at the table. He was simply dressed, in a plain white tunic. He looked tired, she thought, and preoccupied. As he took his seat, his gaze scanned the assembled crowd, stopping when it came to rest on her.

As she had promised herself, she held her head high and looked back at him steadily. Though it took all her strength, she would not flinch.

After a few moments, he looked away, but not before she saw the sadness in his eyes. Whatever satisfaction she might have felt at facing him was as ashes on her tongue.

The prisoners were brought out a short time later. As one, people craned their necks for a look at the four men. All were young, for Helios tended to draw the young. They also were familiar to her, for they had attended the same Helios meetings that she had. In the eager sharing of hopes and dreams, she had come to think of all in Helios as friends. To see the four now in such circumstances was painful.

The magistrate, Marcellus, approached the table where Atreus sat. He held a tablet and consulted it as he spoke.

The charges were direct and straightforward.

"That each did assist in the acquisition of materials used in the bombing of the stadium," Marcellus intoned. "That these actions were taken with prior knowledge of the purpose for which such materials would be used. That these actions resulted in the deaths of eight men and the wounding of several dozen others, including the Vanax of Akora himself."

"Who might have the decency not to hear this case," Polonus murmured, "given his personal involvement in it."

"It is his duty to hear it," Brianna replied. "Atreus always does his duty." As she had bitter reason to know.

The evidence unfolded rapidly. Witnesses testified to seeing one or more of the accused in the vicinity of a wagon, which later turned up stolen and which matched the description of that used in the attack. Others connected them to the barrels. Most damaging were those who testified that each of the four had taken steps to acquire ingredients used in the production of gunpowder.

Long before the testimony concluded, Brianna was deeply shaken. Some of the evidence might be explained away as coincidence, but taken all together it left little hope that the four could truly be innocent.

"I don't understand," she said softly to Polonus. "Helios is a completely peaceful movement. Why would someone willing to use violence be drawn to it in the first place?"

"Perhaps they weren't inclined to violence when they joined. But realizing that nothing was ever going to change may have changed them."

"We all became frustrated, Polonus. We all wanted things to happen more quickly, but that is no excuse for what these people seem to have done. My God, they helped to *kill* people."

"It would never have happened if the Vanax hadn't been so intransigent. He caused those deaths as much as anyone."

She stared at her brother, unable to really believe he had said what she thought she had heard. "You can't mean that?"

"But it's true, can't you see? If Atreus had agreed to Helios's demands, no one would have been driven to take such desperate steps."

"Including killing people? They couldn't bear to wait? They had to have everything right away? And when they didn't get it, they were justified in killing people?"

"Of course they weren't, I didn't say that. Even if at least some of those who died were supporters of Atreus, it was still wrong to kill them."

Had a cloud just gone in front of the sun? It felt very cold suddenly. "Polonus, what about trying to kill Atreus himself? You do understand how wrong that was?"

"I understand he stands in the way of any hope of true reform for Akora."

Long moments passed during which Brianna could think of nothing at all save the enormity of what her brother had just said. Atreus should die. Or at least, his death was acceptable.

Her brother believed this. Her own brother.

Dimly, she heard Atreus say something about the evidence being concluded and proceedings being adjourned until the following morning. The four accused were led away. The crowd began to disperse. Polonus stood up and waited for her to do the same, but she could not bring herself to go with him.

"I'll stay awhile."

"You shouldn't, Bri. If you stay here, you'll still be with

them. Come with me. There's going to be a meeting tonight."

"A Helios meeting?"

"Yes, you should come."

She looked up at him, seeing him for just a moment as he had been, the gentle boy who became her brother. He had hated the thought of any sort of violence. Now he spoke of murder with seeming calm.

She had cared so deeply about Helios, and in some way she still did. But the day had been shattering, and she desperately needed to be alone with her own thoughts.

"Go," she said and somehow, in memory of what they had shared, she found a smile.

Alone, she waited until most of the crowd had gone before making her way to her quarters in the palace. Exhaustion dogged her every step. She had barely slept the previous night, being far too occupied in ways she resisted thinking about just then, and the night before that had been the party. Truly, her dulled mind could scarcely comprehend how tired she was.

She reached her quarters at last. Using the last of her strength, she kicked off her sandals and slumped across the bed without either undressing or pulling back the covers. Moments later, she was deeply asleep.

MOONLIGHT FLOODED THE ROOM WHEN ATREUS entered it. He had waited as long as he could, debating whether to go at all. Indecision was new to him and he disliked it heartily. All the same, he went with caution, opening the door with care and peering in before entering.

She was asleep, as he had expected. Throughout the trial, he had been hard-pressed not to go to her. Her presence surprised him, but also gave him hope. Her obvious exhaustion and sorrow filled him with angry regret.

He had harmed her. He, the leader of Akora, the ultimate upholder of its laws and values, had harmed a woman. And she, the woman he loved.

He should have—what? Told her differently or not told her at all? Refrained from trying in every way he knew to bind her to his side first? Every alternative that came to his mind seemed better than what he had actually done.

The way she had looked at him . . .

You are Chosen, but you might well wonder if that has made you less than human!

Even now, she did not know how terribly right she might be.

He had sought in stone, clay, and metal the means of preserving his own humanity in the face of an experience that, blessing though it was, made him feel set apart from everyone else. But he had found that humanity again in the arms of a woman who now slept, unaware of his presence.

He knelt down beside the bed, studying her. Her face was turned toward him, her lips slightly parted as she breathed slowly and deeply. He wanted so badly to take her in his arms, to comfort and reassure her. But he was trespassing as it was and he should go no further, not while so much remained between them.

Yet the temptation to touch her proved irresistible. He reached out a hand and very carefully moved aside a tendril of hair that had drifted across her cheek.

She did not stir. He had no sign that she was aware of his presence in any way.

That was good, he told himself, and lingered a little longer before finally getting to his feet. Soundlessly, he went from the room, but not before tucking the covers more closely around her and making sure that the shutters over the windows were closed.

The night promised to be unseasonably cool, what with the way the wind was blowing.

He went, dogged by his own weariness, and turned a corner to find his sister coming toward him.

"I was hoping to find you," Kassandra said. She came right up to him, took his arm gently, and kissed him lightly on the check. "You look dreadful."

Despite himself, he smiled. "Honest as always. It's nothing a few hours of sleep won't cure."

She regarded him with frank skepticism. "Really? I'd say it's rather more than that. How is Brianna?"

"Asleep." Deliberately, he resumed walking. She did the same. "Where is Royce?" Atreus asked. "I didn't think he let you wander around on your own these days."

Kassandra glanced down wryly at her swollen belly. "He looks at me as though he thinks I'm about to explode at any moment. I love the man dearly but he's driving me to distraction."

"You know he would do anything for you."

Her eyes softened. "I do know that. I am the most fortunate of women. But I came hoping I might find you. Today was difficult, but I know tomorrow will be even more so."

"Tomorrow Deilos will be tried in open court, in full view of anyone who cares to attend."

The man who had come very close to killing him and who had committed numerous other crimes would face justice at last. It would be difficult, but it was also necessary for the good of Akora. Only when it was done, properly and lawfully, would the people know that they truly were safe.

"Tomorrow," his sister said gently, "you will be remembering everything that happened, even reliving it in a sense. We will be there to support you, of course, but you will face it alone all the same."

"I am accustomed to being alone."

She sighed but did not dispute him. It was understood

in the family that to be Vanax was to be set apart. "Something I—we—hoped would be changing by now."

Atreus stopped abruptly and looked at her. A sudden possibility occurred to him and with it came a note of genuine alarm. "Did Mother send you?"

"No," Kassandra reassured him quickly, even as she laughed. "She's busy with Amelia and thoughts of this grandchild to come, but you can't really expect that to last."

Indeed, he could not. He loved his mother dearly, but Phaedra had been urging him to marry for years, her efforts only heightening as each of his siblings wed before him. If she had any inkling that he had asked Brianna to become his wife—

—and that she was further away from agreeing than ever.

"I would appreciate your discretion," he said.

"You have it, of course, and anything else I can do." She stopped suddenly and put her hand to her belly.

"Are you all right?" Atreus asked.

"I'm fine. It's just that ever since we got here, this one has been making himself known. He's got quite a kick."

Satisfied that she was not in any danger, Atreus said, "I've been meaning to ask you, what made you decide to have the baby here?"

"I'm not really sure. I had assumed he would be born at Hawkforte. He is a he, by the way, I'm quite certain of that. Hawkforte will be his home and his heritage, so it seemed only fitting for him to be born there. But suddenly, about a month ago, I began to believe he should be born here instead."

Atreus nodded. "I was thinking about what you said once, that the future is made up of infinite paths and it is for us to choose which of them we will take. Perhaps this child will have choices to make."

"Perhaps—" She looked up at him, the sister he loved, carrying the child he already knew. "Atreus, are you trying to tell me something?"

He thought back to the caves, the temple, and what once had seemed so clear but no longer did. "Only that there are infinite paths. Come now, let's find Royce before he starts to worry about you."

Kassandra went with him, but not without one or two quick glances in his direction. He ignored them and continued along his own path, not chosen but thrust upon him and inescapable.

THE TRIAL RESUMED THE FOLLOWING MORNING. The crowd was back, and even larger than before, for on this day all attention would be focused on the man whose alleged crimes were of such enormity that they were spoken of in whispers. Brianna herself was unsure of all Deilos was said to have done, but she knew enough to get to the courtyard early and find herself a seat.

Of Polonus she saw nothing, but she supposed Leoni and Marcus were about somewhere. She would have to speak with them eventually but not just yet, not while the sense of betrayal remained so raw.

Atreus appeared just then. She looked at him very quickly and looked away lest she be caught staring. He appeared a little better rested, but his expression was carefully guarded, as though he had withdrawn into himself in preparation for what was to come. He looked like stone, she thought, his form and features perfectly carved, yet lacking all animation, the life and the humanity so deeply buried within as to be invisible.

Like stone, he appeared utterly unyielding. She knew it was his intent to judge fairly, but she could not help but wonder if he had within him anything of the quality of mercy.

He sat and almost immediately the crowd tensed. Encircled by guards, a man was led into the courtyard. Along with everyone else, Brianna stood to get a better look at him. Could that be Deilos? He was hardly a prepossessing figure, shorter than most Akoran men and whippet-thin. His features were narrow and sharp, like the rest of him. He showed no hint of fear, but his eyes moved constantly, surveying his audience. As he neared the dais, he smiled contemptuously and raised his hands. . . .

No, hand. His right arm ended in a stump.

So it was true, the story she had heard about. Royce, the man Akorans called the Hawk Lord, had hunted Deilos while Atreus lay between the borders of life and death. Hunted him with the clear intent of killing him, for the threat Deilos posed to the Princess Kassandra and the harm he had done to the Hawk Lord himself when he held him in cruel captivity. But at the last moment, persuaded by Kassandra, Royce had let Deilos live to stand trial. He had taken from him only his hand and his freedom. It would be up to Atreus to decide if he would also lose his life.

"Hail, Vanax," Deilos called out contemptuously. "Hail, Chosen Ruler of Akora. Here I stand, humbled before you."

Atreus did not react immediately. He leaned back in his chair and surveyed Deilos calmly. At length, he said, "Here you stand, Deilos, in open court to hear the charges against you, refute the evidence if you can and receive fair judgment. Marcellus—" He beckoned to the magistrate, who stepped forward quickly. This time, he did not need to consult his tablet.

"Deilos of the House of Deimatos, the following charges are brought against you: That you did illegally hold Royce, Earl of Hawkforte, then a *xenos*, in harsh captivity without proper authority. That you did conspire to use said captivity to provoke an invasion of Akora by the Kingdom of Great Britain. That you intended to use such an invasion to overthrow the House of Atreides and make yourself Vanax of Akora. That when this failed, you conspired to kill the rightful Vanax of Akora by exploding gunpowder in the vicinity of the stadium during the performance of the Games. That this resulted in eight deaths and numerous injuries. So are you charged."

Long before Marcellus finished, he had to raise his voice to be heard above the startled outcry of the crowd. Much of what Deilos was accused of doing had been known only to the Atreides and their closest advisers. Brianna herself had known of Royce's captivity only because of her friendship with the two couples.

At news that Deilos had tried to provoke an invasion of Akora by a foreign power, many in the crowd cried out angrily. Atreus raised a hand, bidding them to quiet, though they continued to murmur among themselves.

But when Marcellus finished, the crowd could not be contained. Angry men and women shouted out their own judgments.

"Traitor!"

"Murderer!"

"Violator!"

"Scum!"

The guards pressed closer, holding the people back, but it was Atreus who calmed them. He stood and at once they fell silent. He spoke simply, as though addressing friends.

"Deilos will receive a fair trial. It should be in your presence, as it concerns you all, but if you continue to interfere, the trial will be moved into the palace and only a very few will be able to witness it."

He sat down. The people were silent. Marcellus stepped forward briskly.

"If it please the court, the first witness will be called."

Royce came forward to describe without emotion his experiences at Deilos's hands.

"I came as others have," he said, "shipwrecked on Akora's shores. Deilos and his men found me. Rather than turn me over to the proper authorities, they imprisoned me. I was held for nine months and was near death when I was rescued by my sister and Prince Alexandros. Later we learned that Deilos's intent was to use the captivity and death of a British nobleman to spur Britain to invade Akora. He even went to England for that purpose and met with a powerful nobleman there who, at the time, was misguided enough to believe Britain could conquer Akora."

"Deilos took my brother from the cell where he had been held all those months," Joanna said when her turn came, "with the intent of killing him. Only Prince Alexandros's intervention prevented it and stopped me from being harmed as well. Even so, Deilos tried to kill Alex and myself by trapping us in the caves on the island of Deimatos."

"Deilos admitted to me," Kassandra said in turn, "that he believed a British invasion of Akora would make our people turn against the Vanax. He was convinced they would accept him as their ruler instead. When this plot failed, he decided to assassinate Atreus. As we all know, he came very close to succeeding."

The crowd, which had hung on every word, stirred uneasily and muttered among itself. Much of what was said was already known, but to hear it laid out so starkly was disturbing indeed.

Half a dozen other witnesses followed, who added their own testimony regarding Deilos's actions and intent. By the time the last of these had concluded, it was midday.

Atreus called a recess, sending enterprising boys and girls scrambling with their wares through the hungry, thirsty crowd. The better prepared had brought awnings, which they rigged against the bright sun. None showed any inclination to leave. The proceedings held them all riveted.

Brianna did not fully share their fascination, but she had no wish to be alone with her own thoughts. She remained where she was, waiting for the recess to end. Before it did, Polonus found her. He slipped into the seat beside her.

"Quite a performance, wouldn't you say?"

She cast him a quick look, frowning at what she saw. He appeared not to have slept and was unshaven. His eyes were red-rimmed and angry. "I would say it is a fair trial," she replied.

"Fair? How can you say that when almost all the testimony is from the Atreides themselves?"

"But they were directly involved. They have to testify."

"And you think they're telling the truth?"

"I think they have no reason to lie. Why would they? Deilos was a member of the Vanax's Council; he held an honorable position. It was his choice to betray everything he was supposed to uphold."

"Gods, you understand nothing! Don't you see that they are determined to destroy anyone who disagrees with them? Deilos had the courage to stand against the Vanax. This is his reward for it."

A sick feeling was growing within Brianna. She stared at her brother. "Polonus, how did Deilos make a connection to Helios? What brought two such wildly different sides together?"

His cheeks darkened slightly. "Why would you think I'd know?"

"Because you are a member of Helios who seems very sympathetic to Deilos."

"I am merely being fair. You might try doing the same. Open your eyes!"

She had and what she saw troubled her deeply. The testimony against the four the previous day had left little doubt as to their guilt. Regarding Deilos, she had none at all. If Polonus had become involved with such a man—

"Will you be returning to Leios soon with Mother and Father?" she asked him.

He did not answer, but then she could not expect him to. Atreus and the others were returning to the courtyard. The trial was about to resume.

Chapter

SIXTEEN

A KORANS," DEILOS CRIED OUT, "HEAR ME!"
The prosecution had concluded its case. It was Deilos's turn to offer his defense but he had declined to call any witnesses. Instead, he claimed his right to address the court and all those present in it.

He stood in the center of the courtyard, his maimed arm flung out as though to call attention to it. His voice was rich and deep. Brianna thought it difficult to ignore and wondered if it was part of the secret of the attraction he seemed to hold for certain people.

Polonus was leaning forward in his seat, attentive to every word. He was not alone. The crowd was as silent as it had been at Atreus's bidding. Deilos had their full attention.

"I come before you a man defamed. It is said I sought to harm Akora. No accusation, no slur could stab more directly at my heart. I love Akora. I have only and ever sought to protect her."

A few in the crowd jeered at this, but most remained silent, listening.

"My family is proud to trace our heritage back to the very beginnings of Akora, to the time when the Atreides took power. They have held it ever since, while we have served—generation after generation, quietly and diligently, always serving the people of Akora and never asking anything for ourselves in return."

The jeers started again but there were fewer this time and they petered out quickly.

"There were times in the past when my ancestors were troubled by the direction in which the Atreides seemed determined to take us. Troubled as to why our ancient ways were not respected. Troubled as to why the proper role of women in our society became a joke ridiculing sacred agreements. Troubled as to why the outside world—a world in which I have travelled and can tell you first hand of its worthlessness—came ever more strongly to interfere with our own. But *we held our tongues*. We never forgot that we serve, but I say to you, the Atreides have long since forgotten that. They do not serve Akora. They seek only to *rule!*"

This did rouse the crowd, which cried out in denial, but here and there were scattered shouts of agreement, including Polonus's own.

"Now I stand before you accused," Deilos went on. "And to you—my people—I will confess. Am I guilty as charged? Yes! Guilty of loving Akora, of serving Akora, of being willing with my life's blood to preserve Akora!"

This time there were only cheers, not many but more than before. The great majority of the crowd sat silent, clearly shocked by his frank admission.

"Did I take the *xenos* lord captive? Yes! Who is this man

who is now a member of the Atreides family by marriage? In his own land, he is the most trusted adviser of his king, charged by him to carry out missions intended to increase the power of Great Britain. Now he sits here among us, close to the ear of the Vanax, able to influence him in ways that can only harm Akora!"

Kassandra jumped to her feet, looking ready to take on Deilos single-handedly, but Royce urged her down gently and kept her close.

"Why did I not turn him over immediately to the authorities? Because, I am sad to say, by then I no longer trusted them to do what was right. The *xenos* could have simply told me the truth of why he had come, but he would not do so."

"He's lying," Brianna said. "Royce never meant any harm to Akora."

"So they have tricked you into believing," Polonus said.

She looked at him in exasperation as Deilos continued.

"They say I tried to provoke an invasion of Akora by a foreign power. I say they knew the British intended to invade and were doing nothing to prevent it. But I—I went to Great Britain myself and the truth I discovered there filled me with dread. I returned here knowing that drastic steps had to be taken lest Akora fall to the *xenos* invaders."

"Lies," Brianna whispered, but this time Polonus did not hear her.

"Think of it, my fellow Akorans! Even now, this very day, we could be living in an Akora crushed under the boot of an invader. At least those of us who would still be alive, and how many would that be? Would not every true Akoran have fallen in the struggle to keep our land free? But what of our children? How many of them would also have died or be living now enslaved, our temples burned, our homes destroyed, our proud heritage crushed beyond any hope of recovery?"

He was silent for a moment, looking in all directions. He was a master orator and the crowd was with him, unwillingly riveted by the picture of horror he set before them.

"I could tell you of my efforts to reach the Vanax, to make him see the terrible error of the course upon which he was set. But it would only anger and dismay you. Time and again, I was rebuffed, denied even the opportunity to speak with the Vanax, who preferred to spend his time in consultation with his brother, the Kyril Alexandros—who, as you all know, is himself married to a British woman from the same family that serves British interests so very well.

"I despaired, Akorans. I do not say this to you with pride, but it is the truth. And in my desperation, I conceived a desperate plan. I thought to frighten the Vanax, to make him feel firsthand the horrors that invasion would bring to Akora. It was never my intention to kill him, but alas, I am only a man and as capable of misjudgment as any. What was supposed to be only a small explosion was, regrettably, much more. Innocent people died. They may be said to have been the casualties in the war that saved Akora from far worse disaster."

"That's despicable," Brianna said. "How dare he use their deaths to his own credit?"

"Be quiet," Polonus snapped and continued to listen raptly.

That was his choice; she could bear no more. Quickly, Brianna rose and hurried away. Behind her, she was all too aware of the stillness of the crowd and of Deilos's voice, sounding stronger and more confident with each passing moment.

S HE WAS UPSET, ATREUS COULD SEE THAT. WERE she free to do so, he would have followed her without hesitation. No matter what stood between them, he still claimed the right to comfort and protect her.

But he was not free and never would be. Duty demanded that he stay right where he was and listen to Deilos's ranting.

The man was good, he had to give him that. He had the skills of a practiced orator, but there was more than a little natural talent at work as well. When he was on the Council, Deilos had spoken often and with great eloquence. Now he claimed to have been ignored, but that, like all else, was not true.

He made it sound true though. To anyone not directly involved in the events of the past year, Deilos painted a believable and perhaps persuasive picture.

People were listening to him. Many were frowning and shaking their heads, but they were listening.

"I have paid a price for my actions," Deilos proclaimed. He held his right arm high again for all to see. "For them, I have been maimed. That is Atreides justice, my friends. So be it. I accept the price I have paid, for on my oath, I would pay one far higher, even to the ultimate price of my life itself. All I ask, all I demand is that Akora be safe!"

He dropped his arm and bowed his head, the very picture of a man valiant in his convictions and stalwart in the face of all adversity.

The crowd remained completely still. There was no applause, although here and there among the crowd, Atreus saw those he thought were so inclined. Most people merely looked concerned and puzzled.

He stood and they looked at him, to him with obvious relief. No doubt they expected him to refute Deilos, but they were destined to be disappointed. Debate was reserved for honorable opponents and, at any rate, he had to sit in judgment of the man.

"We are adjourned until tomorrow morning," he said and walked away.

Within the palace, he paused for a moment and forced himself to breathe deeply. The effort to simply sit and listen to Deilos had strained his self-control to the breaking point. Artist he was and Vanax as well, but he was also a warrior, and that part of his nature had been hard-pressed not to have it out with Deilos right then and there. The temptation to sink a blade into him and watch his life's blood feed the earth was all but irresistible. Royce had said once that Deilos needed killing, and Atreus knew of nothing to refute that. Nothing except that it served Akora to leave him alive, to bring him to trial, to make the visible demonstration of justice the people needed to see.

The same people who listened to Deilos.

Grimly, Atreus shook his head. He must put aside such thoughts, must not allow himself to be disappointed by people who were simply as they were.

He had to have faith, that above all. There were times when faith came like the gift of a cool mountain stream to a parched throat—a welcome blessing received without question. But there were other times when the clarity of faith was more elusive, even when its constant, unflinching presence was resented.

Deilos stirred that resentment, did he but know it. And perhaps he did, for the man seemed possessed of an evil genius. He knew just how to work the levers of doubt and fear to his own ends.

Yet all his schemings, all his mad plottings and bloody efforts had led him not to the power and glory he sought, but to the very brink of defeat. It would be as well, Atreus decided, not to lose sight of that.

The family would be following quickly and they would want to talk, which he understood well enough. Yet he had no patience for it, not just then. Instead, he went on through the shadowed corridors, letting the quiet and the coolness draw him.

He would never be free. The thought had come to him before, but never with such ferocity. It had its teeth into him now and there was no letting go.

Never. Not while he lived. And afterward? Perhaps not even then. He hadn't thought much about freedom over the course of his life. Duty had always reigned supreme. But he was thinking about it now, indeed could seem to think of nothing else save Brianna.

He needed to see her. Hell, he needed a lot more than that but he'd settle for what he could get. All he had to do was find her.

She was not in her quarters. Briefly, he considered the possibility that she might return to the caves, but he dismissed that almost immediately. She would not seek the place where she had come to such a shattering discovery.

Where then might she go? In England, he remembered, she had enjoyed feeding the birds that came into the garden of Alex and Joanna's London house. There were birds all over Akora, but in the palace there was one place in particular where they came.

There he went. The small garden was nestled against an outside wall of the palace, overlooking the harbor. It was open to anyone who cared to go there, but despite its existence for more than a thousand years, few seemed to think of it.

Brianna was seated on a stone bench beside a small fountain, which spilled into a pond that was home to goldfish. He smiled to see she was doing just what he had expected, feeding the birds.

Even the shy mourning doves with their softly plaintive call had been coaxed to join the darting blackbirds, robins, and the brightly plumed swifters who were native to Akora alone.

Brianna looked up when he entered, and stiffened visibly. For a moment, he thought she meant to rise and go, but she remained seated. After a few moments, she resumed feeding the birds.

He sat down beside her, not close enough to be touching her but close all the same. Now that he had found her, he really did not know what to say apart from the thousand or so possibilities competing in his mind. He resolved to go slowly and chose that which was the nearest to being impersonal.

"What do you think of the trial?"

She glanced up, as though trying to decide what she should—or should not—say to him. He saw her take a breath and let it out slowly. "It is as you said it would be, fair."

That she answered at all, and in a way that held out the olive branch of agreement, was more victory than he had hoped for. Building on it cautiously, he asked, "And Deilos, what do you make of him?"

"I left before he was done, but I had heard enough. He is a snake in the grass, clever, beguiling, and dangerous."

"He spoke well."

She frowned. "He lied well. What disturbed me most was that the people listened to him."

"As well they should. It is important for them to hear what he has to say."

"Even if they are persuaded by him?"

"Even then," Atreus said, "although I do not think there is much danger of that."

A shadow flitted behind her eyes. "How can you be so sure?"

"When a man speaks as well as Deilos does, he casts an enchantment of sorts. For a time, people may seem to fall under it. But when they return to their ordinary lives, they see him in a different light. Deilos stood before all and accused my family, and me in particular, of betraying Akora. He tried to make the case that we have fallen under the influence of Great Britain and have done it to such an extent that we would have allowed Akora to be conquered. That is patently absurd. Further, he tried to claim that it is permissable to murder simply because one is not listened to. He said all he cares about is Akora's safety, but it is he who has violated the laws, threatened stability, and placed us all at risk."

"And you think people will realize this for themselves?"

"I count on it."

"You place great confidence in ordinary men and women."

"I have to," he said simply. "There is no other way I could possibly do as I do. Without faith in the essential goodness of ordinary people, there must be tyranny to force them to behave as it is thought they should. That has never been our way."

She threw the last of the crumbs and brushed her hands clean. "You must know that Deilos has followers. Some of them were at the trial."

Atreus nodded. "He may have a few more by now, those who cannot reason through the fog of his words."

"They could be dangerous."

"Are you concerned for me, Brianna?"

"I—" She did look at him then but her eyes were guarded. "Yes, I am concerned. How could I not be? I would be concerned for anyone in such a situation. But Atreus, you must understand, I went to England to find the child I had been. That did not mean I was rejecting who I had become. I am glad to be Akoran, proud of it. Becoming Lady Brianna Wilcox did not change that, but discovering the truth of how and why my parents died has."

"I had thought you would be relieved to know you had no part in it. That is why I told you."

"Perhaps someday I will feel relieved, but right now all that I can see is that I have lived for sixteen years inside a lie. Those I have loved and trusted most now seem strange and alien to me, as though I have never known them at all."

"Can you not see that what was done was for your own welfare?"

"Can you not see that lies are wrong?" she countered. "That the wounds they inflict may be too deep to heal?"

The sun was drifting westward. In its light, the fiery glints of her hair burned brightly. He stood, looking down at her, staring into the features he had carved with such exactitude back when she was only a vision, not yet reality. Though he yearned with all his proud heart to gather her to him, only his voice touched her.

"It is not lies that trouble you, Brianna, it is truth. The truth that the power of Akora is real, it exists and it must be protected even as it protects us. The truth that you and I are meant to be together as husband and wife. The truth that there is no shadow in you, no spectre of guilt to haunt you with a misplaced fear of unworthiness."

She stood, slim and regal, head high in challenge. "Let us speak of truths. The truth that you expect me to forget how and why my parents died. To set all that aside and serve the very land that cost them their lives. Could you do that, Atreus? If our positions were reversed and it was those you loved dead at British hands, could you set all that aside and love Britain, serve Britain?"

He hesitated, and in that silence she saw truth he could not conceal.

"You cannot imagine doing so," she said. "You certainly have never thought of it. Yet you expect it of me."

"I ask it of you," he corrected. He held out a hand and very gently touched her cheek. "Perhaps it was always too much to ask." Of any woman, to join him in the life he had never chosen for himself, but most especially of her, with whom he shared, did she but know it, truths still un-spoken.

His hand fell away and he with it. He walked swiftly from the garden filled with the dying sun, back into the ancient labyrinthine palace that wrapped him in its remorseless embrace.

Chapter

SEVENTEEN

FOR SOME UNKNOWN TIME AFTER ATREUS left the garden, Brianna remained. She sank down slowly on the bench beside the fountain, her hands tightly clenched. Distantly, she heard the gurgle of water in the fountain and the soft evening song of the birds, but all that made very little impression on her.

Atreus, on the contrary, had made a very great impression. But then he always had, from the very beginning when she watched him step from the ship that brought him to England and felt a surge of joy she could not deny.

Truths, he said, and challenged her to accept them. Yet he also walked away, as though freeing her.

Did she want to be free? Where love existed, was freedom even a possibility?

She did love him, of that she remained entirely sure. If anything, she loved him more knowing now the enormity of what it meant to be the Chosen. His being, the very essence of Atreus, was interwoven inextricably with the land he served. The two could never be separated.

Could she love Akora as she had once thought she did? Could she live that love for every day of the rest of her life? Despite her parents' deaths, despite the lies, despite all her grief?

While yet she believed herself responsible for her parents' deaths, she had been unable to grieve for them properly. But now she could, and the pain was fresh and raw.

She bent her head and watched the tears fall onto her hands. Tomorrow, Atreus would render judgment. Would he put Deilos to death? He was a superbly trained warrior, and she did not doubt that he would kill in battle if the need arose. But to send a man to his death by execution was a different matter. Could he do that?

Death shadowed them both, deaths already done and deaths to come. There was nothing to be done about the past, but the future should not be faced alone.

She stood and brushed her tears aside. As the last of day's light faded and the stars reclaimed the sky, she went from the garden.

Atreus would likely seek solitude. As much as he loved his family, she doubted he would wish company just then. He might go to his quarters, but she thought it more likely he would withdraw to his studio.

She dallied a little, going first to her quarters, where she changed into a fresh tunic and brushed out her hair. At the last moment, about to leave the room, she snatched up a silken stole tossed across the arms of a chair and draped it over her head.

Even then she delayed, walking slowly past the high arched windows looking out across the courtyard, pausing to breathe the evening air that carried the myriad scents of the wood fires burning in the city below, the night-blooming jasmine that clustered in thick bushes against the palace walls, the salty tang of the Inland Sea blown on the wind.

A gentle wind, in no way alarming, no more than a pleasant caress.

She avoided the vast ceremonial rooms and took a small staircase, one known only to the palace residents, whether servants, officials, or Atreides. It brought her to the portico overlooking the courtyard, near to the stairs that led to the roof.

Shortly after coming to the palace she had discovered the roof. It was a world all its own, stretching over the many acres of the palace, planted with its own gardens, crossed by its own paths, which were often the most efficient way of getting from one place to another, and even boasting an observatory from which the stars had been studied for hundreds of years.

The roof would give her an excuse to linger a little while longer, to order her thoughts and, just possibly to find the courage she needed.

But before she could continue on, she noticed a man crossing the courtyard, looking hurried and somehow furtive. When he stepped briefly from the shadows into the moonlight, she saw his face.

Polonus.

She had last seen him at the trial, hanging on Deilos's every word. What was he doing here now?

Curious and more than a little concerned, she turned away from the stairs to the roof and followed Polonus instead.

He was walking very quickly and she had to run a little to avoid losing him altogether. Around a corner of the palace, he disappeared through a small door. Brianna hurried after him but by the time she stepped inside, he was out of sight. She was in a part of the palace she did not know. A corridor ran off into the distance, but several other passageways branched off it.

She stopped, stood very still, and listened, but try though she did, she heard nothing that might reveal which way Polonus had gone. All the same, she could not consider giving up. He was her brother, she loved him, and for all that she feared he was misguided, she would not turn her back on him.

As she continued, she peered down each passageway, but seeing no hint of Polonus, she continued on through the main corridor. It broadened out eventually and she found herself entering a large chamber with a high, arched stone roof. The center of the chamber was sunk a few feet lower than the rest and surrounded by stone benches. Oddly, metal rings protruded from the benches at intervals as though intended to secure something there.

Something . . . or someone? Abruptly, she stopped and listened again. In the distance, beyond the stone chamber, she heard the low murmur of voices.

As she drew closer, the voices became louder. She could make out men talking but there were other sounds as well, the sounds of violent illness. Bewildered, she went a little farther and peered around a corner. A row of cells were set into the stone wall and secured by iron grates. Between the cells there stood a guardpost. It was there that three men, all Akoran warriors, were talking.

Even as she watched, one of the guards hurried off in the opposite direction. The other two turned to regard what was happening inside the cells. She did the same, only to wish she had not. Each cell held a single occupant. She recognized the men who had been tried the previous day and, at the far end, Deilos. All five appeared to be violently ill. They were writhing on the ground, moaning in pain and vomiting.

Caution forgotten, Brianna stepped forward. Although

she had no particular gift for healing, she had received some training from her Aunt Elena, who was a truly gifted healer. Certainly, she knew enough to offer some help. It seemed that these men might be suffering from some sort of poisoning.

That they were prisoners did not matter. Even Deilos, who might soon be under judgment of death, still had a right to proper medical care.

"Lady," one of the guards said when he noticed her, "you should not be here."

"You have sent for help, have you not?"

"Yes, but—" He broke off when she threw back the stole and he saw who she was. At once, he inclined his head. She was known as one of those who had cared for the Vanax and also as one close to the Atreides family. Her presence would not be questioned.

"Lady Brianna, of course your help is welcome."

"Open the cell doors, please." When he hesitated, she said, "You cannot believe any of them is in such condition as to cause you any difficulty."

Truly, it was impossible to imagine that any of the poor wretches could cause difficulty for anyone. Both the guards must have realized that, for they hurried to do as she bid.

"When did this start?" Brianna asked as she bent over one of the men. Distasteful as it was, she did not shirk, but laid a gentle hand on his brow. He showed no sign of fever, even though he rolled his eyes as he looked at her and moaned fitfully.

"Just a few minutes ago, Lady," the guard said.

"When did they eat last?" Judging by what she could see, it could not have been too long ago.

"Dinner was brought half an hour ago."

"Did they all eat the same meal?"

"Yes, I believe so. There was bread, a lamb stew, cheese, wine."

She stood again and looked at the guards. "Did either of you eat the same food?"

Both men shook their heads. "We will eat when we are off duty, Lady."

"No doubt there was something wrong with their meal," Brianna said.

Scarcely had she spoken than the third guard returned, accompanied by her own Aunt Elena, a tall woman of middle years whose strong but pleasant features were framed by snow-white hair.

Elena nodded to her briskly. "Brianna, good, I will need your help. Guards, these men must be moved to the medical quarters."

The senior guard, the same man who had addressed Brianna, spoke with care. "Lady, with all respect, they are prisoners."

"Seriously ill prisoners," Elena corrected briskly. "You know as well as I that by law and custom both they must receive proper care. I cannot provide it here." She looked around at the condition of the cells. "If nothing else, this entire area must be thoroughly cleaned before anyone can be returned to it. Now then, I will send for stretchers."

They arrived quickly, brought by several of Elena's assistants. The five men were placed on them and carried away. The guards accompanied them.

"They became ill shortly after eating," Brianna said as she hurried along beside her aunt.

"Then the meal is the likely culprit, although I cannot remember the last time anyone was sickened by food here."

Neither could Brianna. She had learned the safe ways of handling and preparing food from Leoni, who had not restricted such teachings to her daughter but made sure her sons knew as well. While in England, Joanna and Kassandra both had warned her to be careful what she ate outside their homes, and she had done so. But here on Akora, such caution seemed unnecessary.

Yet the men were undeniably ill. They continued to vomit and writhe as they were carried to the medical quarters of the palace. These were a spacious series of rooms set aside for Elena's use. Her own apartment was nearby, but Brianna knew that her aunt tended to spend most of her time with her patients. Otherwise, she was entirely occupied in studying and teaching.

At the moment, the dozen or so beds in the medical quarters were empty, but, of course, that was about to change. Running down in her mind what would have to be done immediately for the men, Brianna did not realize at once that anything was amiss. It was only when she heard a sudden thud and turned to see one of the guards collapsing to the floor that she understood something was terribly wrong.

She turned just in time to see the other guards ambushed. Struck from behind, both went down hard.

Elena had the presence of mind to run for the cabinet where she kept her surgical implements, many of them very sharp. But before she reached it, Polonus stepped from the shadows and seized her.

"Don't," he said starkly. "I have no wish to hurt you."

"You—" Elena was stunned but no more so than Brianna. Even suspecting as she had that her brother was up to no good, she was still astonished to see him there.

"Polonus, what are you—?"

He did not answer her, but truly he did not have to, for she could see that there were men in the room, perhaps a dozen, some moving swiftly to secure the guards while others helped Deilos and the rest.

"Quickly," Deilos gasped. He got weakly to his feet and accepted a carafe of water one of the men offered him.

Elena stared at him as he drank. "What did you use?" she asked.

"Emetine from your own supply."

"You took a chance," Elena said calmly. "A few drops will bring on vomiting that can rid the body of poison. But more than that can kill."

"As my life is likely already forfeit," Deilos said, "that did not concern me."

His life may be his own, Brianna thought, but what of the others who had also swallowed the potential poison along with him? She had believed them guilty when she heard the evidence against them, and their willingness to follow Deilos proved it. But not for a moment did she think it likely that Atreus would have sentenced them to death. Prison terms, certainly, but with the hope of redemption and eventual freedom.

"It truly did work," Polonus said with evident amazement. "You're free."

"Not yet," Deilos said. He strapped on the sword one of the men handed to him and glanced at Brianna. "Bring her along." Heading for the door, he added over his shoulder, "Kill the rest."

"Kill—?" Polonus stiffened, his exuberence vanishing. "Lord, the guards are unconscious, and my aunt—"

Deilos stopped, turned, and looked at him steadily. "Your aunt will give the alarm as soon as she possibly can. We have no need of her, but this one—" He gestured at Brianna. "She may yet be useful."

When still Polonus stared at him uncertainly, Deilos said, "You are with me or against me, Polonus. Now is the time to decide."

"Don't!" Brianna screamed. Already one of the other men was pulling her away. She struggled frantically, but her strength was no match for him. Her last sight of

Polonus was of him moving toward Elena, his hand on the hilt of his sword.

Shock and disbelief stunned her. Surely this could not be happening. Her aunt . . . the others . . . dying at her brother's hand. Please, by all that was holy, she prayed, do not let it be.

Still struggling, she was dragged along the corridor, through a door, and down a flight of stairs. The man holding her tightened his grip brutally as she continued to struggle. She got an arm free and did not hesitate but slammed her fist into his jaw.

He cursed violently, took hold of her by the chin and struck her head against the stairwell.

She saw pinwheels of revolving light and then nothing at all.

A TREUS?"
      He turned from studying the massive block of rose quartz that had been Brianna's gift to him, and found himself looking at Alex and Royce, standing together just inside the door of the studio.

Before either said a word, he knew.

"Where?" he asked, coming toward them. They were armed, he noted, both wearing swords. Alex carried Atreus's. He strapped it on, listening.

"We aren't entirely sure what happened," Alex said. "But all five prisoners are missing. There are indications of vomiting in the holding area. Apparently, they were taken to the medical quarters. Elena, her assistants, and the guards—"

Atreus listened. He was certain there was more to come.

"Brianna is not in her quarters." Royce spoke. "That may mean nothing . . . or something."

"What else?"

The two men glanced at each other. Quietly, Alex said, "Brianna's brother, Polonus, was seen in a corridor near the holding area a short time ago. Again, it may mean nothing."

"Where do you think he will go?" Atreus asked as they walked quickly from the studio.

Neither man mistook who he meant. "Deimatos," Royce suggested. "The island has belonged to Deilos's family from the beginning and he has used it before."

"Unsuccessfully," Atreus said. "Twice he failed there. And he knows it is the first place we will think of. He will go elsewhere."

Alex nodded. "But where?"

"He knows the hidden passageways beneath Ilius," Royce said. "Those, too, he has used before."

"The question is, what does he want?" Atreus said. "Just to escape, to fight again another day? That, too, he has done without success."

"He is mad," Alex said. "There is no reason behind what he does."

"There is always reason," Atreus replied. "Even in the depths of madness, a twisted reason, to be sure, but reason all the same."

"Then you must think as he does," Royce said quietly. "To determine what he wants."

They stepped through a door into the courtyard. Alex and Royce had given orders before going to find him, knowing as well as he did what would be needed. An army stood waiting for him. The best of Akora, the strongest, the bravest, the most dedicated. The men he had trained with, undergone deprivation with, men he would trust with his life. Men he would die for.

Bathed in moonlight, they stood. Drawn up rank after rank. They were armored, holding their helmets in the crooks of their arms, standing at attention. When they saw him, they cheered.

Their voices rose to heaven, soaring on the wind that had begun to blow with a rare and terrible power.

D AMP. COOL AND DAMP BENEATH HER CHEEK. SHE moved just a little and immediately pain came. A soft moan broke from her.

"She's awake," a voice said. A hard hand turned her over. She looked up, saw faces, but could not recognize them.

"She's barely conscious," another voice said. A man. Someone she had reason to fear.

But the fear was very small compared to the terrible sorrow she felt.

Something was terribly, horribly wrong.

"Sit up." Yet another voice, but she knew this one. Polonus. Her heart leaped. Her brother. If he was there, it could not be so bad, not really.

But wait . . . it was bad . . . very, very bad.

"Polonus—"

"Ssshhh, don't talk. Just sit up." A strong arm around her shoulders, helping her. "Drink this."

The water was cool. She drank thirstily, then remembered. Deilos drinking the water. Deilos vomiting. Deilos—

"Oh, Polonus, why?" She could barely whisper, so great was the pain, but all her fury and grief were in her words.

"I did what I had to." He sounded so young, this brother of hers, but then he always had. Always would?

She wept, despising the tears but unable to stop them. She wept for those already dead and for the dead yet to come. Deilos unloosed would bring terrible things.

Polonus held her, murmured to her, muffled her sobs

against his chest. After a time, he said, "They'll be coming back soon. Don't be afraid."

There was so little light that she could scarcely see him. And she could not understand him at all.

"What?"

"Don't be afraid. I won't let him hurt you."

"But you—" She could not think of what he had done, of them, could not bear it. "You obey him."

"I have believed in him, in what he wants for Akora."

"What does he want, Polonus? What do you think Deilos strives for?"

"To keep Akora safe, to keep us apart, to prevent the rest of the world from infecting us."

He was wrong, of course, terribly wrong. Deilos wanted only power.

"Why would you want to remain apart, Polonus?"

"Because the world is a cruel place. That is why we have to train to fight, isn't it? Why we must always be ready to defend Akora? But the Atreides, they are reaching out too much into the world, becoming too much a part of it. All that is rare and precious here will not survive that."

She thought of the temple and what she had felt there. "Akora is stronger than you know, and the Atreides, Atreus above all, would never do anything to harm our land."

"If only you were right. But he has harmed it. Akora is angry."

"What are you saying? Who told you this?" It must be Deilos, more of his madness, polluting the minds of those weak enough to believe him.

"I have seen for myself." He stiffened suddenly and laid her back down on the ground.

"How is your sister?" Deilos asked, approaching.

"A little better, but not yet herself. I didn't expect anything to happen to her."

"She should not have struggled. You see what occurs when a woman forgets herself."

"Of course, Lord. Even so, I wonder why it was necessary to bring her along."

"Would you rather have killed her with the others?"

Polonus did not reply, but his hands tightened on Brianna.

"She helped to save Atreus's life," Deilos said. "He will feel a duty to try to save hers."

"He would try to save anyone's," she said, faintly to be sure, for the pain in her head still dazed her, but there was steel in her voice.

"Silence," Deilos ordered. "Bring her along, Polonus. See that she does not slow us."

Her brother lifted her, holding her upright with an arm around her waist. "Can you walk?" he asked quietly when Deilos had moved on.

"I have to, don't I?"

"You should not be involved in this," her brother said gruffly. "Why were you in the holding area, anyway?"

"I was looking for you."

He stopped a moment before continuing on. "For me? Why?"

"I saw you crossing the courtyard. I was concerned, worried about what you might be involved in." A faint laugh broke from her. "I couldn't have imagined anything this bad."

"I don't expect you to understand, much less approve, but Deilos is our best hope. We could hardly stand by and let him die."

"Heavens, no, a madman and murderer, let's preserve his life at all costs. But others—" She could not bear to think of them, Elena and the rest, and of Polonus himself, whose soul must surely be doomed.

They went on deeper into the caves. She wondered how

close they might be to the temple, but in the faint light of torches and with her head still throbbing, her sense of direction was gone. She knew only that they were going down.

And that it was getting warmer.

In the caves, it was cool. On hot summer days, she and Polonus had sometimes sought shelter in them near their home on Leios. It was always cool in them and cooler still in the caves beneath the palace.

But not here, not now. Warmth yielded to heat. It was becoming harder to breathe. An acrid smell filled the air, like the sulphur Elena burned to purify a room before surgery took place.

"Polonus . . . what is happening? Why is it so hot?"

"I told you. You didn't want to believe me."

"I don't understand—"

She had never felt heat like this, creeping up out of the earth itself, winding in tendrils of steam through cracks in the ground beneath her feet.

A strange red light appeared some distance ahead of them, growing steadily larger as they approached. She heard a hissing roar, faint at first but becoming louder, as though they were entering the abode of a fiery monster, a dragon perhaps, for what else would live in such a place?

"Akora is angry," her brother said again. He drew her forward to where the passage ended directly above a vast cavern.

Brianna looked down and found herself staring into the mouth of hell.

Chapter

EIGHTEEN

THE MEN WERE DISPATCHED. SOME CAME under the command of Alex to guard Deimatos, in case Deilos did the unexpected after all, and the rest were led by Royce to guard the northern and southern straits leading from the Inland Sea to the ocean. For Deilos, there would be no escape, assuming he sought one.

"I wish I could help," Joanna said. She stood in the courtyard, having just bid farewell to Atreus. Amelia was in her arms. "If I could find Brianna—"

"I do not expect it of you," Atreus said gently. He knew his sister-in-law's gift was—as such gifts always seemed to be—capricious. She had needed all her strength and skill to find Royce when Deilos held him. Since then, she complained she could not find so much as a pin.

Beside her, Kassandra said, "I never thought I would

wish to be able to see the future again, but if I could just glimpse—"

"It would make no difference," Atreus assured her. "As you have said, there are only paths to possible futures. We choose our own fates, all of us together."

As he must choose: stay where he was and wait for some sign of where Deilos had gone or hunt him.

If he chose wrong, precious time would be lost, and with it perhaps any hope of success.

The palace was guarded, not because of the likelihood of an attack but because it had been so guarded for more than three thousand years. It was a tradition no one had ever considered changing.

There were guards on the walls and in the towers, guards who reported seeing no sign of any group of men leaving the palace grounds.

Word had been sent into the city. It was an hour when people were inclined to be lingering over the remnants of dinner often enjoyed on patios outside their homes. The search had only just begun and it was possible there would still be some word of Deilos in Ilius itself, but so far no one reported seeing anything.

No ship had left the harbor. The harbormaster himself was at his dinner, but his eldest son stood the watch at that hour and he was absolutely certain. Indeed, so strong was the wind that Royce and Alex were likely to have difficulty launching their own vessels.

The wind . . .

Eddies of dirt whirled across the courtyard. In the moonlight, Atreus could see white foam on the waves surging against the stone quays in the harbor.

Joanna shielded Amelia's face protectively, hunching her shoulders.

"You should get back inside," Atreus said. He signaled

to the men who formed his personal guard. Several of them took up positions on either side of Joanna and Kassandra.

"Is this necessary?" Kassandra asked.

Securing his sword, Atreus replied, "I think Deilos is still in the palace. It's unlikely he'd make an attempt against either of you, but I want you well protected all the same."

"You really think he's still here?" Joanna asked.

"I think that's rather the point."

As the women returned under escort to the family quarters, Atreus divided the remainder of his men. Some he sent to the caves with instructions to secure them, others to search the passageways that gave access to the beaches below the palace. For himself, he reserved the place he thought Deilos most likely to be.

He chose six men to accompany him, the best of the best. Men he could count on utterly. Men who knew how to hold their tongues.

Atreus led the way back into the palace. He followed the maze of corridors quickly and silently until he came to the door leading to the stairs near the medical quarters. To the casual eye, the stairs ended in what appeared to be an ancient storage room, long unused. To the better informed, what seemed to be an empty wooden rack standing floor to ceiling merely obscured the further length of the passage.

Under ordinary circumstances, the wooden rack would have been snug against the wall. A quick glance showed that it was not. Some effort had been made to move it back into position, but it remained slightly askew. Just enough to tell Atreus his instincts were correct.

"He will have men with him," he said. "Leave them alive if you can, but do not endanger yourselves unnecessarily."

"And Deilos, Lord?" one of the men asked.

"He is mine." Crippled Deilos, lacking his right hand,

the sword hand Royce had taken from him in battle. But formidable all the same. Only a fool would think otherwise.

He led the way, moving quickly but silently. The passage was well known to him. He had come here for the first time shortly after becoming Vanax and had visited regularly ever since. Never had he seen any sign that anyone else knew of it, and he had certainly never spoken of it. But Deilos knew. A discovery in the old records? Knowledge passed down through his family? It didn't matter. All that counted was that he find him—and Brianna—before it was too late.

Behind him, he heard his men, far too well trained and disciplined to reveal their surprise by more than a sharp inhalation of breath.

He sympathized with them, but he was also unrelenting when he said, "You will speak of this to no one."

They murmured their assent and he knew with absolute certainty that they would seal up what they saw, bury it deep within their minds, and not tell a soul. They would do this because they were good men who accepted unflinchingly what it meant to be protectors.

They reached the end of the passageway. Atreus looked out over the vast cavern, felt the heat bore into him, and saw, far below, the surging sea of fire.

"This way," he said and dropped down onto the narrow path running into the hellish landscape.

BRIANNA STUMBLED AND ALMOST FELL. HER LEG brushed against one of the jagged rocks lining the path. She looked down to see blood blossom against the white of her tunic. Numbed by shock and still dazed by the blow to her head, she felt no additional pain. It might as well have all been happening in a dream.

A part of her wanted fervently to believe that she would wake at any moment, but she knew better. Although it violated everything she had ever experienced of the world, she recognized this place in some deep and hidden way.

This was the nightmare vision that lurked behind the beauty of the Fortress Kingdom. The memory all Akorans shared, handed down from one generation to another, recounted in legend, acclaimed in song, the terror gloriously overcome and safely past. Except it was not. It was here, immediate and real.

Close beside her, Polonus said, "You see now why Deilos had to act."

"No, I don't," she gasped, struggling to remain upright. "What has this to do with him?"

"He discovered the volcano has awakened. There is another way into this place, one the Atreides never found but Deilos did. When he saw what was happening, he realized his worst fears were justified. Atreus and all the Atreides are determined to bring us closer to the outside world, but they are wrong to do so. Akora is angered by them, that's why this is happening."

"Polonus, you were a member of Helios. You believed we should become more open—"

"I never believed we should become like the rest of the world. I wanted us all to have a say in our fate instead of it being determined for us by Atreus. But I realize now that was wrong. There is nothing for us to do but return to the old ways, truly honor them, and pray that Akora will relent."

A few days before, she would have said that what they were seeing was a natural phenomena. It had nothing to do with anyone or anything being angry. But since then she had felt the power within the temple. Akora lived, in some vast and eternal sense. Beside that, all things seemed possible.

"Deilos showed you this?"

Polonus nodded. With a young man's self-importance, he said, "Those of us he judged best able to cope with the crisis were taken into his confidence."

"Atreus is best able to cope with this crisis or any other. Don't you see it is only Deilos's overwhelming vanity, his envy of the Atreides, his madness that makes him think he is better suited to lead Akora?"

"I see that what the Vanax is doing is wrong. He will destroy Akora and all of us with it!"

Brianna shook her head despairingly. Polonus would cling to Deilos's lies to absolve the horror of his own actions. She could not reach him, but she could try to prepare herself as best she could for whatever was to come.

Deilos was up ahead, moving quickly as though the heat and fire did not trouble him in the slightest. His men looked considerably less assured, but they followed him all the same.

Polonus had said there was another way in. That meant another way out. Deilos's escape route?

"There is nowhere he can go," she said, "nowhere he can hide."

"He will be protected. You heard him speak, you saw how people responded."

"A few people, very few."

"It doesn't matter. The pure and strong will be drawn to him. His movement will grow. Atreus will not be able to hide this danger forever. When people realize it, they will rally to Deilos."

Granted, her head still throbbed, but even so, she knew this made no sense.

"Why didn't he just tell them?"

Polonus frowned. "What are you talking about?"

"When he was declaiming during the trial, while so many were listening to him, why didn't he tell them about this place then? If he thinks that will bring people to his side, wouldn't he want them to know of this and see it for themselves?"

"He could have done that," Polonus acknowledged. For the first time, a note of uncertainty crept into his voice. But it was gone quickly. "I'm sure Deilos has his reasons."

"None of them good. Oh, Polonus, can't you see—?"

"Brianna, you are my sister, I wish no harm to come to you. But be quiet."

"You wish no harm to come to *me*? What about—?" She could hardly bear to think of what he had done. If Deilos was guilty of nothing else, he deserved the direst punishment for luring her brother down the path of evil.

"Quiet!"

She did as he said, but only because her heart was so burdened by grief that there was nothing more she could say.

They went on, following Deilos farther into the pit. Everywhere Brianna looked, she saw the red glare of lava bubbling up toward the surface. The ground they walked on was just cool enough to be tolerable, but the lava was visible in long, twisted rivelets of fire beneath the cracked earth.

And throughout, steam rose, bringing with it the smell of sulphur.

Her eyes stung. She raised a hand to them and realized she was still wearing her stole, though it had fallen around her shoulders.

Polonus still had hold of her hand, but his attention was focused ahead of them on Deilos and the other men.

She had only a very small hope that anyone would come this way, but any hope was better than none at all. Casting a careful glance at Polonus, she shrugged lightly. The stole slipped just enough for her to grab one end in her free hand. Slowly, she pulled, bunching the fabric up against her side. She took a breath, let it go on a prayer, and dropped the stole.

"Come on," Polonus said and pulled her along.

ATREUS MOVED QUICKLY THROUGH THE SEARED landscape, his men close behind him. He stopped only once to watch a plume of fire erupt from the lava, spewing upward almost to the roof of the cavern. Within seconds, the plume died away and none other followed it, but he could see his men's unease and spoke to calm them.

"Look there, above us. See how the stones are blackened? There have been many plumes like that one. They leave their mark but they do no harm."

The men nodded but their gazes remained watchful as they followed Atreus deeper into the pit.

It needed care to move through such a place, but care cost time and urgency drove him. The path twined around the edge of the cavern before moving deeper within it, but there was a quicker way, straight across the middle where what looked like solid ground could easily be no more than simmering crust.

"Go that way," he said to his men and pointed to the path. "I'll meet you on the other side."

"Vanax—"

Never had he had to repeat an order, but under the circumstances, he could not truly blame them for hesitating. "Go," he said firmly. Without waiting for the obedience he knew would come, he jumped a chasm and moved on.

He had gone only a little way before he misjudged a step. Putting his foot down, he saw it go right through what had looked like solid ground but was not. Fire licked at the sole of his sandal as he pulled it out and only just managed to leap away. Farther on, a plume of fire singed his left arm but he scarcely noticed. He was halfway across the pit, well ahead of his men, when he saw a flash of white against the landscape of black and red.

He reached it, but not before almost going into the fire twice more. Seizing the stole, he held the length of scented silk close to his face and breathed in deeply.

Brianna. She lived. Joy filled him, but only for an instant. Deilos had her. With a low curse, he moved on.

Minutes later, he caught sight of them. Deilos had a dozen men with him in addition to Polonus, who was closest to Brianna. She appeared pale and dazed, but otherwise unharmed. But even as he watched, Deilos called out. Polonus hesitated a moment but then brought his sister over to where Deilos was standing.

"Idiot," Atreus muttered under his breath. He had no real idea of what drove the younger man and frankly did not care. At the moment, nothing mattered except Brianna.

And Deilos, who had taken hold of her and was gesturing deeper into the cavern.

T HE PATH HAS CHANGED," DEILOS SAID. "THE ground is shifting. What was safe before is no longer." He yanked Brianna forward. "You, woman, move ahead. We will follow."

"Lord," Polonus began.

"Do not dispute me, boy! Sentiment is a weakness no true man will tolerate."

Brianna swallowed terror, clung to hope. All she could see ahead of her was thin crust and looming fire. To try to go on was madness. But if she refused—

Polonus moved between her and Deilos. "Lord, I will go first."

"You? You can fight, I presume? I am not willing to lose you."

"She is my sister—"

"What have I said? Did I not speak clearly enough? Are you a fool to dispute me?"

"She is a woman, to be protected."

"She is a woman, to serve, and she damn well will!"

Without further delay, Deilos shoved Brianna off the path. At once, fire licked at the hem of her tunic. She cried out and yanked the fabric away, but not before it was scorched.

"Move," Deilos ordered. "Or die where you stand."

Polonus's hand went to the hilt of his sword. "Lord—"

"Deilos!"

Atreus stood a dozen yards away, sword drawn. He was alone, surrounded by fire and smoke as though he had just stepped from the bowels of the earth. At sight of him, Brianna's heart leaped with joy, but an instant later, dread filled her.

Alone. Oh, God, he was alone.

"Atreus, no!"

He ignored her and kept coming, through the smoke, right at them. "Let her go, Deilos."

"How touching," Deilos sneered. "What did I say to you about sentiment, Polonus. Watch a man die for it."

"Atreus, go back!" He could not do this, she would not let him. Akora needed him, depended on him. Too well she remembered the terrible pall that hung over the people in the days and nights following the attempt on his life. They could not suffer that again. She could not suffer it.

Instinctively, she moved toward him, but scarcely had she taken a step than Deilos grabbed hold of her. His disfigured right arm was hard against her throat. In his left hand he held a knife.

"Drop your sword, Atreus, or she dies!"

"No!" Brianna screamed again, but it was too late. Without hesitation, without the slightest flicker of doubt,

Atreus opened his hand and let his sword fall to the ground. He stood before Deilos unarmed, without even the protection of armor.

Deilos laughed in triumph and called out to his men. "Take him!"

They rushed to obey but before any could reach him, Atreus's own men came out of the darkness, swords drawn. Deilos's men had the advantage of numbers, but they were far outmatched in skill and sheer ferocity. Quickly, the tide turned against them.

Deilos howled in rage and backed up, dragging Brianna with him. No path appeared, save into the fire. He stopped and screamed, "Call off your men!"

"So that they can see you hide behind a woman?" Atreus asked. He came toward them, unarmed, seemingly unconcerned. He did not so much as glance at where he walked, but for him, the ground held firm and the fires remained at bay.

"Let her go, Deilos."

"So that she lives and I die? I think not."

The knife scraped against her throat. Brianna closed her eyes, said a silent prayer—

"No!"

Another's voice, not Atreus's. She was free suddenly, knocked away from Deilos and rolling toward the fire, only just managing to stop herself by digging her fingers into the ground and holding on for dear life.

Deilos was screaming—again. Polonus had hold of him. Her brother had lost his sword but seemed intent on strangling the man he had been willing to follow into the pits of hell.

"You will not kill my sister!" With each word, he slammed Deilos's head down against the ground.

She scrambled to her feet as Atreus leaped across the distance still separating them. He was almost, but not quite, in time. Deilos gave a mighty heave, threw Polonus off, and drove his knife into him.

"Polonus!" All her love for her poor, misguided brother was in that single, anguished scream. She rushed to him, heedless of how close Deilos remained, her only thought to stanch the blood pouring into the earth. The knife protruded from Polonus's chest just above his abdomen. His hands were clenched around it. He looked down at the gleaming hilt and the dark pool soaking his tunic with an expression of disbelief.

"Brianna—" he said softly.

She would have answered him, would have done anything to help him, no matter what crimes he had committed. But in her desperation she had made a terrible mistake. Deilos moved with speed that seemed beyond that of ordinary men. Before she realized his intent, he had hold of her again.

"Back, Atreus," Deilos ordered. "I need no knife to kill her. She will go into the fire before you can have a hope of reaching her."

Atreus stopped but his eyes never left her. His men were dealing with those of Deilos's who remained alive. Polonus writhed at her feet. A plume of fire leaped high.

And was bent as wheat bends before the wind.

It rose in her, she felt it coming, and for once in her life, she welcomed it. The gift that had been a curse, the shame of her childhood, the terror that had haunted her came gloriously and triumphantly whirling out of the unseen world, summoned at her most desperate hour.

"Wind . . ." she whispered and the sound howled, down the long reaches of the cavern, through the passageways, up past the cracks in the fiery ground.

Wind, breath of the earth. Flame bowed before it, sparks shooting off in great whirling vortexes that soared as angels might over all.

Brianna—

She saw Atreus speak her name but she could not hear him. There was only the wind, in her, around her. Her hair was flame of its own, streaming out behind her. Her tunic was flattened to her. She could not breathe. Only a step, the merest step, and the wind would take her.

Brianna, drop! He spoke in her mind and in her heart, this man she loved so dearly.

She stretched out a hand, yearning to touch him, just once more, one last time—

Drop!

The command, born of love, strengthened by trust, reached across the chasm of the wind and took hold within her.

She fell, away from Deilos, onto the ground that received her with the gentle warmth of a mother.

Atreus moved, flowing like the wind itself. He seized Deilos, who fought with the strength of ten, a madman's screams pouring from him. They struggled, lit by fire and smoke.

Atreus was by far the bigger and stronger man, and seemed to have the advantage. But just then Deilos—always clever, always the survivor—reached beneath his tunic and drew from it a small, lethal dagger.

"Die," he said and smiled.

The dagger surged downward and would have struck directly at Atreus's heart had not the wind leaped even higher, knocking Deilos off balance.

Knocking off his aim as well.

The dagger grazed Atreus's arm. Deilos darted back, cursing. "Damn you!"

"You cannot win," Atreus said quietly. "It's over, Deilos, accept that."

"And let you decide my fate? I think not."

He looked behind him at the seething fire, forward

again to the sight of his men dead or in captivity. Raw hatred lit his eyes.

His gaze shifted to Brianna. "How touching that he came for you and yet how strangely right."

He was babbling, maddened by the nearness of final defeat. Yet she could not look away from him or shut out his words.

"What has he told you?" Deilos demanded. "What do you know, *xenos* woman, of how you came to Akora?"

He laughed suddenly, as though it was all an immense joke. "Did he tell you we were there that day, the day your parents died?"

He was a hideous, evil man who wanted to destroy everything that was good and just. Nothing he said should mean anything to her. Instinctively, she looked to Atreus. He was watching her carefully, his eyes filled with sorrow.

In the midst of fiery heat, she was suddenly cold.

"The French admiral was a fool," Deilos declared. "He sought glory but had not the means to achieve it. Still, it was an honorable battle. It tested us well."

Despite her best resolve, Brianna could not remain silent any longer. Her mouth moved stiffly. "What are you saying?"

"We were in warrior training together, Atreus and I, part of the same company. Didn't he tell you that? Atreus, how remiss of you. But perhaps I do you a disservice. Perhaps it is modesty that has kept you silent."

To Brianna he said, "He was the hero of the day, acclaimed by all. Had any young man, still in training, ever proven himself so able? Ever fired cannon with greater accuracy? Granted, he was the Vanax's grandson, and perhaps there were some eager to see the best in him because of that. But to be fair, he deserved their praise. In the midst of battle, as the wind rose, the French Admiral might have had a chance to withdraw had not Atreus acted with such deadly skill."

Deilos grinned, delighted by her dawning horror. "He killed your parents, sweet Brianna. His was the hand that sent them to their deaths. Do you still hear their screams?"

She did, God help her, she did.

Deilos saw the answer stark upon her face. He threw back his head and laughed.

Laughing still, he turned and leaped into the flames.

Chapter

NINETEEN

I T WAS A TIME OF DREAMS. OF THE DISTANT
sense of cool linen beneath her limbs and cool water
between her lips. Of soft breezes and quiet voices.

She woke once and smelled jasmine. It was night.
Through the high arched window opposite the bed, she
saw the sickle moon.

A hand touched her face. She turned her head, saw . . .
Elena?

Dreams.

"I longed for a daughter, prayed for one. My sons were
always precious to me, of course, but a daughter—" It was
Leoni's voice, soft, dearly familiar.

"She was so frail when she came to us, so lost. I slept beside her for weeks. It was for her, but for me as well. I
needed to see her when I woke in the night, to know she
breathed still."

All this she heard in the way of dreams, fragments

falling like petals on a sea of unconsciousness, drifting lightly, descending. This and more.

"She will recover."

"Will she, now that she knows what was kept hidden from her?"

SHE DRIFTED, SEEKING FORGETFULNESS. THE NIGHT aged and she wept, hearing her own sobs as though from a distance.

Someone wiped her face, held her.

"Brianna, hush."

A different voice, not Leoni's. Delphine?

A woman sang softly. *"Sleep, my child, let peace surround you, all through the night . . ."*

Lady Hollister was right, her mother had a beautiful voice. It had died with her, yet lived still in memory.

They were on a beach, somewhere in France? It was near the house where they were staying. Her father had made a fire. They were seated beside it, Brianna in her mother's lap. The night air was cool but she was safely warm, snuggled in a blanket. Overhead, the stars drifted.

Her father laughed, a robust sound all in itself enough to fill her with happiness.

She smiled and tasted the salt of her tears.

". . . all through the night . . ."

Dark night of the soul. She was beyond horror, beyond shock. Even pain was muted. This was the fabric of life, moments of joy interwoven with loss. She saw Deilos go once more into the flames and sank deeper, welcoming oblivion.

* * *

W HEN SHE OPENED HER EYES AGAIN, IT WAS daylight. Joanna sat beside her. She was reading, but looked up quickly when Brianna stirred.

"What—" Was that her voice? That weak croak?

"Easy." Joanna set her book aside and put an arm around Brianna's shoulders, helping her sit up.

But she did not want help, not from any of them.

"You've had a hard time," Joanna said, frowning slightly when Brianna stiffened, moved away from her.

"Atreus—?" She forced herself to speak.

"He is with the Council. How do you feel?"

How did she feel? "As though I am apart from myself." Where she preferred to be. The sense of disconnection protected her at least a little.

"Polonus—" She saw him for a moment, the hilt of the knife protruding from his chest, and bit her lip hard.

"Hush," Joanna said gently and pulled the pillows up behind her. "He is gravely injured, I will not tell you otherwise, but Elena believes he will recover."

"Elena?" This at least pierced her cherished numbness.

"She said you might not know she lives and the others as well. Polonus did not harm them."

"I thought he had. I thought him capable of killing them when Deilos ordered it."

"From what I have been told, it is understandable that you would fear that. But he did not and he protected you."

When Brianna said nothing, Joanna frowned. "Sida has been back and forth a dozen times to see if you are awake. She thinks to tempt your appetite."

"I am not hungry." But she was, and the realization surprised her. Slowly, inevitably, she was settling back into herself.

"How long have I slept?" she asked as Joanna went toward the door.

"Almost a full day. You needed it."

Still, it was odd to think a day of her life was gone and she with scant sense of it. Stirring slightly in the bed, she winced.

"There is a cut on your leg," Joanna said, returning. "Elena has dressed it and says it likely will heal without a scar. There are also a few burns on your feet and ankles, but they, too, will heal."

"Burns . . ." Images flowed back into her mind. For a moment, she felt a flash of heat and thought she caught a whiff of sulphur. "Do you know where I was? Where we were?"

"Atreus carried you up out of the caverns. I assumed you were there." She looked at Brianna questioningly, but did not go so far as to ask how she could have come to be burned there.

"Yes, of course, the caverns." Atreus was so very good at keeping secrets, it was no surprise he kept this one. Yet how long could he hope to manage that and why should he? Perhaps there was time to do something, to flee, but to where? But how could they leave Akora—especially knowing, as she did now, of the extraordinary power dwelling there?

"Come back," Joanna said gently. "You seem miles away."

"I could use a bath." She tossed the covers back and swung her legs over the side of the bed. Rising, she thought for a moment that she lacked the strength to stand. But a deep breath and a firm straightening of the spine cured that.

"Do you need help?" Joanna asked.

"No," Brianna said and shut the bathroom door behind her.

* * *

WHEN SHE CAME OUT, JOANNA HAD GONE. Leoni was in her place. Her mother was taking dishes from a tray and setting them on a table near the bed. Seeing her, Leoni smiled. At least, her lips did. Her eyes were cautious.

"Was it wise to bathe alone? Joanna says you are weak."

"I am fine. How is Polonus?"

Leoni's generous mouth tightened. "Lucky to be alive. Marcus has been with him and your other brothers are coming from Leios. He has said little and none of it makes any particular sense."

"He believed in Deilos."

"He followed a madman. My son . . . I thought I knew him."

"We are all mysteries to one another."

There was bread and honey, a mild cheese, slices of chicken, and an apple tart. Food to comfort and sustain.

She took a little of the bread, broke it between her fingers. Her mouth was very dry.

"Why did he follow Deilos, Brianna? Polonus was closest to you. Did he say anything—?"

Because the confusion and uncertainty of youth overwhelmed him? Because he could see no clear path for himself? Because the revelation of Akora's precarious state sent him over the edge?

"You should ask the Vanax, Mother. He knows all."

"The Vanax? He will have to decide what is done with Polonus and the others from Helios."

She had almost forgotten them, the trial seemed so long ago.

"Were you a member of Helios?" Leoni asked suddenly.

"What makes you think that?"

"I am not blind; I saw your discontent. You used to go

off sometimes when you thought no one was noticing. Elena said that continued once you came to Ilius."

"You did not think to stop me?"

Her mother filled a goblet with water and handed it to her. "I thought you needed to test your wings."

She swallowed the water and the bread with it. A little more strength came back to her.

"I wish I had wings to fly away from here."

It was cruel and she knew it. Leoni winced, but a moment later she smiled gently. "You blame us for not telling you."

It was not a question, but Brianna felt compelled to answer all the same. "It isn't blame I feel, not exactly. It's more bewilderment. I always trusted you. It never occurred to me to do otherwise."

"And you believe Marcus and I betrayed you by keeping silent. Well, perhaps you are right." At Brianna's small start of surprise, Leoni said, "It is all well and good to say we did it for your sake, so you would be better able to settle into your new life. There is even truth in that, but it is not the whole truth, as you must know. We wanted you to accept us, to love us, with no shadow to prevent that. Most particularly, I wanted it. The idea of telling you how your parents died filled me with fear. When news came back from England that no family of yours could be found there, I thought it meant I was right to keep silent."

She sat down slowly, a wistful sadness playing across her face. "I was terribly wrong; I see that now and I am most sorry."

Brianna lowered herself into the chair across from her mother. She stared at Leoni, seeing what was so dearly familiar but also seeing more. The woman within the mother. The being of hopes and dreams, yearnings and frailties very much like her own self.

"You wanted a daughter."

"Oh, yes, I did. After the boys were born, Marcus and I tried three times more. Twice I miscarried early on, the third I managed to reach five months but that was not enough and he, too, died."

"I knew nothing of this."

"Why speak of it? Except now I think I must. Elena told me I would be very wrong to try to have any more children. She reminded me of my responsibilities to the children I already had and to Marcus, who had sworn he would never touch me again unless we took steps to avoid another pregnancy. It was very difficult for me to give up the hope of a daughter, but I thought I had done so until suddenly, there you were."

The memory brought a tender smile. "There *you* were, Brianna. Not just any daughter, but you. You were so very brave. That was what I knew about you before I knew anything else and I never had reason to think otherwise. Through all the long months while you struggled to regain your strength, to learn to walk again, to adapt to a new country and a new home, you never once complained or faltered. You simply got up every morning and did as you needed to do."

"I had no choice."

"Of course you did. You were a child. No one expected you to carry the burden alone and you did not, but your courage was extraordinary, all the same."

Despite herself, Brianna smiled. "I think perhaps you see me with a mother's eyes."

"Of course I do, and what of it? You don't believe that nonsense about mothers only seeing the best in their children, do you? Let me tell you, no one sees as clearly as a mother. We know every little scrape and bruise, inside and out. We see strength and weakness equally well."

She sighed. "All the same, I did not see Polonus as well as I should have."

"You cannot blame yourself for that. You gave him the same chance you gave me and all of us, to test our wings."

"His proved frail."

"Yet he lives, grace to God and Aunt Elena's skill. Let us be glad of that."

Leoni nodded. She wiped her eyes and reached out a hand to her daughter.

"I will say again, I am sorry for my part in the pain that has come upon you. If I could take it from you, I would do so gladly."

When she could trust herself to speak, Brianna said, "Never would I wish you any pain."

They sat a little while longer before going together to see Polonus.

HER BROTHER WAS A PALE WRAITH OF HIS former self. All his young's man assurance was gone, replaced by stark endurance.

"Brianna," he said and tried to smile, though the effort cost him.

The sight of him suffering so filled her with sorrow but she concealed it and spoke briskly. "Look at you. Not bad, I suppose, for a man nearly cleaved in two."

"By rights, I should not be here."

"You owe your aunt much," Leoni said, taking refuge in sternness.

"Skill helped," Elena acknowledged, "but luck played its role. Another inch to the left and we would have lost him."

Leoni's eyes flashed. "Damn Deilos, may he find the hell he so richly deserves."

Brianna met her brother's gaze. Silently, she shook her head. He inclined his very slightly in understanding. Both knew Deilos had come as close to hell as any mortal man could, wherever he might be now. Neither of them would speak of it.

Marcus came a short time later. He looked at his youngest son and sighed deeply. "Polonus, there is much I would say to you but I have no words."

"Father, I am sorry—"

"That is a beginning, I suppose. Brianna, I was told you needed to rest."

"I did that. Now I need to do other things." Although she was singularly unclear as to what those might be.

"The Vanax remains with the Council," Marcus said. "There is speculation about the sentences he will impose, but no actual news."

"Whatever he decides," Polonus said, "it will be just." He spoke without fear, a man accepting of his fate.

"He should sleep now," Elena told them, but did not shoo them out.

Marcus and Leoni lingered, but once Polonus drifted off, Brianna did not remain. She went alone to the garden where Atreus had found her. Had it been only two days ago? Was that possible? It seemed a lifetime ago.

Though the day was fair and the birds eager, she stayed only a short time. The peace and beauty of the place grated on her nerves. She went down to the port, along the winding streets that led from the palace to the quays. People were going about their ordinary business. Housewives tended the gardens that held pride of place in every home, swept walkways, beat carpets, kept careful track of those children young enough to be underfoot, and exchanged greetings with one another. Many did all this while also managing market stalls beside their homes, spilling over with all manner of goods. Several recognized her as being from the palace and nodded in a friendly way. She smiled in response but did not linger. By no account could she be considered good company just then.

In the port, she walked along an empty stone quay green with lichen, rough with barnacles, stopping finally at the distant end jutting out into the water. There she sat, her legs dangling over the edge, and stared across the Inland Sea.

In her imagination, she could see Leios, place of plains, home these past sixteen years. Home still?

She turned the thought over in her mind but quickly knew the answer. Home in memory only. She would find no contentment there now. Yet it was precious to her all the same, it and all of Akora. Despite all that had happened, she loved it still.

And Atreus?

At once, her mind shied away. She could not think of him, not yet, not without hearing Deilos again and again.

He killed your parents, sweet Brianna.

She was not sweet; indeed, she despised the very notion. She was a woman of courage and fortitude. Her mother had told her so. Pray Leoni was right, for she needed to be both courageous and strong.

Off in the distance, she saw the mast of a bull's head vessel plowing the waters of the Inland Sea. It was too far away to know for sure but she thought it was making for the southern inlet. Where might it be bound? Akora's interests were far-flung, if discreet. It could be making for Europe or the Americas, Asia perhaps or Africa. Or it might simply be on patrol, one of the numerous vessels that kept the Fortress Kingdom inviolate.

Protecting it from vain French admirals seeking glory.

Atreus had been fifteen. She had made the calculation in her mind some time before but hadn't thought of it until then.

Fifteen.

At fifteen, she was helping Leoni around the house and Marcus in the stables. The summer of that year, her favorite mare birthed a colt that went on to win every race on Leios and take the gold cup in the stakes held every fall in Ilius. She had not gone to that, although she had been sorely tempted. The storm she thought she remembered, and the guilt that roared within it, still held her chained.

Fifteen—struggling with geometry, arguing philosophy with Polonus, ignoring the appreciative glances of the local boys who seemed suddenly to all be shooting up, gaining inches overnight.

At fifteen, Atreus had been called upon to be a man. Grandson of the Vanax, he must have known great things were expected of him. Plunged into a situation he could not have anticipated, he had nonetheless acted in a manner that fulfilled his duty and reassured Akorans that the Atreides line bred true.

What had he done when it was over? And how curious to think of that. While she lay washed up on a beach, broken and near death, what had he done?

Celebrate? She had never known there to be any celebration on Akora when enemies were defeated. It did not happen often, but there had been an incident only a few years before—the French again—but this time truly bent on conquest. She remembered hearing of their defeat and of the survivors settled on Akora, grateful for the release from war-torn Europe. But there was no boasting, no revelry, only acceptance of the price that must be paid to keep Akora free.

Safe in Akora, glad to be Akoran, she had never questioned that price. But now it had become acutely, agonizingly personal.

He killed your parents.

His the hand on the fuse, his eye steady and clear, his will unswerving. The Vanax in making, the Chosen to come. Had he fired more than once? To destroy a vessel with a single shot was possible but highly unlikely. He must have called out the orders to reload the cannon, all the while keeping the prey in sight. Must have waited, calculated, and fired again.

Fifteen.

The same length of years passed again before he discovered who she was. His intended bride, so he believed, orphaned by his act.

Had he ever, even once, thought that he should leave her in peace, not pursue her out of simple decency for the memory of those he had killed?

The sea had no answers, nor did the gulls whirling overhead. She stayed where she was until the chill of dusk sent her back up the winding road to the palace.

Y OUR MOTHER," ELENA SAID, "WILL NOT THANK me if your recovery is slowed because you are assisting me."

"I will not recover lying in bed," Brianna countered. "I helped you before I left for England. Surely I can do so again?"

"Polonus does need care," Elena acknowledged reluctantly, "and your presence seems to cheer him."

Her brother remained in great pain despite the drugs Elena had given him. More would endanger him, as he understood.

"The pain means I'm alive," he said with a strained smile. "I keep reminding myself of that and then it doesn't seem so bad."

Brianna stirred the soup she was helping him to eat, a little more to cool it. "You were incredibly brave."

He started to laugh, caught himself when the pain was too great, and shook his head. "I was incredibly stupid, listening to Deilos's nonsense. But I tell you—not in my own defense, for I have none—there was something about the man. He spoke with such conviction. He seemed to have all the answers, to understand everything."

She spooned a little of the soup into his mouth. "And he seemed to love Akora."

Polonus swallowed, nodded. "That's what I thought. When he took us down into the pit, showed us what was happening, that was the first time I truly realized how much Akora means to me. I always thought of myself as not fitting in, not being good enough, but suddenly that didn't matter."

He ate a little more of the soup and looked at her. "How many people know, do you think?"

She had wondered that herself. "Not very many, or we would have heard of it."

"I can't imagine how—or why—the Vanax has kept this to himself."

"Perhaps he knows there is nothing to be done."

"But that can't be true. We are a seafaring people. We have enough boats of various kinds to evacuate everyone if we had to."

"And go where? The world is at war . . . Europe, America, people are in conflict everywhere. It is only here we live in peace."

He sighed and leaned his head back against the pillows. Brianna set the soup aside and settled the covers over him. He looked older, she thought, and not only because of his injury. In the last few days, he had confronted evil and defied death. The experience had stripped away the naïveté of childhood that hitherto had clung to him.

"You should sleep now."

"It is good of you to be here."

No, she might have said, it is selfish. It keeps me from other things. But he had drifted off, and, at any rate, she would not burden him with her own concerns.

Even so, they remained with her as she sat beside him,

holding his hand gently, keeping him connected to the world beyond pain and death.

She was still there when her father came. Marcus's face softened as he looked at his youngest son.

"How is he?"

"Better, I think. He is in pain but there is nothing more to be done for it and he bears it well."

"The Vanax has rendered judgment on the four from Helios who conspired in the attempt to kill him."

"What is their fate?"

"Imprisonment until such time as a panal of magistrates, clergy, ordinary citizens, and members of their own families agree they are fit to live among us once again."

Brianna nodded. She did not find it strange that the prisoners' own families would have a say in if and when they eventually were released. It was those families to which they would return when they were free again. If they came without being truly redeemed, they would bring trouble with them.

"And Polonus?" she asked softly.

"The Vanax has not spoken of that yet, but I did meet with him. He said he would take into consideration the fact that Polonus saved your life." Marcus paused. He drew up a chair and sat next to his daughter.

"Brianna . . . what is there between you and the Vanax?"

The question sent a bolt of shock through her. She looked away quickly before her father could see the full extent of her surprise.

"Father—"

"I know," he said hastily, anticipating her reaction. His normally tanned complexion was ruddied and he looked singularly uncomfortable. "You would probably rather discuss this with your mother, and truth be told, I'd rather that as well. But I am here, you are here, and it falls to me. So I ask again, what is there?"

"Why do you think——?"

"Brianna, I am a man. I saw how the Vanax looked when he spoke of you."

"He spoke of me?"

"When he acknowledged that Polonus saved your life."

"Atreus saved my life, too, although I am quite sure he would not tell you that. He threw aside his sword when Deilos threatened to kill me if he did not."

Marcus's brows rose. "Threw aside his sword? It doesn't surprise me. Is that why he was injured?"

She nodded, seeing again the dagger in Deilos's hand, striking at Atreus's heart. Elena had taken pity and informed her that the wound was minor and Atreus scarcely aware of it. But the thought of what might have been still lingered in her mind.

Marcus was watching her. "I see," her father said. His hand, big and hard, covered hers. "Life is precious, love is rare. That is the extent of my wisdom."

She smiled past tears that never seemed far from the surface these days. "Then I would say you are wise indeed."

He muttered gruffly and embraced her.

AFTER THAT, IT BECAME A MATTER OF WAITING. The Vanax was with his counselors. The Vanax was meeting with members of Helios. Member of Helios and the counselors were meeting with each other.

There would be changes; the sense of that was in the air. People clustered in small groups around the palace and in the city beyond, debating among themselves. Sometimes the discussions grew heated, but generally they did not.

There was deeply rooted trust that the Vanax would make the right choices.

Brianna prayed she would do the same.

On the evening of the third day after emerging from the pit, she went in search of Atreus. He was not in his studio, where she thought she might find him, and he was not in the caverns beneath the palace, where she went when she could not find him anywhere else.

Alone in the temple, she hesitated before touching her hand lightly to the stone face wreathed in moss. That she felt only cool dampness did not surprise her, but the memory of what she had felt through Atreus still resonated within her.

So, too, did the memory of what they had shared in this place.

A soft murmur of air moved through the temple, brushing lightly against the skirt of her tunic. She lingered a little while longer, surprised by the sense of ease that seeped over her. So comfortable was she that she might have fallen asleep if the need to find Atreus had not grown even stronger within her.

Was she bold enough to seek him in his quarters, as she had done once before? Rather than consider that, she looked up at the glory of the star-strewn sky. The moon had shrunk to little more than a knife edge of light, scarcely dimming the constellations. As she watched, a meteorite arced across the heavens before disappearing from sight.

It was a night for stargazing. Akora's astronomers, that dedicated band of men and women who slept by day and worked by night, would be at the observatory. But there was all the rest of the palace roof to wander over.

She climbed the stairs quickly but paused at the top. There were no lights on the roof, for they could interfere with the astronomers's vision. Even so, once her eyes adjusted she could see well enough to go on.

She went toward the side of the roof that looked out over Ilius and was sitting there when she realized she was no longer alone.

"I've been looking for you," Atreus said.

Starlight illuminated the carved planes and angles of his face, the broad sweep of his shoulders and chest, the easy grace with which he moved.

Yearning filled her. Rather than lose the struggle to control it, she returned to her contemplation of the stars. "I was looking for you. How are the meetings going?"

He laughed dryly and sat down beside her, stretching out his long legs in front of him. "They are going. That's about the best to be said for them."

She did look at him then, concerned. "Helios and the counselors cannot agree?"

"Oh, they can agree, all right. Each side agrees the other is arrogant, presumptuous, and pig-headed."

"Have they made any progress at all?"

He thought for a moment. "They're shouting less, but it may be that their throats are sore."

"Atreus—" She was still hesitant but the question had to be asked. "Why go to all this trouble to change Akora when the situation is the way it is?"

He looked genuinely surprised. "The situation?"

"The volcano."

He did not respond at once.

"I know what I saw," she said.

Incredibly, he smiled. "And you concluded that Akora is in danger?"

"Isn't it?"

"Brianna, the lava flow you saw has been there for over three thousand years. It appeared within a few decades of the Cataclysm. It is not spoken of because to do so would cause unnecessary anxiety such as you have felt, but every Vanax since the first to discover it has watched it carefully, as I do now. It waxes and wanes, sometimes larger than what you saw, sometimes smaller, but it remains in balance—for want of a better word—with all the rest of Akora."

A vast bubble of relief rose in her. Softly, she said, "I should have known."

"That I would not conceal a danger to Akora? That I would do everything necessary to protect our people? Yes, you should have known."

"Atreus, I'm sorry—" She felt the perfect fool. Deilos had used the threat of the lava flow to convince people like her brother that Akora was angry with Atreus's rule. She would never have believed that, but she had accepted that the danger was real.

He brushed aside her effort at contrition. "There's no reason to apologize. The fact is I came looking for you to offer my own apology." He took a breath, let it out slowly. "Brianna, you must know how sorry I am about what happened to your parents."

"I know you were doing your duty." She spoke very low and in the speaking knew it was so. He had been and she did know. Life could be very hard that way. Sometimes good people died through no fault of their own.

"I was, but it doesn't absolve me of what happened or of how I was willing to mislead you."

To consider a harsh reality in the privacy of her own mind was one thing, she discovered. To hear it spoken out loud, starkly admitted, was quite another.

"Duty again," she said.

"Yes, duty to Akora. It's all I've thought about since I became Vanax. Knowing as I did how completely I did not want the job, I thought I had to work especially hard to do it well."

"You do do it well."

"Perhaps, but it is also necessary that I do well as a

man." He was silent again for several moments. When he spoke again, his voice was deep and gentle, but with an odd note of sorrow she did not understand at first.

"I could not have defeated Deilos without your help."

"Not true. I am sure you would have found a way." He would always find a way to protect Akora, to do what was right. They all counted on him for that and he never let anyone down. She could not imagine that he ever would.

But Atreus, it seemed, felt otherwise. "I don't think so. It was given to me to see you during the trial of selection for a purpose. I think the two of us needed to come together to defeat Deilos. While we did not marry, we did do what was necessary."

What was he saying? This was not what she intended when she went in search of him, definitely not. "What *was* necessary?"

Silently, he nodded. She saw him do it, there in starlight, saw the proud head bend in agreement. Even so, she needed to be told.

"You are saying there is no longer any reason for us to marry?"

He took a breath, held it for a moment, let it go. "Unless you are with child?"

"No," she said and pushed away treacherous regret. "I am not."

"Then you are free. When Polonus is healed, he can join you in England. A time away from Akora, seeing more of the world, would benefit him, and you would have his company."

"You are exiling him."

"It is exile or imprisonment, and I thought the former would be better."

"For him, perhaps. What of me?"

He sounded surprised that she would ask. "You will always be free to return to Akora whenever you choose. But it must be your choice, if the day ever comes when you can put aside the shadows of the past."

He stood and touched his hand very lightly to her shoulder. "When I came for you in England, there was no thought in my mind of giving you any choice, even though I knew that I at least shared responsibility for your parents' deaths. You said I had become something less than human and I think in some way you were right."

"I spoke in haste." Stupid, foolish haste.

"You spoke truthfully. You also objected to lies of omission. What is not said, what is not done can be every bit as hurtful as actions that are taken. I would have no omissions between us. You must be free to make the right choice for yourself."

How very noble of him. She moved away from his touch, stood in chill moonlight. "And what about you, Atreus? Doesn't this choice you are giving me make you free as well?"

"I am Vanax. Freedom is not for me."

A moment longer he looked at her, then he was gone. She stood alone beneath the sea of stars.

She had wished for wings that she might leave Akora. Atreus had given them to her.

Chapter

TWENTY

H E HAD DONE IT. THOUGH IT HAD COST
him more dearly than anything he had ever
done in his life, he had set her free. She deserved nothing less and he could give her
nothing more. He had helped to take her parents' lives;
hers would be her own.

But the cost . . . Damn, he hurt. It wasn't true hearts
could break, not literally, but he felt as though his were being crushed.

He went quickly, knowing if he delayed a moment his
resolve would falter. And he did not look back. Mistakes
he had made aplenty; he would not add another.

Go, but where? No place was far enough from her and
could not be, were she somehow transported to the farthest
reaches of Creation. Still, he was not about to stay under
the same roof as Brianna, no matter how many acres it covered.

Rarely did he take any time entirely for himself, but under the circumstances, that seemed the wisest course. Helios and the counselors could yell at each other just as well without his presence. So busy were they shouting past him, he thought it unlikely they would even notice he was not there.

Eventually, he would step in and sort it out. No one would get entirely what he wanted, but everyone would get something. Akora would take an important step forward.

He had told Brianna they were drawn together to defeat Deilos and he genuinely believed that. But it was also true that she had opened his mind to the need for greater change than he had contemplated. "Sunshine" might not be a bad idea, provided it still left some room in the shade.

But all that was for later. He went back to his quarters, scrawled a note, seized up his favorite bow, and left.

B RIANNA STAYED ON THE ROOF, STARING SIGHT-lessly at the stars. She kept thinking that her mind would clear but it did not. *Life is precious, love is rare,* her father had said, and she had taken his words to heart. She would always grieve for Delphine and Edward, but she could not blame Atreus for their deaths any more than she could deny her love for him.

All well and good. Now this.

He no longer had to marry her. There were other meanings that could be given to his words but those stood out above all. He had gone to England, claimed her, persuaded her to return to Akora, all believing that they had to marry. So convinced was he that he had not allowed himself to be dissuaded even by his part in her parents' deaths.

And yet . . . he could have left her in ignorance until after they were married.

And saddled himself with a wife who might loathe him?

He had set her free for her sake. He had done it for his own. Her sake . . . his . . .

Really, how could she be expected to figure this out without recourse to a daisy?

Something between a gasp and a giggle broke from her. No daisy was to be found, but wings she had been given and she damn well intended to use them.

ATREUS WAS NOT IN HIS QUARTERS. HARDLY SUR-prising, since he almost never seemed to be there. Fine, she would wait for him. Eventually, he'd come back if only for a change of clothes.

The night was old and she was very tired. No effort was needed to convince herself that the best place to wait was in Atreus's bed.

It was morning when she awoke, or more correctly when she was awakened. The slender, dark-haired woman stepped just inside the door and stopped. A startled smile played over her lovely mouth.

Well, really, could this get any better?

"Lady Phaedra." Sitting up, clutching the sheet to her bosom, Brianna stared at Atreus's mother.

Lady Phaedra regarded her with pleasant interest. "I came to have a word with my son. Is he here?"

"No! At least, I don't think he is."

"How remiss of him." Still smiling, Lady Phaedra came farther into the room, shut the door behind her, and settled comfortably on a settee near the bed.

"He's been so busy since returning from England, we've had little chance to chat. I thought I'd steal a few moments before the day took him, but it seems it already has."

"Lady Phaedra, I realize this must look—"

"Hopeful? My dear, Atreus is a grown man. I would not

dream of intruding into his private life. Frankly, I'm delighted to discover he has one."

"You are?"

"Quite. Your devotion to my son when he was injured did not escape my notice, nor did the fact that you are intelligent, sensible, and lovely. Tell me, do you like children?"

"Yes . . . I suppose so. I really should get up."

"Of course, then perhaps we could have breakfast together. Oh . . . what's this?"

Phaedra lifted the note from the table beside the bed. She read it, frowning.

"Atreus has gone off for a few days."

"Where?" What duty had taken him now? What was so pressing that he would leave the palace while so much was transpiring?

"Hunting. He's gone hunting." His mother set the note back on the table. She looked hard-pressed not to smile again. "That's rather odd. As far as I know, Atreus isn't all that fond of hunting."

Brianna got out of the bed with the sheet wrapped around her. She looked around for the gown she had discarded in the night, found it, and tried to shake the worst of the wrinkles from it.

"Where would he go?"

Phaedra didn't hesitate. She told her at once. Further, she provided complete and detailed instructions on how to get there. "I'm afraid you'll have to go on foot," she concluded. "A horse would never make it."

BRIANNA WAS A SENSIBLE WOMAN, SO SHE TOLD herself. She forgot all about feminine gowns and the like, found herself a sturdy tunic and a sensible pair of boots, and set off. Atreus was in the mountains above Ilius, in a place he had discovered as a boy and cherished ever since. He had even built himself a small cabin there.

So Phaedra had told her, and so she would see for herself, assuming she ever got there. The sun climbed and the day aged. She was damnably hot, sweat running into her eyes. She had tied her hair up but it kept flopping down into her face. She pushed it away yet again and kept going.

He couldn't just take a boat out and drift around for awhile on the Inland Sea, perhaps drop a line in the water and snare himself a fish, make a little *marinos*, contemplate the sea birds. Oh, no, he had to go up rocky crags, across chasms, into places a respectable goat would not venture.

It was beautiful, she had to admit when she paused long enough to survey her surroundings. The view all the way down the heather-strewn mountain to Ilius and the sea beyond was spectacular. She could see the three small islands clearly and, when she had climbed a little farther, could even glimpse the ocean toward the north and east.

Off in the distance along the rise, she caught sight of a watchtower. There would be others, she was sure, but none was near. She felt entirely alone save for the hawks that circled above, borne on heated currents of air.

With a groan, she moved on. Phaedra's directions proved dependable. She passed a hidden glen, where every tree and rock seemed covered by black-and-orange butterflies, went on higher yet, breathing hard. The water she had brought was gone. She found a spring, drank deeply, kept going.

All the while she thought of what she would say to Atreus, better yet of what she would do. She was still undecided when she pulled herself up a white chalk ridge and stopped suddenly.

Ahead was a field filled with wildflowers and in the center of it, a small, snug cabin. In front of the cabin was a bear. A very large bear, standing on his back paws and towering a good eight feet in height.

A wooden bear, carved with such attention to detail that she could almost see him breathe.

There were no bears on Akora. She knew that, but even so, the sight was startling. Like the lionesses who guarded the palace gates, the bear was a memory of other places, other times.

No bear, wooden or otherwise, was going to stop her. Breathing hard, she put one foot in front of the other until she reached the cabin. There she slumped against the wall and closed her eyes.

She opened them when she heard the twang of an arrow loosed on its flight. Going around a corner of the cabin, she saw Atreus. He stood with his feet planted apart, the muscles of his bare chest flexing as he drew back a bow almost as tall as himself, took careful aim, and fired.

At a target attached to a distant tree.

The arrow struck it dead center, directly next to its fellow shot a moment before. Another followed swiftly, and another. For reasons she wasn't absolutely clear about, it struck her as a good idea to sit down and watch.

She was still doing that when Atreus walked over to the target to retrieve his arrows. She was watching him appreciatively when he turned, arrows in hand, and saw her.

She was sitting cross-legged on the grass. Her hair had fallen down completely, but she had managed to blow most of it out of her eyes. Her tunic stuck to her. She did not want to think about the condition of her feet.

"Brianna?"

"Your mother told me about this place." She might as well use all the ammunition she had. "I think she likes me."

"Does she?" He came closer, still looking at her for all the world as though she were an apparition. "How did you get here?"

"I walked." Surely he knew that. How else was there?

"The way is dangerous. You could have been hurt."

"This all could have been avoided if I'd found a daisy."

He bent down beside her, looking worried. "A daisy?"

"He loves me, he loves me not. How long do you suppose women have been doing that?"

Understanding dawned, and with it came a smile that stole what little breath she still had clean away. "As long as there have been women and daisies?" he ventured.

"Atreus, do you love me?" A woman who could climb a mountain could ask the question that mattered most to her.

"Yes, Brianna, I do." No hesitation, no pause to think, just straightforward and spine-tinglingly direct.

"That's good. I love you, too."

He blinked, looked away for a moment. "You humble me."

"Never that, dearest. You said I must have a choice. Fine, I have made it." She stood up, dusted off her hands, and swayed. It quite spoiled the moment. She had intended to be indomitable but instead she was in his arms and being carried toward the cabin.

"I don't know what Phaedra was thinking of," he muttered. "She could have sent a messenger."

"Grandchildren."

He looked down at her, frowning again. "What?"

"Your mother is thinking of grandchildren. She has a great desire for them."

He had the most devastating smile, especially when it was directed straight at her. "I am inclined to oblige her, assuming you would be willing."

"I'd like a bath first but I suppose up here I can settle for a bucket."

He shook his head as though mocking her lack of faith

and kicked open the door to the cabin, which, she discovered, he had cleverly built on top of a hot spring.

She was floating in it, unspeakably content, when something white drifted past her. Another followed quickly. A third landed on the very tip of her nose.

Daisies, falling over her, accompanied by crocuses, tiny wild irises, and shy blue violets, bounty of Atreus's field in the sky. Clinging to her bare shoulders and breasts, filling her with laughter and with pure, unfettered . . .

. . . JOY IN THE BRIGHT AND SPARKLING DAY.

"Oh, my dear!" Lady Constance exclaimed. She sped down the gangplank with agility that did credit to a woman of her age, and embraced Brianna warmly. Lord William was right behind her, swiveling his head about in all directions, determined not to miss anything.

"We are so delighted to be here," the good countess said. "When your letter came, we were quite astounded, weren't we, William? William?" She turned around, finding her husband staring openmouthed up the winding roads to the massive palace high above and seized his hand, claiming his attention along with it.

"Of course we were," she replied for herself. "And now to actually be here, to see you—"

"I am so glad you could come," Brianna said softly. She truly was, for the presence of Delphine's old friends completed her happiness. It also seemed right and fitting to her that such honorable and sensible people were the first *xenos* ever to be allowed to set foot on Akora by invitation. It was an astonishing break with the past and it had been engineered by Atreus. Helios and the Council were still arguing over it, although both sides seemed disposed to declare a temporary truce in honor of the festivities.

"They are all quite beside themselves in London," Lord William said with a chuckle.

"We were summoned by Prinny himself," Lady Constance said. She did not appear impressed by the experience. "He spoke interminably about our responsibilities representing Great Britain, the extraordinary significance of this event, et cetera, et cetera. I told him we were simply going to a wedding and intended to have a fine time doing it."

"She did tell him that," Lord William agreed with evident pleasure. "Quite set him back."

Brianna laughed. She tucked an arm through each of theirs and led them up toward the palace, acknowledging as they went the warm greetings of every man, woman, and child they passed.

"Amazing," Lord William said and repeated it at intervals. "Absolutely amazing. I could never have imagined such a place."

"No wonder you wanted to return," Lady Constance said. "Oh, my dear, we are so very happy for you. You know, I did wonder when you came to Holyhood. His Highness, the Vanax, seemed unusually attentive. I said to myself, Constance, there is something between those two. I mentioned it to you, didn't I, William?"

Her husband did not answer. He was occupied by the sight of the lionesses and beyond them, the palace itself. "Never seen anything like that in my life. Makes whatever we've got look like a hovel."

"We must *not* tell Prinny that," Lady Constance said emphatically. "He wastes far too much money on his building projects as it is."

"The palace has been under construction for over three thousand years," Brianna told them proudly. "Nothing has been torn down, the original rooms are still in use, but it's been added to continually."

"Astonishing," Lord William said again as they climbed the broad steps to the immense double doors standing open and towering far above them. There they were joined by Atreus, who welcomed them warmly.

If the sight of him wearing only the pleated kilt of an Akoran warrior startled Lady Constance, she rallied in good order. Curtseying deeply, she said, "Your Highness, we are so honored to be here."

"Your presence does us honor, good lady," he said. Holding out his hands, he helped her to rise. She did so, just a little flustered, and smiled in delight when he added, "Please call me Atreus. We are not so formal here."

"I've a letter for you from the Prince Regent," Lord William said. He handed over a thick missive impressively daubed with seals and ribbons. Rather apologetically, he added, "Goes on a bit."

Atreus nodded and tucked the letter into the waistband of his kilt. "I'll attend to it in due time. Meanwhile, let's get you settled."

When that was done, Brianna breathed a small sigh of relief before hurrying off to meet with Phaedra and Leoni who, praise be, had the preparations well in hand. No Vanax had wed in over half a century and it seemed that every Akoran was determined to share the great event. A general holiday had been declared and people were streaming into Ilius. Every house was filled to bursting, with the excess overflowing into tents set up anywhere they would fit. There was music everywhere, laughter and song, and the delectable aromas of favorite dishes prepared over open fires, to be shared with anyone who happened by.

"Everything is proceeding in good order," Leoni assured her. "The best you can do now is get some rest."

"You really should," Phaedra agreed. "There's nothing more you need to do except catch your breath."

Gratefully, Brianna did as they suggested. She actually

lay down but did not truly expect to sleep. When she opened her eyes next, it was her wedding day.

She might have swallowed some of those butterflies high on the mountain, her stomach fluttered so. Scarcely did she awake than she was swept up and borne as though on an inexorable tide from one moment to the next.

Sida brought her breakfast, hovered while she tried to eat. But the butterflies were not hungry. Leoni followed, her dear mother, claiming a few quiet moments alone to give to her the silver and lapis lazuli bracelet that she had worn on her own wedding day.

"I dreamed of giving this to a daughter," Leoni said softly, "but never did I imagine she would be one as you. I am so very proud of you, Brianna, and I love you so very much."

There were tears then, of course, and tears again when Phaedra came, but this time they were tears of laughter, for she brought with her a wicked store of tales about the young Atreus's misadventures that had them in stitches as Brianna dressed.

Her gown was simple, in keeping with Akoran tradition. The fabric was the finest silk, embroidered over the hem and bodice with tiny seed pearls. She wore her hair unbound except for the garland of flowers Atreus had sent for her. The flowers were from the high field and almost made her weep again. At the very last, she took the Tear of Heaven from the box where she had kept it so carefully and fastened it around her throat.

Then, incredibly, it was time to go, out of the room she would not occupy again, down the broad steps with the two women who would now be her mothers accompanying her. She came out into the vast courtyard, into a wave of cheers that went on and on seemingly without end.

People thronged the courtyard. But they were also on the roof of the palace. They filled the stairs, except where they had been cleared for her, and even, she swore, sat perched in the trees.

They welcomed her with an outpouring of love and acceptance that left her simply stunned. Embraced by it, she went up the steps of the dais to Atreus.

He looked . . . oh, magnificent! Strong and proud, filled with life, younger than he often seemed, as though he had cast off all care, yet solemn, too, as befitted the moment.

He took her hand, raised it to his lips, and the cheers rose to heaven.

Words were spoken, pledges made, but Brianna knew the true vows were in her heart and Atreus's as well, where they would live forever and beyond.

Her hand in his, they went among their people, receiving their congratulations, sharing their joy. She laughed as he fed her honeycakes offered by a beaming old woman, laughed again when they shared a cup of wine the giver boasted was the best vintage from vines he had tended for forty years, laughed still more when he drew her into a dance, passing round and round the circle of delighted couples, young and old, that quickly formed and joined in.

While yet the cheers rang in her ears, they withdrew into the palace and the warmth of family. They were all there—Joanna and Alex with little Amelia, Kassandra and Royce, Leoni and Marcus, Phaedra and Andrew, Elena and even Polonus, who was pronounced well enough to be in attendance. He was a little hesitant, especially facing Atreus, but his brother-in-law quickly put him at ease.

"I appreciate the opportunity to visit England," Polonus said. He looked to Lady Constance and Lord William. "It is very good of you to agree."

"We will be delighted to have you with us," Lord William said. Brianna knew he had met privately with Atreus and had been informed about Polonus's circumstances. His willingness to give the young man a much-needed opportunity endeared the earl to her even more.

Wine and yet more food flowed. When they were at last replete, Kassandra leaned back against her husband and smiled at them all. A bit bemusedly, she said, "I can scarcely believe it is less than two years since Joanna came here. So much has happened, so many challenges overcome, so many blessings received." She patted her impressive tummy. "And so many yet to come. Truly, we are the most fortunate of families."

"As it seems we always have been," Royce said, "back to the beginning."

Silence fell around the table amid thoughts of the generations of bold men and brave women who had brought them, through courage and faith, to this moment.

Then Atreus lifted his goblet, smiled at his bride and said, "To all that has been, and most especially, to all that is to be."

Night deepened. In the palace courtyard and beyond, the revelry of a grateful people continued. Joyful voices floated out over the Inland Sea that washed the high cliffs, protecting the Fortress Kingdom now and forever.

Farther still, beyond where any could see, the future waited.

A NOTE TO READERS

Castles in the Mist concludes my second trilogy, which began with *Dream Island* and continued with *Kingdom of Moonlight*. When I finished my first trilogy—*Dream of Me, Believe in Me,* and *Come Back to Me*—I left the hero and heroine of the final book expecting their first child. However, I neglected to tell readers whether they had a girl or a boy. Oh, my, did I hear about that! I'm not about to make the same mistake again.

As you know, Joanna and Alex are the proud parents of Amelia, who more than keeps them on their toes. Kassandra and Royce will soon become the proud parents of Gavin, who brings his own surprises. Brianna and Atreus don't know it yet but they are going to be parents to twins, a daughter named Clio and a son named Andreas.

These new members of the family will grow up to face their own challenges and embark on their own adventures. I intend to join them and I hope you will, too.

—Josie

ABOUT THE AUTHOR

JOSIE LITTON lives in New England with her husband, children, and menagerie . . . mostly. Her imagination may find her in nineteenth century London or ninth century Norway or who knows where next. She is happily at work on a new trilogy and loves to hear from readers.

Visit Josie at *www.josielitton.com*.

Read on for a preview of
Josie Litton's

Fountain of
DREAMS

Available from Bantam Books
in July 2003

The first of her
new trilogy all available
in Summer 2003

L IGHTS SHINING IN THE HIGH WINDOWS OF THE mansion's ground floor appeared and disappeared between the leafy branches of trees that swayed in the steady breeze off the river. The hour was shortly before midnight. In the walled park surrounding the house, an owl swept soundlessly from its perch. Wings barely moving, it soared over the open ground before descending rapidly to pluck a hapless mouse.

The man waiting in the dark shadows of the bushes saw the catch and smiled faintly. He, too, would hunt soon. Several hours before, he had gotten close enough to the house to confirm that the family was at dinner. He watched them briefly through one of the windows—Prince Alexandros; his wife, Princess Joanna; their nephew, Prince Andreas; and their daughter, Princess Amelia were all relaxed and in good humor. They had no inkling that their privileged world was about to be shattered.

He had withdrawn to wait and now stirred a little, flexing muscles that would otherwise cramp as he remained concealed behind the thick bushes just inside the high stone walls. The night was cool and damp but he scarcely noticed. He had known far worse.

He was a tall man, lean and very fit. For this night's work, he was dressed in the garb of a London office worker, a respectable man who earned his portion in a counting house perhaps or as a solicitor's secretary. A man neither poor nor rich enough to attract attention. His dark trousers and jacket of plain but sturdy wool made him all but invisible in the shadows. He had turned up the jacket collar for further concealment and pulled the brim of his felt hat down close to eyes some had likened to the color of steel.

He was without weapons although to be fair against most armed opponents he would still have the advantage. If he was found by the guards, he wanted to appear a harmless drunk who had wandered where he should not. For that purpose, he had rubbed dirt on the jacket and trousers such as would result from an inebriated climb over a stone wall, and carried a half-empty bottle of whiskey in the pocket of the jacket.

By the look of it, the ruse would not be necessary. While it might be true there was no residence better guarded in all of London, the patrols were at regular intervals, therefore predictable. That was expected. The security around the manor was intended to insulate its inhabitants from the waves of popular unrest that roared through London periodically, not from a lone man intent on gaining access.

Gray eyes flickered in the darkness. He waited, patient and watchful. Lights were extinguished on the ground floor as others appeared on the floor above. The family retired early by the standards of society. They preferred each other's company to the customary round of balls, routs, masquerades, assemblies and the like. According to his information, they had no social commitments on this night. That suited his purposes perfectly.

The patrol was good, he scarcely heard it coming even though he was expecting it. The three men passed within a dozen feet of him. They did not speak and their steps were almost entirely silent. They were, he knew, part of the military force that was among the most feared in all the world. The warriors of Akora, the fortress kingdom beyond the Pillars of Herculeas, had maintained that mysterious land's freedom and sovereignty for centuries. Ancient, legendary and only recently beginning to emerge into the modern world, Akora fascinated many but not him. He cared nothing for the place and hoped most sincerely to have nothing to do with it.

The patrol passed by him. He took a breath, cleared his mind and ran across the open space of lawn. In little more than a heartbeat, he reached the bushes beneath the ground floor windows. Crouching there, he paused and listened intently.

No sound from the house or the surrounding grounds suggested that his presence had been detected. Cautiously, he stood and looked into the now dark dining room. The servants had finished clearing and would be going to their own rest. Soon, only the guards on patrol and on duty in the hall would be awake.

He moved again, around a corner to the back of the house, and looked up. Directly above him were the windows of what he had already confirmed was Princess Amelia's bedroom.

The patrol was returning. He pressed against the wall of the house, blending into the contours of stone and shadow, waiting.

When the patrol was gone, he took a length of black cloth from an inside pocket of his jacket, put it over his face and tied it at the back of his head. Only his eyes remained visible.

He grasped the stones an arm's reach above him, his fingers digging into the fine line between them, and hoisted himself up smoothly and easily. His feet found the narrow indentation that was just enough for him to balance on. Steadied, he reached up again. Swiftly, silently he climbed the wall.

There was a stone balcony outside the Princess's windows. He swung onto it, dropped, and listened again for any sound that would warn he was detected. When none came, he eased the French doors open slowly.

The room was in darkness but he could make out the placement of the furniture, particularly the bed hung with gauzy curtains.

His quarry lay on her side. He could not make out her features but he knew well enough what she looked like, having observed her for several days as she went about London. She was not precisely beautiful but her face had a certain appeal uniquely her own and so far as he had seen, there was nothing lacking in her figure. He had also noticed her to be an exuberant woman, confident and outgoing, given to frequent smiles and ready laughter. That seemed at odds with her reputation, namely that she was cold and proud, an unfeeling breaker of hearts, a spinster at twenty-five despite her family's wealth and power.

If the lady's unmarried state troubled her, there was no sign of it. Lost in sleep, she breathed slowly and deeply. For just an instant, he felt . . . not doubt precisely, never that. Just a twinge of regret that he hadn't been able to come up with a different plan.

He wasn't a man to linger over his shortcomings. In a single movement, he brushed aside the curtains and seized hard hold of her. She woke instantly with a gasp that was smothered by the covers in which he quickly rolled her.

Although she struggled fiercely, within seconds he had a gag in her mouth and a hood secured over her head.

Far from being cowed, her efforts to escape redoubled. She was surprisingly strong. No match for his strength, of course, still she proved more than a handful.

He could have cautioned her to stop but he could not risk her recognizing his voice. Instead, he tightened his grip warningly.

"Lmmmeeemphgo . . . mmpbastarmph . . . !"

Had she just called him a bastard? Surprise froze him long enough for his captive to get an arm loose and land a solid punch on his jaw.

Only a lifetime of self-discipline stopped him from cursing out loud. He contented himself by wrapping her ever more tightly in the covers and moved quickly to the door.

The inside of the house was not patrolled. That, too, he had confirmed during his surveillance. The only guards were stationed in the central hall.

He avoided them by using the back stairs frequented by the servants. The going was difficult because the squirming bundle in his arms refused to desist. Trussed as securely as a Christmas goose, the princess continued to struggle. He had all he could do to keep hold of her without actually causing her hurt.

He reached the ground floor landing and paused. She could not escape him, of that he had no doubt. But neither did he underestimate his potential peril. If she managed to get out more than a muffled expletive . . .

The Akorans would take him prisoner but he doubted very much that they would turn him over to the British authorities. Everything he knew about them said they would handle the matter themselves in their own way, presuming they didn't just kill him outright.

She'd damn well better be worth all the trouble.

He opened the door and stepped outside. If his calculations were correct, he had just under five minutes before the patrol passed again. Enough time to cross the lawn, get through the trees, and scale the wall.

Or it would be if Shadow was on post.

He was, evidenced by the large shape concealed in the foliage of the upper branches of the trees and the rope dangling down the near side of the wall. With an inner sigh of relief, he dumped his unwilling burden into the sling at the end of the rope, secured her firmly and tugged to signal Shadow. Immediately, the sling began to rise. He watched long enough to confirm that his captive was still struggling fiercely before climbing the wall. Settled beside Shadow, who gave him a quick nod, he helped hoist the sling.

Scant seconds before the patrol was due to return, it was done. His quarry slung over his shoulder, Shadow following close behind, he ran down the road and around a corner to a waiting carriage.

The wheels were turning even as the door was closed.

WHAT IN BLOODY HELL? THIS COULDN'T BE HAP-pening to her! She absolutely could not have been taken from her well-protected home in the dead of night, snatched by some lout with hard hands, strong arms and apparently no desire to live much longer.

Not a word, not a sound out of him, not even when she landed a punch that at the very least should have prompted a curse. And that, more than anything, worried her.

Either she'd been kidnapped by a mute or her captor was a man of uncommon self-control who knew exactly what he was doing.

Heart hammering, Amelia struggled against her own terror. At all cost, she had to keep her mind clear. Better to concentrate on anger so great it pushed out fear. There were two men . . . she thought. There might be more but there had to be two at least to have gotten her over the wall. Neither had spoken and the hood drawn over her head assured she could see nothing.

What was their plan? Ransom? Something worse? Her parents had never mistaken ignorance for innocence. All their children, herself included, had a sensible appreciation of the world, both its glories and its dangers.

But so far at least she was unharmed. Even when she struck out at him, he did not retaliate beyond holding her more tightly. What did that mean?

Did it matter? Whoever they were, whatever their intent, they had to be mad. Her father, uncles, brothers, and cousins would never rest until she was both safe and avenged. If she could speak, she could try to convince him to stop now before it was too late for him and anyone else involved but the gag was tight around her mouth. She could breathe around it well enough but could make only the most muffled sounds.

The hood over her head shut out all light while the covers kept her tightly trussed. She could not see, speak, or move. So completely was she cut off from the world that she could smell only the fabric close around her head and nothing else. But she could hear and feel.

The clatter of the horses' hooves rang sharply, telling her they were moving over cobblestoned streets such as were near her home. But in which direction? South lay the river and the docks. Did he intend to take ship, to spirit her far away? Her dread took a further leap forward but she refused to give in to it. If ransom was his goal, as she had to hope, it was unlikely he would remove her very far from London.

If not a ship, perhaps they were heading for one of the coaching roads that ran in all directions from the capital. The roads were much improved of late. Given good horses, great distances could be covered more quickly than ever before.

There was even the new railroad, in operation only a little more than a year, connecting London to Greenwich but surely he would not use that. The railroad continued to attract great attention and besides, it did not run at night.

Whatever his intent, each passing moment took her further from the hope of rescue.

For an appalling instant, tears threatened. She choked them back but the tight, desperate sound penetrated the gag. The man stiffened. She felt it and on a sudden urge, coughed again.

His hand settled on the blankets near her face. Or at least she thought it did. It was damnably hard to tell.

What if she truly was choking? Why would he care unless he had some concern about keeping her alive. If he did, she might be able to use it to her advantage.

Gag be damned, she filled her lungs and summoned a desperate, hacking cough strong enough to convince anyone that she was in danger of expiring.

The blankets were loosened! She still couldn't see anything but she could feel the cool night air. Another deep, prolonged cough set her throat to aching but it didn't matter. She could move her arms and legs. Never mind that punch, he needed a good, swift kick.

She couldn't see to aim but she hit some portion of him all the same. His chest . . . his thigh . . . whatever it was, it felt like steel. She feared almost that she had broken a toe but it didn't matter. His hold on her loosened just enough. Her hand found the latch on the carriage door. She had it turned and the door opened, a rush of air heralding her success. In another moment, she would be out of the carriage. The fall would hurt but anything was better than captivity. Even so, blinded by the hood, she hesitated the merest fraction of an instant.

* * *

DISBELIEF ROARED THROUGH HIM BUT DID NOT dull the lightning fast reflexes that had kept him alive through times far darker than these.

He had planned so carefully, thought out every step, considered every contingency. Or so he had believed. But he hadn't counted on a woman who didn't have the sense to know when she was beaten.

Heedless for the moment of any consideration except preventing her escape, he took hard hold of her. Though she struggled still, he wound the blanket so tightly around her that finally she could not move at all. Any further sounds she made were too muffled for him to hear, which suited him perfectly.

They rode on through the night. Amelia did not try again to escape but she remained stiff and unyielding against him. Another woman, caught in so desperate a situation, might have lapsed into exhausted sleep but she did not. Although he could not see her face, he knew by the feel of her in his arms that she remained entirely conscious. No doubt she was also deeply apprehensive. As there was no possibility of offering her any reassurance, he did not try. But he was relieved when at last, several hours outside of London, they reached their destination.

As Shadow took the carriage and horses around to the stables, he carried his unwilling guest into the small, ivy-draped house and through to a back bedroom. He stepped into the room, set her down on the far side of the bed, and withdrew quickly. As he was about to close the door, he looked back at her. The blanket had fallen away, leaving her in her sleep shift. The finely woven linen trimmed with lace did little to conceal her body. It was, he observed, at least as good as he had thought.

Her hands were on the hood covering her head. She was about to snatch it off when he shut the door loudly enough for her to hear the solid thud that sealed her off from the world.

A ROOM. NOT SMALL, NOT LARGE, LIT BY OIL lamps. A narrow bed with a chest at its foot, a small table beside the bed, a larger table with a basin and ewer, both empty. There were two windows, heavily shuttered, and one door locked from the outside.

She could hardly have expected otherwise. Even so, a tremor went through Amelia as she confronted the evidence that she truly was imprisoned. Sternly, she reminded herself that no good would come from missishness. She was a princess of the royal house of Akora and she could damn well behave like one.

Her fingers tore at the gag, making quick work of it. Even more swiftly, she sought a means of escape. It was hours since she had been taken. Morning would come soon and when it did, her family would discover that she was missing. Her throat tightened at the thought of what they would think and, more importantly, fear. If only she could get free quickly for her own sake but also to relieve their minds.

She was seeking a means of doing just that when the sound of a bolt being thrown back stopped her. Aware suddenly of her lack of proper clothing, she seized up the blanket and was winding it around herself when the door opened.

The man who stood in it was immense. She was used to very tall men—her father, brothers, uncles, and male cousins all being six feet or better—but even by their standards, this man was a giant. Nor was he lacking in bulk. So broad were his shoulders and chest that he seemed barely able to fit through the door. His hair and beard were both thick, black, and unkempt. He eyed her from beneath equally bushy black brows and spoke with an Irish lilt.

"I've brought food and water for ye, lass, an' a bit of advice to go with it. Mind your manners, try nothin' foolish an' no harm will come to ye."

Ignoring the warning, she faced him squarely. "You're mad or suicidal, perhaps both. Don't you realize what will happen to you when my family finds me?"

To her astonishment, the Irishman laughed. "They won't be findin' ye, least not 'till they're told where t'look." He stepped further into the room, being careful to close the door behind him, and moved toward the table. Catching the direction of her gaze, he sighed. "Don't be thinkin' about gettin' past me, lass. That won't be happenin'. Best t'realize that ye're goin' to be here for awhile an' not be fussin' yerself about it."

"You can't seriously believe that I will just accept this?"

He shrugged massive shoulders, set the tray he carried down and returned to the door. Amelia could not help but notice that he moved gracefully for a man of his size. No doubt he was correct, she couldn't have gotten past him. Nor was she inclined to try. There might well be other people in the house—the second man on the wall, for instance and perhaps more—ready to respond if the Irish giant called an alarm. When she escaped—and she had to believe that she would—it would be without anyone knowing until she was much too far away for them to do anything about it.

"Whether ye accept it or not, lass, ye might as well get some sleep." He glanced around at the room. "I know this isn't what yer used to. Best hope yer family pays up soon."

"You're holding me for ransom?" The small spurt of relief she felt faded quickly. He had allowed her to see his face. Why would he do that if he truly meant to release her when her family paid?

"Money makes the world go round, lass." He opened the door, stepped into what looked like a narrow corridor, and shut the door firmly behind him. She heard the bolt slide back into place.

Her shoulders almost slumped but she wouldn't let them. For the moment, at least, she was safe. However many more moments like that there might be, she intended to make good use of them.

But how?

THE GRAY-EYED MAN GRINNED WHEN THE DOOR he was watching bulged slightly. From the other side, he heard a muffled curse. The lady was more than he had expected, much more, but she was now snugly tucked away. For the first time in weeks, he allowed himself to relax, if only a little.

Soundlessly, he went down the corridor. Shadow followed him.

"That's one hell of a princess," Shadow said when they reached the parlor. His words held no hint of the Irish accent he had affected moments before. Instead, he spoke with the flat twang of the Kentucky hills from which he had come.

"She is that." Because he trusted Shadow as he trusted no other man, he added, "Put up more of a fight than I thought she would."

"Did she?" Shadow pulled off the heavy black wig and beard he had been wearing, and tossed them aside with evident relief. "Well, she's here now and that's what counts. How long do you figure it'll be before she gets that shutter off?"

"Morning, maybe? You drugged the food?"

Shadow nodded. "Just as you said. She ought to be dog tired anyway."

"Once she wakes up, she's got to find her own way out. I tried not to be obvious."

"We'll see then. What do you say to a drink?"

"Sounds good."

He was stretched out in front of the parlor fire, a welcome glass of bourbon in his hand, when the first drops of rain splashed against the windowpanes. He frowned, thinking that he had not calculated on the rain. Not that it was likely to matter. He doubted the purloined princess would stir before morning and perhaps not until even later.

And then . . . they would just have to see. So much rested on whether she behaved as he anticipated. If she did not . . .

He would have to start over. It would be unfortunate and difficult, but he would do so. His mission would be fulfilled regardless of the cost.

However, it would all be so much easier if the lady played her part.

HER SHOULDER ACHED. AMELIA RUBBED IT GIN-gerly as she contemplated the unyielding door. She was wasting her strength. The door would not give. Another way out of the room would have to be found.

She ignored the food and water, being far too well trained to touch either, and gave her attention to the windows. She had examined them briefly and discovered that they were covered with heavy wooden shutters. Now she took a much closer look. One set of shutters seemed as immovable as the door. They must be latched very tightly from the outside. But the other . . .

A tiny spurt of hope lit in her when the second set of shutters gave just slightly in response to her pushing on them. True, only a tiny crack opened between them but it was enough for her to see an opportunity. If only she had some means of prying the shutters apart. Perhaps she could weaken the latch securing them and even break it apart.

Quickly, she looked around the room for something that

might assist her but nothing came to hand. Determined, she searched the drawers of the tables, looked under the bed and finally pulled away the bed covers themselves. The bed was of wood but the mattress she tugged aside was supported by thin metal slats. They were tightly wedged into the frame but she managed to pull one loose.

Encouraged by her success, Amelia inserted one end of the slat into the crack between the shutters and pushed hard. At first, nothing happened but as she persevered, the crack widened slightly. She stopped and rested for a moment, then began again. Over and over, she levered the slat into the crack but managed only to widen the space by an inch or two. Frustration filled her. Her hands ached far worse, she felt the first inklings of despair.

That would not do. Angrily brushing aside the dampness that had appeared on her cheeks, she redoubled her efforts. Long, seemingly fruitless minutes passed but finally, just as she reached deep within herself for the very limits of her strength, there was a sudden, rending sound of metal coming apart.

For a scant moment, she thought the slat had snapped but quickly she saw that was not the case. Instead, the latch on the outside had torn away from the wood. It dangled from one of the now blessedly open shutters.

Cool night air revived her instantly. She dropped the slat, gathered the blanket more securely around her, and scrambled over the window sill. From there, it was only a short drop to the ground.

The night was pitch dark. At first, she could scarcely see her hand in front of her face. But after a few minutes, the contours of a garden became evident. There was a wall, which made her throat tighten briefly. But almost directly in front of her she saw a gate.

Barefoot, the blanket fluttering behind her, Amelia ran toward it.